"Captain! Captain. Come to Navcom."

"I found it!"

"No, I found it."

Icabar and Glaze spoke in unison.

"I was just looking and suddenly…"

"The transmitter started flashing again." Glaze's eager voice interrupted Icabar's.

"The alien transmission's reactivated and…"

Glaze's voice rode right over Icabar's words. "He's de-coding them even as we speak and soon, he'll tell us what it's saying."

"Glaze, I haven't a clue. It's complicated and impossibly alien. And different from last time. Captain, it's emitting a different signal series!"

Braden heard the excitement in their voices. It sent a shiver of fear down his spine.

There was a link…and he had activated it.

"On my way," he answered briskly into his comm.

Thank the Creator the signal was back. But what now?

He turned, half floating, half stumbling from sleep bay. With a longing glance back at his empty capsule, he exited and headed for Navcom.

Discover other books

By
Sheron Wood McCartha

Available in print and eBook on Amazon at
https://www.amazon.com/Sheron-Wood-
McCartha/e/B0045K0HD6

The Alysian Universe Series

Caught in Time: Book 1
A Dangerous Talent for Time: Book 2
Cosmic Entanglement: Book 3
Past the Event Horizon: Book 4
Space Song: Book 5
Touching Crystal Book 6
Someone's Clone: Book 7
Time's Equation: Book 8

The Terran Trilogy

A World Too Far: *The Ship*
Somewhat Alien: *The Station*
The Weight of Gravity: *The Planet*

Past the Event Horizon

Alysian Universe: book 4

By
Sheron Wood McCartha

Digital Imagination Publishing
Beaverton, Oregon

Cover art by Toni Boudreault

Published by Digital Imagination Publishing
Beaverton, Oregon

ISBN 978-0-9831066-8-5

Printed in the United States of Americas
http://www.AlysianUniverse.com

Acknowledgements

Many people don't realize how much of a group effort goes into writing a book.

In the early stages, Ted Blasche helped define the story. The Orycon writers' workshop of Gra Linnasea, Kristin Landon and Bill Nolan offered sage advice on how to improve the story.

Then, my Beaverton Evening Writers' Group of Chelsea Nolan, Clayton Callahan, Allie Freeman, Tim Kerber, and Diana Peach all critiqued and corrected it to a better book.

My brother, Scott Wood, helped with the battle scenes and my husband, Bland, served as a science resource and awesome tech troubleshooter. And finally, my editor, Phyllis Irene Radford, offered excellent direction and suggestions.

Finally, Toni Boudreault wrapped it all up in an attractive package.

Thank you all.

After preparing, training, packing, and stowing, this space adventure is ready for launch.

Prologue

Alien! The thing was definitely alien...and everything that implied.

Braden Steele, newly chosen captain of the starship *The Seeker*, stared at the reason for Alysia's deep space venture. His world of Alysia was about to step into the space age, and no one knew what awaited out there among the stars.

He ran a blunt hand through his recently cropped auburn hair, trying to get used to how short it was. Military short. At least they hadn't asked him to wear a uniform for the viewing, so casual black slacks and a blue sweater sufficed.

Braden, his father, grandfather and Solanje T'Kai stood in a white room secured area inside the National Space Agency, a top-secret installation that required thumbprint, a retina scan and blood of the first born, most likely. This sterile room was empty except for a strange craft on a large plasticine pedestal and an object that floated overtop of it.

Floated.

Yes, floated.

Hovering in the air before them, it glowed, a circular band of microfibers woven into a size just large enough to fit on a human head. Only, it wasn't headgear;

it was something else. Something alien. The object had been found inside what they surmised was an extraterrestrial probe, the size of a baby's cradle, that now rested on the pedestal in front of them.

In a covert operation, his father, Chase Steele, had transported the alien capsule to the Democratic Union for study after it had crash-landed in the Ching T'Karre in Salishandra T'Kai's private garden.

Braden's grandfather, Harrison Steele, Director of the Democratic Union's space program, then built the starship through a secret joint program with the Ching T'Karre that would take Braden and his crew into space. Not long after the craft's arrival, strange transmissions were detected emanating from beyond their solar system. Now, both Chase and Harrison stood there explaining what they knew about the alien craft to Braden and Solanje T'Kai, Salishandra's daughter.

Braden glanced over at Chase's serious face with its aristocratic angles and unfathomable gray eyes and knew he would sorely miss his father's solid and supportive presence. Now he was on his own.

He swallowed to clear a closing throat and pulled in a deep breath. His stocky athletic form shifted, and he shuffled restlessly from one foot to another as he stared around the room.

His grandfather flashed a look that signaled for him to pay attention. An elegant hand waved in front of his face and then pointed to the alien machine. His grandfather also looked over a shoulder toward Solanje to see if she were listening, too.

Petit and compact, Solanje T'Kai stood silent and stiff next to Braden. Her long, pulled-back hair made a dark river that flowed partway down her back. Serious onyx eyes stared intently at the glowing artifact and flashed determination in a delicately exotic face of sharp cheekbones and long black lashes. She nodded to Harrison.

Those that knew about the alien probe were a small group, selected on a need-to-know basis. They were an elite bunch who wanted to hold world chaos at bay by preventing the furor such a discovery would cause. So, they kept the alien probe a deep secret from all but a few necessary scientists and high-level personnel.

Braden stared at the silver carriage that held an array of instruments never made on his world and technology that still puzzled their smartest scientists.

"This contains the probe's components." Harrison tapped the top of the silver-colored oblong container and they watched it unseal and open out, revealing nested alien instruments that blinked lights and murmured electronic noises. At the same time, six wheels popped out from the undercarriage, causing the machine to bounce slightly, and then settle. A narrow mechanical lever as long as a human arm unfolded from the interior with something that looked like a vid box at its end. The box swiveled around and made clicking noises. A circle at its center irised open with a whirring sound.

Smile for a picture. Click.

Braden blinked.

"We think the craft has an exploratory function. It moves on its own or by remote control. We're not sure which," continued his father. "Maybe both. The box takes still and video pictures and relays them to a receiver somewhere outside our solar system." Chase ran a hand through his dark mahogany hair, in echo of his son, and squinted at the object under discussion.

"We've finally traced the signal's destination to an area somewhere near the Estride Galaxy," added

Harrison excitedly. "And discovered an odd transmission that we think is sending instructions to the probe."

"And that's where we'll be headed?" Braden asked.

"Best option," commented his father. "We want to find out who, or what, it's talking to."

"And then we return?"

"The favored scenario." His father smiled, but a bit of concern flashed across his face. All stood silently for a moment and shuffled feet.

"Don't worry," Braden responded. "the whole crew trained hard for this at Sunpointe Academy. We're ready." He wanted to fill the uneasy silence and reassure them. "This is my dream. You know how much I've wanted to be a starship captain and explore space."

"More than most." Chase looked at his own father with a wry grin. Harrison chuckled lightly and nodded.

Harrison plucked the glowing halo out of the air and tapped a switch. The light faded, grew dark, and the woven metal circle dropped into his hand. He tucked it away into the carriage. His face grew serious. "We're putting this on board the ship. Solanje will guard and be responsible for protecting the alien device and protecting the crew from it." His grandfather put a hand on his shoulder.

"How much should I tell the crew about it?" asked Braden nervously.

"The device might be dangerous, so we suggest you lock it up and not tell the crew anything until you feel it's absolutely necessary," his father answered. "That would be best."

Harrison lifted his hand and waved it around. "Putting such a thing on board is risky, I know."

Lowering the hand, he stared at the alien craft. "Several were killed during testing, so you don't want anyone near it that doesn't know what they're doing. And you don't want anyone fooling with something this dangerous unless supervised. Don't activate it without both of you being present."

"It doesn't react well to metal probes," informed his father.

"Or combine with potent drugs." Harrison grimaced at him.

"That glowing circle has caused hallucinations for a few that thought to place it on their head," added Harrison. "However, one or two got images of a habitable foreign terrain, not on Alysia. Very interesting images. We've been studying them, and we'll pass along our most recent data."

"Tom put the thing on his head and got a brain hemorrhage." His father gave him a worried glance. "So be careful with that approach."

His grandfather gave Solanje a glance. "We understand the danger it presents, but we feel it might be critically important as you get closer to whatever is communicating with the probe. You may need the probe to signal back or interact with whatever is out there. Or you may be able to translate the incoming signal, if you have the probe to study on the way out."

Harrison delicately pointed with a forefinger into the carriage. "Here's a small monitor and over here a keypad. Unfortunately, we haven't completely decoded the language yet. We're giving both of you a recording of all our discoveries and theories. Study them thoroughly and keep the craft locked up when it's not in your possession."

Braden stared at the contraption. It would be hidden on his ship and it might be lethal. It could be anything from a mind bomb to a means of first contact and communication with aliens.

Wonderful.

Chapter 1

"Everything is under control," announced Captain Braden Steele with satisfaction, as he and his crew plunged through deep space, having left their home planet of Alysia and its cheering crowds far behind. For over three annuals now, they had been following a peculiar transmission emanating from a region outside their solar system

Surrounding Braden, multi-colored lights from the ship's control panels glowed: green for active, black for off, blue for standby, yellow for intermittent, white for monitoring systems and red for malfunction and disaster. The lights radiated a soft glow throughout the ship's Navcom station. Three heavily padded, full bodied, adjustable chairs with sturdy webbing sat in front of three main consoles: helm, the captain's chair, and communications. Two smaller jump seats for navigation and systems were positioned nearby. Above all the colorful electronics on the facing wall, a large monitor revealed an outside view of whirling galaxies, bursting stars, dark matter, lumpy asteroids, and unknown mysterious discoveries yet to be found. Other smaller monitors decorated the captain's board, helmsman, and navigator's stations. Two control ports in addition to three computer hubs sat between the three main stations. Retractable worktables and a multitude of built-in storage bins completed the strategic section of the ship.

The soft whisper of re-circulating air created a reassuring background that the current navigator, Bashar de Fyre Elitas, kept disrupting by absent-mindedly tapping his tan, well-manicured fingers on a recently revised deep space map that lay in front of him. Occasionally, Bashar would emit a humming sound or the words, "Oh yeah, baby," depending on the current musical selection that he was listening to via a small tab stuck on the back of his ear. His coarse, dark hair, native to Sunglast nomads, floated briefly as he shook his head back and forth. Sinewy shoulders swaying in time to unheard music.

Braden glanced at the computer schedule that listed all twelve names of the ship's personnel and their current assignments. The crew was mixed military and civilian, mixed male and female, mixed nationalities, and mixed temperaments. In total, a handful of headaches, thanks to the thoughtful selections of Mission Control. And lately, everyone had been getting cranky with everyone else. Too much long-term close living and boredom. Boredom being the instigator of most conflicts.

The recent water recycling fiasco hadn't helped matters. Thankfully, Robert Armstrong, his weapons specialist and all-around handyman, along with Adam di Adamantine, his engine and propulsion guy, had fixed the faulty pipes and filters.

"We've got it under control now," Adam had said, grinning at him, and patting the now working filters.

Braden hoped so, but he would make a trip out to "the farm" as a courtesy call and reassure himself that the recycling filters were working as reported.

He unplugged from his panel, unstrapped, stretched, and eased out of the center chair. He pulled out a mobile comm unit, activated his code, slipped it over his ear and tapped into the navigator's channel, wincing at the raucous sound of what Bashar called "music."

How could the man stand that noise?

Out in the corridor, he saw the flaxen hair and lean shape of his astrophysicist, Glaze Glissander, heading in from break. Glaze was one of the crew who had been a cadet in Braden's unit at Sunpointe Academy. Several on board thought of him as a quiet crewmember who kept a lot to himself but excelled in finding and mapping unknown space. Glaze understood the universe far better than he understood most people. Braden thought him reserved and competent, while others considered him "standoffish and antisocial."

Braden stretched again and tapped his helmsman on the shoulder. "Bashar, you have the con. Fifth shift will be on deck soon and I'm heading out. Icabar is awake already. He'll come in when he finishes at the scope."

"Aye, aye, Cap." Bashar eased over from the navigation board to the Captain's chair without missing a beat.

Braden said, "Close" and the noise cut out. He heaved a sigh of relief, although his ears still tingled.

Glaze entered and slid into his seat. Braden nodded at him; Glaze nodded back. The half gravity of Navcom caused his hair to float about at the gesture.

Due in Navcom for fifth shift, Icabar had commed Braden to ask for some extra time before reporting in. He wanted to grab a looksee through their high-powered telescope in the observation bay.

The mysterious emissions that had lured them out toward this sector of space fascinated his communication specialist. Now after three annuals on board, they were coming close enough to obtain a better image of the region. Icabar itched to be the first to determine whether the origin of the strange noise was alien generated, or just an unidentified, uncategorized natural noise. He had a bet with Glaze that the transmission was alien and artificial in nature.

Last shift, Icabar had peered so long through the blasted scope that Braden wondered why his eyes hadn't gotten stuck to it. Thinking about the lopsided grin of the long, tall, skinny intellectual they occasionally called "Icky," made Braden smile. He believed Icabar would be the first to figure out the transmission's origins, and most likely win the bet.

Braden headed out toward "The Farm." He would stop first at the hydroponics area where Tessa di Luria grew fresh vegetables and fruits that augmented their manufactured soy protein diet. That's where the water problem had originated.

He was wending his way past tubing and jutting electronics when his comm buzzed red alert. Icabar's voice broke in, full of concern. "The signal's gone, vanished!"

"Are you sure? I was just at Navcom. Everything looked fine, all under control."

"I've checked several times. It's not there," said Icabar with growing agitation. His voice had squeaked at the end of the comment.

Frag it all! Mission Control is too far away to give me any quick answers. Lag time makes effective discussion impossible. We're pretty much on our own this far out.

"We always considered it might stop," answered Braden, trying to project calm. "For now, keep the same heading and try to figure out what happened."

"We need to locate that transmitter." Icabar's voice had a frantic note to it now.

"We're at para-light speed and can't change course easily," answered Braden. "Stay at the scope. Keep an eye on the area in case it starts up again. Maybe a neighboring asteroid field has blocked the signal momentarily. Glaze spotted an unusual amount of debris in the suspected area around the outer edge of the Estride Galaxy."

Braden's comm flashed red. "Standby, Icabar. I've got a red alert. Braden here."

Bashar's voice came on. "We just lost the signal's transmission."

No music now.

"Icabar just commed me the same. Any intel on why it's stopped?"

"There's a heavy debris field near the estimated area. What if our alien transmitter was on a magnetized asteroid that just got smashed up in a collision with another asteroid?" suggested Bashar.

"Let's not leap to assumptions without proof. And remember the signal has never been confirmed as alien," Braden snapped back.

"If it's not alien, then we came all this way for nothing." Bashar sounded unhappy at the thought.

"We're at least half an annual away from the proposed destination, and even after we get closer, it's a lot of real estate to pick through. Anything can happen."

"And probably will," muttered Bashar.

Braden tapped Icabar back into the line.

"Icabar here. What's up?"

"Bashar just confirmed your lost signal."

"Let me stay and try to find it again."

"All right. Check out the debris field and see if you can figure out what might have happened, but don't say anything that will panic the crew," ordered Braden.

Still in the link, Bashar snorted. "Yes, please don't upset them any further. Crew's already on edge and getting on each other's nerves. This won't help the situation. I've been out here cooped up too long in this tin can with crazy people as it is."

Annoyed by the whining, Braden answered firmly, "I know that being enclosed with others like this is hard, but every one of us knew what we were signing up for. If you have any personnel problems, inform Liana. She's the psyche professional. And, by the way, no one is any crazier than you, Bashar."

"Truth there," interjected Icabar. "Talking about crew...I'd like to add that Crystal's in her bitchy mode again. I may strangle her. I'm just giving advanced warning, is all."

Our Lady preserve me, thought Braden.

Aloud he said, "We need her medical skills, so only do so if you have no other recourse, and don't get sick."

Bashar cut in, "Robert's no better. That boy is an arrogant asshole. You need to get him under control before someone gets hurt, and it may be him if he keeps it up."

Braden sighed. *Just what I need.* "Be careful there, guys. He's got the keys to the arsenal."

He heard Icabar's choked laugh. "I'll be here if you need me. I'm going to try to get a better visualization outside."

"Then, get Joel over to Navcom. We're short there and we're going to need an extra pair of eyes out front. Let me know if it starts up again. Braden out."

"Always the optimist. Okay, Icabar out."

"I'm out too," confirmed Bashar.

The transmission had stopped. That was not good. Not good at all.

*

Out in the corridor, Braden grabbed a handhold to steady himself.

So much for things under control! He took a deep breath and considered their biggest problem—the signal stopping.

Solanje. He needed to talk to her right away, especially with the transmission lost.

His attention on recent events, he shifted direction without conscious thought. His feet took the turn inward toward the ship's private quarters, rather than out toward the farming hub. He kept going, and before he even realized that he had arrived, he was announcing himself at her entry, and waiting for a response

The door chorded a musical humming tone, and he burst in. Part of the way in, he noticed that she stood at the center of the room, holding the alien object up over her head. She was staring at the round luminous object as if it were a live snake. The image of her holding it so close to her head burned into his brain, causing him to panic.

"Solanje! No! Stop!" he commanded angrily, as he leaped toward her.

She twisted around in surprise. The glowing object held high, gyrated around with her, making her body move in what looked like a formalized Ching T'Karre dance.

"Put it down, Solanje. Bloody Cryst! What in all that's holy are you doing?" He heard himself swearing. He stepped threateningly toward her. Then, he reined himself in. He had commanded that there would be no violence, either verbal or physical, on board his ship and here he was cursing and shouting.

But what was she thinking? She shouldn't be any where near the alien device without his supervision!

He took a deep breath and tried to calm himself.

"Braden!" The entrance panel slid closed abruptly. Silence fell between them, as both stared at each other.

She should at least have the grace to be embarrassed at being caught red-handed. But no, not her. A royal born Ching T'Karre could do not wrong.

Her depthless dark eyes glared at him and her long, ebony-colored hair swirled around in a shiny mass, finally flowing to a stop, and fanning out around her head to form a dark nimbus. He observed her hair and idly remembered a notation on the Ching T'Karre people that said they rarely cut the hair of their royal born daughters. Solanje had refused to cut it short, even when long hair posed a hazard in low gravity. Instead, she wove her hair into a series of pinned coiled tresses, or alternately, an elaborate chignon in the style of the Ching T'Karre nobility where they believed that the longer the length of a woman's hair, the greater her status and importance. Solanje, adhering to old Ching T'Karre custom, kept her hair long in defiance of shipboard recommendations. She'd rather cut off an arm than a single strand of her exalted hair.

Braden stared in horror at the object she held in clear sight. She brought the radiant piece down from over her head with slender fingers and it drifted and halted, suspended in the space between them. There rested the reason why his world had spent so much time and money sending them into space. There was the awful secret his government kept—and required him to keep.

The alien device.

His eyes now locked onto the round shimmering object floating in front of her. She had taken the piece out of its silver pod-like carriage with its woven iridescent fibers that formed a circular configuration. It must have activated.

On a nearby table, sat the housing for the probe's main components. The woven circlet, detached from the unit, now floating before them. Mission Control thought it had a critical function, still not totally understood.

Several digital images of Alysia had been found on recordings inside the case. These had been photographed from high orbit, and indeed, it appeared that the craft had recorded and transmitted information about their world to a location far out in space that had become the destination for this mission.

Braden looked at Solanje and her agitated behavior, so unlike her. A frightening glitter sparked from her eyes. He wasn't sure whether it was a reflection from the object, or a reflection of her state of mind.

"Solanje! You're not to activate the device without me!"

"I haven't activated anything!" she retorted defensively. "I know what I can and can't do."

"We are forbidden to operate it alone," countered Braden. "Just because you're Ching T'Karre..."

"I know what's forbidden to me. Like Bashar who tempts me with every breath he takes. Forbidden. And you!" She glowered at him.

Me? Braden fell back, surprised by the accusation.

She waved a hand at him. "I cannot give in to one temptation and then expect to be strong enough to resist all others."

What was she saying? Bashar, he understood, but him? A Temptation? Dare he dream?

Hope shone in his eyes, but her returning glare squelched all promise of any reciprocating romantic feelings.

Ah well.

He said as calmly as he could, "Solanje, they're not the same. One is love; the other science."

She wasn't soothed. She looked past him and said, "Both are dangerous. So, I resist. I resist all temptations, so I can remain strong. Even you, Braden Steele, even you I must resist. And the Talent crystals from the Labyrinth! They have put those abominations on board. Do you know that they sing to me? They invade my dreams. Their mere presence tempts me." He noticed her stiff body posture and eyes that wouldn't meet his.

"Solanje they're crystal fragments, pieces from the Master Crystal Stack, and they only enhance what we already are; they don't change us. They make us better and bring forth our full potential. Mission control thought they might prove useful."

"Useful! Ha. They twist and distort the natural self. They change you. You do not understand what they do."

"Yes, I do. They make a chosen few stronger and better. We call those, the Talented. Humans might need every possible advantage when we meet the aliens," he argued. "We have no idea what they're like. We know they can make this." He pointed to the wafting object.

She shook her head. Horror flashed across her face as she leaned toward him for emphasis. "The crystals tinker with your mind and your soul. They're alive," she whispered.

He shook his head and rolled his eyes. "Solanje they're no different than a medicine you'd take to eliminate a genetic fault or cure an illness. We have drugs on board to help us cope with disease and deficiency problems. You don't complain about them."

"Yes! They're like a drug. The crystals are a drug that your people have become addicted to." A hand chopped the air. The floating circle gently bobbed in response.

Braden crossed his arms, frustrated. "No! This is a useless argument. Your culture has influenced your thinking beyond any reasoning."

"And yours has you."

"You don't have to touch the crystals. I said that I would honor your beliefs," he reminded her.

"And your beliefs have been contaminated because of their influence," she shot back.

"I believe in the law of human behavior given to us by Elsinore, Lady of the Crystal, who died for us and our humanity, just as you believe in certain rules of human behavior mandated by your culture. We must honor and respect all beliefs here."

Her shoulders slumped. "And I'm the only one on board who believes as I do. I'm the only one of my people in this entire crew. The others make fun of my awkward speech and ridicule my different customs. How can I hold onto my soul and remember who I am, and where I came from, when all about me wants to change me and wipe out everything I was taught to believe?"

"You're strong, Solanje. Your family house, Hasang T'Kai, is justly proud of you, but we make a new life here and change is not weakness," argued Braden.

"I strengthen myself every moment by placing temptation in front of me and then exercising my will to resist it. The crystals, the alien device, Bashar, you...that is the way of the Ching T'Karre. That's all I was doing,

Captain Steele, if you had taken the trouble to ask." She stared at the sparkling object, her eyes shining.

Braden put out his hand to touch her arm. "I know all temptations are hard, but sometimes if you focus too much on them, you make it harder to resist them. Be careful you don't turn a temptation into an obsession."

She shrugged his hand away.

He dropped his arm and stared off into space remembering things forbidden in his own past that had become an obsession and changed his life. And a current temptation right in front of him. But he would not mention that to her.

Instead he said, "It's a risky game you play. This discovery must remain a secret between us. It's too dangerous for the others—Icabar in particular. With his passion for language and communication, he would be unable to resist tampering with it."

She tapped the glowing object lightly, causing it to bob between them. "We need to study it more, so we're better prepared, if and when, we encounter these aliens you're so eager to find. I think we need to investigate this further to learn more of its secrets. The probe could be a trap, or a bomb, ready to go off at a certain time because of a certain thought, or it could hold the secret to an unknown universe and be a portal to other worlds. We don't know enough yet. We only suspect a little of its purpose. There's too much we don't know and that's just as dangerous."

She waved her hand at him and continued heatedly, "As far as Icabar is concerned, it's only a matter of time before he learns of the device's existence. He only must breathe the same air or be in a room that contains a whiff of a secret to know that it is there waiting for his discovery. On board this spaceship, it calls to him. For

Icabar, all secrets are a siren's song. He holds the most danger and the greatest risk to us. And yet, he may hold the best hope we have of completely understanding what it is."

Braden nodded. "Yes, you're right. I fear that he won't have the discipline to leave the alien device alone once he discovers it. When he finds this, he'll want to solve its mystery, regardless of the danger. He'll want to hear the voice of the alien and communicate with it."

Braden heaved a sigh. "I don't want to lose my communications officer just yet, Solanje; neither do I want my technical specialist to lose her mind. Put it away. Put it away for now. I need you at Navcom. The signal has stopped, and we have to figure out why. Have you done anything to the device?"

"It's stopped!"

"After three annuals of para-light speed velocity, we are drawing near where we think our target is, and now, the signal has disappeared off our monitors. Then, I find you waving the alien device around without me! Have you done anything? I need to know."

"No, nothing! I have changed nothing."

He saw her stare at the shimmering, golden object and then back at him. She reached out and plucked it out of the air.

He gestured at the glowing circle. "One crisis at a time! If we regain the signal, we'll explore this further— but until then, we have more pressing business to attend. Put all your research about the device on a data stick and let me have it to study. I'm hoping that this thing will lead us to an answer, because I believe the signal and this device are connected. But take the probe out only when I'm with you and at no other time. Put it back for now."

She gave him a long calm stare, the light in her eyes receding, or maybe it was only the object moving out of her line of sight, as slowly and carefully, she turned it off, put the circlet back into the pod and slid it into the locked compartment. With a sigh, she turned to him. "For now, I follow your orders."

"You must follow my orders all the time," he answered sternly. "For your own safety, if for no other reason. Forget the Ching T'Karre. This ship is your world now. And I'm its captain."

She gave no response. He watched as she silently locked it away. With no more to say, he let himself out.

Chapter 2

He moved through a connecting corridor toward the farm and tried to calm himself as he picked his way along. If through carelessness, anything was to happen to Solanje, he would never forgive himself, nor would Bashar de Fyre Elitas of the Sunglast who had made his desires for her clear. Still after all this time on board, Braden didn't understand the status of their relationship. Bashar had ardently pursued her while they were cadets at Sunpointe Academy, and since Bashar had been, and still was, Braden's closest friend, Braden had held back from expressing any of his own feelings for her. He had reined in a growing passion for the beautiful Solanje because of his friend. But as time passed in the ship's close quarters, and Bashar's and Solanje's relationship remained unclear, it became harder and harder to deny his own feelings and not to voice them.

He also held back because he felt that, as captain, he had to keep himself apart from the crew in order to command them. Yet, he wanted their friendship and support out here in this lonely void. He found that it wasn't easy to control his desire anywhere near Solanje. The resulting turmoil was a constant secret battle he fought. Whenever he worked himself up to tell her how he felt, the discussion always seemed to veer off into some argument.

Just like then.

His comm flashed red again. *Now what?* "Braden here."

Liana Grace, personnel specialist, came on. "Braden, you need to get to Crystal's quarters ASAP. Something's happening over there. Take Adam for backup."

Fate! More problems. It appears my crew likes to create conflict for no apparent reason other than to alleviate boredom. Blast! I thought everything was under control.

Braden grabbed at a few handholds to help him reverse direction and headed back toward Crystal's quarters. The half gravity lightened as he made his way inward toward the ship's center. He keyed Adam's channel. "Can you take a break? I need you at Crystal's quarters ASAP. Something's happening. Meet you there."

"On it," rumbled Adam. "Heading out now."

Braden breathed a sigh of relief. Whatever the problem was, big blond Adam with his easy-going nature, would have his back.

"Confirm. Braden out."

Braden pushed harder against the wall. He brushed by protruding equipment and danced over wrapped cables and tubing. The heavier gravity lightened, and he picked up speed, barely touching what they now considered the floor. He skimmed past several other crewmember units and stopped in front of Crystal's. On the other side of the panel, a woman's voice shouted, "Take your hands off me!"

He heard a low throaty reply and then a slap. A loud crash sounded, as if someone had collided against furniture. A man began to swear in very descriptive terms.

Braden located Crystal's keypad and heard something thud against a wall inside. "Open up!" he shouted, and keyed in the captain's override.

As the entrance slid open, he saw Crystal staggering backwards, her blonde hair in disarray, and her blue eyes angry. Robert faced her, his back to Braden, angrily shouting at her and oblivious to the man who stood behind him.

"What's wrong with you, bitch? I only wanted a little affection, a kiss, or a smile. Don't you know how to be nice to a man?" He lunged toward her. Crystal's eyes widened at the sight of Braden behind him and she stumbled backward.

"Don't back away from me when I'm talking to you," Robert shouted angrily. "No woman turns away from me when I'm talking to her."

Braden growled, "Leave her alone." He roughly grasped Robert's arm from behind just as Robert reached out to Crystal. "Stop it!"

Startled, Robert spun around, twisting out of Braden's grip. His dark brown eyes glared at him. Malice covered his flushed narrow face. He pushed back damp brown hair and paused. His mouth worked silently, and then finally, he found words. "What? You! I should have guessed you'd show up. Well, you can have her, but don't waste your time." Robert shot her an angry stare. "Give her to Glaze. She's as frigid as he is. Whatever he is. Who knows? Enjoy the cockteaser if you want her, I'm done here." He attempted to push his way past Braden.

Furious, Braden grabbed Robert's arm and jerked him back. Robert fell into him, almost tumbling the two of them. Braden steadied them and raised a clenched fist, coming close to hitting Robert in the face. He stopped himself. His anger was making him act crazy. He held his breath until he could trust his words. He lowered his arm. Then quietly and evenly he said, "Confine yourself to your quarters. I won't tolerate this behavior on board my ship. Do you understand?" He gave Robert a shove that propelled him to the open entrance.

Robert staggered forward, turned, and looked at him as if he were about to explode. A bright red spot the shape of a hand covered one cheek. He took a breath and his face grew cold.

"I mean it. That's Captain's order," growled Braden, waving him out.

Robert huffed, "Snotty bitches, all of them. I know. I hear them talk behind my back. They don't think I hear, but I do. They like it a little rough. Then when I try to give them what they want, they complain."

Braden shook his head. "She said to stop. I heard her. No one forces anyone against their will here, and if you disrupt this ship anymore, I'll be forced to take measures that neither of us will like."

Robert straightened. "Don't start threatening me, or you'll be sorry, Captain or not. And don't pretend you don't want it either. What about Solanje, eh? Think Bashar's going to share that piece of ass with you?" Robert sneered at him defiantly. "Never going to happen. Such a shame for you."

Braden's anger boiled over at the comment. It was all he could do to remain coherent. He spoke carefully, as if dealing with sharp glass, "Watch it, Robert. Do you want me to toss you into lockup and just forget?" Braden glared back at him.

"This ship would fall apart. You need me to fix and repair it."

"Not as much as you think. Adam's good with a screwdriver and tape, too."

There was a long staring match, and then, the anger drained out of Robert. He shrugged his shoulders, trying to appear nonchalant. "Okay, okay. I misunderstood her. I thought she wanted me to seduce her. I thought rough sex excited her. She asked for it, saying what she did. This is her fault, not mine."

A gasp came from Crystal.

"Take Robert and secure him in his quarters," Braden ordered an arriving Adam who stopped abruptly at the entrance. Adam's calm blue eyes surveyed the disaster and widened. Braden waved a dismissive hand toward Robert. "Lock him in his quarters until further notice."

Adam looked down at the shorter Robert and then over to Crystal. His eyes narrowed. "On it," he nodded. His wide forehead wrinkled, and his pale blond eyebrows formed a frown. He grasped Robert by an arm and tugged at him.

"Come on."

Tossing a defiant glare over a shoulder at Braden and Crystal, Adam forced-marched Robert out. The door whooshed closed behind them. Braden could hear Robert's angry voice cursing and complaining and Adam's rumbling reply as they headed away. Then all was quiet.

Braden thumbed his comm. "Liana, Adam's taking Robert to quarters. I want you to talk to him and then see Crystal, too. He attempted to..."

"Yes, I can guess what happened. They're coming in now. Calm Crystal down and I'll come by to talk to her as soon as I finish with Robert."

"Thanks," he said, "I told Adam that Robert is to stay secured in his quarters until I decide what to do with him. Right now, he's acting violent. Go there and keep Adam with you as protection. Braden out."

That done, his attention focused on a trembling Crystal, "It's okay. He's gone. He won't do it again. I promise. Liana is coming by to be with you after she talks to him."

Crystal collapsed into a chair and rubbed her face. She shook her head back and ran her fingers through her hair. "He'll come back. I know he will. His kind always comes back. This isn't the first time he's tried to attack me." Her shoulders convulsed.

He wanted to pat her on the back or something but suspected she didn't want to be touched. His hand wavered in the air above her, then dropped. He tried to think of soothing words, but they all stuck in his mouth. He just stood there as all thoughts dribbled away, leaving him paralyzed and embarrassed.

"Why?" she gulped after a small silence. "I thought that I'd finally escaped men like him. Now I'm trapped." Her words trailed off.

Braden cleared his throat and questioned, "Escape? What are you talking about? Look, he won't try it again. I'll stop him. I can't allow that behavior on this ship. If he even looks like he's thinking about attacking you, I'll drag him outside and dangle him in space until he understands the rules here. I'm the Captain; I'll do whatever is necessary. Or, I can schedule you on different shifts and put a monitor on him that will track his movements if need be. We do have options to control him."

She looked up at him. "Really? You'd do that?" A small smile curved her lips for a moment and then collapsed.

He studied her. This was a Crystal that he had never seen before. She usually did her job well, but with a certain arrogance and aloofness toward most everyone around her.

Her shoulders slumped wearily. "We need him too much," she gusted out. "And he knows it." She put out a hand and touched Braden's arm. "I know his kind. They feel safe in their power, or they don't make the attempt."

"Crystal, he doesn't have the power here he thinks he does. He's more talk and bluster. I'm the Captain and this will be handled. Look, go freshen up, wash your face and get your breath back." He continued, "I'll wait here and guard the door."

Crystal nodded and slipped into the fresher.

The entrance made a chiming sound. Braden distractedly opened it and saw Icabar's inquisitive face peering avidly at him. "Is everything all right?" asked Icabar, his wide brown eyes darting past him and looking into the unit.

"Everything's fine," answered Braden, trying for nonchalance. He eased the panel closed a bit.

Icabar wasn't diverted.

"Oh? I thought I heard a commotion and shouting. I thought it came from here. This is Crystal's quarters, right?" Icabar peered at the outside of the door and back inside at Braden with a puzzled expression on his face.

"Yes, she's changing her clothes. She'll be fine."

A dark eyebrow arched up. Icabar inched forward, putting in his foot, as Braden started to slide the panel closed. Icabar's face looked as if he expected to find something titillating going on. "Is there anything I can do to help?" He practically jittered with curiosity. His eyes blinked rapidly. His breathing was heavy. Braden imagined hair standing on end.

For once, Braden didn't appreciate Icky's prying interest. He continued to close the panel, tapping Icabar's foot back into the corridor. "No, she's too emotional to talk to anyone right now."

"Crystal?" Icabar sounded incredulous.

Braden paused. "Ask Solanje to come here."

Icabar blinked. "She's going on sleep shift after the next shift. Will she be here?" Braden saw Icabar's eyes get wider until they fairly popped out of his head. Suddenly, Braden realized what he had been saying wasn't really what he had meant to communicate.

Oh, what must the man be thinking?

"No, she won't! Did you find out anything more about the signal?" asked Braden changing the subject.

Icabar blinked. "Nothing definitive, but..."

"Go get Joel. I need more eyes at Navcom."

"But..."

"Go!"

The foot retracted.

Gads! Braden slammed the panel, almost pinching Icabar's nose as it shut.

Crystal peered out. She had washed, changed, and looked a lot better. "Who was that? You haven't said anything to anyone, have you?"

"Only Icabar. I didn't tell him anything, although I imagine that he's dying to know what happened."

"No! I don't want anyone to know about this. They'll just talk behind my back and say I'm to blame. I couldn't bear it. I don't want anyone knowing any of this." Her voice grew shrill.

Braden tried to calm her down. "Icabar won't say anything. He likes to keep secrets. Besides, he thinks something else is, ah, going on here. Talk to Liana, though. Then, Solanje is coming over to show you some defensive moves. She has some good ones."

"She's certainly got Bashar tiptoeing around."

"Now, don't you worry about Bashar. He'll get what he wants in due time. Those of the Sunglast understand the power of waiting for what is worthwhile. Do you feel any better now?"

She smiled. "Yes, I'm sorry. I overreacted."

"No. Robert was out of line. I'll talk to Liana and come up with a solution. Right now, he's under lock and key with Adam watching over him. Adam has the brawn to handle him. Liana will be on her way here as soon as she finishes. Any time now."

"Thanks, Captain." She reached out and gently touched his arm. A tentative smile appeared on her lips.

"Stay put until she arrives." He nodded, turned, and left.

Chapter 3

He keyed his comm and called Navcom. Icabar and Glaze were still looking for a restarted signal.

"We've had no luck, as yet, but Icabar has a bet that he'll be the first to find it," said Glaze.

"And most likely you have a bet that you will," stated Braden, knowing his crew. "Has Bashar set the odds and win?"

"There's some disagreement about that," answered Icabar coming online.

"Let's worry more about finding the damn signal and less on the betting. Okay?"

"You bet captain. We're on it."

"Should I be there?"

"Only if you want to give Bashar some money."

"Not probably but let me know immediately if the signal starts again. Braden out."

"We're out."

*

With a sigh, he headed toward the hydroponics module where Tessa di Luria reigned.

She was an opposite problem from Solanje.

He found her in hydroponics among the herbs and vegetables with a frown on her face and a smudge of dirt on one cheek. A stray leaf lay in her tousled light brown hair. She turned as he approached and smiled.

"You came," she said delighted. "Liana said you were delayed with a crisis and might not make it."

"True, but I know you had a problem, and I wanted to make sure it's solved to your satisfaction. Our water supply is critical." He sat down on a nearby bench suddenly tired.

Her eyes showed concern. She touched his arm and sat next to him. "I have sent a menu over for the next meal shift. Some trees fruited poorly, so I improvised, using an old family recipe handed down from Elyssa Telluria. I hope you like it."

He leaned back against a tank that spilled over with greenery. A fragrant leaf tickled one ear. "You know I'll approve it. You're the best cook on board. You're related to Elyssa's line and she's known to have a Talent with herbs and animals, so I'm sure it'll be fine," he answered gruffly.

"Maybe you're just gotten used to shipboard rations after all this time." She raised an eyebrow at him.

"Maybe. People will eat anything if they're hungry enough." A smile curved his lips.

"Oh, thanks so much." She shifted on the seat and snorted.

He shrugged. "It wasn't an insult. I've just never been picky about food. I figure hunger makes most meals palatable."

"Say that to Glaze or Bashar."

"Just keep us healthy and ignore the delicate palates they claim to have."

She sighed. "I'm trying." She rubbed an arm and looked around. "You're letting your hair grow out a little." She put up a finger and delicately brushed his forehead. "It waves in the front now. It's nice. You should keep it like that."

He brushed at some hair. "I need a haircut but haven't had time lately."

"I like it better this length." Reaching out, she plucked a green sprig growing in the hydroponic tub behind them, brought it to her mouth and chewed on it. She fingered in and picked another one and handed it to him. "A new strain. Just propagated it. Like it?"

He indulged in some thoughtful chewing of the minty herb. "Not bad. Are the wide spectrum light panels working all right?" He squinted up at the full spectrum light spilling down onto the surrounding greenery.

"Oh, they're fine. I didn't know if you would come since Adam fixed the filters and we have clean water again. I asked that he inform you." She gave him a shy smile and coquettishly twirled a bit of hair.

"He told me he fixed it, but I wanted to check it out for myself," he said brusquely. "Our water supply is our lifeline, so I'm glad that Adam solved the problem so quickly. Nothing's worse than having your wastewater not get recycled properly and end up in your drinking glass."

"It did attract comments." She wrinkled her nose.

He nodded with a grimace. "You also put in a second request that I come. Are you having any further concerns I need to know about?"

She shook her head and hid behind a veil of hair. Peeking out, she asked, "Do you want a walking tour to check everything out, or would you settle for a verbal summary here? I did clone a couple of miniature goats a while back that look promising. I hope to make cheese. You might want to check them out. They're cute."

An errant air current fluttered several strands of her loose curls and distracted him. He studied her. She had made an easy transition to space travel and seemed right at home here at "The Farm." It was only when she worked in Navcom or engineering that any awkwardness manifested itself. Technology and mechanics daunted her, but the husbandry of growing things fed her soul.

"What would you like to have from my garden?" She cocked her head and blinked light brown eyes at him.

Braden pondered several ribald responses but decided on an innocuous request instead.

No use throwing fuel on burning embers.

"You make a delicious and calming herbal tea," he said, trying to act serious. "We could use this new herb as an added flavor."

"Good idea," she answered back with an impish grin.

He took a breath, feeling the heavier gravity. The ship had been designed with magnetic-electrostatic shields all around and two cylindrical bodies that rotated behind the forward Navcom nose.

Along the cylinders were exhaust jets designed for maneuvering. Expandable sections that contained easily portable furniture and equipment opened out when in deep space to add more interior room.

The two large life support cylinders counter rotated in balanced precession around an axial shaft to provide partial gravity through centripetal acceleration. When needed, the spin could be stopped, and any extended modules collapsed inward. The two-stacked cylinders could be hooked together to form a single smooth exterior if the ship needed to dock or land on hard ground. More likely, one of two shuttles would be the means of transport to any given planet.

Centripetal force acted stronger along the outside rim of the cylinders where the hydroponics and husbandry pods were permanently located. The sleeping bay and crew quarters had a lighter gravity being located nearer the center of the ship.

Braden inhaled the rich fragrance of growing greenery. This area, as well as the sleeping area and Navcom, had extra heavy shielding against damaging radiation or neutrino bursts. Food was survival and needed extra protection. Navcom was also a critical area. He thought of each area, calling them the stomach, the heart, and the head of his ship.

"Actually, now that I'm here, in the heavier gravity, just sitting feels like a good choice. It's been a long difficult shift so far for me. I would rather gaze at beautiful scenery, and maybe have some light conversation." He smiled back at her. "I trust all's well if you say so. Are you saying so?"

"Ah yes, now that the pipes are finally working properly...yes, everything's well. So, what would you like to talk about?" she asked with a coquettish smile. "Farm reproduction? Husbandry?"

Hmmm...

"I asked you to study Professor De Vey's notes on space/time recently, since you have a minor in physics. He proposed the theory that the faster we go, the greater the difference in the rate time passes on board this ship compared to the rate time passes on Alysia. We studied his theory at Sunpointe. So, I thought you might be interested in heading up a group, while we're out here, that would set up some experiments to test out the concept."

"Sounds interesting." She looked thoughtful. "Would you be involved?"

"You would be in charge of selection, pending my approval. If you want me to contribute, I'll see what I can do." He looked at her. "Do you remember the details of the theory?"

She laughed. "I didn't memorize the exact formula, but I remember the theory. It suggests that everyone on Alysia is aging faster than we are. If that's true, then your brother Richard will be older than you when you return. It sounds like you want to see if there's a way to validate Professor De Vey's theory while we're out here."

"That's the idea."

She nodded. "I can detail the theory at our next science meeting and set up some experiments. But Captain, you're already worrying about our return when we haven't even reached our destination." Her nose wrinkled, concern in every crease.

Braden sighed. "I know. Mission Control tried to think of everything when overseeing this project, and yet there are always unexpected surprises in any venture. The truth is that already the reality of space has been far different from what we predicted in several instances. The ice fields on Traigar's moon were a total shock to the scientists back home. So, we must be flexible with our expectations.

"We have already justified this expedition with a lot of surprising new information, and actual success in using dark matter as our propulsion, thanks to Adam. Also, look at all you've done with genetics here. And our food. Your lab creates meat proteins from propagated stem cells that taste like real beef and chicken. Our next mission will already be much more prepared for space survival because of your discoveries and suggestions."

She blushed at the compliment, looked away for a moment, and then returned to his gaze. "Captain, I appreciate your comment on my poor abilities. I will propose an experiment with the others at our next meeting, but right now you're on break and I suggest a soothing massage rather than all this heavy thinking." Her eyes twinkled with expectation of more than a simple massage.

"I'm sure that I would enjoy it, but..." Braden hesitated. Sexual relationships on board had concerned him. Mission Control had given a lot of thought to a mixed crew of males and females. In the end, they had decided that it would be better to mix things up, but it brought a bag of problems to the trip. Braden was captain, but all the others were interlocking pieces with specialties in certain areas. A lot of jockeying for position and status among the crew had started early on and was still going on. Robert had made a desperate attempt to assert power and had lost. He might try again.

As Captain, Braden had been reluctant to plunge into an affair with a crewmember, afraid to upset the delicate balance of crew interaction. He also didn't want to subject himself to manipulation by any crew member. He felt that a captain had to keep a certain distance and a clear head. Still, he considered himself a red-blooded male who was attracted to women, and sex was an itch that wouldn't go away. But so far, sexual contact for him had been confined to a polite pat on the shoulder for a job well done, or an accidental brush with a bobbing breast.

However, Tessa di Luria's lush body and warm manner aroused him, and he wasn't sure he could control his physical responses to things female much longer, especially when the female appeared as willing as Tessa. After his confrontation with Solanje, he needed a release, but he certainly didn't want to use Tessa as a salve for his sexual frustrations. That would be unfair to both, no matter how tempting. Tessa had put out the word that she was interested in the reluctant captain and he even suspected that Icabar and others had a bet going as to which female would be his first. It had been so long, and yet he still held back.

Solanje.

He couldn't have her, so he didn't want anyone else. It might be that simple.

There had been classes explaining how space might affect the human body and specific classes on how low gravity affected sexual interaction. Learning about it was one thing; experiencing it was another. Certain parts tended to bob and float at inconsiderate times and, well, a person couldn't help but notice it, or them. And, of course, Crystal had administered birth control shots to all. A pregnancy in space was a problem he didn't want to deal with.

Although he wasn't sure who was currently having sex, rumors abounded. Bashar and Solanje seemed to be glancing at each other on and off, but he had heard it hadn't gone all the way yet.

But who believed rumors, anyway?

Lately, Solanje had made several sexual overtures toward him, and that bothered him. It bothered him in more ways than one. He had thought that Solanje's and Bashar's romantic relationship, begun at Sunpointe, would have been consummated by now, once they were away from her disapproving parents. Yet, that seemed not to be the case. He wanted a definition on their relationship, and yet he didn't, for without it, his options were still open.

Tessa tugged at his arm. "Don't frown so much. Come and at least enjoy a massage. I'll try not to seduce you, unless provoked." His eyes widened, but he didn't shake loose from her grip either, as she gaily dragged him away. She obviously hadn't heard about Crystal's situation, and he wasn't going to be a fool and mention it now, but it did make things more precarious.

However, his muscles did ache, and he could use a good massage. Recent events had been stimulating, to say the least.

After all, weren't some sacrifices expected of the captain to keep up the morale of his crew? He would start with a massage, and then who knows what might happen? Maybe he would just get a massage, or maybe someone would win a bet.

He checked into Navcom and got an update. Nothing had changed. No one needed him. An argument broke out. Something about changing odds.

Chapter 4

Later after a soothing massage, the deed was still not done, much to Tessa's obvious disappointment. However, he felt much more relaxed. They had come perilously close and improvisation had delayed her expectation. He did thank her profusely, but she pouted disappointment and heaved a great sigh. He laughed and patted her arm, adding in a kiss on the top of her head and a warm hug.

A very talented female indeed, he admitted.

Braden wondered briefly if Tessa might have wagered something along the way. He admitted that he didn't have any proof there was even a bet about him, but the probability was high because he knew his crew. More likely the betting was hot and heavy at this point. They created strange entertainment when they were bored. However, with the signal stopping, they wouldn't be bored any longer. Scared and anxious, yes; bored, no.

He threaded his way through a maze of corridors toward the observation section. Technical equipment, large tubes, and various protrusions impeded his way, but he was so accustomed to traveling through this part of the ship that he barely noticed.

He stopped at an expanded module that they used as a workout room where Adam and Solanje now sparred. At Sunpointe Academy, Adam had achieved a first-degree black belt in several disciplines. Trophies from various martial arts competitions had decorated the dorm room he and Braden had shared. Adam's skills in geology, metallurgy, and spacecraft propulsion were a great asset on board. Having an influential grandfather, such as Hammerslag Obsidian di Adamantine, hadn't hurt his selection for crew either. Politics had played a part in a few crew choices, his own not the least.

Now, Braden peered through the small window and saw the artful Solanje challenging the large and powerful Adam. A big muscular blonde against a tiny, but deadly, dark-haired dynamo made for an interesting match. However, Braden just smiled and signed the schedule sheet posted outside, noting that Crystal and Solanje's names were posted for a coming session. He looked back in. Adam had better watch out, or before he knew it, he would be flat on his back... again.

Braden chuckled as he imagined Adam's dazed expression as he lay flat on his back. Adam didn't take kindly to losing to anyone, especially the diminutive Solanje, but she held a She T'ang Master's belt and was therefore a worthy opponent to the larger Adam. Braden looked forward to his own sparring with Adam, still several shifts away. He would be sure to ask how this current session had gone and note Adam's response.

He eased around to the opposite extended module to peer in at Crystal. She was cycling avidly in the exercise cylinder and was attacking it with more than her usual vigor. She and Solanje must have had a talk, or maybe Liana had suggested the exercise.

The "rat wheel" provided aerobic exercise that helped retain muscle mass and created enough electrical energy to augment the solar powered lights on the farm. Crystal appeared fully engaged, so he decided to leave well enough alone and crossed left, up the corridor, toward the Observatory.

Upon arriving, he slid opened the heavy door and emerged into a breathtaking room with a partially transparent ceiling. Overhead, stars and whirling galaxies glittered against a dark velvet backdrop. The back part of the room also had a clear window that was six spans wide and four spans high and provided a panoramic view of space. Braden strode to the window and gazed out. Whenever he felt restless, he would wander here and stare out enraptured into the vastness of space. When he contemplated the stars like this, he felt the overwhelming fragility of his life descend upon him. Only a few thin layers of an experimental material protected him from the harsh environment of deep space. One small hole in his ship and he would be dead before he could even take breath.

At first, he hadn't been able to sleep on board and had listened; terrified at all the various creaks and groans of the ship, afraid that something would go wrong if he dozed off. His sleep was haunted by visions of asteroids plunging into the ship's frail fabric and opening huge gaping holes, or wayward meteors grazing too close and splitting the ship apart despite the magnetic field that surrounded it. Some people thought that space was empty, but he knew it teemed with everything from huge whirling galaxies to small dense neutrinos, drifting in dark matter.

These nervous thoughts sent a rush of adrenaline through him. The ship seemed to shrink in size and gave rise to a feeling of panic. He wanted to pound on the walls or jump screaming out into space, so that he could be free from the confining grip of the ship and the terror of his thoughts. Sometimes, he felt as if he were trapped in a fragile and dangerous tin can.

His adaptation to space travel had not been as easy as he had expected. What at first had seemed exciting and adventurous was turning out to be exhausting, and too often, just plain boring. Then, at times, he could barely breathe because of an inrushing fear. A claustrophobic captain in deep space was a man with a problem. At least the attacks didn't happen often and eventually, with Liana's help, he had learned to cope with the illness. Sometimes drugs took the edge off.

If that signal didn't start up again, they might be forced to wander out here forever, looking for elusive aliens with no idea where they might be.

Not a pleasant thought.

"Is that you, Braden? Are you sitting in the dark in one of your moods?"

Liana Grace's voice broke the silence. He heard her soft rustling, as she entered the observatory and drifted toward him. She always seemed to find him when he felt like this. No one else knew about his fears. Only Liana had managed to pry out his secret and he resented her for having the knowledge. The first panic attack had occurred soon after lift-off. He had not expected it. A captain of a star ship should not have these feelings, but they came anyway, unmindful of his power to command.

Braden faced her as she came in. She admonished him. "Aren't you supposed to be on your sleep schedule now? Don't you and Glaze have the next shift? I don't want a captain so tired that he can't think properly, do you?"

"I have no appointment with you right now." His voice shook with irritation. He didn't want to be analyzed at the moment or treated like a damaged child. He saw her shape drift toward him through the surreal starlit room and stop by his side.

"Maybe you should."

"Leave me alone. Robert and Crystal need you more than I do."

"My purpose is to help whoever I think needs it."

He gazed at her elegant face. Wide amber eyes fringed with gold lashes stared intelligently back at him. Her short, cropped, white blonde hair brushed across the top of pale eyebrows and fell in a smooth line down the sides of her cheeks. She paused. "Icabar says the signal stopped. Is that true?"

"Yes," he answered shortly.

She laughed. "So, what are you doing out here? Brooding in the dark?" An air of easy calm surrounded her. Her lips quirked into a smile. "Or do you think you can peer out that window and spot the signal generator with your naked eye?"

"There's a telescope nearby."

"Is that why you're here? To gaze at stars?"

"Sometimes I need a moment to be by myself," he said petulantly.

Fate, he sounded childish!

She nodded. "I understand your need for personal space. I'll admit the ship feels a bit crowded. I also know you try very hard to keep an emotional distance from the rest of us."

"As captain, I need to maintain a sense of objectivity. I might have to order someone to do something that could threaten their life in order to protect the mission or save a crewmember."

"Everyone has to make tough choices from time to time." She looked out toward the stars. "You'll know when to do the right thing."

"My having strong feelings for someone could endanger the mission," he added defensively.

"You don't know what's going to happen. You can't predict," she countered.

"I might make the wrong choice because I'm thinking emotionally and not rationally," he argued back.

"Does that frighten you? Making an emotional choice? Sometimes, those are the best choices." She smiled at him.

She motioned him to sit on a nearby bench next to her. A radiant beam of light from some far-off star shone in through the window, causing a rim of white to highlight the side of her smoothly sculpted profile. Her serious, starlit eyes turned toward him. He sat down next to her, gazing at the side of her luminous face.

"You're still a man first," she said softly. "Whatever you tell yourself."

In answer, he expelled out his breath in a short laugh. "Are you suggesting I get intimate with someone as a sort of therapy; rather like one of Tessa's massages?"

"Even a Captain needs love and companionship. Maybe if you would partner with someone, then the rest of the crew would sort themselves out. All this drama is hard on everyone. It reflects the unsettled state of the crew. The Lady knows, Robert needs to learn control. I gave him some drugs, by the way, and strong counseling. I don't like to use drugs very often, but I consider him a special case."

"I thought about space dragging him if he doesn't shape up, or just locking him up until he rots."

"That's a bit extreme. Let me work with him some...but I might mention you suggested it." She lifted an eyebrow and wiggled it.

He waved a hand. "Be my guest if it gets his attention or makes a difference. For now, he stays locked in his quarters until you feel he's capable of cooperating."

"We need him." She looked down at her hands.

"He knows it and uses that fact. I'm reaching a point where his arrogant attitude and stupid actions make him more of a liability than the great asset he imagines himself to be." He tried to throw a captain's tone into the statement.

"Robert said Crystal slapped him and he lost his temper."

"Well, he better find it. You tell him. Find it before I step in and do something drastic that no one will like."

"Give me some more time with him."

"Of course. Let me know when you've had enough of him." He shifted angrily in his seat. "I'll...

"You need to find a mate and get laid."

"Wha..." He rolled his eyes at her. "A bit brash there, Liana. Have you picked her out yet?"

She gave him a quick grin. "Maybe."

"You know I have an aversion to manipulation," he warned.

"A well-known fact."

"Crystal said something." Braden shifted toward her.

"About what?"

"I'm thinking there might have been abuse in her past. Most likely her father. Are you aware?"

"I'm aware," she said firmly. "We're working on it. She can be difficult herself. I blame her father."

"The great Brandon Telluria." He made a sour face.

"Not a nice man any way you look at him but keep it to yourself." She lifted her eyes to the stars and stood up. She put her hand to the glass, as if to touch the shining images, and the touch became a sort of caress. "We might have to spend our entire lives out here. We might only ever have each other." She gazed meaningfully at him. "Therefore, we need to be careful with each other."

He stood up and moved next to her, looking out the window with her. "Among all those billions of stars out there, there has to be intelligent life. We'll find it." He faced her. "And," he continued, "The purpose of this exploration is to return home, so that we can share what we discover. I promised my brother I would."

"That's fine by me. Harrison insinuated that a space wormhole might enable us to travel across vast distances and still return home in our lifetime. Should I believe him?"

He shrugged. "It's a theory. It's not the returning so much I worry about. It's that when we finally do arrive back, I fear things might have changed a lot."

She snorted at him. "Of course, everything will have changed. Nothing stands still in time. Time moves on. We're caught here in our own web of time, just as everyone on Alysia is caught in theirs. Expect it's all going to be different because it will be."

He sighed. "The signal has stopped. Now what?"

She looked at him sternly, her lips in a thin line. "Braden, you of all people, have always known what. Why do you hesitate now? The whole wide universe is out there for you to explore." She threw her hand out in a casual gesture, as a smile played about her lips. "The stars are your destiny. They always have been. And you know that. No need to hesitate, just do."

He remembered that she always seemed to know when something was bothering any one of them and usually knew what to say to help that person feel better.

"Yes, you're right." Suddenly the tiredness, the fear, all lifted from him. "You frighten me with how well you know me. Sometimes, I think you can even read my mind." Almost reluctantly he said, "I better go and check in on Navcom and then, try to get sleep before next shift. We don't want a grumpy captain, now do we?" He grinned and began humming a thoughtful tune, as he slipped out the door.

*

She sighed deeply and gazed one last time at the immense universe floating outside. "You don't know you silly, serious man, but I can read your mind. At least some of it, part of the time."

Liana shook her head. Sometimes having the Talent felt hard. Ever since she had received her Talent crystal, she had sensed other people's feelings and occasionally their thoughts. She considered Empathy a challenging Talent. And added to that, she was the rare Talent that included a touch of telepathy too. That made it harder, given the crew's current state of mind.

She cleansed her thoughts of Braden's tangled emotions and considered Robert. Robert's psyche held the most serious problems. She hadn't realized at the beginning how damaged he was, or she would have barred his selection. Maybe she could straighten him out with just counseling. She would offer strong suggestions. If not, she would have to use the forbidden part of her Talent. She didn't want to alter another's basic personality, but if the safety of the ship demanded that she do so, then she would. Mission Control had no idea the power over behavior that she had. They would have never let her come on board if they had realized her power. But she had needed to come. She had left Bogtown for that purpose. She had made promises to important people, Mother Kat particularly. Kat who had sacrificed most of her long life for this mission. So, she had...influenced their decision, and here she was.

Robert's situation had to change. The situation bothered her while infecting the others as well. She could do it, but there were consequences to changing a personality. She squared her shoulders. Consequences that she was ready to accept. With one last glance at swirling space, she left to sort her own challenges.

Chapter 5

On the other side of the ship, while Braden worked his way to sleep bay, Joel DeLande struggled to wake up. He was dreaming again. This time he plummeted down a spiraling tunnel faster and faster, more and more out of control. At the end of the tunnel, something waited. Something frightening. He saw dim figures haloed in light gesturing at him.

The dream receded, becoming misty, less turbulent. Then suddenly he jerked awake with sweat drenching his face, his whole body shaking. His skin tingled as if cold feathers had brushed the back of his neck. He struggled to awareness and realized that he was on board a spaceship hurtling through deep space. Terrified, he took a stuttering breath. What did this dream mean?

He banged opened the heavy hatch suddenly wanting some space and air. He blinked and looked out to reassure himself that he was safe in sleep bay. Five other green-lighted capsules hummed reassuringly nearby.

"Joel, are you all right?"

Icabar's voice drifted through the darkness.

"I'm fine," he said, grasping the door's edge.

"Was it another one of your dreams?" Icabar's voice held concern and sincerity, and yet, somehow Joel felt as if he were under interrogation.

"Yes, but I'll be fine."

"Tell me about it." The voice came closer.

"It was nothing."

"It might be important," Icabar insisted.

Joel almost denied telling him, but then he remembered that he was talking to Icabar. Denial was useless. Icabar would eventually pry out every portion of the dream anyway, so he might as well tell him, or risk an endless interrogation.

So, he told him.

"Braden needs to know what you're dreaming," said Icabar, rubbing his eyes in the pale green light. "It may mean something. He wants you at Navcom, anyway. I've come to get you. If we see him there, you can mention it." He peered in and the dim green light revealed concern covering his face. He paused. Joel felt him being studied and then, Icabar's expression changed. "Then again, it may mean nothing." Icabar shrugged. "At least tell Liana," his voice trailed off.

An amazing set of circumstances had led to Joel's selection for the crew of *The Seeker*. Mission Control had chosen him unexpectedly when another crewmember had dropped out. They had assigned him to the team because he had received a lot of recognition for innovative systems designs, particularly interior configuration and service functions.

The influence of his family helped. It didn't hurt to be related to the famous Eleanor DeLande Armstrong. The DeLande Talent carried the ability to foresee. Some of Joel's current family held bits and pieces of the Talent. His aunt worked as a stockbroker and his father managed investments. His brother had used the family talent of precognition in his gambling, much to their mother's dismay.

Yet, the Talent had remained latent within Joel, until after he had signed on with *The Seeker*. Then strangely, something began to call to him, and he began having dreams. He had his first dream the night after they passed Kracta, Alysia's second moon. Recently, the dreams were coming more often, and repeating. He didn't understand what was happening to him. Now, he dreamed of alien places and strange ethereal beings. This recent dream bothered him. He was finding it harder and harder to get any decent sleep or to concentrate properly when awake.

Joel sighed and ran his fingers through his curly, light brown hair and climbed out of the capsule. He steadied himself against the side as Icabar left to pick up a hot kauf for both of them from the nearby dispenser.

Joel closed his hazel eyes, now greener than blue in the dim light, and hugged his thin arms to his chest. Medium height, plain features, and shyness made it easy for him to blend into any background or crowd. Hard work, intellectual brilliance and connections had earned him recognition and advancement, but he knew that if they found out about his Talent, they would treat him differently. He had recently taken a liking to a certain female crewmember and he didn't want her to think him a freak. Others had. He remembered several surprising reactions, not all positive, from supposed friends when they discovered that he could foresee their futures.

He recalled how his aunt couldn't go anywhere without someone asking for a foretelling. Many a person's desperate wish for future knowledge, and the unwelcome answer it sometimes contained, would emotionally drain his aunt. "Sometimes," she confided to him, "I hate knowing what is going to happen next; the future isn't always wonderful, sometimes it's awful."

He agreed and understood her feeling. He didn't always want to know the future. Sometimes, he was afraid to know.

Like now.

Icabar returned with two hot drinks and a grim look. "The signal's stopped and the Captain needs you at Navcom. I'll be at the scope, so he wants an extra pair of eyes out front."

"So, who else's on deck?" asked Joel blowing on the hot kauf.

"Well, your highness, the princess of the Ching T'Karre will be there, and after deck duty iz goin' to be entertained in Crystal's private quaarters by none other than ze Captain himself." Icabar brushed at his hair and flung his hands back in a grand gesture as if tossing long strands over his shoulder.

Joel chuckled. "Oh Icky, you're incorrigible."

"Do not call me that, or I'll have my father, the Grand Duke, exterminate you."

"There's no royal blood in your family," countered Joel, shaking his head.

"That's the fraggin' truth, but don't let anyone else know. I'm starting a rumor," answered Icabar sipping the kauf and gesturing for them to leave.

Joel almost choked in mid sip.

Chapter 6

Solanje was at Navcom, but the alien device tugged at him. He drifted down the corridor and stopped in front of her panel. He shouldn't be here. He shouldn't invade her privacy. He should be sleeping in his pod, at least getting rest. It was fifth shift. Instead, he keyed in his override, and heard the tone that signaled admittance. He stumbled to where she kept the device and slid open the door. Fumbling at a lock, he opened the safe and pulled out the pod. He set it out on a table and activated it.

What had grandfather said?

Endless duros of instruction scrolled through his mind. Tapping a top switch, he heard it power up and unfold, revealing an electronically packed chassis full of equipment. Wheels expanded out, found the pad, and the carriage bounced up. He peered inside. Alien numbers and letters were carved on a panel that included switches and a screen. He touched a switch and a light pulsed.

His grandfather believed the device could communicate with the transmitting signal. In fact, when the ship arrived within a reasonable distance of the signal, his grandfather had told him to activate the probe and impute the ship's coordinates on its monitor. He pulled out his personal computer pad and checked their current coordinates. He typed in the ship's position on a numbered keyboard, checking to make sure he got the numbers correctly.

The device flashed a garish green and his numbers changed into strange ciphers on the device's screen.

Alien numbers? What had he done? Had he announced their approach? Did the alien craft link to the signal as grandfather suspected? Grandfather wasn't always right, but he wouldn't bet against him. He copied the strange marks to use for any alien number translations they might have to make.

He wiped sweat off his brow, hastily tapped the hatch shut, stuffed the pod back into the safe, locked it and shut the hidden panel's door. He needed to tell Solanje what he had just done and maybe it was time that the rest of the crew learn what they had on board.

Was it an instrument of destruction, or a whole new era of exploration for the human race?

Time to get some rest. He headed over to sleep bay. His movements felt heavy and his eyes drooped. Even sleep bay's lighter gravity didn't help tired and sluggish muscles.

He no sooner crossed the threshold into the dimly lit unit with its silent blinking capsules when his comm blared an emergency alert. He tapped the response switch and heard, "Captain! Captain. Come to Navcom."

"I found it!"

"No, I found it."

Icabar and Glaze spoke in unison.

"I was just looking and suddenly…"

"The transmitter started flashing again." Glaze's eager voice interrupted Icabar's.

"The transmission's reactivated and…"

Glaze's voice rode right over Icabar's words. "He's de-coding them even as we speak, and soon he'll tell us what it's saying."

"Glaze, I haven't a clue. It's complicated and impossibly alien. And different from last time. Captain, it's emitting a different signal series!"

Braden heard the excitement in their voices. It sent a shiver of fear down his spine.

There was a link ... and he had activated it!

"On my way," he answered briskly.

Thank the Creator, the signal was back. But what now?

He turned, half floating, half stumbling from sleep bay. With a longing glance back at his empty sleep capsule, he exited and headed for Navcom.

*

As Braden entered Navcom, Solanje spun about, her ebony hair swirling around her in the light gravity like a dark enveloping mist. "Ah, there you are," she said, eyeing him sideways. "Look at this. Here's the data I have so far." Solanje gathered up her wayward hair, pinned it neatly to the back of her head, and began to download the numbers onto his handheld. As he pretended to study the incoming figures, his eyes couldn't help but roam over her shapely bobbing body. He shivered.

Blast Liana for suggesting he get laid!

Braden tore his eyes away from Solanje and regarded his gathering crew. Navcom was becoming crowded as the last shift stayed, now totally immersed in their discovery, and the fifth shift came pushing in.

He saw three heads bent over toward each other in conference: Glaze's flopping flaxen tresses, Icabar's dark disheveled mop, and Bashar's black coarse curls. They were all at a computer table analyzing and transferring the incoming data to a star map that Glaze had displayed on the large overhead monitor. Joel was standing, staring up at the monitor, squinting at the developing image, suggesting adjustments.

Solanje murmured something about retrieving ship parameters and moved to another console. She returned with a data stick and inserted it into the computer. The ship blinked into position on the screen.

Bashar looked up, lingered momentarily on Solanje, and glanced away. As if she had felt his gaze, Solanje looked over toward Bashar, but by then, Bashar was busy checking the ship's other monitors. Braden could only grit his teeth and glare at them.

I have more important things right now than thinking about those two.

"So, what have you found?" he asked tersely.

All three heads looked up and studied him intently. He raised an eyebrow at them.

"You seem, ah, relaxed," answered Icabar.

The three exchanged glances. Icabar grinned and rubbed his fingers together and smirked at Adam.

"Not that relaxed, Icabar. Glaze wins the bet this time. By the way, how much did Tessa put in the pot?"

Icabar's shoulders slumped and Bashar smiled triumphantly. He put out his palm to Icabar.

"Aww Captain, you don't think we would ..." Icabar acted the innocent.

"What have you found?" asked Braden irritably.

Icabar waved his hands excitedly and said, "The signal has reactivated...and I saw it first."

"I did," responded Glaze.

"Icabar says the signal is coming from just outside that region." Bashar pointed to a large dark area that had an edge of debris around it.

"Mark it."

"Already done."

Braden studied the spot where Glaze's finger pointed on the monitor. Glaze's vivid blue eyes reflected excitement. "Icabar says the signal is coming from nearby this area." He looked over at Icabar. "I saw it right there before you said anything."

"But I reported it first, officially," insisted Icabar.

"The area looks empty," answered Braden puzzled. He moved closer and peered at the monitor.

Joel shook his head. "Something's there we can't see from this far away."

Icabar continued, "I think so too. Glaze has been taking readings and measurements that indicate an abundance of tachyon particles and intense radiation in the outlying area. There's also strange velocities and perturbed orbits from nearby asteroids."

Glaze's long aristocratic finger circled the large dark region on the monitor as he transitioned into his lecture mode. "See how all nearby planetary masses and gases rotate in a circular fashion here as if around some hidden axis?"

He rotated a finger over the area. "Look at the shadow blocking this particularly large planetary body at the outside edge of the closest solar system, as if something is occluding it along our line of sight. A dark arc cuts into it."

His finger traced a faint dark arc. "It's difficult to see, but something is there that has the configurations of an object more intense than just a dense cluster of dark matter. There's a circular shape to the field." He splayed out his fingers and made a sweeping circular motion.

"We didn't notice it at first because we were coming at it edge on, but now with the new course correction...It's why there's so much matter there. Something is creating a wide debris field along its edge."

Icabar answered from the communications board. "The noise signature is not a natural one and may be something created by an intelligent species to warn incoming ships or mark the area for some reason."

"Sort of like a signal buoy that marks a ship's channel," Bashar added, nodding.

"Or warns of hidden shoals," commented Joel, turning from the screen.

"What does your data say, Solanje?" asked Braden turning to her. "Has anyone found the transmitter?"

Her jaw clenched in concentration as she studied the graphs of sound resonances and the anomalous perturbations in the surrounding matter and gases. "My calculations agree with theirs. There's definitely something there. My first guess is a vortex such as a black hole, but the phenomenon has certain divergences that would make me cautious about jumping to that conclusion. The gravity pull is strong around a central axis and there appears to be abnormal fluctuations connected to the entity. Yet, I wouldn't call it a black hole. Not enough energy. Not the right signature. However, that doesn't mean that it isn't fatal or dangerous. There's been no discovery quite like it that I know of." She looked up frowning. "We'll risk our lives if we go too near it, much less inside the thing. I'd advise we not get too close until we know better what we're dealing with. We need to be careful."

Bashar grabbed Braden's arm. "It's our stargate! Your grandfather's hypothesis was right! We found it. This is what we have been looking for all along." Bashar had a gleam of excitement in his eyes. "What if there's a whole network of gates among the stars? And aliens."

Idly Joel said, "What do you think they look like?"

Everyone paused.

"Surely someone has a bet?" commented Braden.

"I've got money on blobs that float," answered Glaze. "They live in the ether and inhale methane."

"Blobs?" Icabar snorted. "That's ridiculous. You need dexterous digits to build a stargate." He grinned and rubbed his fingers together. "I'll take your bet, and I'll take your money."

"It's not a big bet." Glaze shrugged.

"My money's on a hive mind and insect-like creatures." Icabar looked up. "The leader has a big brain and lots of worker bees."

Solanje shook her head. "Insects stay small on Alysia because they can't support a heavy exoskeleton under our gravity. No, I think, maybe, something with tentacles and eyes that shoot out on stalks. Something tall and skinny that survives in a light gravity."

Glaze twirled around. "Tessa thinks they're living plants with wavy fronds that walk on stalk legs."

"Geesh, she would think something like that," commented Icabar. "She's a botanist."

"Maybe they're all hairy with ugly sharp teeth and red eyes," Bashar offered

"Putting money on that?" Icabar gave a grin.

Bashar shook his head.

"What about ghosts?" Joel blurted out. "Ghosts that glow in the dark."

"I think bird creatures with wings," chimed in Solanje, flapping her arms.

"Yes, wings," mumbled Joel.

Braden pursed his lips and thought. "They need digit like hands so they can manipulate materials and build stuff. The need eyes to see and sensory equipment ... feet and legs to walk with."

"We haven't seen anything they've built yet," Icabar retorted.

Solanje coughed. Braden glared at her. Icabar raised an eyebrow.

"We're getting nearer, and now that the signal is back, we may find out what they really look like. We won't have to guess any more," added Icabar.

Adrenaline surged through Braden at the thought. Exhaustion vanished in the exhilaration of the find. "Then set our course, Bashar. Let's move closer Let's do it carefully as Solanje says, but I'm going in to get a better view, or why bother to come all this way?

"Icabar, try to decode the new signal. Also, send a communications packet back home saying we have found something and attach all our data files. Remember, we're still far away from the target and there's a lot to do. Glaze, update all the maps and get this thing pinpointed. If it stops again, I want a clear location established so we don't lose it." He looked up to see Liana, Crystal, and Adam peering into the bridge, their mouths agape. The rest would be coming as soon as word got out.

And it did.

Word traveled that the signal had restarted, and something unusual had been sighted nearby. Icabar and Glaze still argued over who had sighted it first, and its physical properties, but neither seriously considered where the discovery might lead them, or what they might find once they got there. At the moment, they just thought to collect a bet.

The closer they got to the target, the more nervous everyone became. Excitement and fear permeated the starship. Everyone felt, whether they admitted it or not, very fragile, very mortal, and very insignificant.

Chapter 7

Time sped by quickly by. They mapped and recorded the nearby Estride star system. Glaze studied copious amounts of data on the strange vortex and the surrounding area as he updated his maps. Continuing their preparations, they carefully approached the strange pulsing signal with its accompanying whirling mass. The vortex was throwing off enormous energy, even at this distance, and became more mystifying as they continued to collect information. The staccato electromagnetic pulses remained steady and didn't stop. The ship was still thousands of kilospans away but would soon approach the edge of the dark area...and the circling debris field.

Solanje calculated that the anomaly was at least ninety shifts away. So, Bashar put up a large countdown timer on the bridge. Liana pulled Robert out of solitary, pending good behavior, but confined him to designated areas. Braden assigned Adam to keep a sharp watch on him, but the rebellious crewmember appeared to be entirely focused on the task at hand. Liana's talk with Robert had made an impact, at least for now.

Most important, Braden finally got some sleep.

Glaze filled in more details on the anomaly, aided by Icabar's telescope findings. At first, the debris field didn't appear a problem ... until they got nearer.

"Frag, it's bigger than we thought!" gasped Glaze.

"We'll never make it through alive." Adam studied the images.

"I don't have the stamina to spend five or so consecutive shifts dodging my way through that mine field," grumbled Bashar as he rolled a shoulder and stared glumly at the swirling mass.

"If we go clockwise around it, we might be able to find an area that isn't as dense as the one currently in front of us, and then we can angle a path inward that runs parallel with most of the heavier debris," suggested Glaze. He tapped on a newly revised map of the site.

Braden looked at the monitor and nodded. "We can trade shifts at the helm too."

"I'd only trust the ship to you or Bashar through that mess, Captain." Adam shook his head. "I can fly her but not through that nightmare."

"We'll get a better idea, the closer we get." Braden pointed at the view screen. That transmitter is outside most of the junk. We might not have to go through all of it. Meanwhile there's a lot to do to get ready."

*

Adam and Robert checked and double-checked the integrity of the ship, making sure the structure held sound and the dark matter propulsion unit continued running smoothly. Tessie prepared the plants and animals for hard maneuvers. She secured the stasis box of seeds and embryos and strapped down all hydroponics tubs. She also drained any water not contained or bottled up.

At the forty-first shift countdown, they began to reconfigure the ship into its more compact state. Anything loose got secured or locked away.

With thirty-five shifts to go, Joel became busy reprogramming systems protocol to accommodate the altered shape. Adam reconfigured the exhaust valves so that they would aid in maneuvering the reconfigured ship. The reverse thruster valves were engaged. The ship began to slow. After dropping out of para-light speed, they tried out the ship's maneuvering capability. Thankfully, the ship responded well.

"Damn debris field," complained Glaze. He peered nervously out the portal window.

"I have to drive through it," muttered Bashar. He tapped a hand on the arm of his chair.

"Any way to avoid it?" asked Crystal. A piece of hair twirled around one of her fingers.

Dyra Cantrell looked up. She ran a brown finger over her data pad. "Well, *I'm* not going to be in sleep bay the next time something exciting happens." Her short curly dark hair bobbed emphatically.

"You'd rather see the big asteroids whiz by close enough to touch, eh?" asked Glaze.

"As long as they don't scrape our hull while we're going past," rejoined Bashar. He shot a grin back over to Glaze.

"This hull is tougher than trilenium. Hamm reformulated the material from the alien probe's outer shell," commented Crystal, glaring at them. "Nothing's going to scrape or dent it."

"We also have a magnetic shield around us," Dyra reminded them with a toss of her head.

"Adam says the magnetic shields can get overloaded," added Glaze. "That heap of rubble might do it."

"Then you better plot me a really wide path through it." Bashar looked up and pointed at the monitor. "That stuff looks nasty."

Dyra's lithe fingers tapped out data on her computer. With a sigh of relief, she gave it a final tap. "Here, all downloaded to you and the computers to work out. All your talk is tensing me up. I need a break."

"Did you program the vectors and velocities of all the asteroids and large debris near the transmitter?" asked Bashar. He spun around in his chair and put out a hand. She passed her computer tablet over to him.

"You got all the positions programmed in?" asked Glaze.

"All that Icabar could find with his precious telescope," she answered. "I'm sure there's smaller stuff not visible from this far away."

"That smaller stuff could be larger than this ship." Glaze frowned at her.

"I'll add it in when it becomes *visible*. Okay?" She heaved a sigh. "Transfer what we got into the guidance system and select an optimum course with that. Once we're in, the computers will advise and aid guidance as more data becomes available. I'm done for now. I'm way over my work schedule." She unbuckled and stretched; her slender tan body glad to be out of the restraints. "I need some relaxation."

"Say 'Hi ' to Joel for us." Bashar smirked.

"Yeah, yeah," she answered. She flicked her fingers at them. The middle one wavered and went down last. She whirled and glided out of Navcom.

*

Braden heard the klaxon blare out caution warnings with ten shifts left to go. Already he was feeling the effects of the lighter gravity. Bouncing off a corridor wall, he grumbled at his awkwardness as he tried to get used to maneuvering through the ship's zero gravity all over again. He would have to remind the crew to pay attention to small items that tended to drift off and lodge into critical vents or machinery. Sometimes bits and pieces would just wander off on their own and become lost. He grabbed at a floating object that turned out to be someone's sock, and not very clean. Not what he needed to smell right now. He stuffed it in a pocket to be returned later if he remembered.

Half the fluid in his legs had moved up to his head and his brain felt as if were about to explode. A bad headache was building and a bout of nausea with it. The sock hadn't helped. He palmed a z-cap and dry swallowed it.

Some starship Captain! Space sick again.

Mission Control had mentioned the effect during training, but he had never been concerned for himself. He closed his eyes in agony. Crystal would have to give him something stronger. He needed to think clearly and right now, his pounding head made him feel like he was wading through a fog of agony.

With the centripetal acceleration engines in final stage of spin slowdown, Braden glided his way toward Navcom. Knowing the signal had reactivated, but not knowing exactly what it meant, made everyone edgy. His crew needed to be at top performance, now more than ever, if they were going to get through this. Everyone was exhausted. That thing whirling around outside was dangerous. He had given them recent lectures on the topic of a cooperative team effort. Petty bickering and imagined slights had to be put aside so everyone could work together in order to live through the next critical series of events.

He wanted to stay alive.

He popped another pill.

*

Finally, with one shift to go, everyone secured themselves into their radiation-proof capsules, or strapped in at Navcom, and prepared as best they could for the unknown. Adam and Robert stayed near the power and propulsion units, while Tessa took refuge at the farm. She locked up all living creatures in "the barn," after securing and sedating them. The enclosure was constructed of a protective radiation material and contained enough food and water for several shifts.

Ion particles were spewing out from the center of the spiral, electronically charging the atmosphere. It felt as if they were on the eve of a large thunderstorm. The air was heavy with charged particles and electricity snapped through the atmosphere. Braden could feel his hair standing out in all directions. His skin tingled as adrenaline flooded his body and counteracted the medication. He drummed nails on the console nervously.

"Glaze, have you got an ident on the signal yet?"

"I've located it past a small debris field, and Icabar may collect his bet. Scanning instruments record that it is composed of a metal alloy and the shape is constructed rather than natural."

"Icabar, have you translated the signal yet?" he asked. "Can you identify a defined language?"

Icabar nodded and pointed at a series of markings on his monitor. "This new signal is broadcasting a sequence that repeats in an endless loop. A language identifies if there's a pattern of symbols on a 40% slope of use. This new sequence shows that configuration, so I say it qualifies as an intelligent language. I suggest that it's a warning beacon or marker. That makes it highly probable that it's alien made, and I win the bet." He gave Glaze a grin and held out a hand palm up.

Glaze made a face at him.

"Bashar, you got a path to it?" asked Braden.

"We've worked out the best we can find. I'm going to skim the ship along the outer edge of the debris and come at it on a forty-degree vector. Less of the big stuff along that path and we'll steer clear of the vortex. I'm trying to match speed with the rotation, but the velocity keeps increasing."

Braden nodded. "Let's do it but hang back some. I want to ease toward our target."

"Received and understood that we ease in." Bashar twirled back to his board. "My choice entirely," he muttered.

"Icabar, what's it saying?"

"I'm still trying to decode the language. It's in a numeric sequence. Wait! Something's happening. The sequence is shifting!"

"Oh, bloody frag, it's grabbed a hold of us," yelled Bashar from helm.

"What the…?" Icabar looked up at the overhead monitor.

"Some kind of beam has locked onto us and is pulling us toward that energy mass's center," Bashar shouted.

Braden activated his emergency comm to Adam and commanded, "Reverse engines. Increase reverse thrusters, NOW!"

From the engine pod, Adam's voice could be heard yelling, "I can't! I can't! I'm trying. We're picking up speed. Nothing's responding. It's got a grip on us."

Braden stared at various digital readouts that began to flicker wildly, recording huge leaps of increasing speed. Red lights started to flash all over Navcom. He saw Bashar's hands fluttering over helm's board, as chunks of rock grew larger and closer in the overhead monitor.

Soon, the overhead screen showed bright flashes as bits and pieces of rocks hit the magnetic field and disintegrated into bursts of light. A fanfare of fireworks circled the outside of the ship.

A violent jolt to the left smashed Braden against something hard. He blinked and put a hand to the side of his head. Dark spots dotted his vision. Pulling it away, he saw blood coating his palm.

Sweat poured down Bashar's face as he jabbed at the control board. Blinking red lights flashed collision alert warnings. Another sharp jerk, this time to the right, caused Bashar's fingers to slide over his board. He shook one hand to his side to bring back feeling, while the other gripped a control lever even more tightly.

TAKE HOLD...ALL PERSONNEL SECURE FOR TURBULENCE...TAKE HOLD. The ship's computer blared out warning.

"We are experiencing severe turbulence. Everyone get in and stay secured," announced Braden through the comm.

Bashar's hands started to shake uncontrollably from the strain of holding the ship's course. Bashar bit his lip and bright blood swelled at the corner of his mouth.

Icabar glanced over worriedly.

A path began clearing again. The ship gave a quick jerk to the right to avoid a large asteroid that tumbled by outside.

The computer started flickering and printing error messages.

Frag, no! They couldn't lose the computers at a time like this!

Braden stared across the gaping void and a visible hole began to iris open at its center.

They were going to be swallowed alive!

Suddenly from out of nowhere, an array of blue numbers began to parade across the overhead monitor.

Where had they come from?

Time twisted inside Braden like a snake in its death throes. His sense of time blurred and split. The ship plunged forward, as the navigation computers stuttered and crashed.

"What's that?" Confused, Braden studied the flickering blue symbols.

Bashar tried to turn the ship, but it only slid sideways for a kilospan and then came back around, heading once more for the opening. "I'm losing control of the ship." Bashar's voice cracked. "I'm losing computer assist!" He jabbed frantically at non-responsive controls. "Frag, no!" he swore.

"Go to manual override," commanded Braden.

"You've got to be kiddiiiinng." Bashar's words stretched into tones that dropped octave by octave as he spoke.

Looking over at helm, he saw Bashar moving with lightning speed over his board. Adam groaned over the comm incoherently as the ship bucked and lurched. The air shimmered and everything appeared to stretch like a rubber band, pulled to its breaking point.

"She's piiickinnng up mooore speeeeed. I caann't stoooop her!" yelled Adam from the propulsion unit

They were falling toward some sort of space singularity that was sucking their ship deeper into a vortex of energy. The hole grew larger and larger as they got nearer, and then, it engulfed the ship.

Like a bobsled gone wild, they fell into and swept past the event horizon with increasing speed.

Everything on the monitor faded to black and the ship entered a nightmare. Lightning flashed as gases exploded around them and lit up chunks of rocks and debris that traveled alongside the ship and whirled in an alien dance, as together they spiraled through the churning mix. The atmosphere became surreal and then blanked into gray nothingness, leaving them blind to what was ahead.

"I don't know how much speeeeed this hulllll can takkkeeee," shouted Adam through comm. Braden looked at the hull temperature on the forward level. It read in the tens of thousand of degrees and was increasing at an alarming rate. A red glow covered the front of the ship. Fire flashed off her forward bow.

"Hooollld tiiiiiightt," he ordered.

A strong vibration rippled through the ship. Something shuddered. Something crashed. Someone yelped in surprise and pain. The ship groaned in protest.

"O h C r y s tttt," swore Bashar through gritted teeth.

"A m e nnnnnnnn," added Robert through the comm. The word stretched in the air and floated.

Thrusters smoked and failed. Power controls fluctuated and choked.

Their speed increased.

"Matrix burning ng ng ng ng." Adam's voice slid and slurred. "Hulllllll heat in redddd dd. Braden, how do slow w w w w?" Adam's lament tore through the comm link in crazy tonal stretches.

"Keep ussss tooogettttttherrr," Braden shouted above the roaring that penetrated the ship. He felt his own words draw and stretch across the air. He doubted that Adam could understand, even as he tried to voice the words. His fear shimmered in front of him as sweat bathed his body. Frantically, his mind leaped for a solution. He realized that the incredible speed at which they now traveled would not only stretch and expand their physical components, but time itself could be twisted and distorted in this swirling energy.

The ship lurched to the right, suddenly snapping him into the pressures of the immediate present. Electricity sparked from his panel, as magnetic forces tugged and pulled unevenly from outside the ship. Solid objects appeared to stretch and twist inside the ship as the strange forces played tricks with reality. Time slid in a way he could not explain.

Unexpectedly, he felt a strange mind inside his head as someone suddenly linked onto his thoughts. His concentration expanded, and he saw a narrow path through the gray vortex. The ship bounced against a side of the strange energy mass and flared. It shuddered with the impact. Then another link snapped into place. His mind expanded again as he saw a pattern in the strange blue numbers floating across the overhead monitor. They were coordinates that identified a path through the swirl. They gave declension and drift ratios using base six rather than base ten. Icabar had tried to translate using base ten. The idle thought that base six was Carbon and made total sense drifted through his terrified mind.

Braden looked over toward Bashar and focused his concentration. Bashar looked back at him startled. *Bashar was in the link!* Braden visualized the meaning of the coordinates streaming across the monitor and flashed it mentally to Bashar.

Bashar nodded sharply and delicately punched a key as they tore by another curve, barely missing the energy field swirling by that side of the ship. They plunged down into a deep roiling abyss and began a frightening spiraling rotation. Bashar's fingers, responding to Braden's directions, literally danced over the control board in a blur as Braden's translation appeared in his brain and he tried to navigate the ship manually.

Braden's fingers danced a fandango of their own at his board, as he plugged in to helm and began inputting the coordinates. Faintly, in the background of his mind, Braden felt a continued presence that held their link together. He drew on its strength as coordinates blinked in and out of existence in front of him, while his mind struggled to keep up.

Forcing his concentration to the path ahead, he widened his perception. He shifted his mind into timed increments and pushed ahead of the current time. His instructions must be plucked from future time in order to relay fast enough to Bashar and give navigation time to respond to the whipping speed. And, he must keep them in the center, or the edges of the whirling energies would tear apart the ship. The path veered. The ship twisted with it.

Objects flew and crashed against red-lighted panels, but neither noticed, because they were tightly focused on their task.

Both men looked like concert masters playing on wildly blinking instruments.

The vectors changed again as new data coordinates flashed into Braden's head. He stabbed at the board. The ship slued around, missing another wall of energy as the relayed coordinates arrived, timed in from Braden's future vision.

Bashar nodded, as if understanding his instructions, even as they formulated in Braden's mind. His hands skittered over the keyboard and the ship centered. Just then, Braden saw the path straighten out. Bashar, with sweat pouring off his forehead, gently eased the ship upward by punching the next series of coordinates that Braden fed to him.

"Ahhhh..." Bashar gave a cry.

Braden made an answering correction on his board, nodding like some daft puppet. The ship started to curve upward, groaning in the sudden heavy gravitational shift. Everyone sank deep into their seats, squashed under the forces weighing down on them.

"Ohhhh... Arghh..." Braden didn't know where the sound came from or who said it.

Bashar inputted another series of coordinates and the ship lurched past an energy wall, grazing its side briefly. Sparks flashed off a thinning force field. Then, they were through another turn and the ship was straining against the wild forces that surrounded it. Suddenly, a clear area opened in front of them as the ship shot out the back end of the vortex, spilling them into an unknown region of space.

A strange vast universe confronted them. Ahead, unidentified planets and stars whirled.

"Brake, brake!"

At Braden's command, Bashar immediately activated all reverse thrusters. The ship bucked and shook, sluing from side to side like an enraged animal as Bashar tried to rein it in.

Braden heard Bashar cry, "Oh frag, bloody shards. NO!" He looked up. He saw that they were headed toward what could only be described as a convoy of alien vessels.

The Seeker, totally out of control.

Chapter 8

"Brace for collision!" yelled Braden.

COLLISION ALERT! TAKE HOLD! TAKE HOLD! blared throughout the ship. Sirens and klaxons screamed warnings of immediate danger.

"Prepare for impact," shouted Braden over comm. Everyone gritted teeth and braced.

Out of nowhere, an invisible energy field sprung up around them. It caught them like a ball in a net and bled off their speed before they reached the other ships.

Everyone lurched violently forward, but the safety harnesses and padded webbing limited the serious damage to mostly a few deep bruises. Soon, the ship slowed to a more maneuverable speed as Bashar made a course change away from the impact zone.

"Yahoo!" The voice sounded like Adam's, but it was hard to tell. It could have been Robert's. "What a ride!"

"Holy shit. Look at those alien ships!" Icabar appeared shades paler than normal.

"Frag! Frag! Frag!" Bashar gasped.

"What happened?" several voices shouted in unison over the comm.

"Looks like a dispersal energy field," answered Icabar. "Maybe they were expecting us."

"Maybe we aren't the only ones to come charging out of that hole," added Bashar.

"Well, there are a few ships nearby." Bashar eyed the assembled vessels.

"All stations report in," Braden croaked.

"Anyone hurt?" asked Crystal. "Med lab's operable, or I can be there in one."

"I'll run a systems check," responded Joel in a warbling voice.

"Some damage here, but most systems are functioning. We were lucky!" said Adam breathing heavily. "We're alive and our power sources didn't implode. Thought they might."

"Damage at the farm," Tessa was trying to sound brave. An animal bleated in the background. "But recoverable."

"Arming weapon array," signaled Robert crisply.

"Wait for my order, Robert," commanded Braden. "Stay at standby."

"Armed and ready," Robert confirmed

"Activate scanning," ordered Braden.

"Surveillance systems activated. Scanning unknown objects now. Looks like either alien ships or some sort of orbiting space station, Captain," reported Glaze. "No life forms apparent yet. Neither are those ships powered up."

"Continue scanning," Braden ordered. "Let me know if you have anything. Hold helm steady, Bashar. Continue forward at Mach 1 speed. Steady as she goes. Let's get a good look at them."

"Affirmative."

"Come to Navcom, Solanje," ordered Braden.

"On my way."

"I haven't identified the constellation configurations at this close range, but I'm running the data through the computers right now," informed Glaze turning around toward Braden. "Wow, notice the gorgeous planet behind those ships!"

"Find a match on that planet, if you can," ordered Braden. "Let me know when you have a good guess as to where the frag we are."

"Working on it." Glaze radiated excitement at the extraordinary find.

They all stared at the monitor as an amazing planet came into sharper view, rotating behind the orbiting spacecrafts. Enhancing the image, they saw white, blue, green, and other shades that suggested a living world.

"All systems back online and functioning," Joel sighed with relief.

Crystal came into Navcom with Solanje and Joel. "I checked the sleep pods. Liana's unconscious, but her vitals have stabilized. Everyone there appears to have survived. How's everyone here? I've got a med kit with me."

"Holy Lady," breathed Icabar. "Look at those ships!" As they got closer, the alien ships loomed larger in their monitors. They floated lazily in orbit around a turning planet that lay behind them.

"The structures appear attached to one another. I would say it's been reconfigured into being a space habitat of some sort," observed Adam.

"I'm getting nothing here," Icabar grumbled. "Is anybody getting anything?"

"Nothing here," Solanje, responded now at her station. She had started running search programs.

"Nothing here," said Braden with a grunt. He peered at the forward monitor, and then rolled a shoulder to release tension. "Icabar, are you picking up anything?"

"Zero," came the answer. "Zilch." He made a humming noise under his breath.

They all stared. Humanity's first encounter with aliens and no one was meeting and greeting.

"Helm ahead slowly," ordered Braden.

"Adam how is our power and maneuverability?"

"It's coming back online, Captain. Using the fusion drives now. A few thrusters burned off. She's limping, but repairable. We'll be able to make a few turns. Not much else."

Slowly they drifted toward the cluster of large alien vessels orbiting around the vibrantly colored planet.

"Reduce speed to 1000 KSP," ordered Braden. "And match orbit speed."

"Affirm, Cap," responded Bashar. He ran a shaking hand through unruly damp curls and shifted in his seat. Flexing fingers, he lightly pressed the control lever.

Braden rubbed a sore shoulder and dabbed at a bloody face. "Glaze, have you scanned any movement or activity from the area yet?"

Crystal came over and cleaned out the cut at the side of his face. "There," she said stepping back and evaluating his condition. She gazed around. "Anyone else?"

Several negative shakes of the head.

She handed Braden a pill.

"Still negative," announced Glaze. He rubbed his eyes tiredly.

"Well, something stopped us from colliding into those things and killing us and everything within range!"

exclaimed Bashar. His gaze flickered off his board to Braden and then up toward the big monitor.

Icabar frowned into his headset. "That may have been an automated response to any ship coming out of the vortex at too high a speed."

"Hey, I want a study done on that planet," said Tessa breathlessly coming through the entrance into Navcom. "Look at all the green and blue. Water and vegetation. It's beautiful! It reminds me of Alysia. Life's down there, folks. I'd bet book on it."

"Are you a betting woman, Tessa?" inquired Braden looking over at her. He raised an eyebrow in question.

She shook her head at him and made a face. "Not anymore."

"Look at those cloud formations," exclaimed Solanje. All eyes swiveled around and studied the monitor that revealed more and more of the approaching planet. Excitement mounted all over the ship as closer observations announced more new discoveries.

"That means rain and weather," added Adam.

"Glaze report," barked Braden. "Tell me where we are."

"We appear to be in the Galorian Galactic Cluster M51073."

Braden's eyes widened. "That far out?"

"Infinity and beyond."

Silence filled the area, quiet as vacuum.

"Will we be able to get back?" someone finally stuttered.

"If I have anything to say about it ... yes," answered Braden firmly. He scanned the room; they just looked stunned and panicked. "But now, let's see what we have *here*. Solanje, fire off a robotic probe to sample the atmosphere and get me data on this place. Everyone get to your stations and gather data on this place."

"Yes, sir." All responded with alacrity.

Navcom woke to action.

Solanje's nimble fingers tapped in a sequence and a spidery looking mechanical apparatus shot out of the ship and floated down toward the planet. Everyone stopped momentarily to watch the probe ease past the alien ships and eventually penetrate the planet's atmosphere.

Dyra looked up. "I'm checking the data now. Temperature's in the habitable range. Gravity's at three-quarter Alysia's gravity. Lower atmosphere's 74% nitrogen, 25% oxygen, small amounts of carbon dioxide, traces of neon, helium, methane, hydrogen, nitrous oxide, and xenon—some others. It's remarkably similar to Alysia's atmosphere."

"So, *don't* hold your breath," hooted Icabar.

Pause, pause.

"Don't hold your breath?" questioned a puzzled Braden.

"Because it's breathable," choked out Bashar and shook his head in dismay at Icabar's attempt at humor.

"So funny," retorted Solanje dryly. "You boys are so funny."

"I'm turning bl...uuu ee," warbled Adam. "Got to breathe. Got to breathe."

"Take a deep breath of that, then," someone answered.

"All right, you clowns. We're at first contact and all you're doing is joking around," admonished Braden. "Get serious."

"Comic relief, captain," explained Icabar solemnly.

"Anyone called Icky would know about that."
The voice sounded like Robert's.

"Aw, captain. They're picking on me again."

"Stop it, all of you. Get serious. How about a closer surveillance?" asked Bashar. "Those are alien ships out there ... big ones."

"I'm getting nothing here, Captain. All I'm getting is strange photonic shifts and incomprehensible energy surges on the planet's surface." Glaze tapped on his board.

"Bashar, get a little closer, but slowly and carefully." Braden peered at his monitor.

Bashar brought them forward toward the strange vessels suspended in orbit around the mysterious planet. Still nothing stirred. Nothing moved. Silence fell within the ship; silence prevailed out in space. Icabar looked up from his headset shrugging his shoulders. He opened all channels throughout the ship so that the sound of any outside noise could be heard. The only sounds heard were the hum of the ship's electronics, human breathing, vent noises and something bleating plaintively from off the farm. Braden found himself holding his breath so that he could hear better. His ship drifted in space, staring at the silent shapes.

*

They waited, watching the fascinating planet, taking measurements and pictures for duros until their eyes watered from the effort. Still nothing happened. Not a trace of movement occurred anywhere.

Finally, everyone grew restless.

Tessa left and came back with drinks and food. Harnesses came unbuckled and a few went to change sweat soaked clothes and shower. Others fiddled with repairs.

"Captain, let's put together an exploration team and investigate one of those things," suggested Glaze finally. "We need to try out those rovers to see if they work, anyway."

"I volunteer to go," offered Joel immediately.

"I want to go," added Crystal.

"Okay, you three," said Braden, quickly pointing to Glaze, Crystal, and Joel. "Exercise extreme caution. Remember procedures for first contact. This is a peaceful mission. Take aggressive action only if provoked, and then get out fast and back here," he ordered.

Crystal, Joel, and Glaze began immediately to suit up and prepare for the excursion. Adam left to help get the rover ready. Soon the three were opening the airlock door, entering the shuttle, and exiting the shuttle bay

Dyra entered Navcom to replace Glaze.

On the view screen, Braden watched the shuttle loom large as it left the exit bay, and then gradually diminish in size, until the sheer bulk of the alien structures swamped it, and it became a mere dot against the orbiting spacecrafts.

Time slipped away as they waited for the shuttle to glide its way to the large alien ships. Tessa and Robert surveyed their ship for damaged and dislodged items. Everyone tidied their workstations. Bashar tapped his fingers in a staccato rhythm on his board and stretched. Solanje ran more computer programs from data supplied by Icabar and Glaze. Dyra massaged the numbers and organized it into a reportable form. Braden studied the results and cracked his neck.

Icabar turned from his communications board. "The shuttle is getting no response from the alien station, either. I've been communicating on a broadband frequency and have received nothing but low-level static.

The shuttle team should be arriving at the nearest structure anytime now. If they want to try entering, Captain, do they have your permission to knock on the door?"

Braden studied his readouts on the console. *Nothing. There had been nothing for duros now.* He didn't understand, but they had come too far to quit now.

"Tell them to knock gently and investigate carefully," he ordered. He wondered why nothing showed life.

"Do you want me to prepare a standby crew?" asked Adam. "We might need some backup over there. Just saying."

"Good idea. Robert, Solanje, and Bashar, suit up and stand by. Prepare the second rover. The rest of the personnel stand by your stations. We have no idea if there are aliens there and what their intentions might be if we find some."

Suddenly Liana came through the door. "What can I do?" she asked.

"Liana, we were missing you," commented Braden. He arched an eyebrow at her. "You're missing all the excitement here."

"I'm not missing much and I'm here now," she responded. "Aside from a pounding headache, I'm ready for duty. What do you have out there?"

"You're not the only one with a headache." He cocked his head at her, but she ignored him, and instead, turned to gaze at the overhead monitor. Wonder and excitement lit up her face. "Look at that!" she breathed. "Those are huge alien ships."

"That they are, and we're trying to make first contact, but no one is answering," Braden responded as he gazed once more at the monitor and out the portal window.

Time passed some more as all waited for what the first away team might discover.

Chapter 9

As the away team's rover approached the alien ships, Glaze saw three large, cylindrical structures that had circular units attached to them by connecting tunnels, much like beads on a matrix necklace. At the perimeter, floated several other sleeker, smaller ships. He agreed with Adam's suggestion that it was a convoy of spaceships converted into an orbiting habitat. Somehow, it had that feel to it. Immense flat panels sprung out at various locations along the wider hulls and rotated to catch light from a nearby sun. The whole arrangement reminded him of a connecting toy that he used to play with as a child. There were too many attachments and protuberances for the larger structure to be a warship. Warships were sleek and moved fast. This thing looked like it hadn't gone anywhere in a very long time, and wasn't about to go anywhere soon, much less at a high speed. However, the smaller ships looked dangerous, and they looked fast. Another convoy circled the planet farther along the orbit's path and possibly still another ahead of that.

With a start, Glaze heard Braden's voice in his comm. "Describe what you see."

Glaze gave a quick overview and added, "The large flat panels attached to the hull look like a solar array. There are also several openings that appear to be landing platforms underneath the larger ship. We're heading toward that."

"Proceed with caution," responded Braden.

Glaze guided the rover into what appeared to be a landing bay and parked. Static fizzled in his comm and Braden's voice broke up. Glaze paused, and then, the line cleared. "Are we ready?" he asked, putting on his helmet. Crystal and Joel nodded with serious faces and did the same.

*

On board *The Seeker*, a frustrated Braden asked, "Can you get a clearer signal on him? I'm getting interference here."

"I'll try." Icabar switched channels and tried Crystal's comm. Finally, Crystal's voice broke through a surge of static. "It looks like an abandoned space colony," they heard her say.

"Crystal, adjust your headset. We're getting interference." Icabar tweaked a few dials and frowned. "We can't hear you." He tapped back into Glaze's link.

"What's your assessment, Glaze?" asked Braden over the increasing noise.

"I agree with Crystal. It appears to be a...hiss...squeak...hmm."

"Glaze, you're dropping out." Icabar rotated a few more knobs and pounded the console.

Liana entered Navcom with a concerned look on her face.

"We have problems."

*

On board the shuttle, Glaze turned to Crystal and Joel. "Some static is interfering. I can't hear Braden or Icabar anymore. Think we should go back?"

Crystal's helmet shook from side to side. "We're here now and we can hear each other simply fine. Maybe it'll clear once we're inside. Are you getting any signs of movement or heat signatures in this landing bay or from anywhere further inside?" She waved around a sonic detector and then switched it to infrared.

"Nothing," answered Glaze pointing his in all directions. "All clear."

"I vote we go in," said Crystal. She turned a definitive gaze on him through her helmet.

She liked to be in charge.

"Let's not stop now," added Joel. "We're here. Might as well continue."

Outvoted, Glaze opened the shuttle door and all three eased out into the ships' hangar. A convenient hook provided a place to tether the shuttle. Farther along, several small shuttlecrafts sat huddled together near a large door.

The three explorers jetted their way through the vacuum to the entrance, which had a large round handle similar to a bank vault's. A strong twist and jerk caused the shuttle bay's door to open into a medium-sized chamber. All three peered in. Crystal held out a detector to test the air. "Nothing appears to be toxic, so far."

"But we're still in vacuum." She closed the heavy door, causing a muffled clang.

Crystal and Joel looked nervously at Glaze. He gave a weak grin back through his transparent faceplate, hoping it would be enough to calm them.

On the opposite wall was a door with a large dim button at its center. They pushed it and air whooshed in, filling the chamber.

"It's an airlock," said Joel looking around.

"Pretty obvious," grunted Glaze.

The button turned bright purple and the door slid open.

After being confined so long in a smaller ship, the sheer size of the alien ship overwhelmed Glaze. Once inside, gravity tugged at his limbs, weighing him down.

How did they create gravity on a ship?

All three stared at each other.

Across an open area in front of him a wall held several colored ledges tiered up to a vaulted ceiling that faced a central stage or platform. Crossing to the ledges, Glaze noticed several doors to other parts of the structure.

Sliding a door open on his right, an adjoining room held banks of equipment that stood silent. Another door opened onto metal corridors that led in various other directions. One, he concluded, was a connecting tunnel to another craft.

The air tested breathable, but the entire interior appeared abandoned. The dim interior held no scattered items to indicate that anything lived there. Everything was utilitarian with the feel of a workplace. Not a sign of life stirred or showed up on their detectors.

Glaze watched Joel drag a gloved hand over a wall decoration with wavy colored lines as he wandered over to investigate an alcove in a corner of the room. He saw Joel put his hands up to his helmet as if to shield his eyes from a strong light.

Crystal stood nearby fiddling with her comm.

"Lines of light radiating at all angles. Can you see them?" asked Joel, turning to stare at them from the niche in the wall.

Glaze shook his helmet. He didn't see any lines of light. The place appeared to be just an empty dim interior.

Braden's voice came on asking for a report. Through her faceplate, he saw Crystal's face smile as she gave a thumbs-up, due to the now working comm.

Glaze composed his thoughts. "This area appears to be deserted. I don't see any signs of life yet..." His headset emitted a high protesting whine. He shook his head in exasperation at the annoying noise. Icabar would hear from him when they returned. The comm system wasn't working right.

Something caught his eye and he looked over and saw Joel bathed in light. The man positively glowed. He must have stepped near an opening or an illuminated surface. He was smiling. Come to think of it, Glaze suddenly felt surprisingly good himself.

At last things were getting exciting! Look at this fantastic place! What a find! Finally, after all the boring travel through endless space, they had discovered something amazing. Glaze smiled, and he was smiling when he saw Joel waver, fragment into light particles, and disappear right in front of his eyes.

He blinked.

What the frag? What had just happened?

Panic rippled through his entire being. He shivered.

"Crystal!" He turned to search for her, finding she stood reassuringly nearby.

"Glaze!" she shouted, alarmed. "Where did Joel go? Braden told us to stay together and not let anyone out of our sight. Where did he go? Captain said that's the protocol. We have to report..." She stamped her foot and fiddled with her headset. "This ship is causing too much interference. I've lost contact *again*. Try yours, Glaze. Is yours working?"

Glaze fiddled with his comm with no better results.

He had to report to the Captain! This was serious.

"We have to locate Joel," he agreed.

He didn't like it one bit that he was also having a hard time staying in contact with the ship. The situation was deteriorating rapidly. They should retrieve Joel and go back. He moved over near the spot where he had last seen Joel, careful not to enter the alcove, but looking around for clues as to what might have happened. He was shaking badly, but he couldn't see anything but a highly decorated *empty* alcove.

Calm. Calm. Joel might just be around a corner or behind a panel and not aware of the panic he was causing.

Glaze tried to deal with the shock. Putting his hand out to steady himself, he leaned on the wall for a moment to catch his breath and think about what he should do. He moved to tell Crystal that he had decided they should go back when the wall in front of him gave way and he fell into darkness.

*

On board *The Seeker*, Icabar was sweating and frantic. Communications was breaking down *again*. "They've boarded," he said. He rubbed his face and cast a glance of apprehension at Braden.

"I need to know what's happening," responded a concerned Braden. "Do not lose contact."

Crystal's voice broke in on comm saying, "It looks like an abandoned colony.

"I hear them." Icabar turned back to his board.

Braden leaned forward. When nothing came through after a while, Braden grew restless. He leaned toward Icabar with a question on his face and drummed his fingers impatiently.

"Wait! I'm getting something. They're in safe!" exclaimed Icabar. He eased back in his seat, gave a wide grin at Braden, and put a thumb up.

"Put them on speaker." Braden unplugged out of his board and gestured to Icabar.

Icabar flicked a switch. Static filled Navcom.

"Glaze, I need more information," urged Braden. "I need to hear voices."

Joel answered, "I see lines of light everywhere..." A loud whine filled Navcom. Braden clapped his hands over his ears.

Static. Silence. Braden and Icabar stared at each other. Then....

"Joel ... where's Joel?" Crystal's voice broke through, and then faded.

"Icabar ..."

"I'm trying, Captain. Something's interfering." Icabar's face got red and he rubbed his hands down the legs of his pants.

Crystal came back online. "I saw him staring at something just a moment ago. He said he saw lights." The sound of her voice faded as static interfered again.

"Glaze, report immediately. Answer me! What's happening?" Frustrated, Braden unstrapped from his chair and moved to stand over Icabar, as if the answer were etched into his console. Only silence answered his commands.

"I've lost them again, Captain." Icabar rotated in his seat. "Give it a moment."

"I don't like this. There's a bad feel to it," said a worried Braden. He crooked a finger at Bashar who floated over, half suited up. "Prepare the second team. Follow them exactly and bring them straight back. No sightseeing excursions. Maybe it's just some static caused by those structures that's interfering with the communication, and you'll be able to get a clearer line on them. Just get in, secure them, and get out. I want to hear their voices as soon as I can, and I want to hear yours the whole time, or you come back. Understand?"

"On it, Captain."

"Bashar, take Dyra to help your team prepare, then send her back here."

*

Crystal blinked. Joel had gone missing. Now where was Glaze? She hadn't been able to raise Braden over comm so she had rotated to see if another direction might clear her headset of static and when she had turned back, Glaze had vanished. Braden said something about a second team, and then her comm went quiet.

Going in search of Joel had caused Glaze to disappear. She shook her head. All her training concerning away teams had emphasized staying together, or failing that, staying put. Well, she would stay put for a while, hoping the others would come to their senses and return. She would not leave them stranded ...just yet... but they'd better not keep her waiting long, or she was going back on her own, and they could deal with the consequences of their carelessness.

Suddenly tired from all the tension, her legs gave out from under her, and she sat down on what looked to be a molded seat. Leaning forward, she scrutinized the amazing, but odd, curving teal and aqua designs on the walls in the main room. She tried to adjust her comm again. As she settled into place waiting for the second team to arrive, she experienced an odd feeling that she was not alone. She glanced up. At that moment, her eyes met those of a wondrously luminous being who smiled at her, as he came gliding toward her surrounded by a nimbus of light.

*

On board the second shuttle, Bashar watched Robert nervously fiddle with his laser gun and then his headset. Something strange had happened to the first team, and they weren't responding. Their team had gone quiet. Solanje stayed focused on the operation center, keeping in touch with Icabar and Braden.

Bashar followed the first team's path, varying it slightly if he heard static, and listening to the steady cadence of Icabar's voice, as he maintained voice contact by counting. Robert had armed the rover with an arsenal of weapons, but Braden had stressed that they were to be deployed only in the gravest of situations.

Picking up an extra weapon, Robert smiled grimly and tucked it into his belt. He caressed a few raster guns and tucked one of those into a hidden sheath.

"Braden said use weapons only if attacked," Bashar reminded him.

Robert nodded and waved a hand at him. "Rasters have a stun setting," he replied. He turned to peer out a window and shifted in his seat, then shifted again.

"They also ricochet off metal," Bashar added irritably. "Not good inside a ship."

"I'll use stun if we're attacked. Rasters don't need reloading," Robert argued back. "I'm the weapons specialist. It's my choice." He rubbed his face and glowered at Bashar.

"They went over there," said Solanje crisply, as she tried to distract everyone from an escalating argument. She pointed ahead to the looming vessel "See that opening?"

"Got it," answered Bashar, steering toward an opening under the craft.

"There's two here," said Solanje.

"Pick one," answered Bashar.

Solanje pointed to the one on the right and Bashar guided the shuttle in.

"Have you heard any more from Glaze?" Robert asked Braden as he put on his helmet.

"Nothing, only static. However, now, you're coming in clear. Just proceed with extreme caution and don't lose contact with me. Either we are talking, or Icabar is counting," responded Braden.

"I knew your math skills would finally come in handy. How high can you count, Icabar?" Bashar quipped.

"As high as you need me to go," came the dry response. "Try to keep up, if you can."

Bashar snorted. "What if the aliens out there communicate using number sequences? You might be saying something dirty or even insulting," countered Bashar with a wink at Solanje.

"Let's hope not, for Icky's sake," Solanje responded and returned a grin.

"Hey! Cut it out."

"Maybe he should sing rather than count?" suggested Liana leaning into the onboard speaker.

"Please no!" replied Solanje and Robert unanimously.

"All right, stop it," interrupted Braden. "You're just about there. Do you see the other rover yet? Can you still hear me?"

The captain sounded anxious.

"Yes, but you're coming in fainter," answered Bashar. "It must be the ship, or whatever this large construction is, blocks our communications." At that point, some static sounded on the line.

"Frag! If you start to lose me, come back immediately," ordered Braden.

"Affirmative. The plan is to board, retrieve, and return," answered Bashar.

"That's exactly right. Return if you have any trouble. I want no dead heroes," ordered Braden, his voice full of tension.

"Affirmative. We're entering now," responded Bashar. He carefully edged the rover into the open bay.

"Proceed. Repeating one, two, three ... be careful, four, five ..." Icabar restarted his count.

"I don't see our shuttle," said Robert nervously, peering around the cavernous area.

They had entered the landing bay, settled the shuttle, and began scoping out the place.

"They probably entered the other side. We came in an adjoining bay. That means we'll be entering from a different direction," Bashar suggested.

Several intervals passed as they shut down, put on helmets, and cautiously exited. After they tethered the shuttle, they scanned the area It appeared empty. No air, no gravity. Cold. Silent. Still.

"They must be in the other bay," suggested Solanje.

"Let's hope so," Bashar responded. He gestured to Robert. "Lead on," he ordered. Nothing showed up on any thermal scans, so they wrestled opened the ship's outer door, passed through an airlock, and entered the interior, hoping to locate their missing crewmembers.

Chapter 10

"Wow!" Solanje's voice interrupted Icabar's cadence. "What an interior! This looks like the work of an advanced culture. Notice those blue and green geometric designs on the walls and the odd symbols. I wonder what they mean? Dyra would love this place. I bet she could figure out what they meant."

"This technology appears pretty advanced too," responded Bashar. "Solanje, look at this! What do you think this does?" He gestured to shelves of mounted equipment.

Meanwhile, Robert strode across the main room and slid open a door. "Let's hope they're friendly. Cast your eyes on the high-tech stuff in here! Wow! I want to study their power source to see how they make this baby go."

"Keep together," ordered Bashar. "Solanje?"

"Right here."

"Robert, you're our point man. Everyone set your weapon on stun and stay alert. Lead on Robert."

Robert pulled out a raster and moved forward. "Hey! Wait! I think I saw something moving over there!" Stopping, he put out an arm to halt the others and spun to his right, raising his weapon. His eyes flashed and his jaw clenched. His hand shook briefly as he aimed, and then he flicked his gun about, searching for any signs of movement. Warily he moved his weapon in a broad sweep, and advanced haltingly down a corridor, until he reached a partially opened door. After looking in, he waved the others to follow him.

Bashar pulled out a thermal detector and swept the room. "I might have something! There's traces of animal heat registering."

"Wait!" crackled Braden's voice in their comm. "Remember we have people in there. It could be them."

"I hear you Captain," Robert said aloud, but under his breath he muttered, "Yeah, and where are you, Crystal dear? Where are you, bitch? Just let me find you. Come on out, I have a surprise for you." He waggled his weapon. Louder, he said, "It could be coming from in there." He pointed and waved the group on into a new section and down a dim corridor.

"Robert what's wrong with you?" asked Bashar suddenly alarmed at Robert's aggressive words and nervous actions. Robert was acting strangely, but the man had trained in initial contact situations and was a front-line military weapons officer with combat experience. He hoped Robert knew what he was doing, but Bashar felt concerned about Robert's behavior.

Really concerned.

"Glaze, Joel, Crystal, report." Bashar put his mike on outside speaker and shouted into the dim corridor. Their names echoed back faintly, and then the walls swallowed the sound.

Bashar noticed Robert unconsciously flicking his gun's safety switch on and off several times. His eyes were darting nervously from wall to wall. Robert scanned the area and then moved ahead in jerky forward motions. He signaled the others to come on, as he led the threesome deeper and deeper into the alien ship's bowels.

They followed him as he slid opened a door into a room that contained a wall of silent electronics with a large console in the middle. The other walls were composed of a gray gun metal material and the room echoed the sound of their entering. Several shoulder high canisters were stacked among various computer stations. Three exit panels led into other areas, one stood partially open. Robert motioned for Bashar to cover the right side while he moved left.

"Solanje, stay by the door and guard our flank. Watch the corridor for any sign of the others." Their footsteps whispered into the room.

Solanje stopped and stepped back out to scan the corridor. "Got it," she murmured back at them.

"I see something moving. There!" Robert pointed. A strange distorted humanoid image undulated along one of the metal walls across the room and crawled up the side of the far opening.

Robert spun around, dropped down to one knee, and fired his raster at the opened panel, screaming obscenities all the while.

The panel tore away.

Solanje stumbled in from the corridor, "What's going on?" she yelled.

"Stop! Robert! Don't stream laser fire in here!" ordered Bashar.

Too late.

Energy beams tore through the room and hit the hard metal wall at the far end and ricocheted. Lethal rays rebounded off surfaces everywhere, scoring walls and equipment.

"Solanje, get down!" Bashar shrieked, whirling around to shout at her.

Weapons fire bounced in from the adjoining room and exploded a panel near Robert.

"Aliens attacking!" Robert shouted. "Commence firing!" He shot through the open doorway with his second weapon, throwing down an empty cartridge, and tearing out a new one from an outer pocket. Wild energy beams crisscrossed each other all over the area like some frantic, glowing, spider web.

Across the room, Bashar yelled hoarsely. Energy beams were ricocheting off hard interior surfaces, creating a deadly crossfire. One beam ripped open his suit's hard fabric, scoring his leg, and causing him to scream in pain. He watched Robert fall to the floor and fling explosives toward the open doorway.

What was he doing using explosives in an enclosed ship?

A loud boom followed. Debris flew in from the other room. Bashar dove behind the nearest protection he could find, while Braden's voice crackled worriedly in his headset, buzzing in Bashar's ears like an angry bee.

"What's happening? Report, Bashar!" ordered Braden frantically from *The Seeker*.

Bashar sucked up the pain and responded, "We may be under attack!" He peered out from behind the base of a wide console in the center of the room. Its top formed a flat glass surface, filled with alien digital lettering and numbers.

A flare of energy tore past Bashar just missing his head and taking out a chunk of the console. Metal and glass flew everywhere. Pain lanced up his injured leg as he leaned back on it, trying to escape the lethal path of fire, and instead, caught the console's hot, ragged edge. Several pieces of glass slit open his suit at the front. A sharp pain scored his chest. He muttered a string of curses and began to fire into the open panel just out of pure irritation, confused as to whether he was under attack or not.

Smoke drifted in from the other room, creating poor visibility. A return fusillade met his volley, but he couldn't tell whether the hits were ricochets or enemy fire. The attack seemed to be coming from all angles. Bashar tried to get a glimpse of what he was firing at. He reached to reload. Explosions rocked the ship, but the durable structure appeared to continue holding air. There still was no breach to space, or maybe the alarms no longer worked.

Fate, I don't know.

Light skittered and sparked along a wall. He peered down, noticing red liquid dripping onto the floor at his feet.

I'm bleeding.

His now smoke-fogged helmet made it hard to see clearly. He could make out Robert lying very still not far away. Bashar moved to have a closer look and groaned from the intense pain that lanced though his whole body. As he moved forward, he dribbled a trail of red blood behind him. It took everything he could muster to stay conscious. His suit flashed a warning light indicating that his oxygen supply had been disrupted and was running low. Most likely his oxygen cartridge had been damaged. His eyes blurred and he felt light-headed. Images of burning filled his agonized mind, as he tried to hold onto consciousness. Angry static sounded in his headset. Then, another explosion reverberated nearby, wracking his already battered brain.

I'm going to die in here, he thought angrily. *A really stupid death.*

His headset mumbled against the background of his burning thoughts. Fire danced across the inside of his eyelids, searing his vision. A wave of anger at the stupidity of it all built up inside him and erupted. A blast of heat exploded, in front of him and everything began to slide away into darkness. His last image was of someone's fingers enveloped in flames right in front of him.

"Bashar?" Solanje heard chaos erupt inside. Looking in, she saw the room stitched in fire by ricocheting energy beams. She pressed her comm to her ear listening for any reports from anyone.

Nothing.

She peered into the room, but searing light and enveloping smoke obliterated her sight. Stumbling forward, she tried to see ahead, but her smoke-occluded helmet made that impossible while the bulky suit made her movements clumsy.

What were these fools thinking to use that kind of firepower **inside** *a ship?*

She hadn't realized that Robert had packed so much weaponry. Ducking back out, she looked behind her, and then peered back in again. Another explosion made her pull back. "Report, Bashar," she begged. A spurt of flame erupted nearby. She whirled around; her weapon held before her.

Careful, careful. See your enemy first before firing. Proceed with caution.

Angry words issued out of her comm as Braden's voice demanded to know what was happening. Static and fear blocked her answer. The flare flickered and burnt out. She crept further into the room. A piece of equipment fell over with a loud crash. She spun around toward it, swerving to find the direction of the noise, and sucked in her breath as she surveyed the area.

Nothing.

She stumbled past flames, weaving to avoid any errant energy beams still ricocheting randomly off the walls. Somewhere, something exploded, causing more flames to flare up, and then gradually everything subsided. A line of fire licked across the bottom of one wall and then flickered out. Quiet descended on the littered area.

"Bashar? Where are you? Be alive," she pleaded and crept toward a low guttural moan. She heard a small noise. Somewhere, someone, or something still lived.

Was it alien or human?

*

Back on *The Seeker*, Braden hovered over Icabar, talking frantically into the onboard speaker. Suddenly, Liana gave out a strange moan and collapsed at his feet. Dyra leaned over her murmuring. She looked worriedly up at Braden. "Bashar's been hurt. Find out what's happened."

"What does it look like I'm trying to do," responded Braden irritably.

Liana screamed. The sound curdled his blood.

"What's wrong with her?" Braden peered over at her, bewildered at the commotion. Liana's hands had developed a strange mottled red color.

"Liana has telepathic and empathic powers. She's been in contact with Bashar, and I suspect that he's been badly hurt," Tessa answered. She knelt and murmured at the convulsing woman.

"Has what?" Braden stopped in mid-speech. The implication stunned him. "You mean she reads minds?" He paused. "Can she read my mind?" His ears flamed bright red, while his eyes widened at the idea of all his hidden feelings and thoughts exposed. He recalled a few and winced. Then he recalled the trip through the space gate and remembered a mind inside his. So, it might have been her mind that had linked with his and Bashar's. He recalled that had been helpful.

"Most certainly, Captain. I would venture a guess that she probably has read all of our minds at one time or another." Dyra nodded.

Braden gestured to Icabar and said, "Put the ship on red alert. Then talk to anyone you can get a hold of in either of the away teams. I want to know what's happening out there."

He turned to stare at Liana, as if *she* were the alien.

"I'm talking. I'm talking, but no one is talking back." Icabar waved his hands over the console in frustration.

Braden roughly adjusted his headset. He was angry and confused, but he would deal with the Liana situation later. Right now, he had a top priority emergency on his hands.

"Wait. Quiet everyone," said Icabar, leaning into the console. "I'm hearing something."

*

"Bashar, speak to me!" Solanje's voice disrupted the silence.

As if in answer, something nearby exploded. She crouched down. A fire broke out across the room throwing a lick of flame up the wall. Then she heard something move.

Through a haze, she saw Robert lying at the center of the room. Energy burns scored his suit. He wasn't moving. She looked away.

With Glaze and Joel missing, that would make only nine of them left against whoever or whatever had built these ships. Highly advanced entities had created these complicated structures, and she didn't think them human.

She shivered.

Solanje called out again. Her headset mumbled a static noise. She couldn't raise Braden. In the room, only silence answered her calls. She caught a glimpse of a red trail over near a console.

Bashar!

She crouched down and crept toward it, staring at the growing red puddle that had a charred human hand splayed across it. At least, she assumed it was human. Gloves had been blown clear off the hands and lay singed and smoking less than a span away. Then she got closer and saw his familiar silver suit and *The Seeker*'s insignia.

It WAS Bashar.

His oxygen monitor was in the danger zone and blinking. She read the outside monitor on her suit that indicated a borderline breathable atmosphere. She would take the chance. She dropped down next to him and pulled off her helmet and gloves. She took a tentative breath. The air smelled stale and smoke filled, but breathable. Then, she took off his helmet and lifted his pale silent face with her bare hands. She sucked in air. The smoke made her cough. She felt light-headed, but she remained conscious. She took his pulse, finding it weak and thready. She paused to catch her breath and reached out to caress his still face. "Oh, Bashar, don't die!" From somewhere, tears splashed down and splattered onto his face. She wiped the wetness away tenderly. More dripped down. He wasn't breathing. She took a gulping breath and pressed her mouth against his, tasting a salty wetness on his eyes and lips.

"Bashar," she whispered, lifting his head. "Wake up." She inhaled and put her lips back on his mouth and pushed her breath into him. His blood smeared her silver suit, painting it with red blurred streaks. Her hands slid in sticky wetness, trying to hold onto an unsteady head. She looked down at him and terror clawed at her heart. Moments ago, he had been alive and vibrant. Now, his face looked lifeless and blue. She bent over and breathed into him. She pushed his breath out by centering her palm over his chest and pushed. Then she breathed into him again and pushed. She did it again. And again. And again.

He responded with an inhalation and a low moan.

"Don't die on me," she pleaded. "Bashar!" she wailed, hearing it echo and re-echo throughout the quiet of the ship. Then she heard a rustling noise.

And froze.

"Who's there?" said a voice from the doorway. Solanje slid around at the noise and thumbed her blaster to lethal intensity. She was aimed and prepared to fire when she realized that she recognized the words.

No alien would be speaking Unis! Alien couldn't possibly know it!

She halted and peered through the smoke.

"Who's there?" she asked back. She saw Crystal's face emerge from the haze and come into the room. Under her arm, Crystal carried her helmet and looked thoroughly put out.

"Crystal!" she cried out in relief. Never had she been so glad to see Crystal's disgruntled face.

Crystal stared at her in shock. "Solanje, is that you? What are you doing here? What's happened?" In disbelief, she surveyed the disaster in the room.

"Help me!" Solanje pleaded. She flicked off the blaster and slid it back inside her suit. "Bashar. It's Bashar. He's hurt and not breathing well. I just got him breathing, but he looks awful." Solanje gasped, as if she couldn't breathe herself.

Crystal moved quickly to Bashar, stooped down to feel his pulse, and checked under his eyelids. "Tell me how he got hurt," she said abruptly, as she pulled out and ripped open a Med kit she carried inside her suit.

"Laser fire. I think it was an accident. Do you remember the training session we had with that jerk Rutlege? We messed up badly. Do you remember?"

"Solanje, we had so many training sessions at that blasted academy, and they're all rather a blur in my mind," said a distracted Crystal, as she tried to stem the blood oozing from his damaged hand. She gazed in concern toward a nasty tear on his suit, a cut on one leg and a gash over his chest.

"It was the exercise when we fired into a mirror array."

"Oh yeah, are you saying that Bashar attacked a mirror?"

"No, no. Robert did. He thought he saw aliens, but I think he just saw his distorted reflection off the metallic walls. He started firing all over the place. He's over there and probably dead, and if Bashar isn't, he's awfully close."

Crystal glanced over at Robert. "I'll check him after Bashar," she said in an uninterested tone. "Bashar's alive, but critical. Help me get him out of his suit, so I can work better."

They peeled the suit off and Crystal checked his vital signs. "This isn't looking good," she muttered. "He needs an adrenalin shock." From her med kit, she took out an injector with a stimulant and plunged the needle into his heart.

Solanje felt her heart stop as Bashar jerked violently in Crystal's hands. He caught a stuttering breath and then inhaled roughly. Crystal ran a hand over his body and dabbed a medicated cloth at a profusely bleeding gash on his leg. Solanje recognized worry flashing across her face.

Solanje stroked Bashar's forehead and brushed some hair back off his face, feeling useless.

Crystal shook her head and pointed to her kit. "Hand me the cream. He shot a mirror?" Crystal made a face of disbelief.

Solanje took a deep breath, trying to steady her mounting panic. "Something like that. Maybe not. Maybe there are aliens in the next room, but they're not there now. Or if they are, they're awful quiet. I've been listening for a while now ..." Her voice broke off with a sharp inhale. Solanje glanced down at Bashar as blood drained from her face. She started shivering. She reached to grab Crystal's arm, shaking it. "We've got to get him out of here. You must do something!"

Crystal shook off her hand roughly. "I'm trying to do something. Move back. You're not helping." Crystal reached in and got the cream herself, all the while casting a worried eye on Solanje.

Crystal muttered, "Too much blood. We have to get him to *The Seeker* stat." Crystal frowned at her as she wiped away more blood and wrapped his leg as tight as she could. Then, she delicately applied burn cream to his ravaged hands and squirted some on Solanje's shaking hand. Solanje dabbed at his chest, her whole body shaking now.

Solanje looked up to see a puzzled expression on Crystal's face as she rummaged for something more in her med kit and came out with a needle.

"What's that for?" She looked at Crystal.

"You. Give me your arm." Solanje felt a needle jab into her arm and soon calmness settled over her. She took a deep breath.

Crystal nodded at her. "That's better. I'll ask Rafael to help. He says he has helped humans before." She looked around, as if expecting someone to be nearby. Then, she gasped, and her eyes widened. She stared at Solanje as if she had just realized something momentous.

"Who's Rafael?" asked Solanje still a bit distraught, and now confused by what Crystal was saying. She was having a hard time understanding what the woman talked about. Her thoughts felt foggy.

"He was right behind me," said Crystal, glancing over her shoulder. She paused when no one appeared to be there. "I think I met a real live alien," she stuttered. "And he talked to me. I understood him. He said I'd have to do this on my own ... and he showed me how." She rubbed at her face and heaved a sigh. Leaning into Bashar and laying a hand on each side of his face, she muttered something.

"What're you doing? What's the matter with you? We need to get him to the ship." Solanje couldn't understand why Crystal just held his face like that, wasting precious time. Then she saw a blue light start to glow around Crystal's hands and begin to pulse.

"Crystal! Your hands!" gasped Solanje. She leaned back, eyes wide.

"Wow!" gasped Crystal in awe. "I didn't believe I could do this, but he said I should try if I got desperate, and it's working!" An intense expression came over Crystal's face. Solanje's waited, barely breathing. Crystal appeared to go into a trance.

Solanje watched Bashar's face transform from a deathly white to a flood of pink. A distorted grimace of pain replaced the slack, dead appearance. He screamed and jerked. Then, as Crystal murmured and stroked his brow, his expression smoothed. Next, she passed her hands over his wounded hands, chest, and leg. Soon they showed signs of healing. He opened his eyes and reached up to gently touch his healer's face. A smile appeared. Then he closed his eyes and sighed.

"He's going to live!" croaked Solanje hoarsely. She could barely speak for the incredible joy she felt. She reeled backward. "He's going to live, isn't he? How'd you do that? What just happened?"

"It has to do with the arrangement of subatomic molecules," mumbled Crystal, a bit surprised as the words came out. "I have to effect their realignment before degeneration sets in and protect the undamaged cells by increasing antibodies in the immune system. Then I sub-atomically rebuild the damaged cells. Rafael showed me how. I was sick and he cured me, so that I can heal others. It's my path, he said."

"What are you talking about Crystal?" asked Solanje. Her eyes widened.

"Healing people. It's my destiny," said Crystal as if Solanje were an idiot.

"Never mind." Solanje felt hot tears on her face. "Whatever you say. He's going to live. That's all I care about right now." She wiped them away and took a huge gulping breath.

"He will." Crystal squeezed her hand. "Now I need to check out Robert. Stay here and watch Bashar. Get him back into his suit because we're going to have to get them back to the ship. Find something to carry them on. She moved over to Robert and within moments, Solanje heard a low moan that became a series of gasps.

Solanje's headset squawked, startling her. The static cleared. She inclined her head to listen as Braden asked for everyone's position. She looked up at Crystal.

"Crystal, where are the others?" she asked.

A bewildered expression passed over Crystal's face as she said, "I don't know. I just stayed put where they left me until I heard a commotion. If I had gone tearing off after them, I would have lost myself in this labyrinth of a ship. I decided the best thing to do was to stay put until your team came to rescue me, but it looks like I'm the one doing the rescuing."

"We need to find them." Solanje looked around. "The Captain is screaming to know where they are, and I don't know what to tell him!"

"Tell him to get help over here fast."

*

Solanje stared down at the sleeping face of Bashar. Braden had sent over Liana and Adam to help bring back Robert and Bashar.

Now Crystal had them both in the med lab applying medicine and bandages to what injuries still needed healing. Neither Crystal nor Solanje had mentioned Rafael yet, as they had been focused on taking care of the wounded. Solanje cast an apprehensive look over at Crystal who was busy putting away antiseptic cloths and towels after she'd wiped Bashar down and gotten him into clean clothes.

Now Solanje sat watching over him while Crystal prepared a final scan.

She caressed his face and touched his still hand. "Oh Bashar, I don't care anymore. I just want you to live. I'll accept disgrace. Let me be the one punished, not you." The wall she had built to hold back her emotions began to crack and crumble. Now that she was safely back, the enormity of what had happened overwhelmed her, and she realized how much she cared for the wayward Sunglast nomad.

Crystal tossed a worried glance over at Solanje. "What are you talking about Solanje?"

Solanje sat back and tried to explain, but anguish stuttered her words. She gathered strength and said, "They said if I loved Bashar, I would bring shame down on my family. They'd cut my hair. The Tang would shun all Hasang T'Kai, *my family,* because of my contamination."

A blurry Crystal paused and gaped at her. She put the scanner down.

Solanje started again, but Crystal interrupted her. "Cut your hair? You're worrying about hair at a time like this? Do you realize what has happened, is happening? Look the frag outside!"

Solanje blinked; her mind froze.

Crystal sighed and gathered a smile. "Whatever are you ranting about? You're making no sense." Puzzlement crossed Crystal's face.

Grief and guilt washed through Solanje. "The Royal Council of Honor ... the Tang. Honored men who make the rules." She gasped and choked. "They arrange the match of husband and wife, and a royal wife must come to her husband as a pure vessel. A royal of Hasang T'Kai cannot choose for herself the one she marries, and they have forbidden me to marry one from the Sunglast. Especially this one."

She pulled at her hair with frantic fingers. "The discipline says clearly that one must control emotions and body, but I have failed. I chant the mantra, I whisper the promise, and I do the exercises, but my feelings do not go away. I'm unworthy to be chosen guardian of the sacred communicator. The Tang decreed that if I mate with Bashar, they'll dishonor my name; they'll cut off my hair. They'll call down disgrace on my family. My parents will wail in shame. Doesn't anyone understand?"

Crystal's eyes widened. "You're worried *here* about a bunch of old men from some Ching T'Karre council?"

"They are the Voice."

Crystal put down the scanner and crossed to Solanje. "These men from this council you talk about, they are *nowhere* within light annuals of us. Do you see them anywhere here? Show them to me."

"Ahhh," Solanje hesitated a moment. She cast her eyes around, expecting them to appear suddenly through the door, shaking an admonishing finger at her. "They'll punish me if I dishonor ..." Her voice faded out and her face clouded over. She stared at the entrance panel. It remained closed. No one stormed through.

They weren't here, and they weren't coming here ... ever. They no longer controlled her life. They had no say here in space, on the ship.

She gave a hiccup and stopped, as blazing realization swept through her.

Crystal shook her head. "This Tang you talk of reminds me of my father. Some men like to control others. But Solanje, they can only hurt you if they are anywhere nearby, but I don't see any of them anywhere within a million light annuals of us. Do you?" she asked tartly.

"No," whispered Solanje, blinking her eyes.

"Solanje," responded Crystal in exasperation, "We may be out here in space for an awfully long time. We have no guarantees that we will ever return, and if we do manage to return, Braden has worries that it will be a far different world from what we left. We, trust me on this one, we are on our own out here. You should do what you believe is right, rather than follow the insane wishes of a group of shadowy old men who may not even exist anymore, and are very, very far away. Shipboard rules are the rules we follow. That's all that counts now. Get a grip girl!"

Crystal paused and gazed at her as if she suddenly understood something important herself. "Funny how clear it seems when it's someone else's life," she said with a laugh. She continued sternly, "If you care for him, Solanje, then pull yourself together. You must help me if he and Robert are to survive." She gazed down at Bashar.

Crystal started talking again. "Solanje, I saw an alien. We're at first contact." Crystal touched her arm lightly and shook it.

"We have to tell Braden."

"Yes, as soon as I finish with Bashar and Robert. Icabar will be upset that I saw one before he did." She smirked at her.

"He'll live." Solanje shrugged and then grinned back.

"And so will Bashar, thanks to Rafael." Crystal clapped her hands and smoothed down her top.

Solanje laughed and sobbed at the same time. "You've met a real alien! We have finally found them. What was it like?"

Crystal nodded. "It was an amazing experience. I'm going to tell Braden now. Go. Go check on Robert for me while I talk to the Captain. Pull yourself together. Bashar needs your strength, not your fear."

Solanje stiffened. All thoughts of councils and honor were wiped away with the thought of Bashar alive and aliens out there waiting.

Chapter 11

Glaze awoke in total darkness. He breathed in a thin, stale, chill air. He first thought that he was trapped in some ice cave in his native Islia. Hidden caves and crevasses posed a constant danger for travelers in that cold land. Blocking the panic that threatened to overtake him, he slowed his breathing and contracted his blood vessels, trying to conserve every particle of energy in his body. Easing to a sitting position, he assessed his surroundings and began to take control of his body, as befitted a disciple of the Maentran Sect. They had taught him how to master certain bodily functions in order to survive in the hostile environment of his native land. He listened for the howling wind, or any other sounds that would orient him. His pupils widened so he might see through the pitch black. He began to doubt where he was. No natural sounds echoed in this dim cavern. There existed only empty silence and utter darkness.

He remembered once almost going mad in a howling wind, as he huddled in a dim frozen cave for what seemed like an eternity. Darkness and the sound of wind would ever be twinned in his mind, but now, he heard nothing. He moved tentatively forward. His body ached from a rash of bruises, but he was basically unhurt.

He saw an odd round object nearby and the thought of a space helmet popped into his mind.

What would a space helmet be doing in an Islian cave? He reconsidered the current data. The air registered breathable but smelled stale. The temperature felt cold, but it was above freezing. He puffed out a cloud of breath that dissipated quickly.

How long have I been here?

He removed a heavy glove and reached out to feel his surroundings. The nearby wall felt smooth and metallic, not rough like natural rock.

As his recall came back, in that previous time, he had been rescued from the cave and the experience had happened long ago. The memory of his being caught in an avalanche while on a spy mission in Islia and being trapped for a long time in a deep cavern poured into his mind. He recalled that at the height of his fear, when he thought he was going to die, a glowing apparition of a beautiful woman had appeared out of the darkness. She had smiled at him and told him to hold on a little longer because he would be rescued soon. Because of her, his will to live strengthened. When the rescue team finally appeared, he had been near death, but he had hung on. They were amazed that he was still alive. He had babbled on and on about the beautiful lady who had saved him, but they told him it was only a hallucination brought on by oxygen starvation, and the effects of prolonged exposure. He refused to believe them, and never forgot her. For him, she had been more real than anyone alive. After that any other woman had paled in comparison to the vibrant image that he still carried in his memory.

Thinking of her after so long a time, he called out to her, as he had in other critical moments of his life. Silence had always answered him before, but now, the dark began to glow and a light appeared brighter and brighter until once more she stood in front of him, glowing and radiant.

He shaded his eyes from her brilliance She dimmed, and a smile played over perfect features. "You seem to find all the dark holes in your life ... and fall into them," she chided him. Light fanned out from her, filling the space between them.

His hand reached out to touch her. "Tell me you're real and I'm not losing my mind. I need you to save me again." She shrank back from the touch. Then reconsidering, she put out her hand as if in a benediction, or a warding off.

"I didn't save you the last time. You saved yourself. You can save yourself again if you want to. Concentrate on your ship. Envision a place there. Close your eyes and see the space in detail and imagine you are there." She smiled at him. "It can be that simple ... for you, at least. You have the control and the ability. You just have to push it a step further... with my help."

With a shake of his head, he, dropped his hand as his sight adapted to the light. He studied her like a starving man, starving for sanity. "I can't leave you. I won't. I never forgot you, you know. I can love no other woman, once knowing you. No other woman compares to you," he babbled. "Tell me you're real. Please, tell me you're real."

She smiled at him. "If you do this, I'll come to you soon. Don't be afraid. Close your eyes and think of a place in your ship. If you want to see me again, do this."

Her voice breathed against his closing eyelids with a light tickling touch as she leaned over to kiss his forehead. The heat of her lips left a warm spot that began to spread outward. A burning sensation swept through his entire body. As he became warmer and warmer, the cold existence of his life started to shatter under the weight of her soft, hot kiss. He felt like he was cracking up and melting, as the ice in his soul transformed through her touch. His spirit, long dead and frozen, began to vibrate in the joy of new life, and then it splintered into a million glowing and rejoicing pieces.

Obeying her firm command, he imagined his room. He envisioned the images of space and stars and planets displayed on his walls. He saw the exquisite, miniature starship given to him by his father, the desk cluttered with pictures of galaxies. He remembered the soothing comfort of his cozy chair and heard the gentle humming of the power grid that fed him oxygen.

He realized that he was truly happy for the first time in his life, basking in the glow of her attention.

She had returned to him. He had not been crazy. She was back after all this time and she had promised to come again soon.

He exploded in the pure bliss of that thought.

Chapter 12

"Ow, ow, ow."

"Shut up. You'll wake Bashar."

"Ha! He's out cold. They're going to attack us. You told Braden about the attack, didn't you?"

"Shut up."

Robert sat in the medical unit with his right arm in a sling and his left leg splinted. Unfortunately, his mouth wasn't damaged. Solanje wished it were, so she could slap a bandage across it right now.

Crystal came in and frowned at him.

"He's all yours," said Solanje, giving him a glare.

"But you have to tell Braden how they attacked us," he protested.

"You fired into an enclosed area and used a grenade, for crying out loud. What were you thinking?" Solanje countered. "The whole 'attack' was your laser fire ricocheting off the walls. You're an idiot."

"There *are* aliens. Tell her, Crystal. You saw one. Just look at those ships and then tell me there aren't any aliens."

Crystal shook her head at him and glared. "I did see one, but he wasn't hostile. In fact, you'd be dead if it weren't for him and what he taught me. So, don't go shooting off your mouth about what you don't know."

"I'm done." Solanje rolled her eyes and left the room.

Robert smiled at Crystal. "We'll, here you are again, my dear. Like she said, I'm all yours and my poor leg really hurts. Could you do that touching thing again?" He rubbed his groin area with his undamaged hand and smiled at her. "Heal a fellow crew man. You're going to need me now that we've lost two. Come closer. Ummm. Touch me."

"Liana," murmured Crystal into her comm. "I need you here at the med unit ASAP."

"Hey, no, now don't do that." Robert struggled to get out of the unit, but Crystal shoved him back in.

"Look I know that you're pumped up with painkillers and that makes you less inhibited, but it's still no excuse to talk to me that way." She'd had enough.

"Naughty, naughty, Robert. Maybe you should spank me. Might like it, too. Some do, I hear." Robert made a scrunched-up face at her.

Crystal just shook her head. She hesitated to cure him fully for fear that he might come after her again. As a healer, she shouldn't think like that. But he was so ... damn ... aggravating.

Liana poked her head in and shook a finger at him. She entered, shaking her head.

"Ah, the dragon lady. Come to scold me for my bad boy ways?" Robert grinned at her. "I was just showing Crystal where it hurt. You want to feel it too? It's starting to swell up a little."

"Little is right."

"Crystal, leave us for a moment. It's past time that I straighten this boy out."

"I'm shaking in my boots," sneered Robert.

"More than happy to leave him with you," gritted out Crystal. "Please do something with him." Looking at Liana, she added, "Before I do something deadly." She left without turning back.

"Listen Robert, you're out of control and we can't have that anymore," she said sternly.

"I was only trying to protect my fellow humans from hostile aliens. Can't anyone see those ships out there?" he protested.

"You were trying to kill them and that would be a terrible mistake," she said taking his face firmly between her two hands.

"What are you doing?" he jerked in her grasp. But her mind was already entering his, as she reached for her forbidden Talent to alter him and fix the problem before it was too late and too many died... aliens and humans alike.

*

After Bashar and Robert got settled into the med unit with Crystal and Solanje attending them, Braden and Adam took the first shuttle over to search for Joel and Glaze. They spent an extensive amount of time combing the large ship, but they found nothing except more equipment and a section with oddly human facilities. There they found beds, dishes, alien electronics and familiar furniture with an alien styling, but there were no signs of live aliens, or lost crew. The investigated the pods but found nothing. They were empty and smelled bad. Finally, they returned.

Crystal told them as much as she could remember about her mysterious friend, who called himself Rafael, but they didn't find him anywhere on the alien ship either. Her description of him indicated that he was humanoid in shape and could obviously communicate with them in their language, or through their mind. He had a nimbus of light surrounding him that made details of his body hazy and hard to describe.

She said that Rafael had told her that the large space crafts had been a convoy of ships at one time, but they were now abandoned and no longer needed. He had been eager to exchange information about medicine, imbedding high level healing instructions through mind-to-mind contact. Crystal had been in a trancelike state when she heard the explosions. As far as she was concerned, the alien hadn't acted hostile at all. On the contrary, he had been polite and informative. Then all the commotion had diverted her attention and she had gone to find Bashar and Solanje. Her mysterious stranger had vanished. The rest of the story everyone knew.

Braden called a ship-wide conference. He left Icabar at Navcom manning the communication board in case either Joel or Glaze tried to report in. Robert continued to stay in the med unit with a mysterious relapse, heavily drugged. Everyone else jammed into a work module that they had enlarged by removing an adjoining partition. Braden poured himself some of Tessa's special tea. After making sure that everyone had something to drink and plopping a sprig of newmint into his tea, he scanned the area. He shook his head sadly. "I'm responsible for what happened. As Captain, I must take the blame," he said.

Still weak, Braden struggled up to a sitting position from a recliner and protested. "I was the leader of the team. I take the blame for his actions. I should have …"

Braden waved him down. "You did everything you thought was necessary at the time. We all did. We learned a hard lesson on how inexperienced we are at first contact procedures. It shouldn't have happened. ROBERT forgot his training. We trained for first contact eventuality, but I should have insisted on more reviews during the trip out. I grew careless. So, I have decided that everyone needs to study the first contact directives, and Liana will set up a schedule for each of us consisting of possible emergency scenarios and suggested responses. I do not want to lose any more people. No one here is expendable. We're a small ship, especially compared to what's out there.

They all looked in the direction of the alien ships and went quiet.

Braden continued, "I'm also putting Dyra in charge of collecting any data she can find that might help us discover what these aliens are like. All bets are off, except for a significant reward to the person who makes a convincing case of what the aliens look like and what they want. And blobs are not even close. We have Crystal's description, but I want to know a lot more."

He sighed and grabbed a handhold near him. "I also want Bashar to reevaluate our weaponry tactics and defense system. He'll take over Robert's job for now and refresh everyone else's training. At no time is any one to fire any kind of weapon indiscriminately inside a ship, much less toss grenades. That is basic training ONE."

He looked around. There had been murmurs about Robert's senseless action and general agreement about the new rigorous schedule. *Good.* The frightening episode had focused everyone on the dangers of the mission and what they might be facing.

Then he straightened up and cast a determined look at each one of them. "I will not count Glaze or Joel dead until I see their bodies as proof. We must continue to hope that they're alive somewhere and we'll get them back. If anyone has ideas on what we can do, see me privately."

Everyone nodded grimly in agreement.

Their attention then turned to the world in front of them. Photos and radar sweeps from the earlier probe revealed that the planet contained a myriad of seas and lakes. Dense vegetation covered a large portion of it. The atmosphere was analyzed as breathable for humans. Still, a few unknown gases caused concern. What effect might they have? Could they have caused hallucinations? The wealth of materials on the planet's surface excited Adam. He pointed out that using their existing equipment, certain minerals he had identified might provide an additional source of fuel for power. The planet appeared to teem with possibilities. He wanted to go down, explore, and see what other resources the planet contained.

He wasn't the only one. Other adventuresome crewmembers wanted an exploration of the planet right away. Indications of abundant plant life with new and exotic varieties she had never seen before excited Tessa. They had also sighted several lower level animal forms, some hot blooded and mammalian, but so far nothing that indicated intelligent life, nor any indications of buildings, roads, or electronics. The planet looked pristine—like a well-cultivated garden.

"Captain I have an observation." Crystal offered a comment.

"What?" Braden nodded toward her.

"Have you noticed that we have changed somewhat?" she asked.

"Changed? What do you mean?" Braden frowned.

"Physically, we're not the same as we were on take off," she explained. "On a molecular level we're slightly different than at the beginning of this trip."

"Different?"

"Yes. I ran a series of physicals not too long ago and there are some unusual chemical changes in our bodies. We're extraordinarily healthy. I assumed that was my fine doctoring, but now I'm not so sure. Also, there are my new healing powers. Then, someone commented on the fact that Liana was empathic and telepathic. That startled me. I don't remember that being a Talent of hers at launch. What else? Are there other strange Talents that have emerged since takeoff?"

"Do you mean that something that we are being exposed to is enhancing latent Talents within us?" asked Dyra.

Braden jerked back at the thought. "Now that I think about it, yes. Some of you are different. Liana has a talent I certainly wasn't aware of." The idea of her being aware of his every thought stabbed at him uncomfortably. He wondered if the others felt the same discomfort.

"I can only read someone's mind under special circumstances. I would never eavesdrop without permission," protested Liana.

"So how did you know just then what I was thinking?" he retorted. "You read my mind!"

"I said that because everyone in this room just had the same thought and group shouting like that is hard to ignore. I understand your concerns but believe me; I really need dire circumstances to invade an unwilling mind. However, I can and will if necessary. So, this crew needs to shape up now or...face the consequences. I do not want this mission to fail because we acted like idiots, and a few have been appallingly idiotic recently."

Uncomfortable looks were exchanged.

"What you did in the gate..." Bashar looked at Braden. "That was unexpected..."

"Yeah, my brother Richard had the Tellurian Time Talent, but they said I didn't. He eventually became the Timelab Director. Not to be outdone, I thought that being a starship captain would be almost as good and lots of fun. So, I decided that's what I wanted to do."

"Yeah," commented Bashar... "lots of fun."

"But now, I think that I do have a bit of the Talent. I can sense space/time."

"You changed it!"

"I only timed events forward a fraction. Even so, it's unnerving to be able to do that."

Quiet fell over everyone, and then, "What about Crystal's healing hands?" Solanje looked at Crystal.

Crystal looked down at her hands and turned them over. "Rafael is responsible there. I found it a bit unnerving also, but I should think Bashar's grateful for it."

Bashar grunted and nodded.

Braden raised a hand. "Now that I think about it, Icabar mentioned something about Joel dreaming things not so long ago, but I didn't pay too much attention. He tried to tell me that he thought his dreams might foretell the future, but I was too preoccupied and just dismissed it. Maybe there's something to them. We should ask Icabar about Joel's dreams. It might help us find Joel and Glaze."

Braden stood up. Adam had stopped the ship's rotation before they had been sucked through the gate. He had not started the rotation again, so they were still in light to no gravity. Braden wanted to be ready to move the ship out as fast as necessary if he had to, and to do that, he had to keep the ship compacted and the gravitational spin at minimal. Consequently, they all were still trying to re-adapt to the effects of near zero gravity. The strong push to stand up translated into Braden drifting toward the exit. He grabbed the handrail and rotated out the door. Everyone followed floating behind him. He traveled down the corridor, clutching handholds, wending his way toward Navcom. He palmed the panel entrance into the area, looking over toward the communication deck. Icabar wasn't there. Braden tumbled into the room, looking wildly around.

Now Icabar was missing!

A bubble of fear rose in Braden's chest.

"Icky. Where are you! Icabar!" he yelled loudly. He frantically activated his comm.

In his ear, he heard an answering shout. "Braden. Here! Quickly! Come here! Come to quarters."

Braden spun around colliding into Adam who bounced right behind him. Adam lost his grip, stumbled backward, and flailed wildly before he stabilized. Braden reached for and gripped the handholds, propelling his body as fast as he could toward the sound of Icabar's voice. The others followed him like bobbing ducklings. He found Icabar standing just outside Glaze's quarters with a strange expression on his face.

"I came here to see if I could find any clues as to his whereabouts. You know... maybe he left a note, or ummm a diary, but .... but ... look ..." Icabar, for once, seemed to have run out of words. He just stood there pointing, his eyes wide. "Do you see what I see? He's glowing. I swear by Our Lady, Braden—he's glowing."

Braden peered in and there leaning at full recline was Glaze. He appeared sound asleep with a beautiful smile on his face and a glow all around him that winked out as he opened his eyes. He stared up at the ceiling briefly, and then frowned. Taking a deep breath, he twisted his head to squint over at the newcomers.

"Where am I?" He rubbed his eyes and peered over at the gathering cluster of crew, all gaping at him from his doorway. "Can't a fellow get a nap around here without everyone coming and staring?" he said, but a stupid grin lit his face.

"Glaze!" shouted Braden. "How did you get here?"

Chapter 13

"I'm good to go, Captain." Enthusiastically, Adam voiced his opinion on the proposed expedition down to the planet. All their scans had shown a world that contained large caches of precious stones and rare metals, not to mention sightings of potential fuel reserves. A treasure trove of raw materials lay beneath her crust and exotic plants and animals covered her surface, tempting all on board despite a wary captain.

Crystal had done a complete physical on Glaze and pronounced him fit. He still couldn't or wouldn't come up with a good explanation of how he had gotten back on board. He had said that he remembered nothing about the incident, but he said it with a strange expression on his face. Then also, they noticed a dramatic difference in him. He acted warmer, more open, with less edginess and cutting sarcasm. He smiled too much. Definitely not the same Glaze. The constant smile was unnerving.

"Lock him up with Icabar for a while and we'll find out what happened," suggested Bashar.

"Liana did a mind read," Braden informed them. "What did you find?"

"Nothing. There's a big blank from the time he was in the ship until he woke up here." She frowned at Glaze who returned it with one of his goofy smiles.

Finally, the discussion came back to the proposed expedition to the planet below.

"I know how much you want to get out and explore. I feel the same way, but it could be dangerous," Braden warned his crew. "I have already lost crew, and Robert isn't fit for duty. He's out of any expeditions until he improves. I can't afford to lose anyone else. Dangerous aliens could be down there."

The crew clustered around the viewing screen as he pointed below. "In fact, it's more likely that, if there are aliens anywhere around here, they're on that planet. I think they deserted the ships once they got a colony established. Looks like a nice place to live, actually."

"Well, they haven't shown up on our scanning," retorted Icabar. "Except for a multitude of strange photonics surges." He frowned. "Just lower animal life forms for the most part, although..."

"We can't just stay up here and rot," interrupted Adam. "We came all this way to explore new worlds, and that down there sure qualifies." He waved a hand toward the monitor.

"The air is breathable and analyzes out safe. Crystal and I took samples." Glaze looked eagerly at Braden. "As far as finding a planet comparable to our own, it doesn't get any better than this one."

"I want to go down there and sample the plant life and observe the native fauna. There's bound to be some new exotic species," added Tessa eagerly. "I don't know about you, Braden, but I want to feel the wind against my face once more and put my hands deep into some real dirt. With that soil, real soil, we could grow fresh lettuce, pears, corn, and strawberries. Think of the possibilities!"

"It's been so long that I have forgotten what a fresh strawberry tastes like," grumbled Adam. "Makes my mouth water just thinking about it."

"Mmm. Yum," Icabar added with a smirk.

"So far, there's been no evidence of anything threatening." Dyra looked at Braden, pleading with her expressive brown eyes. "Robert hallucinated and brought on that catastrophe. No matter what he says, aliens didn't attack us. He just went berserk."

Braden put up his hands against the onslaught of eager faces in front of him.

"What about your friend, Rafael?" he queried Crystal. "Who knows what he or his friends, if he has any, are capable of doing?"

"He seems capable of disappearing," snorted Icabar. "Are you sure you saw him?"

Crystal answered angrily, "No matter what you may believe, I did see him. I didn't make him up. I wish you would believe me. And, if all the aliens are like him, then we'll be lucky if we find them." Crystal glared at them, her hands on her hips.

"But where is he? And where's Joel?" Icabar shook his head in disbelief. "Has anyone seen anything? Maybe something in the ship's air contains unknown elements we haven't discovered yet that affect our brain chemistry. We have done very little chemical analysis inside the ships because we have been so busy looking for aliens and surveying the planet. What if there's some element in the artificial environment on the ships that causes hallucinations in human brains?" Icabar looked skeptical.

"I know what I saw!" exclaimed Crystal. "It was real."

Icabar raised an eyebrow at her.

"Glaze, what about you?" asked Braden. "What do you have to say?"

"I didn't see anything," Glaze snapped, looking suddenly nervous.

Liana cocked her head toward Glaze and sent him a puzzled expression. Braden noticed the gesture. He frowned at him. "I was just requesting an evaluation of the data you found on your latest air samples from the alien ship. Didn't you recently sample air in there? I just wondered what you found. Or, did you see something like Crystal did?" asked Braden, suddenly realizing how Glaze had misinterpreted his question.

"I told you that all my data says that the air's safe to breathe," answered Glaze, turning away to study the console. "I'll go re-check my sample now if it will make you any happier." He whirled around, steadied himself and abruptly left Navcom.

Braden frowned after him. Glaze was hiding something, and Braden wanted to know what. Liana had been disturbed by the comment also.

"Suppose Joel is down on that planet and needs us to rescue him," suggested Dyra.

"How in all the world would he get there?" asked Braden.

"Maybe like Glaze," suggested Adam.

"And how would that be?" Braden gave him a studied gaze.

Adam fell silent and looked uncomfortably away.

Crystal interjected, "Icabar told you that we haven't scanned any intelligent lifeforms down there, at least intelligent as we would evaluate them. Also, there's no buildings, communications, streets, anything we would call evidence of intelligent life. Although, things might be organized differently here, they would still need shelter, food and technology." She waved a hand toward the alien ships.

"Well, we didn't record any life forms on the alien ships, either," said Dyra. "But Crystal says that what she saw appeared intelligent and humanoid."

Crystal nodded her head vigorously. "I did see him. Thank you for not calling me crazy, Dyra."

"You're welcome." A grin.

"How about if we only send two," asked Adam. "I'll go. The power grid is stable now. The ship's in orbit and on automatic systems. Bashar's well enough that he's capable of handling any engine room emergencies with some help. Besides, I'm the official geologist and that planet looks to have some interesting rock formations and energy resources. All I have been doing lately is helping Tessa at the farm."

"Helping? I'd call it something else!" snickered Icabar.

Tessa blushed. "Adam helps me with chores and I'm grateful, so don't start with your snide remarks." Tessa's bright red color gave a lie to the protest. "We work hard there."

"Sure, Tessa," smirked Icabar. "I'll bet you do."

Tessa turned to Braden, "Captain, we should both go. Adam can sample the geology while I, as the ship's botanist and zoologist, can catalog the flora and fauna. Now that we have established orbit, we do seem the logical choice."

She gave Adam a big smile that dimpled her cheeks and went all the way up into her eyes. Startled, seeing them standing there together, smiling at each other so foolishly, Braden realized that Icabar was on to something. That relationship had become something more than platonic. He felt a flash of regret for an opportunity lost.

"Crystal might be right. The animal life could be intelligent, even vicious in a way that we don't understand," argued Braden.

"What isn't dangerous out here?" asked Tessa. "Every moment in space is dangerous. We knew that when we signed up for the trip."

She has a point, he thought.

"Then, I'm leading the expedition," he said, surprising himself.

"What!" several voices protested.

Braden found it hard to articulate how he felt. He just knew that more than anything; he wanted to be the first human to step on alien soil. As Captain, he should be the one to meet and greet the first time.

"Bashar will be in charge of the ship," he said firmly.

"Can we afford to risk our Captain?" asked Liana with a frown.

"Make no mistake. Out here, as Tessa just very aptly pointed out, everything is a risk. I just want to lead the expedition. It's my decision to make," responded Braden firmly.

And that was that.

Braden ordered the crew to activate the rotation to get them used to the heavier gravity. While they prepared, the planet below enticed them with photographs of lush greenery, winding rivers, and broad oceans. The weather remained consistently perfect with an occasional spring shower sweeping across the landscape. Temperature varied only a little from night to light. Colder temperatures existed at either pole, but not cold enough for ice and snow to remain.

After multiple shifts of observation and preparation, and nothing further to discover, the only thing left to do was to send out a manned expedition. So, Braden, Tessa and Adam suited up and boarded a shuttle. The planet revolved beneath them like a jewel against the dark velvet of star-spangled space. They left the ship, eager after so a long a voyage to make their first landing on firm ground. Closer and closer they came, dumping speed at a rapid rate, snatching glimpses of green landforms and blue water opening before them in breathtaking beauty. The planet's winds buffeted the rover like a mother rocking her child as they prepared to land.

"Look at those formations over there!" exclaimed Adam peering out a window.

Braden cut the thrusters and carefully landed them in an open meadow, edged by giant trees and a tumbling stream. They looked around, sampled the air again and then satisfied with the results, unsealed the rover. Braden gingerly climbed down and halted on the bottom step. He pulled out a piece of paper and read, "I dedicate this planet to humanity's spirit of adventure and exploration. With this small step, we have leaped the void of space and discovered paradise."

Captain Braden of *The Seeker* officially touched down with a deft tread. But then, uneven ground and high gravity made his legs wobble, so the second step wasn't quite as accomplished. At first, he could only stagger about like a drunken sailor just off ship. Gradually he got his legs working satisfactorily.

"The air tests fine for us to breathe without helmets. Do I have permission to try, Captain?" questioned Tessa.

"Let's wait and look around a bit," countered Braden.

All around them flourished lush flora with brilliant flowers. Tall olive stalks with purple feathery clusters at the end waved a welcome. Small lavender petals hid amid fern-shaped viridian leaves and spread out over a wide meadow, forming a vivid rustling carpet. Large, prolific, sunburst blossoms at tips of dense verdant bushes all danced and fluttered at the meadow's edge. Soaring thick pines swayed in a nearby forest to their right, and waving chartreuse grass rippled at their feet. It was difficult not to want to throw off the bulky helmet, much less the entire space suit, and go skipping through the glorious landscape that greeted their eyes.

"Look at this!" exclaimed Tessa. She wandered over to a stand of branching trees and picked something red off a bough.

"We can breathe without the helmet, I'd bet on it," protested Adam. "It tested safe every time we tried."

"All right, but be careful," said Braden reluctantly.

Adam gave a happy shout and yanked off his helmet. The wind ruffled his hair as he took a deep breath. A wonderful smile lit his face. "The air smells sweet and fragrant. I forgot what real air smells like. It's fantastic!"

Braden eyed his enthusiastic crewman and then tentatively lifted off his own helmet. After the stale metallic air of the ship with its musty human stink, the fresh breeze, filled with the fragrant aroma of flowers and ripe greenery, did indeed, smell like heaven. He felt the sun warming his face. He had forgotten how good it could feel. With no ill effects for either of them, he signaled Tessa that she could take off her helmet too.

Tessa followed suit. Adam lurched over to where Tessa was studying some flora.

"I want to explore that rock formation over there. Come with me, Tessa. Directive Three says that we should stay together, right Captain?" Adam tossed Braden the question over his shoulder as he headed over toward a rock formation.

"Yes. Everyone keeps together with your channel open on your headsets, so you don't lose contact. Remember what happened to Glaze, and Joel is still missing. I don't want to lose any more crew."

"Aye, Captain," responded Adam eagerly. He waved at Tessa who stumbled enthusiastically along in his wake.

They had trained hard recently on planet exploration procedures. Adam was pulling out his sample box and forceps. Tessa brandished clippers and testing tubes filled with various liquids. Braden looked around and took a few readings of his own, but the beauty and power of the planet distracted him. He felt energy flow through him as he gazed at a particularly large stand of trees that ringed the base of a high hill. They reminded him of the legendary giant heartwood trees of the Great Forest back home. He sighed, remembering the distant dreamlike memory.

Braden listened to the sound of a small stream nearby that bubbled and splashed. Staggering over, he plopped heavily onto a nearby rock. The trees outlined against the sky seemed to vibrate in every shade of green imaginable. The whole place felt wonderful. After annuals of being confined on shipboard, they had found paradise.

He couldn't really be mad at his crew for wanting to explore such a glorious world.

They had discovered an alien planet! And it was magnificent!

The idea of his life's dream finally being realized rocked him, and a rush of wonder enveloped him.

Over in the distance, Adam held up a rock to show Tessa, and she waved a flower in his face. They were babbling happily into their data set as they recorded all their discoveries, but with their helmets off, he couldn't hear what they were saying. He decided to let them be.

The moment alone gave him an opportunity to think. Things were just not adding up. Crystal claimed to have seen something that looked a lot like a human; only none of Icabar's scanners had recorded any lifeforms on board the alien ship. However, maybe it had fled because of all the excitement. He wouldn't blame it. There had been enough time and available shuttles on the ship. Bashar said the technology on board was annuals ahead of anything they had; only it appeared to have been abandoned ages ago. By whom? And why? What had made them leave? To colonize the planet? Solanje appeared confused as to whether they had really been attacked, or whether Robert had panicked. But what had spooked Robert? And where was Joel? Yes, that worried him the most. Where was Joel? And how had Glaze gotten back without the rover? That gave him pause. Questions. Too many questions with nothing making any sense.

Braden yawned. His eyes grew tired. They had been through several intense shifts and he had barely had a moment to relax, much less rest. Crystal had supplied sleeping medications, but it hadn't helped much. His head nodded and he stifled a yawn. Then without realizing it, he fell into a deep sleep.

*

He was dreaming. In his dream, he heard someone calling his name. He rubbed his eyes and opened them, noting the position of the shadows and saw that they had moved around and were much longer than before. He groaned.

He had fallen asleep! How careless!

He looked for the others, but they were no longer nearby. The light felt cooler on his face, and the heavier gravity made it hard to breathe easily. Trying to readjust his position, his muscles screamed pain at him. He must have slept for a while because he felt stiff and sore. He blinked his blurry eyes and stretched out his arms as he surveyed his surroundings.

Where were the others? They should have kept in touch with him. Then he heard a voice. It sounded like a woman singing.

Well, at least he had found Tessa, and if he had found Tessa, then Adam lurked nearby.

He took a deep breath of relief and scanned the area. Suddenly, he noticed a strange woman emerge from the trees and walk right toward him as if it were the most common occurrence in the world.

She glowed. Light bathed all around them Her eyes smiled at him. "You're finally awake. The physical body exhausts too easily, I'm afraid."

He stared at her. She wore a loose white top with a flowing shiny gold skirt. She had long swinging blond hair, and a stunning face that had the most striking luminescent golden eyes. Her beautiful smile made him feel good. He found himself smiling back at her before he realized that she was a total stranger and most probably alien. Still she acted human. In fact, she felt familiar.

He scrambled back from her. "Who are you?"

She laughed. "Don't be afraid. I'm a friend." She fluttered her hands toward the horizon of trees. "The natural energy of the forest amplifies your capabilities much as the energy in the crystal does. She pulled out a sparkling crystal from a deep pocket. "Don't you recognize a Master Crystal? There are only a few Master Crystals left, but they are more potent than most ordinary crystals combined. They are sentient entities that generate a level of energy and can act as a catalyst on certain species. Yours is one, but not everyone in your species can bond with them. However, you can." She grinned at him. "You're already familiar with them. You have a few on your ship. Here's one especially for you." She pulled a second crystal from within her gown and held it out to him.

Braden found the glowing crystal irresistible. He reached out to touch it. A shaft of light bounced off the crystal turning it into a rainbow of colors. The crystal warmed, and suddenly his mind received a jolt of tremendous energy. Synapses expanded and connected throughout his brain. Chemical reactions occurred at tremendous rates causing thoughts that had been hazy and half-formed to clarify into understandable concepts. The crystal acted upon his mind to refine, restructure, and re-sort it.

Vaguely he heard her say, "Now work with me, Braden. At one time in your life, there was a popular art form that when you first looked at it, you saw only an abstract picture of pretty colors and patterns. However, when you de-focused your eyes and looked at it in a different way, the picture became three-dimensional and creatures and objects that you had not seen before suddenly appeared. We're going to do that now. I want you to concentrate on certain areas around you and de-focus your eyes a little. Relax and let the three-dimensional patterns that you see near me become four-dimensional. Do not be alarmed at what you see. No one will hurt you."

Patiently, she watched him. He glanced where she indicated but didn't see anything unusual. Nothing happened. He tried again. It wasn't working. Everything appeared blurry and hazy.

"You're trying too hard. Look at something beyond your point of vision. Stare at those trees over there. Then relax your eyes. Look at the crystal and then as I draw it away, pull in the outside surroundings with it," she said.

He tried again. Suddenly the vague images fell into focus. Once he had the shapes, he focused harder on them, and they became clearer. Light radiated around certain areas that grew more and more defined. The light resolved itself into the forms of glowing beings that revealed a shimmering humanoid form. He saw them watching him intently.

One drifted over, reached out to the woman and touched her on the shoulders. Braden marveled at the beautifully luminous creatures made up of what appeared to be mostly light and air. A few wafted delicate wings at their backs.

The being smiled and said, "Elsinore, he sees us! The human can see us. If he can do it, then his whole species has the potential."

Braden stared at the creature trying to keep it in focus. Then the words the creature had uttered connected within his brain, and he gaped at her and gasped, "He called you Elsinore! You're Elsinore, Lady of the Crystal!" The shock of the revelation exploded within Braden's brain, stunned, and overloaded his synapses so that his entire mind shut down.

He fainted.

Chapter 14

As he entered the alien vessel with his away team, Joel stared in awe at the immense area. Gazing at the walls with their odd glyphs and splashed dark blue designs, he shivered at the surreal beauty. He also studied aqua and cream tiered balconies that rose along the far wall and faced a central platform. Although quiet now, he could almost hear strange alien voices rebounding throughout the room, and an echo of lives no longer present.

The first larger, more decorated room led into other smaller areas via various angled corridors and sliding panels. He wandered away from the team as he randomly traced dark wavy lines on a wall, feeling rough ridges and bumps under his sensitized gloved hand.

Following the lines up to a private alcove, almost a small room, he studied an area no bigger than a large walk-in closet.

Looking out, he observed Glaze and Crystal fiddling with their headsets and scanning the awesome interior. Glaze had taken off his helmet. Joel then checked the air quality and it checked out safe. In order to see better, he removed his helmet too. Attaching his helmet to his suit, he shook his head, glad to be rid of the cumbersome headgear. The air smelled stale and metallic. He wrinkled his nose and coughed.

Blinking his eyes, he scanned the odd cul-de-sac where a wall of electronic equipment nestled further in. The alcove contrasted with the rest of the room having a darker blue hue. A complicated maze of connecting yellow, red, green, and black colored lines snaked along the wall. Strung on the differently colored lines, red, blue, purple, green and yellow embossed circles hung like loose beads on a bracelet. He stepped inside to study it closer when he heard a humming noise start up.

A tingling sensation passed over him. Rays of light shot out all over the alcove. He shouted to Glaze about the glowing lights and got a mumbled reply. His head started to buzz, and his knees buckled. He leaned against the wall, causing a finger to accidentally brush one of the colored circles. The light pulsated faster and faster, making his eyes blur. Light started flashing everywhere.

Abruptly, everything went dark. Now, he was disoriented and falling through emptiness, tumbling, and spinning through a black void. He reached out trying to grab onto something to steady himself, but he only flailed wildly at empty air. After a few moments of heart-stopping freefall, he slowed, and solid walls closed back around him. A floor bumped hard under him, jamming his helmet brutally against his side and bruising a few ribs.

He opened his eyes. Wincing, he stood up. He stood in the same space with the same electronics blinking at him, but when he peered out, he saw a totally different view. All these walls were gray. Also, a greater array of technical equipment filled the area. No tiers climbed the wall, no platform stood in the center. The area appeared smaller. He let his eyes get accustomed to the dimness before he stepped out of the decorated structure and into a whole new area. Glaze and Crystal were nowhere to be seen.

"Glaze!" he shouted frantically.

The sound of his voice bounced in lonesome echoes and died out.

The new room smelled musty and stood silent and empty, giving off an air of abandonment. No residue litter of life could be seen, and dust motes swirled around his feet as he shuffled forward. Gravity felt heavier. Panels of electronic equipment jutted out from the walls. Monitors and switches clustered together on a console in a curving corner. All stood dark and silent.

Across the room, near the edge of a partially opened wall panel, shone a lighted rectangular button with strange encryptions etched on it. It was half the size of a small playing card. He moved slowly across the room, scanning the area, trying to find an exit. Curious, he touched the bright square. Somewhere far away, a rumble sounded. Then, he heard a harsh grating noise, as if some old unused machinery was trying to start up. A soft light came on. The panel slid completely open. He jumped and looked around but saw nothing.

"Halloo. Is anyone there?" he shouted into the quiet. His voice echoed back in dying repetitions. He drew out his raster, set it on stun, and held it loosely in his hand. After a few moments, he gathered up some courage and decided to explore further. Peering inside, the partially opened panel, he stepped through into a corridor. The top brushed his head, so that he had to dip down at times, and he could barely swing his arms without hitting the sides. A soft glow of light appeared on the floor ahead of his footsteps. As he walked, a pool of light appeared in front while the light behind him winked out. Amused, he decided to see if it would follow him into a room to his left.

He wrestled open a heavy door with an airlock that led into a huge two storied holding bay. Finding himself on a second story balcony, he surveyed stacks and stacks of silent oblong capsules about as high as he was tall. They filled the bay below. Odd markings decorated each front. The capsules appeared empty. No activated power was apparent, but a dim light pervaded the area. Seeing nothing further, he decided to explore the corridor some more and backed out. The heavy door clanged shut, setting up diminishing echoes all around him.

The light winked on ahead of him, and the hallway behind him grew darker. He slid open another paneled door. A light clicked on and lit the area, revealing four rows of fifteen seats each that formed a semicircle around a center platform, much like a stage. He heard a noise. Nearby, a motor stuttered into life and a green light began to blink on a large electronic panel against the wall to the right of the entrance. Joel decided to investigate. As he stepped closer, racks of cubes within the now glowing machine lit up with alien symbols on them. He studied the strange cubes until he came to the words, "Homo Sapiens." Seeing that word among indecipherable alien lettering startled him. He pulled the cube out and rolled it over in his hands. Looking around, he noticed a matching indentation on the machine and placed the cube in it. Immediately, light sprang up over the platform.

A glowing holographic image began to form in the middle of the stage with various distorted sounds coming from it. He squinted to see what it was. It blurred and wavered. Alien symbols sprung up on a small glowing monitor. He leaned into it and pushed a button to the right of it. The sounds changed tonal values.

The scene on the platform came into better focus. Six humanoid beings were sitting around a conference table with a colorful vid screen built into a console next to them. They were talking in a strange language. Joel pushed the button again. The tonal values changed some more. He frowned as he strained to hear what they were saying, but it sounded like gibberish. Pushing the button again, he suddenly heard a familiar dialect. It sounded like T'Kest. Excited because he recognized the language, he pushed the button once more and the words became decipherable, even though heavily accented, so that he had to strain to understand what they said. Still they were speaking a dialect of Unis, his native language.

The holographic images flickered in and out as Joel angled in closer to the platform for a clearer view. The images glowed, yet their faces looked human having two eyes, a nose, and a mouth in all the appropriate places. However, the bright glow over the scene made it hard to see defining facial features. Each wore a luminescent, loosely draped white garment that disguised any closer details of bodily form. The vid screen next to their table started pulsing a tapestry of colored lights. Electronic strands of lights danced and winked back and forth, weaving an elaborate pattern across its monitor.

The images steadied a bit as Joel found a front row seat and leaned forward to peer at the odd group. He heard one talking and listened intently to what they were saying. He wondered if he were about to see some strange vid show, or an alien virtual reality presentation.

"Humans are a violent, dangerous lot. They should be annihilated," a stern voice blared out.

Joel jerked back in his seat stunned to greater attention.

The speaker continued, "Look at that dark sequence." Five digits, long and slender, revealed a delicate, but human looking hand that flicked at a weaving pattern on the monitor. The hand waved around. "They kill living creatures of all species ... even each other ... more often each other. How can we continue to encourage such a species?" The being leaned forward. A murmur arose from the other images.

There was a flutter and a protest from one across the table. Joel thought he saw a beautiful woman. What he could see of the face appeared exquisite. He strained to listen for her answer.

She shifted in her seat. "Yes, but other genetic markers are brilliant and unique. Many of the humans are creative and daring. They contain a strength and an energy that we've lost."

An angry, deep voice came from across the table and said, "We know your love for humans, Angelique, but their energy and strength could destroy us if they ever knew we existed. They're dangerous. These emerging new powers, called Talents, are causing great concern in council."

"Dangerous? Gabriel, they could be our cousins, if the ancient stories are true."

"Bah! Never! Blasphemy!" A voice from farther down the table protested.

"We seeded that colony. My father transported them to their world from Earth." Angelique refuted his disclaimer.

Joel sat up, startled by the statement. He leaned in to focus more intently on the heavily accented language. *Could this be true?*

"The first Earth colony was primitive, almost barbaric."

"That primitive energy enabled them to survive," said a voice. From outside of the hologram, another being entered the room. The being named Michael looked up and irritably waved him to a vacant seat.

Joel shifted uncomfortably, wondering what they would say next.

Michael slapped his hand down. "The codes of Judgment are clear. These humans are barbarians. It's a miracle their race has survived so far. Time after time it has been our interventions that has saved them from extinction. They have yet to learn how to control their violent nature. We cannot permit them to spread across all universes and contaminate existing lifeforms."

A new member spoke up. "We must wait for the tribunal's verdict. We should hear from all sides before deciding. That has always been the way."

"Yes, Ariel speaks true. Do not judge them so harshly," said Angelique. "Remember that we evolved from depravity. Surely you recall our Great War. You led our legions to victory against The Fallen. So, we too, were violent once, and some still need to curb those impulses." Here she looked pointedly over toward Michael.

She continued, "Now, we hope to transform and escape the stresses of our physical world entirely. No longer need we be trapped like them on a physical plane of existence. It's time for us to evolve just as they are evolving. We have run out of time. However, we won't evolve successfully if we don't raise our minds to a higher plane where mercy and forgiveness reign."

"Why do you fear them?" Ariel asked. She gestured toward Gabriel.

There came a shifting movement and quiet. Finally, Gabriel answered, "You know that I'm only considering what is best for all the sentient worlds, not just our own species when I say these words. Now, these beings are an uncontrolled violent lot, and we are forced to deal with them, *as they are now*. Maybe in some far future they'll be able to curb their natural instincts and dwell in peace, but in the meantime, they pose great danger. They could ravage solar systems while we wait for them to reach enlightenment. Remember, those we sent to guide and help them received violence in return for their efforts."

Here, the monitor next to them showed an image of a bloodied young woman being clasped in a human's embrace. Another image flashed on the screen that showed a dying man savagely nailed to wooden planks on a rounded hill.

"They murdered the one and might have also killed Elsinore, if she hadn't been rescued by us." Sadness and anger tinged Gabriel's voice.

"The humans react with violence when they feel threatened," objected Angelique. "It's a natural defense. We bred them that way as part of their basic nature to ensure their survival. Notice this genetic coding here."

Now the monitor showed a magnified view of a DNA strand. Angelique pointed to a highlighted section of the strand. "My father was asked to encode an especially strong survival instinct into them. How can you blame them for something we did?"

Joel blinked. *Interesting information. Were they saying that they created humans or just changed them?*

Ariel shifted in his seat and leaned toward Angelique. "Do you love them so much that you would bring them here into your own flock, knowing their nature and what they are capable of?" she asked.

Angelique waved a hand and shook her head. "I'm not saying that! I'm just saying that they have great potential. The harder you try to suppress and control them, the stronger they become. Look at the latest evolutionary advance in the Eastern sector of their world. They were isolated out from the Crystal Talent experiment to serve as controls, yet even they learned greater ways to manipulate their abilities without the crystal's catalyst. Now, they are evolving also. These humans are no longer chattel that we can keep penned up like wild animals. Some have escaped the pen, and soon they may find the gate that leads to our world. For some reason, their eyes have turned toward space despite all we did to delay them. What will we do if they come through our gate?" Seated next to the console, Angelique looked down as once more they all gazed fascinated by the intricate patterns playing on the monitors.

"They're too primitive to survive the gate. Before they even get that far, space will destroy them," said Michael defiantly. "Space may be dangerous for frail humans with such short life spans. I have allies who could help there ..."

"Speak not! You will call down a penance for such thoughts. It is unworthy to ask for their death. We forsook murder long ago in our quest to attain a higher spirit." Ariel shifted in agitation.

"Truly," another answered timidly. "We do not advocate confrontation, do we?"

"Just quiet species annihilation," Angelique answered sarcastically. "Michael, do you not see how wrong it is?"

Several murmurs ran around the group. Then Gabriel spoke up, "You applaud their strength and abilities, but what if they were to link up with our old enemies? The vicious minds of those *Fallen* sinners joined with the developing power of these humans ..." The sentence dangled menacingly in the suddenly quiet room.

Again, Angelique spoke up, "Where is your code of love and forgiveness? We told them they must love each other. Might not we show the same compassion that we demand they show others? Were they not given free choice by God to decide their own fate? Doesn't that mean they can choose the path of good *or* evil?"

The beings moved restlessly causing still more flickering in the holograms, so that Joel still could not see any of the beings clearly. They were vague images discussing the fate of the human race as one might discuss a naughty pet.

"Should we not try to save them? Are we not on a higher plane of enlightenment?" responded Angelique.

"Michael doesn't sound like he's on any higher plane," Ariel sniffed. "I believe that he's jealous of your possible interest in these creatures, one in particular."

Down the table, Michael glared at them, his former smile becoming a thundercloud. Waves of energy rippled the hologram, disrupting the scene. Out of the turbulence came a voice, hard and angry. Joel jerked back from the burning energies swirling within the platform.

Michael half rose in his seat. "It's precisely my knowledge of them that makes me say these things, not any ridiculous personal and inappropriate emotional response. Remember also that their world is rich in resources we and others desperately need. They are unaware of what they hold, but its value is immense to certain species." Michael looked around sternly.

Ariel gasped, "You will kill them because of greed? I had thought that you, of all people, had overcome such vile emotions."

"Already they contaminate us," murmured still another. "It's been a long time since we've argued like this or heard such evil thoughts."

"Their existence is but a mere hiccup in time to us. Might we show continued patience? We have learned from them, even as they have learned from us. They have so much to offer." Angelique fluttered in her seat.

She stretched and traced the patterns on the screen. "Their race is vital, thriving ...."

"They breed all over the place with disgusting abandon and no thought to consequences," retorted Gabriel. "Their mating rituals confuse even them. No logical reason is apparent for the actions they take. Both male and female do ludicrous things to attract each other's attention. Then, it's incomprehensible the acts they commit on those they claim to love."

Silence enveloped the room.

Angelique gestured and said, "What does our wise head counselor Uriel say? He's not added to our discussion."

The hologram moved across the group to a lone being slouched in a large corner seat.

"He just sleeps," commented Gabriel sarcastically.

"I am awake," grumbled the being. His eyes popped open. Slowly the viewpoint shifted until it centered on a dazzling and interesting face. "I find that closing my eyes and ridding myself of your sight helps me to focus on the grains of wisdom that you so sparingly offer. These humans provide interesting possibilities. They are coming sooner than you expect. We should take responsibility and greet them. Maybe this ship would be an ideal way to evaluate their new talents and their worth. We could test them and see whether they are ready, or not, without disturbing a whole planet. We have watched and shepherded this species for centuries, even transporting them to other worlds in order to insure their survival. They have meant a great deal, for some strange reason, to God and the higher circles. Our own comings and goings have been kept secret from them, so as not to attract their attention. Still, some learned of our existence.

"Now something has happened to bring them here. They have leapt from their world and changed from the simple creatures to something far different. And they continue to evolve. Why now? There is more at work here than you might imagine. Think well your thoughts and weigh them wisely before you speak. These creatures are a catalyst and may affect our future far more than you suspect. I adjourn this discussion until you have attained more wisdom than you show me at present," Uriel said with scorn.

He stood up, shook himself and began to stretch. Up until now the holograms had been diffuse humanoid beings with glowing gowns and human features. They could almost have been a group of high-level senators discussing world events. Then the being stood up, and as he stretched, he seemed to grow larger and larger. Enormous white wings unfolded and expanded out from his back until they stretched the length of his arms, dominating the hologram, swooping toward Joel. Joel rose awkwardly and stumbled back as the apparition loomed toward him. A glowing radiance expanded out and bathed Joel in its light. The being's perfect face turned toward him, looked directly at him, and winked

Abruptly the room blinked black, leaving Joel stunned in darkness and silence.

Chapter 15

The image of the creature standing up and stretching out those magnificent wings shocked Joel. He stumbled backwards. Hair rose on the back of his neck and arms.

His reeling brain searched through his memory, plucking images out of his mind. His mother had been reading him a story from the Holy Book given to them by The Church of Our Lady of the Crystal. The book had mentioned fantastical creatures that supposedly helped the Great Creator. He had considered them just fairy tales, stories of mythical beings that those in the Space Academy had scoffed at. Therefore, any faith had drifted away in the glare of scientific inquiry and peer ridicule.

Now, he had seen with his own eyes a recorded hologram of these creatures on an alien spaceship. He couldn't breathe. *What if it were true!* They had been saying terrible things about humans. *No one would believe him, unless...* He glanced over at the glowing cube.

He backed past the rows of seats and spun around, stumbling blindly through the dim light to the door. He jerked the cube from the slot, grasping it tightly in his hand. The machine turned off as he opened the door. The lights blinked on in the hall and glowed at his feet, showing him the way back to the main room.

He recalled the old story, where an Enjelise, some even said the Creator himself, had supposedly come and taken the Lady Elsinore to heaven. The old stories had talked of something dressed in white and bathed in light, reaching out, and then she had vanished.

Did those beings really exist, or was this just some drama in a library's archive? The hologram had looked real, but when he thought about it, all that he had seen could have been an elaborate play or a virtual fairytale created for public entertainment. Maybe it was only an entertainment room full of imaginary stories kept on holographic cubes—that had to be it.

Joel shook his head. He came to the main room and stopped, trying to steady his heartbeat and calm his roiling thoughts. He tried again to raise anyone from the ship to no avail. His only recourse was to go back where the others were by going through the transporter. He crossed the room and stepped into the alcove. Searching around, he held his breath as he touched an aqua circle.

*

On board *The Seeker*, Solanje walked to her quarters and paused. Her panel was open. Someone rummaged inside. A stirring in the air along with a breathing sound alerted her. She stepped inside. There she encountered her worst fear. "Icabar! What are you doing?" She moved swiftly over to him.

Of course, I know what he's doing.

She had dreaded this inevitable moment ever since coming on board with the alien device. She still wasn't sure what she was going to say to him.

Damn the man!

Icabar whirled around like a small kid caught with his hand in the tasty jar.

"This is it," he shouted at her triumphantly as he faced her. He held up the alien artifact, waving it under her nose. "I knew it! I figured out that something like this must exist, but I wasn't sure. *This* is the catalyst that got us sent into Space. *This* is what forced the Ching T'Karre to work in a joint venture with the Democratic Union despite blatant animosities. *This* is the reason Hasang Dark Shadows allowed you and your brother to come back to the Academy! Those events baffled me. Only some powerful reason would make people behave in such an illogical manner. *This* is it, isn't it?" Icabar waved the luminous article at Solanje. "This is not from our world. Someone found an extraterrestrial item. What is it?"

"It's deadly," she warned him. "Put the device down, Icabar. Put it down carefully."

"If it's so deadly, then why have it on board?"

"Because it's evidence that other sentient life exists. Also, it may give us clues toward understanding them or enable us to contact them. I haven't activated it yet, but I have vowed to protect people from it; people like you! Dangerously curious ones. Put it down!"

Icabar stared at the object, turning it over in his hands, then placed it reluctantly on her dresser.

"What happens when it IS activated?" he asked.

She sighed, walked over to the piece, and picked it up, caressing the golden circlet. "I think it's a communication device. If a human places it on his head while activated, he can see strange images from an unknown world, very much like the one down there. Our scientists experimented with several of my people who bravely volunteered to test it. A few dropped into a coma and never woke up. Others had brain hemorrhages and were paralyzed for life. Don't even try it!" She stared at the object in frustration. "The carriage it fits into has archived images of Alysia. We think it's part of a package designed for space exploration with a purpose to study other worlds. However, the language is alien, and we're still working on a translation." She shrugged.

"What else?" prompted Icabar eagerly.

She closed her eyes and shook her head.

"Solanje!"

She opened them. "Okay, the construction is indestructible. Hamm analyzed it and from a study of its molecular pattern, he was able to formulate the special material that he used to build this ship. It is lightweight, yet tougher than any material we know. They built this ship using a technique that's a rearrangement of silicon molecules, sand actually." She sighed and frowned at him.

"If it's a communications device," Icabar stared at it hungrily and put out his hand. "I must try it. I'm the communications specialist on board."

"You can't. I promised," she said firmly. "It's my responsibility to protect this crew. And that includes you. It could be deadly. We have lost enough crew already." She firmed her shoulders.

"I'm the Communications and Security officer. It's my job to investigate such things. You MUST give it to me." Icabar glared at her.

"It belongs to Hasang T'Kai. You have no claim."

"Belongs! What are you talking about? You're holding an important alien communication device and you're claiming ownership? No one nation or person can own such a thing."

"My *mother* found it," she yelled at him.

"What're you saying? Finders Keepers, Losers Weepers? That's a kid's game, Solanje. It may contain the secret of communicating with an alien race!" Icabar breathed heavily, as he pointed at the device.

"We have no proof of that. It could be a lethal mind weapon for all we know. Maybe an alien mind triggers an explosion. Could be it's a booby trap. I was made responsible. I gave a vow to guard it, a sacred vow."

"Fine, but you can't just hide it away when it could be a critical factor in our understanding of what's down there. That IS what this mission is all about, isn't it? To find the aliens that built this probe and make contact in order to protect Alysia. You realize that we have found what we went looking for, don't you? For let me tell you, Solanje, no humans made those ships out there. And it was no human that Crystal saw. I may have sounded like I believed that she was hallucinating, but I really don't believe she was. I said so to calm the others. Intelligent aliens have been here, and we may have to deal with them sooner or later. More likely sooner."

She waved the artifact at him. "Why do you think I have been studying this device so intensely? Don't you believe that I can investigate as well as you? If you press me on this, Icabar, it *will* be on my terms," she said aggravated.

A noise at the door caused them both to whirl around and notice a distraught Liana.

"Where's Icabar? He's supposed to be at his board. He can't keep leaving his post!" she shouted. She saw Icabar standing next to Solanje.

"There you are!" She exclaimed. "Something's happening to Braden. Something's in his mind! I can't find Tessa or Adam either." Liana stopped when she saw the object in Solanje's hand and Icabar reaching for it.

"What's that?" she asked staring at the object.

"Great!" exploded Solanje. "Look at what you've done, Icky! Now everyone will know. The entire crew will want to see it, and then, vacuum will be in the airlock!"

"It'll have to wait," said Liana abruptly, as she curiously eyed the object that Solanje and Icabar were struggling over.

Solanje saw Liana stop and blink. Liana would have to be mind-blinded not to sense the feelings of fear and anger swirling around the room.

"The Captain is in trouble, and you were supposed to be monitoring him," Liana accused Icabar.

"I left Robert watching the communications deck. Braden said that you said that he was fit for duty."

"He's wandered off into the observatory. I found him gazing out the window at the planet."

"Frag! What's wrong with him?" asked Icabar as he dropped his hand and gave the device one last look before turning to face Liana.

Liana sighed. "Too much." She rubbed a hand over her face and then, gathered her composure. "Find Braden. Find him now. Call him back to the ship. Something is tampering with his mind. If we lose the Captain because of your negligence ..." Liana let the threat dangle in the air unspoken.

Solanje glanced at Liana and then Icabar. "We'll finish this conversation later. You'd better see to the Captain." She stuffed the circlet into the probe's compartment, slid that into the storage area, and twirled the dial on the vault's lock.

"I *know* the combination," threatened Icabar.

She spun around and glared at him. "Be careful, Icabar. You want to know every little secret. That's your problem. And if you don't know the answer immediately, you worry at it until you do. One time you'll get an answer, and it will be your death. Go." She pushed him toward Liana, who dragged him toward the bridge.

Chapter 16

Braden moaned. "Oh, Sweet Lady E, my head!"

He detected a quick intake of breath next to him, and with a start, he sat up peering blurrily around. Suddenly, the whole episode flooded into his aching brain. The lady in question gazed calmly back at him with a smile.

Ooops.

She shook her head at him. "My name's become a swear word?"

"Ahhh..."

"Are you all right?"

"You're Elsinore, Lady of the Crystal," he accused. "And that is the Master Crystal!" He pointed at the luminous object in her hand.

"Yes." She smiled again at him, as wonderful feelings of joy rippled through him. A warm energy enfolded him with a soothing calm. He realized that she was broadcasting, trying to put him at ease; only it made everything worse. She was using mind control on him! He took a deep breath and pushed her out. "Stop it!"

She jerked and her eyes widened.

"How can you be here? The church claims that you ascended to heaven," he said bewildered.

"It's a complicated story," she sighed.

"This is a hallucination, right? I'm hallucinating— just like Crystal did in the alien ship. Does something in the air make us see strange things?"

Elsinore sighed. "No, it's … I'm real. This is my world. My species vibrate at a higher energy level than yours. You can't normally see us. The Universal Mind, the Creator, *he who is*, has as many aspects as he has names. He deemed it necessary to multiply many of these aspects throughout the universe. We are one facet of his glory, and you are another. He made your species in his own image, although as much the same as a candle flame is to the sun. He designated a special order of Enjelise to watch over you."

She settled next to him on the ground. Flowers swayed nearby giving off a sweet perfume. The brook gurgled a cheerful melody

wasn't soothed.

She continued, "A few broke the rules and implanted their genetic code in various of your females. Some used force: others used manipulation. Some just wanted to improve the breed and managed it scientifically, while others were only interested in the physical pleasure it gave them. Any way you say it, it was species rape. They knew they had disobeyed a direct edict of non-intervention, and their defense was that the new creatures tempted them, although some felt justified while others actually insisted it improved the human race."

"Sounds like they abused the humans." Braden clenched his jaw and tore at the grass. He closed his eyes and felt the warm sun on his face. Then, he peered over at her, his emerald green eyes angry.

She took a breath and said, "When my leaders discovered the transgressions, my side became outraged.

Two factions developed and plunged my people into civil war. In the end, they exiled the transgressors to a world on the other side of our galaxy where they were damned to a harsh life. Meanwhile, humans changed and evolved to a level where they could think and imagine. They could make choices that affected their fate." She put a hand on his arm and sent a soothing thought to him.

He pulled away and shifted his position. "I don't see how that helped us any."

Making a face, she rubbed her forehead and tried to explain more. "To prevent the new humans from causing any more trouble, we transported them to a far world, called Earth, at the outer edge of a large galaxy. This was difficult because we could only find one planet that was inhabitable. Unfortunately, the environment was harsher than they were used to. We created a nearby gate for easy access. The humans struggled there. Sometimes we intervened to help them, but only very carefully. Not only could we be dangerous to them, sparking a panic, but also, they could spread their disease and contamination on us. One time a disease we unsuspectingly contacted from them wiped out a large portion of our people. After that, we resorted to mind thoughts and holographic images to communicate with a few selected humans."

"Most likely, we considered those people crazy," he added.

"Most likely." she nodded. "As we discovered other habitable worlds, my father devised a plan to transport selected humans from Earth to other places such as Alysia. The ships that transported thousands of humans now orbit us. However, that task has been completed."

He stood up to stretch tingling legs and gazed down at her. "But you didn't stop with that, I imagine."

Shrugging, she stood with him. "No, we didn't. Later, we discovered the crystal creatures on Beta Centauri could form a symbiotic bond with some of the humans and accelerate their evolution. I was designated as the one to take the Master Crystal to your world. "

She gazed off into the distance.

"The experiment went beyond our expectations, and then, it went wrong. The Master Crystal fell into the hands of malevolent Talents who used it to develop and gather destructive powers. A war broke out on Alysia between those with Talent and those without."

"A devastating war." He turned his back to her and scanned the tall trees swaying nearby.

She reached toward him, agitated. "That was not our intent. To correct our mistake, I used my Talent, to stop the war and left the sacred laws behind as a guideline. My body was altered to a lower vibration, so that I could live among you. It worked. I did good. But your species continued in violent ways. Many Enjelise wanted to stop humans from exploring space, but you, in particular, were too strongly focused."

Braden shifted around and murmured, "Exploring space has always been my dream." He flicked a hand to the sky.

"Yes, and now you have found us, and we are forced to decide your fate earlier than planned. With humans able to travel the stars, many other species have become afraid. My father, who has defended your race in the past, is dying and unable to speak for you. It will be up to you, Braden Steele, to prove to the council that humanity has a right to exist."

"What! Of course, we have a right!" He straightened in disbelief at the words.

"You must convince the council of that."

"Who! Me?" Braden shook his head and put out warding hands.

"Yes. I'll offer help, but it will be up to you to save humanity."

"Why me?"

"You brought humans to our world through the stargate. As a small boy, you influenced your grandfather, suggesting the existence of a gate. He bent his studies in that direction and found our signal. So, you made the difference."

"I wanted to captain a starship!"

"*Yours* was the desire that propelled humans out into space. *You* were the catalyst."

"I was a kid. How can you say that!"

"Events shifted because of your energies pulling at them. As long as your species stayed put, we were safe. Now you come to our front door and we have to decide whether to let you in as a welcome guest or slam the door on a dangerous beast. You proved that you can vibrate to our level, that you have the potential to advance, now you will have to convince my people and the others that you're worthy."

Stunned Braden stared at her. The creatures around him began to waver. He put his head down between his hands to regroup his thoughts. He felt woozy and nauseous. The shock of her words churned his stomach and made him light-headed.

The air popped and it was like waking up from a dream. He looked up and Elsinore was gone. Only the fragrant flowers and the swaying trees remained.

Had it been a hallucination?

Picking up his helmet off the grass, he saw where the receiver had been closed by the drop. He put on his helmet and toggled the receiver open.

"Captain!" His comm sputtered to life. "Answer me, Captain. Come in. Where are you? Away team report in." Icabar's voice sounded hoarse and filled with worry.

"I'm here Icabar. I'll round up the rest and return."

"Braden, they're missing. Everyone, particularly Liana, is worried. Thank the Lady, I found you."

"I'll be sure to mention it to her," mumbled Braden.

"What?" Icabar's voice held a bewildered note.

"Never mind."

She had vanished. No surprise there. A chill wind blew over him, dragging a curtain of rain after it. He lifted his face to the strange feeling of water splashing on skin. It had been ages since he had felt rain on his face. He closed his eyes.

Adam and Tessa were missing ...on an alien world. Right here. A Dangerous world. Opening his eyes, he scanned the landscape. The planet still vibrated with the same color and light, but he was changed.

His shoulders slumped under a heavy weight. It wasn't just the gravity.

Chapter 17

"Joel?" Liana's frightened voice whispered in the dark.

"Where is he, Liana?" came Icabar's voice in answer.

She jumped as he emerged from the shadows of the Observatory. She had been standing in the dim light, staring out the view plate toward the cluster of circling alien ships. Then something had called for her. She thought it might be Joel. She turned to Icabar.

"I thought I heard him calling out from somewhere over there," she sighed. "But I don't know for sure. It felt very faint."

"Do you know what I'm thinking now?" asked Icabar, coming up to the window to stand beside her. He softly touched her arm and gave her a nervous look.

"Please don't, Icabar. Don't start with me. I can't help what my Talent is. I try not to read minds if it means invading a privacy. I know what a private person you are. Besides, your blocks are the strongest of any from the ship."

"What would make you try?"

"There would have to be a good reason. Safety of the mission or danger to lives on board. Okay?" She shifted uneasily next to him. "It's who I am, Icabar just as you are who you are ..."

"Okay, okay." Icabar paused. "Fair enough. Fate knows I can't help my own strange actions at times. Where did you hear this calling come from?"

She felt his hand touching hers. It relaxed against her arm.

Good, she thought. *It might be all right.*

Smiling, she said, "I felt his mind. Over there." And pointed to the bigger ship. As she did, she moved closer to him as if to gather some of his warmth to her. Almost as if it were an unconscious move, he put his arm around her shoulders. She exhaled slowly.

Perhaps he understands my situation and could handle it. If I moved carefully, I might win him over. It didn't take mind reading to know what he has been feeling. Well, it took maybe a little because he hid himself so well, but finally, he has made his move. About time.

She grinned fondly at his serious face. She wanted his affection to be real, not something she manipulated .She needed to move carefully.

He nodded to himself. "Maybe it's time for another search. Let's ask the Captain to go on board again." Icabar grabbed her hand and squeezed it. "Let's go find him. Let's find Joel."

*

Braden stood in Navcom and stared at the two of them.

They had to be kidding! Another ship search?

"We've already looked for him everywhere on that ship," he said frowning. "I need to use our resources to find Adam and Tessa. I can't believe they're missing, and our sensors aren't locating either of them."

He clenched his fists and a muscle jumped in his jaw.

He was angry, but mostly at himself for falling asleep, and he was having a hard time containing his frustration at the entire confusing situation.

"Well maybe Joel wasn't there then, and he is now," answered Icabar in his usual stubborn manner.

The man has got an idea and won't let go. But what if he were right?

"Also, I would like to nose around to see if I can learn anything more about who made those interesting designs, or what can be found on board. I haven't gone there yet. Solanje said that the technology was extremely sophisticated; using stuff she didn't understand. I might discover what others overlooked. There may be clues over there that someone didn't notice. I'm good at finding clues and figuring out mysteries. Besides, I'm Security and Communication. It's my job to protect this mission and investigate dangerous things. Crystal insists that they communicated in her language. Maybe it was just telepathy. Maybe it wasn't. I want to know why we still haven't heard anything. I want to know …"

"All right. All right," Braden waved his hands to stop Icabar's flood of "I-want-to-know" words. "As usual, you want to know everything and as usual I don't have all the answers. I will not let anyone out of my sight. You, Glaze, and me. We stick together no matter what," said Braden. "We stay awake and we only stay a short time. If anything goes wrong, then, Bashar, you pull the ship out of orbit and take everyone away. The mission must survive."

Bashar frowned, "Captain!"

"That's an order!" They glared at each other. Braden won the battle as Bashar nodded stiffly and looked away mumbling, "Yes, Sir."

Braden caught Bashar rolling his eyes and shaking his head at Icabar. "Bashar, I take this mission seriously, and I expect you to do the same."

Bashar nodded sheepishly and put his attention on the navigation board.

Icabar cleared his throat and said, "Liana should go with us, but you should stay here. Last time we could have lost you and did for a while. I left my post. I plead negligence in my duty. I will not let that happen again." Icabar tried to look contrite.

"There, I agree with you," Braden responded harshly. "You were negligent, and I can't afford that kind of behavior. Do it once more and you're off the communications deck for the entire mission. However, I *don't* agree with Liana going over there."

Icabar's eyes widened and blinked. He stepped back, looking shaken. Taking a deep breath, he kept going in his argument. "If Joel's really there, she's the best bet to find him. She has a unique, er, ability and is the most likely person to locate him."

"This 'unique ability' wouldn't by any chance be called mental telepathy, would it?" Braden glared at her.

"Sometimes. Sometimes it's called intuition," said Liana calmly. "I think he's there now, Captain. Just a hunch I have."

"You and your 'hunches.' All right. All right. Let's go quickly before the whole crew wants to go. Suit up as soon as you can and meet me at the shuttle."

"Yes, sir. Right away!" Icabar waved Liana forward.

Braden grabbed him by the arm. "I want this mission to go over there, find him, and return intact. I'm going to see that it's done exactly like that. So, I'm going. Get suited up before I change my mind about anyone else."

Icabar nodded stiffly.

Within a short period of time, Glaze, Liana, Icabar, and Braden had suited up, met at the shuttle, and traveled over to the alien ship's landing bay. Once there, they exited and tethered the shuttle, floated over to the outside door, and eased into the airlock. Once the airlock had filled with breathable atmosphere, they entered the main room, and scanned the area.

The place was a disaster. Consoles and computers were gouged and scored with burn marks. Pieces of metal littered the area. Chunks of wall lay about the floor. It looked like war had been waged recently.

"We need to clean this mess up," Braden muttered. He tapped a foot against a broken piece of equipment. "My Sunpointe training instilled in me the danger of loose equipment in low gravity, not to mention my mom's constant nagging at keeping my room clean. We make the mess; we clean it up. Get somebody who isn't missing on it. Maybe Robert can handle this."

"Don

"Don't bet on it," Icabar murmured.

Icabar ran his fingers lightly over faded geometric designs and alien symbols decorating the immense walls. He tapped at them with a thoughtful expression.

"Interesting," he mused as he gazed up at a multi-tiered balcony construction with each tier a different color, much like seats in a vid show. "I wonder why different colors."

"The various colors might symbolize different social standings," Liana suggested.

"Maybe they just like a variety of colors," retorted Glaze.

"Or it could be family lines," Liana added, craning her neck up to study the higher rows.

"Has anyone seen any children?" Icabar asked.

"No, no children, or old people, either," muttered Braden. "Where are they?"

"Maybe the different colors are different price points for the audience like at our ice games. There might be a financial component. At home, sometimes, different colored seats signify a different cost." Glaze gestured at the tiers. "You psychology people always think in terms of social interactions. It may not be that."

"We're trained to think that way," responded Liana evenly.

"Adam was studying their power sources to see how the ship's drive works," informed Braden, as he peered into what looked like an engine room. More rooms could be seen farther down an adjoining corridor. "Could prove useful if we figure it out. Need to get him back. It might provide a breakthrough in interstellar travel."

"I want pictures of these glyphs here and those odd patterns over there," commented Icabar, tapping the walls. "Most interesting. They could be part of a language."

"We have been photographing and labeling technical equipment already," said Glaze. "Bashar is trying to understand some of their physics, and Adam says they have a unique propulsion system. He's studying the smaller ships that he says are warships designed to protect the mother ships."

"Liana have you gotten any indications of any human thoughts or emotions around us, yet?" asked Icabar.

She paused, looking at him thoughtfully. "There's something in that direction. It's very faint." She pointed back toward the main room.

Icabar looked at Glaze. "Let's check it out."

Glaze flicked out a stun gun.

"Now, Glaze, no shooting until …" Braden started to say.

"…you see the whites of their eyes," interjected Icabar. "Or whatever color they may be—if they even have eyes. Maybe they have long tentacles that suck thoughts from your mind and cause weird hallucinations, driving you totally …"

"Shut up," Liana interrupted, waving aside his flood of babble.

Icabar paused, allowing them to distinguish a low moan that came from an out of the way enclosure they had overlooked upon entering. They hastened over to it.

"Joel!" Liana exclaimed.

She stooped over a silver heap that they had thought was melted metal but turned out to be a decidedly worse for wear version of Joel DeLande.

"He's alive! Let's get the med cart and move him out of here. Inform Crystal that she needs to ready the Med Lab."

A bit of static sounded and then Crystal's voice crackled in the comm. "On my way now. Good work! I'm glad you found him."

"Great! Really great!" yelped Dyra, who listened in at Navcom. "Hang on, Joel. We got you now. You're going to be okay." Her voice quivered.

Joel moaned again, fluttered his eyes, smiled, and passed out again. They moved him into the shuttle and back onboard *The Seeker*. When he awoke, they would find out what happened.

*

Braden paced up and down listening to Joel's breathless recital of his adventures. They were all grouped around him in the small meeting area, having slid a wall panel back to allow them more space. Braden stopped by a folded-out table that now featured an assortment of refreshments and poured a second tube of tea, tucking two sprigs of newmint into his drink. He stirred the tea and took a sip. Not even Tessa's famous tea could sooth his frazzled nerves right now.

Dyra shifted in her chair uneasily. "This hologram you brought back. Do you suppose it could just be a play, or virtual vid, rather than a recording of a real event? I'll try to get it to work on our equipment if I can."

"I hope you can. It could have been a weird dream for all I know. I seem to be having a lot of them lately. I'm not sure," said Joel bitterly, as he popped a few knuckles and scanned the group nervously.

"Is there any information from our history on these beings?" asked Icabar.

Dyra sat up. "Now that you mention it, there were several old manuscripts that I read before we left that mentioned winged supernatural beings called Enjelise. I thought it interesting and made a disc. Anyone can borrow it to read if they want." Dyra looked over toward Icabar. "We need to know if this was real, or a hallucination."

"... or a dramatization. We need more information and quickly." Braden sigh and rubbed his hand across his face. "I'm also interested in the capsules Joel saw. Adam says there's a whole bay of them in the first ship. They may be how humans got to Alysia from a place called Earth. That would support what Elsinore told me."

He then related his experience with Elsinore, and what she had explained to him. Events had progressed so quickly that he hadn't found time to tell anyone yet. Crystal had said the Enjelise helped humans, now Joel was saying that they wanted to eliminate them. The hologram that Joel had witnessed seemed to support the idea of dissension in the ranks. He didn't have an accurate picture of what was going on, but pieces were accumulating into a great big pile that somehow, he had to fit together soon.

"Elsinore wants you to prove to some sort of tribunal that we are worthy of admittance into an intergalactic society?" questioned Liana with a frown.

"It appears that they consider us no better than vicious savages, and they are better off rid of us," said Braden, looking at Joel who nodded in agreement.

"No, I don't believe that," Crystal argued.

"The comment about the Master Crystal intrigues me." Icabar stared thoughtfully at the far wall.

"The crystals *have* had a powerful effect on our world," said Liana. "But a sentient being?"

"A living rock? Who would have figured that out?" Icabar murmured.

"Some historians and others mention that very idea," Dyra reminded them.

"Is it all just alien mind games, or are the Enjelise as we see them?" Braden stared out. "Should we believe what they tell us, or are they trying to mislead us and confuse us as to their real purpose?"

Crystal sipped tea and said, "My experience with humanity makes me wonder how we could ever convince any species that mankind is a danger to their existence. What would you think of humans if you were the Enjelise? I think men are awful—and I belong to the species." She reached for her tea. Her hands were shaking so much that tea splashed in her tube, a few drops escaped and fell to the floor.

The room grew silent.

Chapter 18

"Adam and Tessa must still be alive somewhere. But where? Nothing has shown up on our scanning." Dyra made a face and tapped a computer monitor.

"I would know if they were dead. I just feel like they are asleep somewhere," commented Liana.

Dyra had been combing the computer, pulling out any information about Elsinore and the Enjelise. Particularly interesting was the account of the giving of the law at the Great Battle where eyewitnesses claimed Elsinore had been taken into heaven.

"It says here that a white-robed being took Elsinore up to heaven surrounded in light," read Dyra. "Some versions claim it was The Creator himself. A few translations use the word 'God'. Some call Elsinore an Enjelise, but most believe she was just a human who had a Talent for mind control and used it to stop the war. There's nothing about wings or anything else Enjelise. However, the church wants to make her a saint and argues for her divinity, calling her the daughter of God."

"I'm not sure that she isn't a higher spiritual being," Braden replied. "What makes a spiritual being? What makes a saint for that matter? If another life form performs a saintly act, should we call them a saint? Who's to say that there wasn't divine guidance for what she did?"

Dyra nodded agreement. "She helped our species when she stopped the Great War and gave us the Divine Law. The Talents were finally redirected and integrated successfully into our society—for the most part." Dyra leaned forward toward Braden. "These beings fascinate me. I would like to learn more about their literature, history or art to see what it tells us about them. I want to study them."

"I'll have Bashar take us down in the rover. I want to talk to Elsinore more too." He was thinking that a lot had been left out of Elsinore's explanations.

Glaze arrived at the entrance. Braden waved him in.

"If we're going down to the planet, I want to go," said Glaze firmly. "Leave Bashar up here. He's still recovering, anyway. Besides, I can drive a shuttle better than he can."

Braden glanced at him. "Everyone seems to want to go, and I'll admit the place has its attractions, but remember that there is an intelligent species down there that we know very little about, not to mention various alien animals that could also be dangerous. In addition, the place has a way of relaxing you and putting you off guard."

Glaze nodded, not daring to offer a comment. "I'm still requesting permission to go. Of course, I expect it will be dangerous, but I'm *well rested*. If anything happens, I'll be alert." Glaze gave him a smile.

Braden frowned at him. There was a hidden agenda here somewhere. He wondered what. Glaze appeared adamant about visiting that planet.

"I can keep an eye out in case Elsinore, or her friends try to kidnap you," said Glaze earnestly.

Kidnap him?

Braden looked amazed at Glaze's suggestion. "I doubt if the Lady of the Crystal would kidnap me. Why would she do that?"

Icabar appeared at the entrance just in time to hear his last words.

"Who's going to kidnap you, Captain?" he asked.

"No one!" Braden a little too loudly.

"Adam and Tessa are still missing," suggested Liana. "They haven't reported in for a while now. Maybe they were kidnapped."

"More likely got distracted and then got 'lost'." Dyra gestured quotes with her fingers. "Tessa probably offered a massage in some romantic little grove. Those two have been making eyes at each lately."

"No, something's amiss," contradicted Liana.

"That's why I just offered to go and protect the Captain. How well do we really know Elsinore, anyway?" Glaze asked. He raised an eyebrow.

Icabar nodded. "Glaze has a point. We really don't know these aliens at all. We only know the myth that we created about them and Elsinore. She was in the same area that Adam and Tessa were in when I last communicated with them. She might know where they are."

"Then we go ask her!" encouraged Glaze.

"Or even better, I could go and try to read her mind," Liana murmured

"Could you do that? Do you think that you can read an alien mind without the risk of damaging your own?" Braden wondered how strong Liana's Talent truly was.

"Hasn't she been re-calibrated to human, so to speak?" Liana quirked an eyebrow.

"Remember that she admits to being alien," said Icabar. "She's not human."

"You said that you don't invade another's mind unless ..." reminded Braden.

"... it's vital to the mission or it might save lives. Don't we want to find Tessa and Adam?" Liana responded. "Aren't they vital to our mission?"

"Absolutely ... I want them here, but ..."

Braden noticed Icabar move over and touch Liana in a way that suggested intimacy. "Do you think reading an alien mind is a good idea?" Icabar asked her with an agitated voice.

She reached up and smoothed a wayward lock of hair from his forehead. "I think there's a good chance I can." She smiled at Icabar. "It could be helpful. I don't think I'll be put in danger."

What was happening to everyone? Danger seemed to be drawing couples together and everyone was pairing up all of a sudden.

He thought of Solanje, and then, the alien device that she guarded.

"We're in a sorry state when we begin to question the Lady of the Crystal," Dyra muttered, distracting him from a developing idea about what that glowing circle might be. Somewhere, something reminded him of the device, and it tied in with an image of an Enjelise he had seen in a book a long time ago. What had he seen? Braden frowned.

"Until our lives aren't threatened and until we know more, then I think we should question everything here," said Icabar firmly. "I need answers and she has lived among humans and understands them better than anyone, or so she says. Elsinore is our best bet to get inside information on these beings. I'm just concerned about the danger to Liana," he continued. "What we think as Elsinore could be a dangerous shapeshifter, posing as Elsinore and trying to lure us in."

"Hardly likely," Braden snorted at the idea.

"You never know."

"I'll get an opportunity to read an alien mind," Liana enthused. "I could go down in history," she said with a smug grin.

"You could go mad. Be careful and remember that she's an alien, not human. We'll have to careful." Braden turned to Dyra. "This will be your best opportunity to ask about their history and anything that might help learn more about them. Let's go. We don't have much time left."

*

They landed near a grove. Braden assigned Glaze to guard the shuttle and stay near enough so he could keep an eye out. Braden exited first and walked toward the stream where last he had seen her, while Liana paused a moment inside the shuttle gathering her handheld. Dyra scrambled out after Braden, a recorder in hand.

Among the flowers by a stream, he saw Elsinore awaiting their approach. "I'm so glad to see you," she said. "I sent out a broadcast urging you to come, and now you're here."

"You beckon and I come," he bowed to her. "But I want to keep near the shuttle. I still don't trust this place."

As he spoke, Liana stepped out of the shuttle and strode toward the group. Elsinore pivoted in her direction and caught her breath. Seen side-by-side, Liana bore a striking resemblance to the Lady of the Crystal. They stared at each other out of identical amber eyes and a similarly shaped face.

"Who are you?" husked Elsinore in shock. "Your eyes are gold like mine. Your hair ..."

"I'm Liana," she said stiffly, staring at Elsinore.

"You're one of them?" Elsinore waved her hand at the group in general.

"Who else?" Braden countered. He also noticed the similarity now that they stood together. Why hadn't he connected it when he first had met Elsinore? Distraction?

Liana said nothing but smiled as if she knew a secret.

"You look so like...Do you know who your mother and father are?" murmured Elsinore.

"No, why do you ask?"

Elsinore looked around distractedly. "Do you know a place in Bogtown run by a woman named Kitty?"

"Her daughter, Kat." Liana nodded. "Kat Love was my foster mother. She raised me."

"Kat! It can't be," Elsinore mumbled to herself.

Braden looked at her. Something was going on here. He could see that Elsinore didn't know what to say. She looked at them distractedly and finally said, "You have to understand the chaos the Black Talents created on your world. The place where I first arrived was attacked. One of their "Searches" found me, and sensed I had Talent. They wanted to recruit me to their army, but I refused them.

"To teach me a lesson, they raped and beat me, leaving me for dead. I survived because I broadcasted a Repulse."

"Humans do bad things at times but weren't you strong enough to control them?" asked Braden.

"Not entirely. I was young and my talent wasn't developed for humans yet. After they left, I fled to the caves along the coastline. I hid there, and then I found myself with child."

"What!" Dyra looked horrified, while Liana nodded as if she had heard the story.

"I was terrified, confused, starving, and shocked by the intensity of the physical realm. I wanted to give the whole plan up. I didn't understand how I could be pregnant, except that our genes had been mixed in the old times. There were stories about it. No one accepted the idea, but I realized that I had proven the whispered rumors. Pregnancy and childbirth are very physical. I was reduced to a level I had never experienced before. I was terrified.

"When I was with the Enjelise, saving the human race sounded noble and romantic, but up close it soon became horrible ... and painful."

Liana nodded sympathetically.

Elsinore continued, "Then, after I gave birth, the war still raged hotter than ever, and the Talent Searchers continued hunting for those of Talent. Nowhere was safe for the child or me. My Talent was increasing in power and that protected us in one way, yet in another way it also attracted their attention.

"I wandered north and collapsed one night on a Bogtown doorstep. A kind woman named Kitty Love took me in. She was a generous and wonderful human being. She ran a house filled with women and her young daughter Kat took a liking to my child. We named her Lilith and Kat promised to keep her safe. I gave her precious jewels and stones to help defray the cost of her care, but I never found out what became of the child. She had golden eyes just like yours and golden hair and looked a bit like you. I would guess you are one of her descendants."

Liana's eyes smiled knowingly. "We're distantly related. I have always wanted to meet you in person for a long time."

Elsinore rubbed her face and stared intently at them. "It was too dangerous for Lilith to go out into a society who banned those containing Talent, so she stayed there. As for me, I had a mission and I couldn't take a baby into battle, nor could I send her back to my people, so I left her safe with Kitty."

Liana nodded mutely. Elsinore looked at her. "I would have liked to have known my daughter better, but I'm glad to meet her descendent, at least."

She paused and frowned. "But now I must warn you that things have gone from bad to worse. I have bad news. My people are very disturbed. There's a faction saying that you have already desecrated the sacred garden and they're furious. Is this possible?"

"I can't imagine any of my crew deliberately destroying anything considered sacred," began Braden.

Elsinore frowned. "They claim that your people have eaten forbidden fruit and ripped precious plants and flowers from their rightful places. They have stolen valuable rocks and minerals too."

"Well, we're supposed to take samples of the local flora and any mineral resources we find ... for analysis and evaluation," he said hesitantly. "Scientifically, we're bound to examine the alien lifeforms we find and perform routine scientific experiments to determine their construction and function."

"Do you also steal sacred crystals and precious stones?"

"Well, Adam is a geologist. It's his job to take samples to determine the contents of minerals and metals of a planet," began Braden. "He said that he wanted to analyze for possible fuel sources. Does that have anything to do with why they're missing?"

"Some of the Enjelise are calling it a sacrilege. They're saying that already you defile their land and steal their property. It's causing quite a stir. There's talk of immediate expulsion and reprisals!"

"But Adam was only following required protocol. Any new unknown planet must be explored, and samples taken. Don't they understand that?"

"No, they don't know, or care, about your procedures. All they see is the desecration and count it as just another act of violence. I'm afraid that certain factions are putting pressure on father. Some want immediate death and expulsion. In two cycles, they will call a full tribunal and you must answer these charges."

"Well, we won't attempt any more sampling. You have my word on it. Tell the Enjelise they did it in ignorance of their laws. They can release them on my word of honor," Braden offered.

"They will not release them until the tribunal says they can go," she said with conviction.

"Elsinore," responded Braden just as firmly, "I'll not have my crew held hostage, no matter what the circumstances. Tell this tribunal of yours to release them. Explain the misunderstanding. Tell them that I'll be forced to act if they aren't released. Holding a human prisoner is an act of violence against his personal right of freedom. I'll be forced to try to free them."

"Be careful what you do," she whispered.

A tense silence ensued. Then Liana cleared her throat. She noticed the Master Crystal glowing in Elsinore's hands.

"May I touch it?" she asked.

Elsinore appeared surprised. "Have you never touched a crystal?"

"Not one like that. Not a Master crystal." Tentatively, Liana put her hand out toward it as if drawn by an intense force. She touched it and closed her eyes. Startled, she jerked her hand back and stared at the crystal.

"It's sentient!" She looked upset. "It's quite powerful and invasive. It tried to take over my mind!"

"You blocked it?" Elsinore pulled the crystal back. "That's unusual," she said in a wondering tone.

Dyra cleared her throat. "I have many questions that I wish to ask concerning these histories that I found," she began. Braden leaned in to listen, relieved that the unpleasantness had been temporarily diverted by Dyra's questions.

*

Because they each were intent on their various agendas, Glaze languished in the shadows by the shuttle waiting. After a while, when he saw that they were deep in conversation, he slipped away.

He wandered through the swaying trees, wondering if they hid alien beings from his sight, or if they truly were as absent as they seemed. At least in the snowy bleakness of his native Islia, an enemy stood out plainly against its stark white landscape. He missed Islia's icy cold sting that blunted passion and focused a man's attention on survival, rather than chase after a hopeless love.

This haze of emotions enveloping him caused confusion and exhaustion. One moment he craved a glimpse of his mysterious lady's glorious face, and the next he dreaded the encounter, knowing it would only increase his hopeless addiction. Then, he would be yearning for still another glimpse and another touch. He couldn't help himself. He wanted to be with her all the time and when he wasn't with her, he felt miserable. She had promised to see him again, so he had insisted on coming down to her planet.

His constant state of upheaval unsettled him. He yearned for his old, calm, cool, dispassionate self and yet, not at the cost of losing her. He could not live without her. Finally, wrapped in misery, he perched on a nearby rock and listened to the bubbling of the stream over rocks and pebbles. The air shimmered as she appeared in front of him. His heart leaped up in excitement. His feet followed.

She shook her head, hiding a small grin. "What? No dark caves? No deep holes in the belly of a ship? There is a fine black cave over there you might like." She pointed in a direction.

"My mood is black enough," he replied angrily. He plunked back down on the rock.

She became serious and still. "So it is." Her image flickered and she seemed only light and air—a fragile insubstantial being. He willed her back into being, not caring if he was losing his mind. Braden had talked about focusing. She grew clearer as he attempted to concentrate his attention better. She smiled as if she knew what he did.

"Tell me your name. Do you have one? At least I'll have a name to remember," he retorted hotly.

Sensing his strong emotion, she drew back a little as if its intensity was too much.

He calmed himself.

Then, hesitantly she moved forward. "I am called Angelique." She smiled a sad smile. "They're convening a tribunal soon. They have secured two of your kind. They want to keep you here for some reason. I think they're delaying, waiting for something to happen. They say that holding your people is only a precaution, but they don't realize that serious consequences could result."

"I thought your species abhorred violence. Has it all been lies?"

"We try to avoid violence when we can, but our history contains a struggle for power. We were an aggressive race once. We have the capacity. They say that we have overcome that flaw, but some are still capable of it. I fear it's more a part of our nature than we want to believe."

"Ah, yes, I understand. Destroy the barbaric lower beings because you are worthier." He snorted.

"Oh Glaze, you make us sound so awful when all our lives we felt that we were only doing the greatest of good, evolving to the highest state of bliss, becoming the perfect creature for God. How can that be so wrong?"

"You talk about destroying a whole species and you don't consider that immoral? You claim you are a nonviolent people, and this is a course of action you are contemplating?" He looked incredulous.

"On your own world, humanity has destroyed thousands of species already without a second thought, and you would destroy us too, if we threatened you. How can you hate our actions?"

"I don't hate you; I love you." He shook with the intensity of the feelings warring within him.

"There's a legend among us that you are part Enjelise. That you come from a long-ago stock of our people mated to yours," she said.

"A distant cousin? Where's your morality there?"

She grimaced at his jab. "The Enjelise argue that they made you, and thus are responsible for you."

"Do you believe that we are monsters?" he asked.

"No, I believe you are important for our survival."

"Wait. Necessary for *your* survival? Answer me this: why did Elsinore's father start a new world, and why did he hide us on Alysia? Why was he so intent on continuing our species and keeping us hidden?"

Startled she looked at him. A range of emotions crossed her face. She looked away. Her wings fluttered in agitation.

"Why, Angelique?" he insisted feeling that suddenly an important question needed to be answered.

She sighed and looked at him. "I should tell you. You need to know."

*

"Glaze. Where is he?" Liana looked around.

What was it about this world that everyone always seemed to be wandering off?

Just as she was about to call the ship and ask Icabar to locate Glaze, he appeared.

Braden strode up next to her and glared at Glaze. "I told you to stay with the shuttle and guard it, and you go wander off." He hauled back his arm and cracked Glaze on the chin with his fist.

"It seems that words aren't enough for any of you. You only seem to understand physical violence. You left your post!"

Glaze rubbed a bloody mouth, stunned at Braden's anger. Then, he realized that the shuttle was their only ticket back to the ship, and he had left them vulnerable.

"I'm sorry, Captain," he mumbled wiping his mouth.

"Where have you been?" Braden demanded of him.

Glaze gazed off into the woods, a smile forming on his swelling face. "Getting answers to important questions," he replied cryptically. "It was worth the risk. It was even worth the hit."

Chapter 19

"What did you do to him?" demanded Crystal.

She had asked Liana to meet her in the observatory alone where she would confront her directly.

"Who?"

"Don't 'who' me. You know who. Robert. What did you do to him?" Crystal put her hands to her hips and scowled.

"Hypnotism?"

"Ark dung!" Crystal shook her head. "I was in Navcom with Icabar when Braden took you down to meet Elsinore. I heard. You were on speaker. You're genetically related to Elsinore. You're also telepathic, among other possible Talents. I know she stopped a raging battle using only her mind."

"So? Everyone knows that ...now. The result was worth it, wasn't it?"

Crystal leaned forward to tap Liana's chest. "I researched each crewmember's background after they picked me. I discovered your association with the Riviera Medical Center, but I never imagined you were a designed crossbreed of Elsinore's daughter."

"A bit harsh there, Crystal."

"Tell me it isn't true, then. Tell me I'm wrong."

Elsinore shrugged. "I was included to ensure this mission's success."

"The Captain should know what you can do, and most likely did to Robert."

"No, he shouldn't. It would just needlessly upset him."

"Did Mission Control know about your abilities?"

Liana nodded. "Of course, they knew. Well, not about the telepathy or mind control, certainly, but they knew that I was good at curing and alleviating behavioral problems. They knew about my empathetic Talent but only suspected telepathy. Look, all the studies we did on enclosed small space interactions showed that after a certain length of time, given the boredom factor combined with the stressors of space travel, humans manifest aberrant behaviors. We shut down a few of the simulations because the actions of the test subjects became too dangerous."

"They acted stupid and childish like we sometimes do. So what?" Crystal tossed her head.

"They went berserk. They tried to kill each other."

"The thought *has* crossed my mind."

"Most of this crew's behaviors, so far, are within acceptable parameters, and a lot of the stuff they do just helps relieve the intense stress of space travel, but Robert's behavior was compromising the mission."

"What did you do?"

"I moderately adjusted his aggressive tendencies. We don't want a rapist and paranoid personality running amuck while we try delicate negotiations with the Enjelise, especially given their complaints about humans. The outcome of that would be unacceptable."

"We're too violent." Crystal sighed. "How did mission control know the aliens were Enjelise?"

"They didn't, but the Enjelise were the only candidates they knew about. Even though most of the mission decision makers considered them imaginary, a few believed they might exist. They tried to get proof, but those who ran Mission Control didn't buy in to the idea, consequently nothing was done about it."

"So, how did they come up with you?"

"Madame Kat put my name forward. I was perfect. She saw me as the hybrid Enjelise who could control minds, go out to negotiate with aliens, most likely Enjelise, and who might be able to convince them humans were okay. I could also adjust extreme behaviors and keep the crew functioning effectively. Lady Elsinore controlled several hundred violent men and stopped a battle cold. I can only sway one at a time, but I can do that. Most of Mission Control considered me just an exceptionally talented behaviorist, but that was enough to get me on board. Besides, I can be very persuasive if I need to be."

"I'll just bet you can." Crystal suddenly felt a shiver of fear run up her spine. She backed away.

"No one on board this ship is going to compromise this mission. It's too important." Liana took a step toward her.

Crystal stepped back some more.

"I only want what's best for both species." Liana took another step toward Crystal. "Please understand that I only do what I do for the good of all."

Liana reached out and grabbed her arm. Crystal felt her touch, and then, a sensation of something invading her mind. She tried to scream but couldn't. Then she heard Liana's thoughts as they swallowed up her own.

Braden needed to find Solanje so he could open the vault and study the halo some more. The glowing object might provide a clue to their predicament. It was almost as if the probe had been tossed into their laps for a reason. He was beginning to think that those kinds of coincidences weren't really coincidences, but deliberate acts. The discovery of the device somehow tied to these beings, and he felt strongly that it was not an accident that the Ching T'Karre had found it, throwing their two nations together and thrusting them out into space. Well, they had found what they had gone looking for.

What was that saying his father often quoted? "The wise seeker knows he may regret what he finds. The fool looks anyway."

The aliens, they had been so eager to find, now threatened humanity's existence. He needed a way to save them, and he didn't have the first clue as to how he was going to do it. He only knew that it was up to him, as their captain, and he needed a workable plan. He also needed to believe that he could do it Unfortunately, he had his doubts. He would start by warning Alysia, and then he would get the rest of his crew back. And then, well, he would face what needed to be done next. A step at a time.

Gads, I'm tired. And scared. He ran a hand through his hair. *I need a haircut*, filtered into his thoughts.

He also needed a crew better focused and working together, instead of chasing after their own agendas. He wasn't sure what the right thing to do there was, only that he had to craft a plan of action and do it ... something that would keep them alive and protect Alysia.

Can I do it? He sighed. *I must. I have no other choice but to move forward and do what is necessary.*

He bounded down the hall to Solanje's quarters. He pressed the entrance signal and got no answer. Her entrance panel stood partially open, so he stepped in. She wasn't there. The vault, where she usually kept the device, stood wide open. The probe was missing. The danger of its loss almost took his breath away.

Where was it?

He thumbed his comm. "Solanje! Braden here. Report immediately to Captain's quarters."

"Her comm's turned off," answered Liana, coming into the link. "She's with Bashar."

"Bashar?"

"Yes, they're in his quarters. But Captain ..."

He flicked off his comm and headed out.

What's she doing with him?" He hoped she wasn't showing him the alien device. She was not supposed to take it out of her quarters. She wouldn't do that. Bloody Frag, this could be a disaster in the making!

Braden hurried down the hall, bobbing and weaving through scattered attached equipment and snaking tubes. He ducked overhead pipes. Passing an unsecured computer pad and drink box, he fumed at the negligence. His mission trainers would throw a fit, anytime they saw unsecured items in a low gravity ship. It was dangerous. He made a verbal note in his recorder to get someone on it.

He arrived at Bashar's quarters where the slide stood partly opened, so he charged in, without a chime, and landed in the middle of an argument. Voices were high and the occupants didn't notice his arrival. He stepped back and went quiet in order to listen.

Bashar was speaking angrily. "Solanje, you have worn me out with all your delays."

Bashar stood with his fists clenched and his shoulders hunched. "I don't even know how I feel anymore--if I do feel anymore." He gestured outward with a hand. "You aren't what I thought you were when I first met you, but I accepted that, and once we were in space and away from your father, I thought you and I could have a real relationship. I was wrong. It's still wait, wait, wait. Now, I've waited long enough. I'm through waiting." He crossed his arms over his chest and glared at her.

Solanje straightened. "You said you loved me and promised patience!"

"Yeah, back at the Academy, ages ago!" Bashar responded, agitated. "Everything's different now. I'd hoped that we would be different too, but you still cling to the old ways and the prejudices of your father. I'm no longer a lowly nomad of the Sunglast; I'm a man of the universe, a starship pilot! I'm worthy of anyone; but you ... make me feel ... unworthy. No one likes that feeling. I want a relationship where I'm valued."

"I do value you! I always have, but my family refused you," she reminded him.

"And you always do what they say, like a good girl."

"Yes! I do," she exclaimed indignantly. Then, her face softened, and she reached out to touch him. "Did," she amended. "Not now. Now, I realize that Hasang T'Kai has no sway here, and it doesn't matter what the Tang think. I just thought that if I gave in to you, then I would be weak and give in to everything. I wouldn't be strong enough to honor my oath and duty. I thought the Tang would shun me when we returned. Also, I thought that would matter to me. I have already lost more than I can bear. But when you almost died, I realized how much I loved you, that I didn't want to live without you."

"You have a strange way of showing it."

"I know." She caressed his flinching arm. "I realize now that shipboard rules are the only rules that matter out here, and we should live our lives each moment, holding close to those we care about. Who knows what will happen tomorrow? Do you understand what I'm saying?" She smiled at him brightly.

Bashar sighed heavily, dropped his arms to his side and turned up the palms of his hands. "I don't have the slightest clue. That's the problem. I don't understand you at all—and I've tried. The women from my family were vastly different. They wore the abela and obeyed their husbands. Their thoughts seemed simple and their deeds centered around taking care of family."

He flailed his hands around in agitation and blinked rapidly. "They were easy to understand. They cooked, cleaned, and raised the children. They never traveled out into the world or showed their faces to others. Now everything has changed. You're different. You've been schooled at the Space Academy; you have a brilliant technical mind. You have traveled farther than most *men* dream of ever going. I saw you face death without fear and kill a man with delicate, elegant, *hands*...I don't know. I only know I fell in love with you the moment I first saw you, but I didn't know anything about you. I still don't. You're unlike any woman I've ever known. You're very confusing."

"I have obligations and honor, Bashar. I am royal Ching T'Karre born. It makes things complicated."

He blew out a breath. "But we make a new life out here. We're not bound by old ways and traditions, me as much as you. I'm trying to accept that, and you must too. Here you are a woman, and I am a man ... no more than that." Bashar raised a hand to lightly stroke her arm.

"But it's become too hard. I'm a patient man, but my patience has blown away like smoke in a hard wind."

"Okay, Bashar," She leaned in toward him. "I love you and nothing else matters. Maybe you will understand this." She began unfastening her shirt.

Oh frag! Braden's heart dropped into his stomach when he realized what she was about to do. He wanted to grab her and scream stop, but all he did was clear his throat before anything could go further. They both turned to stare at him, startled at his presence.

"I knocked. I did. You just didn't hear. You were talking too loud." His voice quavered as he tried to hold onto his composure and focus on why he had come.

They stepped apart. "Yes Captain," they said simultaneously. He could tell they were embarrassed. No more than he.

"Where's the device?" he asked hoarsely.

"In the vault." She looked at him with a question as to why he would ask.

"No, it isn't."

Her eyes widened in alarm. "No!" With a cry, she lunged at the door, exited, and in a few graceful strides negotiated the corridor to her quarters. She flung herself in, scanning the area in apprehension.

"Bloody Cryst!" She saw the open vault and spun around to stare wildly at Braden. Then understanding lit her face. "Icabar! He has it. Where is he?" She whirled and tore back out into the corridor.

"Check his room." Braden trailed after her.

"I knew this would happen. I knew it!" she shouted. "He sent me to Bashar. He set me up."

They hurried to Icabar's quarters. It was locked. Braden pounded on the door. Using his Captain's override, he burst in and saw Icabar crumpled on the floor. Part of the alien device was bobbing erratically over him.

Solanje knelt next to him and picked up a limp hand. "He's gone and killed himself. I warned him...but did he listen? No, he never listens. He's so..."

Liana strode through the entrance. "Icabar!"

Braden knelt down to feel for a pulse.

"He's dead," said Solanje with grim finality.

"No, just an idiot," rejoined Liana, standing over him.

Icabar's eyelids blinked erratically. "Liana, that you?"

She sighed.

Icabar sat up groaning and rubbed his face. "It's an instantaneous transpacial communicator." He pointed at the glowing object. "The key is to tune the frequency properly for *humans*; then you can holographically transport to anywhere in any universe you direct your thoughts to and communicate with whoever you're thinking about. This is a powerful piece of equipment. No wonder they're looking for it. They must be very worried that it's missing." He smiled triumphantly at them.

*

Not much later, Braden hurried down a passageway to their meeting just outside of Navcom. His mind roiled with thoughts concerning Elsinore, aliens, spaceships, teleportation, and a dozen other immediate crises when someone called his name.

"Captain, Braden. May I have a word?"

He stopped, startled at the tone in Crystal's voice. She chased up to him, flushed and breathing hard. "Braden, I have to talk to you a minute about something important."

Ever since his meeting with Elsinore, Crystal had been sending him urgent messages that she needed to speak with him. He had been so busy preparing for the upcoming trial that he had shelved talking to her until after. Palming the door open, he entered the work mod and ushered her in. He began to gather up his tablet and laser pointer.

"I'm limited on time. What is it?" He tossed her a harried look.

Crystal paused and an expression of confusion slid over her face. She put a hand to her head and closed her eyes.

"Tell me quick. There's a meeting here soon. You got the alert?"

"Yes, yes. It's just ..."

"Just what?"

"I'm trying to remember!" Crystal sounded exasperated. "It's important!"

"Okay." Braden took a breath and waited.

She was acting odd.

He cocked his head and gave her an impatient look.

She took a breath as if gathering thoughts or trying to figure out what to say. "Okay, ah, Rafael said I was cured of, you know, my problem."

Braden's mind scrambled to think of what problem she talked about.

She saw his puzzled expression and attempted to explain what she meant. "I have no proof that I've been cured. Robert said that I was frigid, or that I probably liked women. I need you to prove that I'm not ... like that." She blinked at him.

What was she talking about? Then he remembered her problem and froze. A tingle skittered up his spine.

The walls began to close in on him. He broke out in a light sweat.

"Ah … this may not be a good time." He backed up; did a bit of hand waving.

She stepped toward him. "Well, I'm not sure I'm cured, but I figured if anyone could prove that I was, it would be you. Then everything would be fine," she explained, but she shook her head and put her hand to her mouth.

Fine? Didn't she realize all that was going on?

He hemmed and hawed a bit. "Crystal, you're a very desirable woman, but right now isn't the time."

Her eyes went wide, and she shook her head again.

"Sex isn't something that I can do like a scientific experiment at a moment's notice." He fumbled for words that would get him gracefully out of the current situation yet leave a door open. After all, he didn't want to be totally stupid.

"No, I didn't mean what I said. It's just you need to know …" She struggled with words. "Elsinore …"

She was acting very strange.

"Er, now I'm rather busy. Can we talk about this some other time?"

He needed time to think about this, opportunity—would that be the right word?

"Yes, you need to think about it. I … oh …" She stood on tiptoes and quickly kissed him on the lips. Then, she backed up, shook her head, turned, and fled, leaving him flabbergasted.

He arranged the equipment that he would need for their discussion, barely aware of what he was doing. He wanted to run and hide suddenly. Never in a million lifetimes did he think Crystal would suggest … It was very out of character, but she had been acting odd lately. He put it down to the attack and the stress of their situation. Still, Robert hadn't made another attempt. In fact, he barely talked to any of the women at all. He kept quiet and did his job without energy. *Lethargic.* Liana had admitted that she gave him drugs. So, Braden had relaxed his restrictions a bit but still monitored him. Liana had been working with him and reported great improvement. She hinted that he might be "cured." He acted competent, just quiet for Robert.

As if she had heard him thinking of her, Liana appeared at the module. "Am I too early for the meeting?" she asked, looking around.

Startled, Braden eyed her warily. Crystal had blurted out her name and then acted strange.

She could read minds. Had she just been reading his?

"No, I'm putting it together now," he said, trying to block out his thoughts. Vigorously, he focused his mind on the task at hand, shelving all thoughts of Crystal for later when Liana wasn't nearby.

Liana smiled at him and offered to help set up.

*

The rest of the crew began filing in. Glaze stayed on watch at Navcom, so Braden put him on speaker for the meeting. Bashar opened a few modules to form a larger conference area, enabling everyone to fit in comfortably. All the crew eagerly showed up to hear what Liana would say about her attempt to read Elsinore's mind.

"Hey, Robert, what's all that scruff on your face?" The question drifted through the gathering.

Robert ran a hand over some stubble on his chin and threw out a fake grin. "My new look. The razor is overrated."

Braden signaled for attention and waited for his crew to find seats and settle down. Then he began, "First, I want to say that I realize that this is not a military mission. That each of you were selected for your high level of skill and ability"

"That are getting weirder by the moment," said a voice from the group. It sounded like Robert's or Icabar's voice. He wasn't sure which.

Mumbling and murmuring followed the remark.

He held up a hand for quiet and surveyed the room. "Okay, but I want you each to remember back to why you joined the space program in the first place. For me, as I watched the night sky off my grandfather's deck, I knew, even then as a child, that I wanted to explore space and find alien planets and lifeforms to learn what was out here. That dream has stayed with me and brought me here to this moment.

A rustling and murmuring of voices followed his statement. "Why are *you* here? To make a difference? To do something with your life that no one else has ever done? We are at a precipice *right now*. We represent humanity and the Enjelise want us to prove humans is worthy of survival."

He stopped to take a breath and rolled a shoulder. "Are we? Look out there. There, they are. What do you see? Powerful ships, evolved aliens, one of which stopped a battle cold with her mind."

"Just one." He put up a finger.

"But," Here he paused, as complete silence and all eyes riveted on him, "if we can put aside our separate agendas and focus on what needs to be done, we can band together and stare them in the eyes and show them our worth. Humanity has a right to exist and I plan to prove it, but I need you at my side, ready to act with me and support me, because I can't do it alone."

"I'm with you, Captain," Bashar breathed.

"Me too." Icabar nodded.

"I need you all." Braden gestured outwards. "Our lives are on the line. Alysia is on the line. Frag, the entire human race, as we know it, is on the line. We may not survive what we must do, but it's up to us. There's no one else. We're the ones here and now. We're the ones who can make the difference; we are the ones who can save humanity. Are you with me?"

Braden's eyes roamed the room and landed on Robert. Everyone held his or her breath.

His scruffy face went still, then serious, and he gazed back at Braden. "You can count on me, Captain," he said in a soft voice that echoed in the small chamber. "I came here to make a difference and I still want to do that."

The room breathed a sigh of relief.

Robert gazed around and raised his tube of tea. "To humans."

Bashar raised his. "To Alysia!"

Every hand in the room went up as every voice joined in. "To humanity!"

Tears glistened in Braden's eyes as he looked proudly at them. He let the moment linger and ease. He cleared a choking throat. He circled a hand and flung it out toward the planet. "First we save Adam and Tessa and get out crew back!"

"Yes," they all shouted.

"Then we stand up and prove we're worthy."

Clapping and shouting broke out. A few drummed on nearby computers.

He put up his palms and got immediate quiet.

Braden cleared his throat. "Okay, now to begin. Liana, did you get a reading on Elsinore?" Braden turned to her and gestured her to his side.

Liana shrugged. "She contains strong mental blocks, but at times I did catch her thoughts. I must wonder if she fed me information, or if I received a true reading. Don't forget her mind control is strong, but she appears to care about humans. She endured a lot on Alysia that wasn't pleasant. There may be some emotional scars from her experience."

"Was there anger against humans because of the rape?" asked Braden.

"A little anger, yes, but she blames the individuals, not the whole species. Bringing the Master Crystal to Alysia was more dangerous than she expected. Her feelings of outrage have been lessened by time and other more positive relationships. Someone named Kitty treated her well and showed her that humans contain the capacity for goodness. Her father's duty was to protect humans and guide them, and that duty has been passed on to her. It's her mission."

Dyra picked up a tube of herbal tea and took a sip. "They're justly afraid of us. We're a violent race. We want to dominate everything. No wonder the Enjelise feel threatened and react with fear."

Liana shook her head. "No, that's where I'm confused. I think the Enjelise are more powerful than we imagine, and there is no reason for them to fear us. Something else frightens them. Something from their past. Somehow, I got the impression that she was covering up something that will soon happen."

"What?" asked several voices at once.

Braden waved a hand to settle the interruptions. "Go on," he said, nodding at Liana.

Liana looked at Braden and searched through her memory. "When she talked about a Great Battle, she experienced an emotional surge. I felt strong apprehension in her but not about us. Another race of beings occupied her thoughts. She has a memory of a conflict from their past."

"Another alien species?" asked Braden.

"No, not really. They're Enjelise, but she thinks of them as 'The Fallen.' These Fallen committed an atrocity and were punished. And, somehow, we're involved. The thought was fleeting and covered up quickly. She didn't give me details, but they're more threatening than humans."

Braden slapped a hand to his head. "She explained what happened to me. She told me when we first met." Then, he briefly described the story that Elsinore had revealed, concerning the conflict over the humans and the banishment. "What else bothered her as she talked?" he asked.

A thoughtful looked flashed across Liana's face. "When you two were alone by the stream, she saw in your mind a circular glowing object that frightened her."

"Why was she afraid?" Braden asked interestedly. He leaned forward.

"She didn't realize that you knew it existed or that we had possession of one. She recalled images of Enjelise visiting our world with that round glowing object over their heads. They use it to communicate and to visually record what happened around them." Liana snapped her fingers. "It's exactly like the object Icabar and Solanje's were arguing over."

"What?" Dyra blinked. She shifted a puzzled look over at Icabar.

Braden straightened up in a burst of inspiration. "Of course! We called it a halo! Why didn't I see that before?"

"A what?"

"A halo," he explained.

Dyra straightened up and nodded. "In the old manuscripts, pictures of holy beings often are drawn with a glowing circle over their heads," she said slowly. "Is that what you're talking about?"

"There are so few renderings of them in our records that I didn't recognize it either," exclaimed Icabar, clapping his hands. "But they are there in the old records.'

"I want to study it some more and try to figure out what it does and why it's important," said Braden. "But I don't want to let them know we possess one."

"We have one?" Bashar gasped.

Icabar grabbed a breath and held it.

"We do?" Crystal appeared as confused as the others.

Everyone began talking and asking questions. Braden raised his hands for quiet and flicked a glance at Solanje and nodded for her to bring in the alien device.

Braden scanned the murmuring crewmembers, while they waited for Solanje to come back and realized that he was taking a tremendous risk. Yet, he felt it was time. Time to let his crew know what they carried. Time to act.

"Yes, and here it is." Braden gestured at the probe as Solanje placed it on a table and tapped it open. Braden proceeded to explain what they knew, even downloading the information from the disc into each crewmember's handheld. Several times he gave strong warning on how dangerous the probe could be and that they had to be extremely careful with it on board. He emphasized that only he and Solanje could experiment with it, unless otherwise authorized. He flicked a glance at Icabar, who nodded.

Their dangerous secret was finally out.

Chapter 20

Joel groaned, trying to fight to wakefulness, but the dream held him in thrall. And just when he thought he had finished; the dreams began all over again with a strange new ferocity.

He stood on a blasted plain, red dust beneath his feet, the atmosphere so thin that he gasped for breath, so hot that the heat sucked out air, even as he breathed it in. Ahead in the distance, molten lava spewed up in fiery vengeance and dripped down the sides of a string of pulsing volcanoes that lined the edge of a dry flat plain. Heavy gravity pressed down on his bones, bending them so they became misshapen. He saw the effects of radiation, burning his wife's face, turning it old and ugly with scars. The child within her twisted in agony, as it grew warped and damaged by the cruel radiation and pressing weight. He saw a once beautiful people, now torn and ravished, by the grueling effects of a God-forsaken world.

Alien thoughts that he had no control over tumbled into his mind, his thoughts melding with those of a stranger. He kept his own thoughts, but he was someone/somewhere else too. The name Lucien vibrated in his mind. He had become linked to some strange creature whose eyes he now saw out of.

Where am I? Who am I? Lucien.

Lucien's thoughts overwhelmed his own. *I deserve so much more than this, had so much more than this. I was the best of the chosen.*

He felt the creature's indignation.

Joel learned of Lucien's people: humiliated and resentful. Only their pride and iron will pushed them forward to survive, to rebuild, to wreak vengeance back against those who had done this to them. Every small step forward had been bought through anguish and pain. But he had kept his people going. Every small accomplishment had been won because of determination, fueled by burning hatred. They would win back their lives. The lost world would be theirs again. He vowed vengeance against those who had put him here. He hated those who cloaked themselves in righteousness and sat in judgment. They had no right to judge his people!

Scarred and ravished faces worshipped him, listened to his fury, bent to his will, because they had nothing else to sustain them. Nothing else but his voice to fill their lives of hell.

Joel struggled, screaming in his dream. From the sky, raindrops began to fall. Turning up his face for the cool moisture, Joel saw the rain bleed to acid—its poison etching the people who looked up for answers, shaping them in blood, molding them into something different, changing them as they fought to survive, making them hard, tough, formidable, violent, and driven.

With that horrific vision, he awoke.

Chapter 21

Braden paced up and down in the Captain's quarters. He couldn't sleep. Drinking tea no longer proved helpful; it just gave him the jitters and kept him awake. He felt exhausted, but his thoughts kept racing around past the speed of space, and nothing he tried to do stopped them. Fear drove them. He started all over again to marshal his arguments for the hundredth time when a chime sounded at his entryway. "Who is it?" he asked warily.

"Icabar and Liana."

Braden let out a breath of relief and said, "Enter." So far Braden had managed to evade Crystal and her situation, but he knew eventually that he would have to deal with her. Meanwhile, he excused ignoring her under the guise of duty.

The door opened and Icabar slid in, followed immediately by Liana. Braden shook his head. "The man who likes secrets and the woman who reads minds. What a pair you two make." He watched them glance guiltily at each other and, in a flash, he realized that they, indeed, were a couple. Something had happened between them. He coughed into his hand, hiding his surprise.

"I didn't realize you were that perceptive, Braden. Interesting," mused Liana. "I find that Icabar's mind is amazing. I have never met a man with such clarity of thought and intelligence in reasoning, or such a smart ass, but he has always been the most difficult to read because he contains such strong blocks. You also have a strong mind, which has been recently strengthened by an alien's touch."

Braden waved them to seats. She arranged herself primly into a nearby chair but reached out to caress Icabar's hand. Braden noticed her unconscious gesture and envied their apparent happiness. Icabar sat down next to her, wearing a foolish grin.

"You two probably resonate to the same frequency. I often considered that Icabar might be able to read minds at some level. He always seemed to be able to dig out secrets and solve mysteries no one else could," admitted Braden. "His mind is unique."

Icabar looked startled at the high compliment.

Liana smiled. "I use the intuitive approach. He uses the rational. He is all reason and deduction and sneers at my technique. I get a feel for what I think the answer might be and then I test it against his logic. We make a good combination, actually."

Icabar snorted. "More intuitive? That's *all* you use for your conclusion, while lacking any shred of evidence. I propose a good logical argument and your answer is that it 'feels' wrong." Icabar glanced at Liana. "How can anyone counter that argument?"

"And who is usually right? I am! My intuition comes up with the right answer more times than your so-called rational approach," she countered. "Being an empath helps."

"Don't forget the telepathy thing either. It's cheating." Icabar pouted.

"Okay, is there some reason you two are here bickering in front of me?" asked Braden.

They stopped short and looked at one another. An understanding passed between them and they leaned toward him. "Maybe we can help," said Icabar eagerly. "We have formulated some thoughts on the situation."

"I'm surprised you two took so long to voice an opinion," said Braden sarcastically. "So, what are these great thoughts? Should I retrieve my electronic notepad? Last time I had this sort of discussion with Icabar, I tried to take notes on paper, which ended up totally smeared with ink and fragged illegible. I wanted to eliminate the innocent, but by the time Icabar stopped talking, everyone was a suspect. Since then, I have resorted to digital devices. How should we proceed this time, Icabar?" Braden sat down behind his worktable and crossed his legs, looking at Icabar with a small smile as he pulled out his electronic tablet.

Icabar sighed, "Whatever suits you, Captain."

Captain was it? Ahh, there's a good start.

Braden nodded and looked attentively at Icabar.

"Let's consider what we are calling 'The Enjelise.'" Icabar rubbed his hands together smiling. "I read what little material we brought about them and feel that, although they may be higher spiritual beings than we are, we should try to consider them as just another species. What do we really know about them? Are they divine beings that appear to be aliens or aliens that fit a mythology that humans created?"

Braden leaned forward perplexed. "I thought we were trying to defend humanity. They said that I must prove we're not a violent destructive race or we get annihilated or kicked out of some universal alien association. At least, that's how Elsinore put it to me."

Liana shook her head. "Be careful there. Remember that Elsinore's Talent is mind control and she may be directing your thoughts to that argument. She and the Enjelise want to hold us here, I'm sure of it. I'm not sure why, but it has to do with something that happened long ago but threatens them now."

Braden nodded. "I've been talking with Joel and Dyra quite a lot recently about what Elsinore said, and have some conclusions as to what happened. The pieces of the puzzle are starting to come together, but no matter how I look at it, I can't refute that we are violent."

"Don't let yourself be put into that position," said Liana.

Icabar nodded. "Starting at that point gives us a poor defense. Who says these Enjelise have the right to judge us one way or another? I would start by questioning that right and what they have to gain by having us here."

Liana added, "Besides, don't forget the Master Crystal. Elsinore knows something that is important about it. The thought was quenched, but the Crystal is more than it appears. The Crystal is sentient, and we keep forgetting that fact."

Braden looked at her with a frown. "The most important thing is that we are in a weak position as long as they have Adam and Tessa. I want them back, and I have a plan."

Liana put up a hand. "Be careful there too. They may be bait for a trap or a test of some sort. I had some strange impressions about their motives for the kidnapping. I didn't get the impression that they were serious hostages, more that it was a test or a trap."

Braden laid his palms flat on his desk. "I thought the same thing. We should be able to bring them back easily. The Enjelise make a big deal of not being violent.

But we are, and they know it. If we can locate Adam and Tessa, I think we are more than a match for any Enjelise. We find Tessa and Adam, walk in and take them back. What are they going to do to stop us? Point a finger and waggle it at us while making a disapproving face?"

His communicator buzzed and Bashar's voice came on. "Heads up. Glaze is on his way to see you. By the way, have you seen Icabar anywhere?"

Braden put the comm on speaker, so Icabar could hear and answer.

Bashar continued, "I've been sitting here at this forsaken board forever now while he's off on some mysterious mission. Nothing's getting done at my watch and my butt hurts. You ordered that this post not be left vacant, so I'm covering for him, but he needs to get his butt back here."

"You're on speaker now and Icabar's here. He'll be along soon. Be patient." Braden grinned at Icabar.

"You're just used to the soft-cushioned chair of Helm," retorted Icabar leaning forward. "And all the pretty visuals you get there." He winked at Braden.

"Ah Icabar. So, you're with Braden, are you? I should have guessed. Hey, next time I'll let you try piloting us through the stargate. See how well you like the soft cushion of Helm and my pretty visuals then."

"I talk better than I fly. I'll admit that any time."

"I do have my own work to do, you know. Captain, he just can't keep his nose out of everyone's business. He has to be handing out opinions for every situation while leaving the grunt work to others."

"I know. He's actually arguing with me at the moment," said Braden. "I'll be relieved to send him back as soon as we're done."

"He needs to help me unstick the extender panels on pod C. A little help with some chores on the outside would be appreciated now that Adam isn't here and Robert's unreliable. There's some maintenance work yet to do to have this ship ready if we need to…"

"I'll send him back as soon as I can," Braden, interrupted him. "We aren't just having a social visit. Hang tight a little longer. Get Robert to take the con and take second seat. He's recovering well and should pick up more responsibility, anyway."

"That's no better."

"My, my… grumpy aren't we?" countered Icabar. "I would think that one who has ridden over the hardpan of the Great Desert on a Lompir could sit awhile at the comm deck. Now you know why I get testy after sitting there so long. It's no picnic; believe me. Maybe Solanje can soothe your nerves. You two should try a little sex to put you in a mellower mood, or am I late with that suggestion?" Icabar let the barb fly and they heard an ear-deafening squeal as comm cut off abruptly. No more was heard from Bashar, but a parting garbled sound.

"Okay, back to our ideas," responded Icabar, patting Liana's arm. "Braden, you have to turn the tables on their argument."

"I don't know how to explain humanity to aliens. I can't understand the species myself." Braden gestured with his palms out to them.

"Don't doubt yourself," answered Liana firmly. "I have every confidence that you can do this."

Startled, Braden felt convinced that she had just read his mind.

Ack! Maybe this thing with Icabar was just as well. Having your lover read your mind whenever she wanted could be very unsettling. Bad enough having her as a crew and wondering if she were reading his thoughts.

Liana laughed. He glared at her. And Icabar appeared suspicious, as if he thought they were having a secret conversation without him.

Braden heaved a sigh. Just then the entry chimed. Glaze and Crystal joined them. Glaze appeared changed, too. He looked strung out. Something was bothering him. He was acting odd, not his usual unflappable self. Braden took a deep breath. Twelve humans facing an infinitely superior species with humanity hanging precariously in the balance, and his entire crew was acting strange.

Glaze found a seat and sat down. "Braden, humans by nature are sinful, greedy and destructive. I know of no moment in our entire history that isn't fraught with violence of some sort."

"Yes, and fearful and loving and innovative. Complex, I would say," said Liana, shifting toward him in her chair. "Don't give up on us just yet."

Glaze's shoulders slumped. "Sometimes, I wonder if we're worth saving."

"Of course, we're worth saving. That's why we're going to go in and rescue Adam and Tessa," said Braden stoutly. "I need them back and a good captain always looks out for his crew. Glaze found out some important details while on the planet and has given me some ideas. Tell them what you know."

Glaze nodded. "I know where they are. They're in a guarded hidden garden."

"Can you get us near in the shuttle?" asked Icabar.

"Yes, but I should go in alone first," responded Glaze. "I think I can teleport there without alerting the aliens. That way I'll be able to scope out the situation."

"Teleporting? I'm curious about this teleporting idea," said Braden rocking back in his chair. "You really did it?"

Glaze nodded. "It's an ability I've recently discovered. I'm hoping it gets easier with practice."

"Won't you need backup to help get them out?" asked Liana. "They can't teleport. They're going to need the shuttle to get out."

"Yes, but I should scout the area before we do that," argued Glaze. "They aren't there because they want to be. If I can get in and contact Adam, then we can set a pick-up time."

"It might work," Braden answered slowly. He tapped his teeth with his nails.

Crystal eyed him worriedly. "Glaze, are you sure that you'll be all right? Can you teleport by yourself there and back safely?"

Braden watched her eyes soften and her gaze trail over Glaze tenderly. A strange feeling came over him.

He pushed the feelings of jealousy away.

Maybe Glaze had been willing to try her little experiment.

"I'll be fine, Crystal. Don't worry. Tessa, Adam and I need to work out the details of our plan."

Braden noticed that he looked uncomfortable.

As captain, Braden called a meeting to detail the rescue plan. Glaze explained to them how he would imagine a place that he knew and then will himself there. They watched as Glaze stood in a cleared area, closed his eyes, and remembered the quiet glade where he had talked with Angelique.

As they watched, Glaze glowed and shimmered until the air tingled, and then, in an explosion of light, he shattered into a million pieces and nothing remained but drifting dust motes and empty air.

Chapter 22

Glaze closed his eyes while his crewmembers watched. He tried to remember the spot where he had last seen Angelique. He visualized the swaying pines and the splashing stream. He imagined the warm sun on his face, the soft breeze and recalled the small ash sapling which had caught his earlier attention. He called up the yellow sunburst blooms and the blue sky. When all was fresh and felt right in his mind, he willed himself there.

A ripping explosion of pain shot through his entire body. Flying apart, before he knew it, he was reassembling his mind and body in another place. He now stood somewhere on the planet amidst swaying pines and sun yellow flowers. He looked down and gave his body a poke to make sure he had reassembled properly.

Yep. Incredible.

He took a deep breath. A sigh of relief.

Still alive and sane.

The experience scared him, but he felt more confident with the ability each time he attempted it. He heard gasping and wheezing nearby. Following the noise to its source, he found Adam asleep with one arm flung over Tessa. They were in an enclosed garden, curled up on a bough of soft greenery.

He looked around nervously and kicked urgently at Adam's foot. He crouched down and murmured in his ear, "Adam! Wake up, mighty warrior."

The snoring changed into a snort. Next to him blissfully asleep, Tessa murmured unintelligible noises.

"Wake up, you two. Now," Glaze whispered. He leaned over and shook Adam by the shoulders.

"Leave me alone," Adam moaned, flailing at him.

"Shhh ... It's Glaze."

Tessa stretched and yawned. She sat up startled.

Glaze shook his head at them. "Wake up! We've got humanity to save, and you're just lying about. Get up." He prodded them some more.

"Wzaa at? Where'm I?" Adam rubbed his eyes. Next to him Tessa peered around puzzled.

"How can you sleep when the human race needs saving? Wake up." He bent over and shook Adam again.

Adam frowned and sat up drowsily next to Tessa. "Wzaa's hap'ning?" He shook his head as if to clear it.

"Quietly. They may be nearby. You've been drugged. I knew you wouldn't go easily any other way. Braden said as much too."

"Drugged? I do feel a bit woozy," mumbled Adam. He looked around, and then squinted at Glaze. "I also have a terrible headache."

"I'll bet it was those berries with that sugary coating on them." Tessa shook a finger at him.

"I ate a lot of those," Adam admitted.

"Right," reiterated Glaze. "Your sweet tooth got the best of you."

"Oh, My Lady!" said Tessa.

"I'd rank her the number one suspect," responded Glaze dryly.

"Cripes! What do we do now?" Tessa looked alarmed. "Are we prisoners or something?" She brushed leaves and twigs off her arms and out of her hair.

"Yes. First, we need to de-tox you. You aren't any good this way. We have to figure out a way to cleanse your system without them knowing that you're onto their game."

"That's easy," said Tessa. "We only eat natural fruit and nuts. I saw what tested out to be apple trees near here. We'll just eat those and pretend to eat their food." She pointed to some trees laden with fruit.

"Good idea," said Glaze. "Then when they give you food, kick it under the bushes for any prowlers."

"Prowlers!"

"Shhh … I'll be back in two transits near dusk. You should be better awake. Lie low but be ready to make a run for the entrance. Fill your spacesuits with pine boughs so it looks like you're here, and leave them in case they have inserted trackers, or monitors." He grabbed a breath and scanned the area again.

"We don't have any other clothes. We'll be naked." Tessa rubbed a hand through her hair, smoothing it down and gazing about.

"I promise I won't look."

"Oh please." Tessa gave him a disbelieving glare.

He pointed southward. "I'll divert the guardians at the gate. The shuttle will be parked just a little way off from the entrance in some trees. Go to your right out the gate. Braden and Bashar will be nearby."

"We'll be ready," agreed Adam. "We'll keep each other awake but pretend to be drugged." Glaze left them yawning and standing up. Adam started bouncing on one foot and then the other.

*

Glaze managed to teleport back up to the ship and report his conversation with Adam and Tessa. Braden called a meeting to lay out the completed plan and assign tasks to each person.

"Bashar, Glaze, and I'll shuttle to outside the spot where Adam and Tessa are," said Braden. "There's a grassy meadow we can land in behind some trees. The rest of the crew will stay here on standby. Icabar and Liana will maintain a link with the ground forces."

"Robert you're to monitor the surrounding area near the shuttle. Do not leave your post for any reason. Contact us if either of you see trouble. Pull out of orbit if anything goes wrong and the ship is jeopardized. Remember to protect the remaining crew and the ship, even if it means sacrificing the team on the ground. Bashar comes with me to the rendezvous. Solanje stays on ship to guard the alien device and also give Bashar incentive to return safely."

Braden gave them a grin.

"Hey," protested Bashar.

"Best way I know to guarantee you'll get back," he said. Bashar grunted at him. Solanje had the grace to say nothing. She only blushed.

*

Braden, Bashar, and Glaze landed at dusk. Then, Braden and Glaze crept through foliage toward the area that Glaze had indicated the Enjelise held Adam and Tessa, while Bashar manned the shuttle. Sure enough, two glowing beings stood guarding the entrance. The guards peered into the rising darkness and then at each other, as if deciding whether to investigate the disturbance, or not.

Glaze disappeared into the dense greenery. He made a rustling sound off to the side. The guards looked around and signaled to each other. They waved glowing objects in Glaze's direction and soon left the entrance to pursue him. Wild noises erupted from inside.

Moments later, out from behind bordering bushes, crept a semi-naked Adam and Tessa. A few bits of greenery covered strategic body parts.

"Hurry." Braden rushed up to them and took Tessa's arm, dislodging a green fern. She stumbled and reached to grab some replacement leaves from a nearby fig tree and held them against her body as they fled past.

"Forget it," murmured Braden irritably.

Distant waving beams of light cut the darkening sky and indicated more Enjelise entering the garden from another direction.

Glaze was attracting attention.

"Enjelise entering from north entrance," whispered Robert in Braden's comm. "Get out of there!"

"On it."

Soon sounds of fighting and flashes of light lit up the greenery. The two investigating Enjelise arrived back at the garden's entrance and pointed towards the shuttle.

All modesty tossed aside; the three humans made a mad dash for the waiting shuttle. Braden pushed Tessa in as Adam appeared beside him. In the distance, they heard a human battle cry erupt out of the center of the garden and the crash of falling trees and tearing foliage. Streams of light flashed and waved violently about.

"Yahaaa..aaa!" They heard Glaze screaming. "Come get me you bastards. Look over here; look at me."

"Glaze!" Tessa started to shout and turned toward the commotion, but Braden put his hand over her mouth.

"Quiet. Get in," he whispered. His hand was shaking.

She climbed in, looking over her shoulder. She brushed some more leaves out of her hair and clutched her seat in a white knuckled grip.

Next to him, Braden grabbed Adam's arm and pushed him forward into the shuttle. As soon as Adam fell through the door, Braden followed and made a whirling gesture with his hand at Bashar who sat helm.

"Lift off!" he shouted into his comm, sending Glaze the signal they were on board.

The shuttle roared to life. At the controls, Bashar grinned fiercely at them. Before Braden got the door completely air-locked, the transport lifted. Looking below, Braden and Bashar saw a swarm of lighted beings around a single point of blazing incandescence that appeared to explode into a fireball and scatter on the wind. Gradually, everything looked smaller and smaller until the garden disappeared and the only thing they could see was a large round colorful planet and a looming spaceship, growing larger and larger in their view.

*

They emerged from shuttle bay bedraggled and covered with bits of greenery. Braden waited impatiently while the lock cycled the atmosphere in and practically ripped off his suit in his haste to get to Navcom. He tossed his clothes into a pile, while in the sterilization container, not bothering to dress. After a cursory decontamination, he strode through the corridor with Adam and Tessa trailing naked and out of breath behind him. Bashar stayed back to shut down and secure the shuttle.

"How'd it go?" Braden burst into Navcom. "Did he make it back?"

A singed and battered figure whirled around near Icabar's console and flung out his arms. "What took you so long, Captain?" A muddied and scorched Glaze grinned triumphantly at him.

"I had to go the long way around, you fool." Braden stumbled over, grabbed Glaze by the shoulders, and fell into the outstretched arms.

Glaze winced. "Easy, Cap. The shoulder's a bit tender."

"You made it. It looked bad, and I hated abandoning you to face them all alone, but you said …." Braden stuttered to a stop.

"I thought we left you for dead," put in Adam astonished.

Dyra hastily threw shirt and pants at the naked crewmembers.

"I don't think they've experienced that much excitement since the last time man was there," chuckled Icabar.

"Glaze sure stirred them up," Robert agreed.

"Remember, they said that they were not a violent species." Glaze shrugged. "I'd imagined they would have a few guards at the garden's entrance and some re-enforcements but wouldn't really muster a violent force. I got out as soon as Braden gave the word."

"I was frightened," quavered Tessa as she tugged a top on.

Glaze made a face. "It was mostly a light show."

Tessa grabbed a hairbrush handed over by Liana. "Surely now, the tribunal will vote that we're a violent species. It was a political trick. We just sealed our doom. We proved that we're not worthy. You should have just left us there," she said, waving the brush at Braden.

"No, Tessa, I think that you were deliberately put there to see if we would come and get you," responded Icabar.

"You're saying I was bait!"

"We demonstrated we were violent," moaned Robert.

"We failed the test," Liana mumbled.

"We passed with flying colors," answered Braden. He slid into a pair off pants and brushed a hand through his hair, then smiled at them.

"What!" exclaimed Robert. "How can that be?"

Braden answered smugly, "You just have to understand what the test was all about. They were testing human nature. They wanted to know if we would risk our own lives for each other. We proved to them that we'll fight to survive and save others of our species."

"However, tomorrow we must face the tribunal and prove that we're not violent," protested Adam. "Tonight, we just proved that we are." He rubbed a sore neck and smoothed down his top.

Braden smiled. "Of course, humans are violent. What fool would argue otherwise? I have to approach the problem from a different angle, as Icabar so wisely pointed out to me."

Icabar nodded.

Braden explained, "We need to go on the offensive if we want to win. Glaze and Dyra have given me some good points to argue. Tomorrow will be "their trial." We humans stand together or perish together. Right?"

"We're with you Captain. We said that," rumbled Adam. All heads nodded.

"Good." Braden clapped his hands. "I'm going to need you at my back for what comes next."

Chapter 23

Braden sat on stage in a full-dress navy-blue captain's uniform at the center of the large room in the alien ship. Next to him sat the rest of his crew. They, too, wore a formal dress for the occasion. Several tugged nervously at a collar, while others smoothed down an imaginary wrinkle or two. A row of seven Enjelise sat at the left side of the stage, Braden and crew on the right.

The Enjelise's glowed in white and gold. They looked uncomfortable also, because they had to manifest in the physical realm, and a few had a hard time maintaining their physical form.

Braden's crew had cleaned away all signs of the earlier disaster and the area looked presentable with dust and accumulated debris swept up. Fresh air circulated.

Braden looked up toward the multi-colored tiered walls, now packed with agitated Enjelise. Because of the excitement of the trial, those that could manifest on the level of human vibrations did, so that to the humans, the room appeared full, although portions often flickered in and out of visual context.

A circular halo, like the one from the probe, hovered in mid-air over a sitting Enjelise's head. Braden surmised that this was the moderator and one of the halo's functions was to translate what was said into other alien languages.

Elsinore broadcasted for quiet, and the room fell silent. Braden's crew looked at each and a few eyebrows raised. The haloed Enjelise glided forward out from the row of seven. His large wings fanned out over the stage and then tucked back and down to his sides.

"I am Remiel," he announced to the audience. "I'm the head of the council which has come to present charges against the homo sapiens."

Murmurs rippled through the onlookers. Remiel motioned for quiet. He continued, "Homo sapiens originated from Earth, found within the Milky Way Galaxy. There, they contaminated their world with war and blasphemy. Because we saw what was happening, long ago, and at the Creators command, we selected what we deemed were the best of Earth's humans and seeded other habitable worlds with them in hopes of saving and improving the species. Alysia was one of these worlds. Unfortunately, they soon followed Earth's path of destruction, proving that humans cannot be changed."

This comment caused a stir in the gallery and fluttering and murmurings rippled among them and then quieted as Remiel continued.

"Many say that humans should be forbidden space travel so that they can't contaminate the rest of the worlds. They vote for interdiction. Others go so far as to say that they are too dangerous to exist, and they threaten other species. They want eradication. They conclude that humans would try to subdue and destroy all they meet."

The Enjelise turned to Braden. "What defense do you propose to these charges?" He motioned the Captain forward to speak.

Stepping smartly out to the middle of the platform, Braden smiled out at his audience, and then, turned to Remiel. "Aggressiveness is part of our nature," he said simply. "Why would I say otherwise?"

Mutterings and shiftings occurred in the room.

Remiel waved for quiet and continued, "We have tried to show humans the path of enlightenment. Those we sent were met with cruel and vicious treatment. We offered prophets to sway your masses and single beings to touch individual lives in hopes that you would change, but to no avail. I charge that it would be impossible to assimilate your species into our universe."

Remiel leaned forward. "We charge humanity guilty of violence and evil, and a contamination to all other worlds." He glared at the humans on the stage.

Braden took a deep breath and wiped sweaty palms along side his trousers. He thought of Glaze, Icabar, Liana, Joel, and Adam; all his crewmembers that he cherished, even the foolish Robert. He thought of Dyra and Tessa and her love of growing things and Bashar, who always steered a straight course. He thought of Crystal with her healing hands and beautiful face. He thought of Solanje and how she moved elegantly through space carrying the heaviest of burdens lightly on her slender shoulders. They were all dear to him and had helped him to answer this charge. He knew that he did not carry this burden alone, and he gathered calm and strength from their presence. He gazed over at them and then raised his head to glance at rows of radiant beings who had only known peace and love in their life. They'd never had to face what most humans faced in the form of disease, death, and despair. They didn't experience or understand pain or loss, so now they were afraid, and fear made them dangerous.

He cleared his throat. "We're exactly that. We're guilty of being a violent, destructive species."

A loud uproar broke out in the galleries. Strange alien words mingled and clashed in the room. Elsinore stood up to beam calm. A surprised expression flashed across Remiel's face. "Then you accept judgment and agree that you should be destroyed?"

Braden laughed. "Oh no, we're only violent because you created us that way, and for what you thought were good reasons."

Whispers skittered around the room. Images flickered in and out of human perception.

"What makes you say such a thing?" thundered Gabriel leaping from his seat. Remiel motioned sternly for him to sit down. He nodded at Braden and palmed out his hands in question.

Braden took a shaky breath. "Before, when The Creator, the one you call God, first made man in his own image, he was made here. Here is a beautiful easy place to live and thrive. Here humans lived in peace. And then something happened. The humans were manipulated and changed by the Enjelise, *for selfish reasons.* Challenges were thrown at humans. Indecencies forced upon them 'Do not do this. Do not do that. Stay only here. Go only there'. They used our women and committed species rape. Alysian myths claim so. Dyra researched our ancient scrolls and Elsinore admitted it to me.

"So how did the new creatures react to this treatment? They rebelled. I believe it was a test. When humans proved that they were not pliable and could determine their own fate, they were banished to harsher worlds where they faced hardships. First, they were put on Earth and then some were taken to Alysia. Why? Because by then, the Enjelise needed a hardier version of themselves with a strong survival instinct. Man does not necessarily have the instinct for killing; he has the instinct for survival. That was the key element you wanted bred into them. Disease, pestilence, famine. The Enjelise sent those too. The Enjelise, you," Here Braden pointed to his audience, "sent those horrors to our world so that we would become hardened, tougher. You guided us and molded us to become what we are now, so that if you needed us, we would be strong enough to protect you."

"Protect us? We protected YOU," rasped Remiel. He looked confused.

Braden continued in a firmer tone. "You protected us because you might need us. You deliberately bred certain traits into our DNA. Some Enjelise just bred with humans. However, that was against the rules and those who did were punished severely.

"Meanwhile, you lived the good life in your paradise here where there was no disease, no violence— only love and peace. You built a spiritual golden path for yourselves that would lead straight to the Creator, undisturbed by adversity. You have a life of perfection and you don't want anything to upset it. Only a few of you still carry the remnants of a once violent nature. The rest are incapable of defending themselves against attack. The trait of violence has been bred out of you and you wish to be left alone with your safe and peaceful world. Violence arises out of fear, and here fear has been banished, or was, until recently. Now for some reason, you're afraid. What are you suddenly afraid of?"

"Searching for peace and tranquility is not an evil act!" argued Remiel. "We want a world without conflict that your species has brought back to us. The Creator asks that of us."

A muttering rose again in the gallery.

Braden shook his head. "No matter how you name yourselves, or what you try to tell us, you're not immortal. Your race is long lived, but it does die. Some still fear death, although many have been taught that it's just another step to God. You vibrate to a higher energy level, but you cannot breed anymore. Where are the young on this world? Tessa pointed that out to me. Your race is dying. You cannot afford a war. A war would decimate your species and your leaders realized a long time ago that could happen if they pursued the peace option." Braden glanced at Glaze with a short nod of his head. Angelique's comments had been enlightening.

He swung around and continued to address the now gallery. "So, after our creation, we were tempted and tested. Could we make a choice for ourselves? Could we set our own destiny? When we did, we showed that we had the potential for the kind of strength you might need some time. Then we were removed to a harsh environment to become your little side experiment. Ask Glaze what a harsh environment does to a man. It toughens him. Love and harmony are all well and good until threatened. Then what? Where are those who will protect you from hostile enemies if they come? How many galaxies are out there? Do you think that we're the only violent species among the stars?"

"You're the most violent we know about," answered Remiel. "And we want to be rid of you."

"Ark dung!" Braden shook his head. "Both Elsinore and Dyra mentioned to me that there was a great battle that divided your world and almost destroyed the Enjelise. Your side won. Histories say we were the cause. Some of you became too involved with us and had to be removed. You punished them. They had crossed the Enjelise moral line. What happened to them? What world did you drop them on? Might they not seek you for revenge?"

"They deserved punishment. They knew they had transgressed God's law," protested Remiel. A few of the council who were sitting nearby stood up but were pulled back down.

Braden faced Gabriel with a firm expression. "Elsinore's father formed a contingency plan for that eventuality—a plan that would protect the Enjelise if The Fallen grew strong enough to threaten your world.

"Joel came to me, telling me about his dreams. He dreamt of a harsh world and a race of beings full of hate. I remembered the great battle that Dyra mentioned and suspected that your old enemies were not destroyed, but still survive, hoping to return and wreak revenge. While you pursued peace and enlightenment, they learned how to be strong, tough, and worse—they fed their hatred until it now consumes their existence.

"Meanwhile, in case they returned, you molded us to make us violent enough, desperate enough and powerful enough to defeat them, if you ever needed us."

Exclamations and open comments ran around the room once more and subsided.

Braden shifted from foot to foot and clenched a fist. "We would have to destroy a species advanced enough for space travel, but you had to deal out carefully the weapons we might wield for fear we might turn against you too.

"The power of the Master Crystal was a gamble, but you wanted us to evolve at a more rapid rate. You found a way to do that using the crystals. Elsinore took it to our world to accelerate our transformation and bring forth new powers we call Talents.

Braden pumped his fist at the gallery of increasingly disturbed aliens. He raised his voice and shouted, "This trial is a mockery. You'll not destroy us. You need us too much, but you want to frighten us enough so that we'll do anything you might. After all, survival is the foremost characteristic you designed in us. You staged that kidnapping to see if we would risk our own lives in to save each other, and we did, because for us each human life is precious."

Liana jumped up and shouted, "We're your step-children. Why would you want to destroy us?" Many felt the force of her mind and recognized its touch as one of their own. Several gasped at the realization.

Braden waved her back to her seat.

The room looked toward Remiel for denial. The Arch Enjelise shook his head vigorously. "We are not as cruel as you describe. As your guides, how could we teach you to fulfill your own destiny if we protected you from every hurt, every challenge? We cannot be around forever to watch over you, and we didn't want you to make the mistakes we made. But yes, we wanted this world to be in total peace and harmony. You brought dissension. Here's a place where all can shed their baser nature and evolve to a higher existence. We enter the body to learn certain lessons, and then, there's the higher dimension where only the pure spirit exists. Dissension weakens our higher energy levels. You're not the only species able to evolve. We also have been evolving. And we're close at last."

"Yet you threaten us with extinction? How could you?" demanded Braden

"We wanted to force you into a position where we could negotiate our survival now that everything has become critical."

Braden leaned toward Remiel. "Critical? Why did you accelerate our evolution by exposing us to the Master Crystal? Lately, we have been changing at a rapid rate. These strange new powers that frighten us."

Braden made a sweeping gesture with his hands. "Ah, let me guess what this pressing matter might be that would cause you to show yourselves to us and pull us here to your world from across the stars."

He paused and gazed around. All eyes in the room focused on him. The silence became absolute. He put up both hands and then flipped them dramatically outwards.

"Why have you brought us here? Now? We didn't stumble here; we were lured. You threw the alien device into our laps, knowing that our curiosity would get the best of , and we would come here once you sent out that signal. So, why?" he asked angrily.

"Could it be that your old nemesis is coming *now*, after all this time? That those exiled have finally mastered space travel and seek you out? Your leaders banished those you call "The Fallen" to the other side of this galaxy. Now they're returning and you can't stop them. They've evolved also, but they have taken a path of hate and anger, rather than love and peace. They have been baked to perfection in their hell of an existence which you gave them, and now, they're stronger than you are. And you're afraid. Judgment may be at hand; but it's a different Judgment than you would have us believe. We may be your only salvation. You can't afford to eliminate us. Who else could possibly fight your battle when you have become unable to fight your own?"

The room broke out in chaos. Many were shouting, "Is this true?" Others cried, "No! No!" Most exclaimed in unintelligible alien words that needed no translation.

Gabriel tried to get them under control. Then he gestured for Elsinore to calm everyone. A peaceful radiance filled the room. Noise abated to a low murmuring.

When they had quieted, Braden continued. "You have a dilemma. After all you have done to us, dare you trust us to protect you, or might we decide to join sides with your enemy? Are you now going to expect us to hold you blameless for all you have done?"

"Yes," exclaimed Gabriel indignantly. "We have enabled you to be what you are now. We have raised you up to aspire to be our equals. As Liana pointed out, humans are part of our genetics. Elsinore proved it was possible for us to interbreed. You're our children. We bred in our own enhanced genetics. You are *more* than you were because of it. You're no longer barbarians who grunt and stomp around. You share our heritage and have shown that you may be able to vibrate to our dimension and eventually transform yourselves, as we now are transforming ourselves. Would you prefer *The Fallen* as your allies? Do you wish to lower your species to what they have become? They live lives filled with hate, anger, and violence. Is that the path you want for your people? Is that your choice? Or will you let us guide you to God?"

Wearily, Braden answered him. "What alternative do you have? We're the only ones that can defend you. And your enemy is coming. Who else will save you? You dare not kill us. We're your only hope."

Pandemonium broke out yet again. This time no one stopped it.

Chapter 24

"Braden Steele! Now what do we do?" Solanje's dark eyes snapped at him. He twisted around from his monitor to glance over at her and saw her fierce stance. He would stop breathing if she continued to look at him that way. Easing over to her, he put out a hand, hoping to gentle his fierce tiger. His lips parted.

She sighed, shaking her head.

He put up both hands, palms out. "At least I got us a stay of execution until I can figure out what to do next." Her hair brushed against his hands. His fingers reached out to feel its soft texture and caress it before he released it to float away.

"You still wear the hair of the royal born daughter, so long and silky. You flaunt it as a sign to all who understand that you are of the Ching T'Karre, know the discipline, and can call upon its strength."

"And all who are left to understand what they see may only be you," she murmured, stepping toward him.

"We're missing something." Icabar entered briskly into Braden's work module. "Something's wrong."

Braden dropped his hand, stepped back, and abruptly spun around to face him. "You buzz my entrance first, Icabar. Do you understand?" Braden used his irritated Captain's voice. "And you wait for permission to enter."

"What? Oh. Oooooh. Yes sir, sorry sir. Next time I'll buzz more loudly." Icabar stared, startled at the two of them standing so close together. "And I'll get permission, so that I don't interrupt something that I shouldn't be interrupting." Icabar's eyebrows lifted.

"Say what you have come to say," gritted out Braden.

Icabar's brow furrowed in thought. "That trial could have ended badly for us and would have, if you hadn't been able to figure so much out...with my help, of course, Captain." He darted a quick smile at Solanje.

"Your suggestions were much appreciated." Braden raised an eyebrow.

There was a commotion at the entrance. Adam entered the module behind Icabar and joined them. "I agree. It could have really gone badly for us." He gave a curt nod and shifted his eyes to Solanje who stood shaking her head.

Braden looked at the two of them with a stern expression. "Did I hear an entrance chime, or is my hearing going?"

"I thought your reasoning fairly solid, but I have to agree with Icabar. We're missing something," said Glaze, filing in behind the other two.

Braden rolled his eyes at Solanje, as his crew began flooding into his work quarters. He threw up his hands and waved them in.

"They're wrong in their actions, but the temptation to play God is sometimes overwhelming. We might have been tempted to do the same thing given their situation. They must be terribly frightened," said Dyra, now coming in through the entry. Braden had to step back to make room for all the incoming bodies.

"I need to tell him something," said a voice outside in the corridor. Bodies shifted aside to let Joel enter. He wiped his hands down his sides and choked out, "I have been having more of those dreams," He swallowed hard and rubbed his forehead. "I think they're important. I think they're telling me what's happening with the ones they call 'The Fallen'."

"Doesn't anyone ask permission to enter the Captain's quarters around here anymore? Have we vented all procedures out the airlock?" Braden glared at his crew who shuffled their feet. Eyes glanced down. He heard a few mumbled apologies.

Looking around, he heard Crystal and Tessa coming down the corridor, arguing loudly.

"It would seem that a meeting is in order." Braden made a short chopping motion with his hands. "Everyone find a place to settle and we'll get on with it." He headed to his desk with a sigh and scanned his crew. He waited for the laggards to come in and find a place. "I assume someone is on watch ... other than Robert."

"I'm here." Robert came breezing in through the door with a growing beard and a smile plastered on his face. He gave everyone a nod and slid into a spot in a corner near Adam. Adam shifted over to give him room.

"Liana and Bashar are manning Navcom," offered Icabar.

"Hey Icabar, we've noticed you seem, ah, mellower lately. Got a big smile on your face all the time. Working on those human relations, are you, huh?" Dyra gave Crystal a wink and a nudge.

Icabar gave her a finger.

Braden cleared his throat as he waited while everyone squirmed, rustled, and fidgeted his or her way to a place. Finally, all were settled.

With a nod from Braden, Icabar glared at Dyra and then began speaking into the pause. "What if there really is a hidden faction that wants to eliminate humans? I smell a deeper game here. Remember, I'm a Tygelian, and I can sense the play of a game. Something instigated that farce of a trial. Something powerful pushed it to happen quickly before we could mount any reasonable defense. That trial could have gone wrong in a nasty way. Thank the Creator that we did as well we did. If we presume that the beings, we call Enjelise, are good, just misled, then what's left?"

"*The Fallen* and Lucien?" asked Joel. "Why would they want to eliminate *humans?*"

"Lucien? Are you on a first name basis now?" Braden cast a worried glance at Joel. "How much has he influenced you through these dreams of yours?"

Joel looked down and mumbled, "I need to tell about the latest dream." Joel described his recent dream and explained their leader called himself Lucien.

"I believe we were the catalyst for the whole conflict," Dyra suggested. "That's why they want to get rid of us. I've been studying what history and myths Alysia has accumulated."

Icabar grimaced. "Possibly, but in every mystery, I try to solve, I ask the question, 'Who benefits?' Or who gets the money on the death of the victim?"

"And who does?" asked Solanje, leaning forward, suddenly intent on his words.

"Well, if humans are eliminated, then Alysia's up for grabs," Robert croaked out with a shrug of his shoulders, as if it were obvious.

"Alysia!" More than one voice sounded their home world's name in surprise and anguish.

"Elsinore's people already have this world. It's a perfect place to live. Why would they want Alysia?" asked Tessa, puzzled. "And according to Joel's dream, this world is Lucien's target. Why would they want us eliminated? They shouldn't hate us. *The Fallen* want the Enjelise's world, not Alysia. Or a reasonably habitable world of their own. Most likely they don't even know Alysia exists." She shook her head at the idea.

"But I don't think that the real target is the Enjelise," mused Icabar. "Lucien's group is coming here because this is the world they left and the source of their revenge is here, but we were led here. WE WERE LED."

Murmurs and mumbles followed that remark.

"What do we offer?" asked Dyra.

"We provide the way to Alysia and *the Fallen* provide the transport for a sentient being that can't fly itself. We know how to get back," answered Crystal. She shifted in her seat and firmed her shoulders.

Glaze held up a hand. "About this being a perfect place, I wouldn't want to live here, necessarily. I was thinking recently about how I miss the snow and the high mountains."

"Yes, you mentioned that to me," said Icabar. "I wondered what is it that our world has that this world, or any other planet in this galaxy, might lack?"

"Snow?" asked Braden. He looked over at Glaze with raised eyebrows.

"No," Glaze shook his head. "Too many other planets and asteroids have ice and cold. That can't be it."

Adam cleared his throat. "Most of the ones we passed were gas giants, or either extremely hot with lava, or extremely cold. I mean *extremely* cold."

"Deserts!" said Bashar, snapping his fingers and suddenly sitting up. "I miss the Sunglast with sand and the sound of the dry wind blowing. We haven't located any deserts here. I miss my desert world."

"Well, there's wind here, but sand is an idea," offered Tessa. She angled her head and pursed her lips.

Adam nodded. "Sand! A common commodity—common to our planet at least. Silicon is the second most abundant element in Alysia's crust. Joel said that Uriel talked about the riches of our world, and yet, I found plenty of precious gems and stones on his world. Maybe silicon is precious to this world."

"Haven. I've named the Enjelise's world Haven," Tessa spoke up.

Bashar rolled his eyes and Icabar snorted. Braden gave them both a glare. They put their heads down, suddenly interested in a blemished belt buckle or a shirt wrinkle.

"That's the name I put in my reports next to the scientific notation," agreed Dyra. She patted Tessa on the arm and smiled.

"Okay, Haven." Bashar waved a hand at them. "I, too, wondered what riches Uriel spoke about in Joel's little drama."

"Most of the systems that we passed didn't have much silicon," informed Glaze. "Most were uninhabitable hard rock, or gases, but not sand."

"Other than Bashar, who would want to live in that much sand?" asked Tessa. "That sounds strange. Surely not Joel's friends."

"They're not my friends! I just have some sort of psychic connection to Lucien. Only him. It doesn't make him, or them, my friends," protested Joel. He pressed his lips together and clenched both fists, as he glared at her.

"Alysia is habitable, but frankly," said Adam, looking around. "If I were given a choice, I would prefer living here. This is paradise."

Tessa nodded in agreement. "Haven is rich and very fertile."

"Yes, for us," said Icabar thoughtfully. "However, what about an alien race that would die if they didn't have enough silicon?" He smiled smugly. "Actually, Liana mentioned it. She said that the Master Crystal blocked her mind because she felt its thoughts. I considered that odd. What might she read that the crystal didn't want her to know?" He looked around for her, but then remembered she was on duty.

"The Master Crystal!" yelped Crystal excitedly. "We don't think of it as a living thing, but Elsinore said that it is a sentient life form. The crystal is composed of silicon. I know; I studied it. Silicon is essential to their survival, I'll bet." Her mouth dropped open, and she inhaled sharply. "Could be that!"

"Yes," agreed Braden. "A silicon-based being. What if their race is starving to death and dying because they have used up all the silicon on their own world and all nearby worlds lack that mineral? Wouldn't they be interested in our world? What precipitated our evolution, so that we would arrive now, just in time to confront this Enjelise enemy and lead them to our world?"

"The Master Crystal!" exclaimed Adam.

"Exactly." Icabar smiled. "It's worth thinking about, at least." He crossed his arms and gave them all a smug expression.

"You're suggesting that the Master Crystal has spearheaded a plot to destroy humanity and take over Alysia? Why?" asked Robert.

"Maybe not destroy humanity as much as get access to our world with its abundant silicon. Survival of the species," explained Icabar. "It's a theory to think about."

"The Enjelise will be destroyed if we don't do something. They may be incapable of surviving a direct attack from Lucien's people. But what if we're the real target? They may be manipulating both Alysian and the *Fallen* so that they can get to Alysia," suggested Braden. He glanced over at Adam and Bashar to see their reactions to his comment.

"They already know about Alysia," countered Solanje. "Elsinore took the Master Crystal there, and then, she brought it back."

"Not without seeding the Labyrinth," offered Crystal. "And the Talent Crystals have survived very nicely on our world. Maybe they liked what they saw and have been planning a reunion."

"What do you mean?' asked Joel.

"There's a motherlode from the Master Crystal's matrix that has been found in the Labyrinth. and is flourishing. It's from Elsinore's time and is used for developing Talent in genetically disposed individuals."

"Elsinore may not have been fully aware of what she was doing when she brought the crystal to Alysia," protested Solanje's in her defense.

Icabar interrupted, saying, "The innocent often are not aware of the evil that manipulates them."

Braden put up a hand. "Okay, okay. Maybe the Enjelise have been maneuvered into focusing on how dangerous we are. Something was working hard to convince the Enjelise to judge us as violent and pushing to have that trial happen quickly before we could think of a good defense. The trial may have been an attempt to eliminate us, but that didn't happen. Since that plan didn't work, another plan may be in progress."

"A plan B?" Icabar stoked his chin thoughtfully and rubbed his forehead.

"Yes," answered Braden. "Here's the new hypothesis, which may or may not be true: The Master Crystals are dying due to lack of silicon on their world. We have plenty of silicon on Alysia, and they know they can survive there. They bring *the Fallen* to Haven. They draw us here also. Somehow, they get information on how to get to Alysia and *the Fallen* take them there since they are rocks and can't drive. Sound about right?"

"But *the Fallen* want Haven," protested Crystal.

"So somehow, they must get the Fallen to take them to Alysia," muttered Icabar rubbing his face. He cast a glance over to Glaze who shrugged.

"The Enjelise keep talking about evolving and changing." Braden steepled his fingers together and gazed out. "We need to talk to Elsinore again."

"The halo may be more important than we realize. I think it's their means of a virtual reality into other worlds," said Icabar. "I've been doing some investigations into the halo device."

"You scare me to death with your 'investigations'," countered Solanje. She glared at Icabar and gave an I-told-you-so expression to Braden.

"Do you realize the halo device is made of a silicon compound similar to the material found in the crystals? Where does it come from?" asked Adam.

"What if the halos are created by the silicon beings and they are low on materials?" asked Icabar. "That would be important to a lot of sentient creatures." Icabar raised his eyebrows and wiggled them suggestively. He sat up and smiled triumphantly.

"Without the halos, their communications system breaks down. Not only can the aliens not talk to humans, but they can't talk to other species," mused Braden. "If we aren't condemned for being too violent a race, we are faced with fighting *the Fallen* for the Enjelise and die that way. In both cases, the crystal beings end up the winners."

"Only if they can attack and surprise Alysia," corrected Robert.

"I must use the halo and warn Alysia," said Braden. "If we're the real target, our world is in danger."

Solanje inhaled abruptly. "No, not you. I'm responsible for the artifact. I have pledged my honor to protect others from its danger." She looked panicked.

"As Captain, it's my responsibility," he retorted. He hit the desk with the flat of his hand.

Icabar jumped up. "No Braden! You can't do this. Someone else must. ME," argued Icabar. "I'm communications. I know how to work the communicator. Sort of."

Braden shook his head. "We must be incredibly careful who we contact. Right now, our world is helpless to an outside attack, but we don't want to start worldwide panic. I can tell my brother or my father, and either one has access to the right contacts and knows how to use them wisely. I have a psychic link to the best people who can remedy the situation. It has to be me," answered Braden. "Because they would only believe this bizarre tale if it came directly from my mouth."

Chapter 25

"Tessa what you're doing is very dangerous." Liana frowned as she watched Tessa pulling out herbs and vegetables and adding them into the sealed cooker.

Tessa gestured at Liana to hand over a carrot. "I think this soup will be delicious, now that we have access to planet grown food," she answered. "My new discoveries have really expanded the menu."

"Tessa!"

"I've found, and am now cultivating, some amazing new foods. While Braden and the others were concentrating on the trial, and other stuff, I put together a little garden of native plants. Adam helped. What do you think we should call this one?" Tessa held up an odd purple object that looked like a cross between a grape and a tomato. "It's tasty."

"Stop ignoring the question and answer me! What are you going to do about your situation?"

Tessa spun around and glared at Liana. "Nothing. What kind of person do you think I am? I'll not murder a human life...and that's that."

"If you go through with this, it'll most likely kill you. You have to do something...soon."

"I'll get Braden to let me work more on Haven. After all, I've already started a small farm there that I expect will yield some amazing things." She held up the object. "Gramato, or tomape?"

Liana snorted.

Tessa smiled. "The goats are thriving, and I'm attempting to domesticate an animal from Haven very much like our gebbit. I plan a stew soon. So, you see, I can be a bloodthirsty killer if I need to be."

"You heard Braden say that a hostile invasion is on the way."

"It could be extremely far away. Nine phases is nothing when traveling in space. How many shifts would that be?"

"And then what?" Liana swirled her hands around in exasperation. "A starship is no place for a baby. The radiation dangers, the low gravity ..."

"The farm has gravity and the baby goats are doing just fine. I'll keep it here and take care of it."

Tessa's chin had a decidedly stubborn tilt to it.

"You might not have enough time. Joel says they're on the way, and if we're forced to fight in space, it could be very dangerous for you."

"And what *isn't* dangerous out here? There isn't a shift ever where I have felt safe. Only down in that grove have I ever felt safe. Look, somehow the sterilization medicine that Mission Control injected into us wasn't effective down there when Adam and I were, ah, trying to alleviate a little boredom while waiting for you to rescue us. Something in the air, the food, or just not drinking shipboard water may have been the reason I got pregnant. It may be a false positive, or I could still abort naturally ... but I will not actively kill my own child."

"Tessa!"

"What I really want to do is stay on Haven. I have nothing to go back to, but Adam would have to want to stay too. It would be hard, but we could make a great life there."

"It would be easier to ..."

"No! I do not murder. My mind is made up. I doubt even you can change it. Don't make me. I'll hate myself forever. I've heard you do things ...well, don't!"

"Will there be a marriage?"

"I expect to marry him. It'll give the kid a name and legitimacy. He's a great, big, wonderful lug, you know. Can you talk to him? Maybe use those great persuasive powers that you have. If we fight these *Fallen* and lose, they could go after Alysia and wipe out all humans. Talk to him, Liana. Work your magic ...for me?"

*

"Joel. Joel. Are you all right?" asked a distraught Solanje. She had gone looking for him and found him curled up with a blanket in his private quarters.

Shakily Joel stood up and stared at her.

"Was I having another dream? They've been coming more frequently lately," he mumbled almost incoherently. "It's almost as if I'm drawn there by some compulsion." Joel looked down at his feet, his cheeks flaming from the awful admission.

"I know it's hard on you, but it's also important. We need to know what's happening. We believe that you're able to see what he's doing in real time. You're like a human remote viewer. What did you see?"

"They're building ships."

Joel knew that soon, much too soon, attacking ships would be upon them. The desire for vengeance and the hope of finding a better world would propel them forward. He saw them spread out like a swarm, descending toward Haven, bent on destruction. He squeezed his eyes shut and wiped out the vision. Solanje patted his hand.

"It'll be all right. It'll be okay," she said worriedly. He wasn't sure who she was trying to convince, herself or him. She left to tell Braden this latest vision.

*

Solanje found Braden in Navcom and caused a worried frown to furrow his brow when she relayed Joel's most recent vision. He studied her and reached out to touch her. "Solanje, the alien device is the answer. I plan to use it and warn Alysia of danger. I must let them know, so they can prepare a defense. The halo is the only way. You knew that it would come to this."

Solanje looked at him. "I promised my mother…"

"And I promised my father that I would find the owner of the alien device, and if they proved dangerous, I would warn Alysia. He feared something like this might happen. If you and Icabar are right about this thing, then we can use the device to warn our world."

"All right, *Captain,* but if you die, then I must sacrifice myself to atone for your death. I swore the oath."

He grabbed her and shook her. "No! Solanje! Two deaths don't make it right. I must take this chance in order to protect Alysia. This stupid vow of yours must be put aside. Bashar becomes captain if anything should happen to me. He'll need you. Our Lady knows what he'll do if you die that way."

"I won't *want* to live if you die, so you better survive your *little expedition.* Do you understand?" she said with watering eyes and a quaver in her voice. One drop fell on her perfect cheek and quivered there.

He brushed it tenderly away as he looked at her. Seeing the expression in her eyes, suddenly he needed to blink. He needed to blink a lot, and he needed to leave now to find the communicator immediately before she saw his face and realized how vulnerable he was to her.

*

He commed Icabar and Liana to meet him at Solanje's quarters. The crew knew what he planned but were ordered to keep to their posts and out of possible danger. When the four of them were all together, Solanje unlocked the cabinet. He took out the carriage and removed what they now called "the halo." With shaking hands, Braden touched the panel inside the probe's main housing where its intricate switches and circuits nested.

Solanje pointed out the various controls in the pod. He nodded. Grandfather had given them detailed notes, and he had studied them. Still, he was terrified.

She held the halo, showing him. "That button adjusts the halo to the *human* mind and enables us to communicate without damage across deep space instantaneously. That's critical. Space warps and changes time. This switch compensates for the fluctuations. These intricate dials and buttons here control the volume; these control the field of vision and the depth. Here's the scanning array, and you key this mike so that the one receiving your message can hear you. Then you squeeze this nub to talk. The computer samples the language and if it is stored, it translates automatically. I'm not sure how far the voice range goes. It may be only the one contacted hears what you say."

"Only certain high-level leaders of the Enjelise are in possession of this instrument and have the clearance to use it," added Liana.

Solanje looked at him worriedly. "It's most important that the mode that conforms to the human species is activated. When it crashed on Alysia, the mode had been set for an alien species, causing the device to impose different thought patterns other than human on earlier subjects. Created some problems."

"They died ..." snapped Icabar.

"... others went into a coma or became mentally damaged," added Liana. "Icabar fiddled with it so much that he pushed the right switch, and luckily, it didn't destroy his mind," she concluded.

"Luck had nothing to do with it," retorted Icabar haughtily. "I'm an amazing investigative scientist and detective."

Liana slitted her eyes at him. He smirked back at her. Then, she raised an eyebrow and drawled, "Although I fear some damage may have occurred if recent actions and conclusions are any indication of his current mental state."

Icabar's smirk transformed into a glare.

"All right you two." Braden looked at the device and flipped the switch that activated it. A hum began.

They all stared at it. Braden felt sweat pop out on his forehead.

Icabar broke the silence. "Liana says that Elsinore knows a halo is missing and is panicked about where it could be and who might have it."

"You didn't tell them that we had it?" responded Braden apprehensively.

"No, I agree with you that we need to keep this our secret for now. It seems that these high-minded beings haven't been all that truthful," Icabar pointed out.

"You think?" muttered Braden.

"Lying is a sin," said Icabar sanctimoniously. "Gives you bad karma. They should behave better."

Liana rolled her eyes.

Braden nodded at the comment. "It shows a crack in their 'perfect behavior' argument. There's some sort of division within the Enjelise."

Liana grimaced. "They're not all in agreement."

"No, and other possibilities. We're running out of time and we must warn Alysia. My brother will need time to prepare in case we fail to stop them," said Braden, running his hand over the halo.

"Which them?" asked Liana.

"Any of them," answered Braden.

"So, the sooner I start, the quicker, we'll be able to take the next step." He took a breath and his voice firmed as he eyed the device in his hands.

"Which is?" asked Solanje.

"To use this," answered Braden with finality.

Braden placed the halo over his head. It bobbed a bit and then settled just above the top of his hair. Solanje reached up and nervously adjusted and checked the dials and buttons. She brushed a quick kiss over his cheek. Startled, he squeezed the knob he held, and the halo began to glow.

Everyone stepped back.

Then light flared out, swirling around him. He felt as if he were breaking up into millions of vibrating string-like particles that flowed outward from the ship. His mind skimmed on a matrix of dark matter pushed faster than the speed of light by gravity waves. He soared past whirling galaxies, exploding novias, and lifeless moons, as he glided through the quantum of space.

He concentrated on imagining Richard or his father. If he had a chance to contact anyone, either one would know what to do and do it without creating world panic. If warned in time, either one would have the clout to convince others to take action. However, Richard was his strongest link and held the greatest possibility of contact. Braden focused on his brother, building a picture of him, as he directed his thoughts toward Alysia.

As his thoughts carried him away from the ship, he experienced time wrapped around the limitless galaxies, holding together everything like flour in a dense cake. Time appeared not as a thin ribbon of events strung out, but a uniting force. The past, the present, the future all were there, all at once, woven into a vast tapestry. Man traveled along one track, skimming along the surface, weaving in and out like a wild surfer on a board, navigating the tricky ocean and rivers of time and matter. Dark matter permeated through an infinite number of galaxies and held worlds together, while dark energy pushed everything apart, sending worlds and galaxies catapulting outward. He tried to understand it all, but it went beyond his comprehension.

Then he was falling toward a familiar, whirling galaxy, containing a known planet. Behind him, the glowing stars faded, while Alysia brightened and formed before him. His planet's lush vitality came into view, then the region of the Democratic Union, and finally the bustling city of Tygel. As he thought of his brother, he soared into the cathedral of Our Lady of the Crystal, stopped, and found himself staring at the top of Richard's dark blurry head. Things appeared out of focus, but he could make out Richard standing in front of a long gold table full of ornate lighted candles, his head bent.

What was he doing?

"Richard!" Braden twisted his volume button so Richard could hear him. "Look up, it's me, Braden."

The top of the head jerked up. His brother's eyes stared upward toward him and widened. Braden felt as if he were looking at an out of focus, younger, version of his grandfather.

This was Richard? When had he gotten so old?

"Richard, I'm calling you!"

Braden fiddled with another dial and the hazy scene in front of him came into sharper focus. The lens only clearly showed what was right in front of him while the farther field of vision was still quite blurry.

He didn't have time to play with all the dials. He had to contact Richard quickly and convey his message.

Richard's mouth dropped open.

Braden was having trouble looking past a white obstacle on the other side of Richard that kept blocking a farther view. He raised and widened the field a little to see better and realized that the white obstacle was someone's broad back, covered by a rich white and cream embroidered fabric. He elevated the view. Candles flickered below. He looked toward Richard and fiddled with the focus some more.

Time was short.

"I have to warn you. Hostile aliens are planning to attack Alysia. They got the location from our data banks." As he said the words, he felt the frightening reality.

Richard paled and choked out, "Braden is that you? Are you dead?"

Braden realized that the hologram must appear like a floating ghost. To reassure Richard, he answered, "Dead? Hardly. No, I'm alive." He paused, thinking that he might not live all that much longer if things went bad. He took a mental breath.

"I'm using father's alien device, which allows me to cross time and space instantaneously, so I can talk to you without a time lag, but I only have a small window of opportunity. We found what we went looking for. We found the aliens, but they aren't all friendly. Some may try to invade Alysia. I'll try to stop them, but you must prepare Alysia in case I fail." He choked out these last words.

Understanding flickered across Richard's face, then puzzlement. "Why tell me?"

"The device is thought directed. We're connected because we're brothers. Besides, I trust you to do the right thing. Others may not. You know the right people to contact ... discretely ... to avoid world panic."

Richard's brow furrowed. "I don't have time to create a military space force, much less build a bunch of spaceships in secret," he whispered harshly.

Why was Richard whispering?

Braden answered, "Yes, you do. You still have several annuals before they get to Alysia. The space/time dilation will provide you with time."

"Space/time dilation?"

"I can't explain now."

Then Braden became aware of a murmuring of voices behind Richard.

"Richard, what's that noise?" The voices were getting louder and he heard the rustling of clothes and bodies.

What was going on? Where was he?

Richard's pale face gazed around. "Braden, I'm in the middle of bearing witness to the divinity of Elsinore, Lady of the Crystal. Father Will is performing the sanctification." Richard gestured at the wide white back.

Braden widened the field a little more, tweaking the focus again, and realized that he had accessed Richard at the Church of Our Lady in the middle of some fancy ceremony.

Oh no!

Frantically, he sharpened the focus to a deeper field of vision and looked out over Richard's dark head to see hundreds of worshipers gaping at him. Some had begun to point and shout. He remembered the effect that Richard had caused when he had used the time gate and snatched Elsinore from the battling mob centuries earlier. They had thought her supernatural and built a whole religion around her. This church.

Oh dear. Now they would think ... I must get out.

The congregation began to shout, and the large white obstacle started to turn toward him.

Hurriedly Braden finished, "Begin now! The time dilation effect gives you time, but you must start soon. Alien devils are loose in the universe and threaten Alysia. You must ready a defense. All of humanity could be in jeopardy."

Was his message getting through?

The large congregation behind Richard burst into pandemonium. Some began to scream about the end of the world. A few started fainting. Others were yelling something, but he could not make out the words. People were getting extremely agitated.

Belatedly, Braden realized that he must look like a weird glowing spirit, floating over the high altar. *What have I done? I might have created more damage than I hoped to prevent. I better get out of here.*

"Richard, listen to me!" Braden thought of his dear brother, whom he might never see again. Braden focused his concentration. "Protect Alysia. Protect humanity." The scene before him flickered. The halo transmission weakened.

As he said the words, the wide back completed its circle, came toward him, and he found himself staring into the jowly face of Father Will. Father Will's eyes opened wide in shock.

"It's a sign!" Father Will whispered hoarsely and flung up his arms. "Praise Our Lady!" His face began turning a mottled red. He gasped for breath. "It's a holy visitation," he whispered, peering intently at Braden.

"Prepare your people before they come," admonished Braden.

Father Will inhaled sharply at his words. "A second coming!" he choked out. He gave Braden a terrified stare, grabbed his chest and began to collapse

What? No!

The flickering increased. The connection faded.

Looking past the slumped body of Father Will to Richard, Braden said, "I'm counting on you."

As he said the last words, the scene winked out, and Braden fell up and out into space, as his consciousness returned to *The Seeker.*

Eventually, he felt the hard, cold floor of the ship under his back and heard a murmur of indistinguishable words circling around him overhead.

Had Richard understood? What would he do? Would Alysia now be safe or in worse danger?

Chapter 26

Braden looked up into a ring of blurry faces peering down at him. He blinked and rubbed his face, trying to remember where he was and what had happened. His thoughts felt like mud.

Where am I? Oh, I'm on a spaceship.

"Who's at helm?" he asked worriedly.

The remark caused a collective sigh of relief.

"Are you all right?" asked Solanje, as she laid a hand on his cheek and put a pillow under his head.

"I think so," he said, struggling to sit up. His head felt as if it were going to explode and his body felt like it was made of rubber. Gasping, he slid back down. Maybe he needed a moment.

"So?" Solanje asked, impatience edging her voice.

"So what?" He tried to clear away the cobwebs.

"What happened?" asked Crystal, looking around at the others with frustration written on her face. She waved something with a strong odor under his nose, and he choked violently as the sharp smell slammed into his senses.

"Whew!" his head jerked back. Sinuses roiled. "Geesh!"

"Here, try this." Icabar leaned forward as Crystal lifted his head and offered a tumbler of a potent liquid that contained large amounts of alcohol.

Braden took a sip with shaking hands and sputtered. "Where'd you get that?" he demanded, choking.

"A guy's got to keep something for emergencies," Icabar answered blithely. "It's the finest we have."

"I thought stuff like that wasn't supposed to be on board." Braden gave him an official Captain's glare.

"It's for medicinal purposes," Icabar, blinked innocently.

After a look of disbelief from Braden, Icabar added reluctantly, "Okay, truth is that we put together a small still, and Tessa recently revealed an unknown cooking skill handed down from her father. An ancient recipe. Most potent."

"I see." Braden felt life returning to tingling limbs. The stuff was working. "In that case, give me some more." He waved a hand at Icabar and leaned in for another sip, this time steeling himself for the kick. A violent explosion hit his mouth, and a warm glow suffused his body, as he took another sip, and then a strong swallow. Clarity began to return and then strength. He sat up and tried to manage a shaky stand, leaning against a chair. Energy ebbed. He slumped to the chair with a grunt, breathing heavily.

"Are you going to tell us, or do we just keep wondering?" This time it was Liana demanding an answer. Everyone stood around him as he tried to remember what it was they wanted to know.

"The ship. Is anyone watching the ship?" He tried stalling for time so he could collect his thoughts.

"Adam's at captain's seat." Icabar waved a hand in the direction of Navcom. "Glaze's on comm. Bashar's nearby, or he might be with Robert at the converter."

"Okay, then," mumbled Braden.

Memory was returning. *The alien device. I used the alien device and created a riot on Alysia.* He sighed and saw six eyes riveted on him, demanding a report.

Taking a deep breath, he said, "I would suspect the thing works like a virtual reality communicator and recorder that uses gravity waves for instantaneous spatial transit. I really don't know the science, but I talked to my brother Richard in what I believe was current space/time. He looked funny, but it was him."

"You actually spoke to him?" Icabar asked. Voices started chattering all at once, confusing him with all the noise.

"Yeah, I'd say I did." Everyone paused to listen. "He looked old, like a grown-up man, not a kid who just graduated."

"There's some data for DeVey's relativity theory at least," Icabar offered helpfully.

"Did you warn them? What are they going to do?" Solanje queried.

"I warned Richard, but my timing could've been better. He appeared busy." Braden looked away. He cleared his throat.

"Busy? Doing what?" asked Liana with a frown.

"He was in some important religious ceremony at the Church of Our Lady of the Crystal."

Memory of what had happened flooded in.

Maybe it had only been a dream, but it seemed very real now that he remembered it. Especially the way Richard had looked and acted. Very much like Richard would look and act. He wished it had only been a dream, but he was very much afraid it had really happened.

"Oh God, what have I done?"

"Why do you say that?" asked Solanje worriedly.

He put his face into his hands as he remembered the experience. "I made contact, but a ceremony was in progress. Father Will collapsed at the altar. I might have startled him into a heart attack. I might have killed him."

"He thought you were some divine visitation, didn't he?" accused Liana. "He was always a bit of a fanatic about that stuff. It wouldn't surprise me if he saw you hovering about, he might think you were a holy witness or spiritual being come to visit."

Braden lifted his chin, firming his voice. "As hard as that concept may be, yes, I expect that's what most of the congregation was also thinking. I heard Father Will say it, but Richard knows better."

Crystal groaned. "Father Will! Oh Fate, he'll make it into some big splashy miracle. You know how he's been after Richard for years to consecrate Elsinore."

Braden sighed, "That's what the ceremony was all about. Father Will was making her a saint."

"What a mess." Liana rubbed her forehead.

He firmed his shoulders and looked her in the eye. "Well, what's done is done. I just hope that Richard understood what I said and will build a defense system in case we can't stop what's coming. I did what I could. I might try again, just to make sure there was no damage done, but right now, I need rest. Then we take care of business here." Wearily, Braden looked around. Alysia seemed far away—like some faraway dream. It just didn't seem real. Reality was here, on this ship.

"We need to formulate a plan before Lucien arrives," said Icabar.

"Does anyone have any ideas yet?" asked Dyra.

"They came out of the Enjelise's past, why can't the Enjelise deal with them?" asked Crystal. "Aren't they supposed to be powerful spiritual entities?"

Braden straightened up abruptly. "Wait, forget the past, how about the future? Where's Joel?" He stood up with a bit of wobble.

"Here, here." Joel pushed to the front. "What?"

"About your dreams—what do you see? Isn't that part of this foreseeing Talent Icabar tells me you have? Let's use it." Braden looked at him expectantly.

"Er, maybe that's not such a good idea. I've become linked to this Lucien entity, and I better warn you that he's out for revenge on both humans and Enjelise. He blames the humans for causing their conflict and hates the Enjelise for punishing his people. He acts like a jealous sibling, the way I see it. He may be trying to take over my mind, and I don't know how long I can ward him off and maintain control. If he succeeds, then it might be better for all if, if ..." Joel choked. "If you just kill me. I don't know what I might do if he gains control. He's trying to."

"Kill you? We need you! You have a link that tells us what they're doing." Braden cast a glance at Joel and raised an eyebrow. "Besides, you're an important member of my crew and on my ship, life is considered sacred, right Robert?" Braden looked around.

"He's at the converter, sir," coughed Dyra.

Braden swayed and he put a hand on Joel's shoulder. "Tell me, Joel, what's happening with your friend?"

Joel stiffened. "He's not my friend, but I do feel a certain sympathy for him. His life hasn't been easy. None of their lives have been easy. I can understand their rage.

I'd be angry too. They were dumped in a horrible place and left to fend for themselves."

"I'm not going to give him a lot of sympathy when he's rampaging our way with murder and mayhem as his agenda," Braden argued.

Joel rubbed his face with shaking hands. "Okay, but you might not like it. In the last dream I had, we were in a swirling tunnel. Flashes of light were everywhere, and stuff was floating around. I saw explosions. Then, I woke up. I didn't want to upset everyone, so I didn't say anything."

"Yes!" Braden grabbed a surprised Joel. "That's the answer."

Joel looked shocked. "What do you mean? I wasn't too happy with the vision. Things looked pretty scary."

"We didn't all die, did we?" Dyra tried to sound optimistic.

"I didn't see that exactly, no," hedged Joel. His shoulders relaxed a bit. He grimaced a tentative smile.

"So, that's good." Dyra looked around defiantly.

Braden clapped his hands. "No, you saw the stargate. We'll use it. Remember how we came here? I bet we can lose a lot of them just going back through that hellhole."

Liana protested, "We don't need to kill them, just divert them to somewhere else, away from Alysia."

"Some of them will die. Some of us may die," interrupted Braden firmly. "It could become nasty for everyone, especially the Enjelise. They're defenseless. Also, don't forget that some of *the Fallen* might eventually head to Alysia if we only divert them. No, I want Alysia safe and them gone." Braden clenched a fist tightly.

"Besides, if these *Fallen* are coming to attack us, then we have a right to defend ourselves," interrupted Solanje.

"Don't you think that the Enjelise feel the same way about us?" added Liana. "They feel we threaten their way of life."

"We haven't attacked the Enjelise directly. It's different," argued Braden.

"Lucien's lot hasn't attacked us at all, yet," countered Joel.

"Better we're prepared, because it sounds like he plans to attack us," countered Braden. He scanned the group. "Glaze?"

"Yes, sir," the comm crackled. "Right here."

"Ah, right, at Navcom. Glaze, you're the master of the star map. You know this universe better than anyone. Find us a route back to that gate and see what else out there we can use to get rid of these folks. Each one of you is here at this precise moment for a specific reason, and to survive we're going to have to pull together."

Braden began firing out orders. "Adam and Robert will need to retrofit four warships from orbit that we can use. Elsinore offered them, and I'm accepting. I don't want us to be one target. We need to split up and spread out. We need as many ships as we can crew safely. I'll talk to Elsinore and have her get some of her people to train us on them."

Nervous glances passed around the group. Icabar wiped at a sweaty forehead and blinked.

"Bashar," Braden looked around. "Where's Bashar?"

"We said he was at Navcom, Captain," answered Icabar defensively, "or with Robert at the converter." His voice quavered at bit.

"Oh, right." Braden combed a hand through his hair. "Get him to find us something to use for our counterattack. *The Fallen* are aliens and will most likely have different weapons than we're used to. What we have is limited since this wasn't exactly a military mission and we aren't armed for battle. We'll have to get innovative and even borrow some from the Enjelise if they have anything. Maybe Joel can rummage around in Lucien's mind to find out what kind of weapons *the Fallen* are carrying and what attack strategy they have. Hearing that, Bashar?"

"Yes, sir."

"Liana, you and Icabar need to talk with Elsinore's people and find out what they can do to defend themselves or help us defend them."

"On it." Liana straightened up and rubbed her hands together. She canted her head at Icabar, and he joined her to head out in her wake.

"Joel, you need to interpret your dreams for clues as to what weapons they have. Also, we need to know how far away and how much time we have until these *Fallen* arrive. Divert his attention away from what we're really doing. If he gets curious again, try to read his mind. Find things that we can use against him."

Joel grimaced. "Don't tell me any of your plans, then. I'll help all I can, but Lucien may be able to get inside my mind and find out what we're doing. So, the less I know, the better."

"Right. Solanje, I'm putting you in charge of watching over Joel," ordered Braden.

"Yes, sir."

"I'll help too." Surprised, Braden saw that the voice belonged to Dyra. Joel smiled at her faintly, a red stain creeping over his cheeks.

What was this? Dyra and Joel? Past and future. Oh well. Of course—it made a weird kind of sense.

Next, Braden faced Crystal. "Crystal, we need to know everything we can about these crystal life forms. You and Adam are the experts there. Work with Adam to find out what we can about them. I want to know if they are the enemy or not."

"Yes, sir."

"Solanje, you need to also come with me to put numbers through the computer. Once Glaze locates the gate, then I need to know the exact trajectories that will get us there and home. It'll require precise computations. I want to preset what I can."

"Okay, everyone. Let's get ready."

*

Braden, Liana and Bashar met with Elsinore on the ship. Braden shuffled some star maps and waved the two to a seat, as he pushed his monitor toward them and sat down, stretching his legs out under his desk.

Elsinore leaned forward. Braden blinked. She appeared to be flickering in and out of his vision. "Our energy barrier will slow them down once they enter our system," she said, sketching a line on the map he had pulled up on the monitor.

"Is that the barrier that stopped us when we came out the gate?" asked Braden.

"Yes," Elsinore answered. "The net protects us from unfriendly invaders with the gate so close to our world. However, Lucien's people will come from within our system and won't come through the gate. They'll come from the other side, but the net will still be effective."

"So that provides a warning and will be our first line of defense." Bashar tapped the areas on the screen.

Braden nodded. "We're still too few, however. How about we throw holographic images of ships up onto their screens or onto objects that we float in space to make them believe we have more ships than we do?"

"That's an interesting idea." Elsinore nodded. "Clever. We're also working on energy transmutation."

"Energy transmutation?" Braden asked, puzzled.

"I explained that all living things evolve through layers of energy, seeking to reach higher levels. We've been able to visit your lower level when the need was great, but always our goal was to transform to a higher level. Your species lives at a certain physical level and then at death, you decide whether you're ready to ascend to a higher vibration, or to go back and learn further lessons from the physical. Sometimes it takes many lifetimes to gather the understanding that enables an entity to move up into a higher energy ring."

"What happens to those who 'transform'?" asked Liana.

"They enter a different reality, or a different universe. We're the same in reality as ants and humans. You share DNA and environment with ants, and yet, both remain mostly unaware of each other's daily existence. We're occasionally aware of your existence, yet most humans are seldom aware of ours. Most often our attention is elsewhere, and we're in another dimension."

"You're comparing us to ants?" protested Bashar.

"You'll have to evolve a lot more before you reach our current level." Elsinore shrugged.

"What happens in this other reality?" Liana asked.

"We help run many universes. Every energy level has a role to play."

"Universes! More than one?" exclaimed Bashar.

"Yes." Her eyes widened in surprise at his lack of knowledge. "Surely, you knew that there are many."

Braden, Liana, and Bashar all stared in astonishment at one another.

Braden cleared his throat. "So, when are you planning to transform to this 'higher level'?"

"Soon."

"Soon! How soon? And how many will transform?" asked Braden.

"Most of us hope our transformation will work. We've been evolving for a while and now it's time. However, some are not yet ready and will be brought back into the body to stay behind, but most hope to go on."

"It sounds like you're leaving us here to face *the Fallen* alone," complained an irate Braden. The humans exchanged panic-stricken glances.

Elsinore explained, "You showed us that you'd be willing to jeopardize your own lives to protect your species. We feel that you're ready. We didn't want you to make the mistakes that we made. We focused so much on peace and enlightenment that we no longer could, or cared, to fight. Besides, we don't want a war. Violence begets violence and opens the door to evil and chaos. We're not interested. We've other things we must do. Now's your time to grow and learn to take care of yourselves without our interference. We wanted to see if you would make a choice that showed us that you were ready to take care of your own and you did that when you sought out Adam and Tessa."

"Yeah right, I thought it smelled too much like a test," commented Braden bitterly. He crossed his arms and went silent.

"You're abandoning us," protested Bashar.

Elsinore shook her head. "We don't think of it as that. We think of it as letting you grow up. You want to wage war, then wage war. Both of you are so eager for violence that we decided to let you confront each other and let the stronger, more intelligent, species survive. It's time for us to let go and move on.

Braden uncrossed his arms and slammed a fist into his other hand. "Not yet! Not now! We need your help. This isn't our fault. We didn't create this war, your people did," he protested.

"Many have already translated."

"They may try to move Haven, too," said Liana.

"What!" Braden stared at Elsinore in disbelief.

"It's a popular option," she answered.

Chapter 27

Joel closed his eyes wearily. He never thought anyone would want to encourage those awful dreams! He'd been surprised at Braden's reaction and now wished he had said something sooner about the repeating dream of the swirling tunnel. The gate—of course. Not recognizing it before; it was now obvious. He had thought his dream foreshadowed death. Dying might be like that--spiraling down a tunnel and meeting shadowy beings on the other side, but now the dream presented a possible different interpretation.

Braden wanted him to connect to Lucien to get information. That scared him. Gulping down the sweet concoction that Crystal had assured would induce a dream state, his last thoughts before he dreamed were elation at Dyra's warm feelings for him. He had admired her from afar and was excited that she might return his affection.

He felt Solanje come in and sit by him as his consciousness ebbed. She said something about Icabar having duty, and Dyra coming as soon as she finished talking to someone. Picking up his hand, she patted it softly. Then the drug kicked in, and he began to dream.

*

His body floated out of awareness, hovered in the void, and slid through dark space like a magnet drawn to an iron core. In a blink, he was standing under a red sky. Crimson fire blazed along mountaintops and flung plumes of smoke into the roiling caldron they called an atmosphere. The land burned. Surely these poor beings deserved better than this hellhole. Surely, there were other worlds in the vast universe that would have been more suitable.

This was extreme punishment.

He witnessed their warped bodies, mutated by radiation; felt their twisted minds, transformed by hate. Powerful feelings blocked out rational thought. Pain and agony fueled their anger.

Joel felt a link snap into place. He suddenly saw the world through Lucien's enhanced vision. Emotions flooded his thoughts in a tide so overwhelming that he could scarcely breathe. He felt a mind so powerful, so coated with rage and despair that it was as if he rode a wild beast. Something was different. Lucien felt stronger than before. A Crystal sparkled in a rough grip in front of him. Lucien clutched it so hard that Joel watched blood oozing between his white fingers and felt a sharp sympathetic pain.

The results of the Crystal's influence in accelerating their evolution could be seen all around in the vastly altered landscape. Sophisticated cities nestled in hollowed out mountains; domed fields protected flourishing crops beneath them. Factories added their smoke and ash to the clouded atmosphere.

Then Joel saw the ships out a window and realized that he stood on the bridge of the largest one. An explosion of rocket blasts sent winds whipping and whirling around the metal beasts, causing the ground to shake beneath him. The backlash of flames from their igniting engines razed the edges of fragile greenery, scorching the earth as a phalanx of ships rose with a mighty leap into the thick atmosphere. Outside the ship's viewplate, space grew closer and closer, dark and dangerous.

Joel counted rapidly and estimated some thirty ships in formation around him. He probed to learn what they carried in weaponry and technology. Flames, heat, fire would be useless in space. He noted projectiles with chemicals that exploded on impact and laser weaponry. the like of which he had never seen before. Delicate crystal beings rode at the front on the bridge of each ship, guiding them, linking them together through electronic pathways, enabling all the ships to work in unison. Each one was tuned to Lucien's ship, as he led them out, at long last, to wreak their revenge. They'd found the Enjelise's home world and now soared toward it, bent on destruction. Lucien's exultation flooded Joel's senses.

Joel felt Lucien become aware of his presence. With a surge of exultation, Lucien wrenched control from Joel and mentally examined him in a firm grip.

"I have you now, human," he heard him shout.

*

Solanje looked at Joel's sleeping face and saw it twitch and moan. Something was happening and she wasn't sure what. She leaned over him to study his reactions when suddenly his eyes popped open.

"Joel?"

The face was Joel's, but what looked out at her were no longer Joel's eyes. They cast around, as if taking in the surroundings, and then, finally settled back on her face. A feral grin stretched across the mouth. His cheekbones appeared sharper.

"Ah yes, the Enjelise's pet human, I see." The tone was harsh and guttural, not Joel's voice at all, and the eyes ... the eyes were demon eyes with flashes of red deep inside.

"You're not Joel," she stated, trying to find courage, somewhere. Her whole body shook as she eased out away from him, never taking her eyes off his face. She felt her heartbeat start racing and sweat slicked her forehead. She scrambled back.

A cunning expression shifted across the creature's features as it stretched its arms and sat up. It rolled his shoulders and stretched out Joel's arms looking at them curiously. "Solanje." It paused a moment as if tasting her name, then studied her. "You're computer systems. You work Navcom."

It appeared to be able to access knowledge from Joel's memories. A shiver ran down her back.

What had happened to Joel?

Fear for his sanity flickered across Solanje's thoughts. Somehow Lucien had taken possession of Joel. This was the enemy, not Joel. She took a deep cleansing breath to prepare. She called up the way of the Shetang and readied her mind and body for whatever this creature might attempt.

The entity smiled at her. She wasn't fooled. He raised an eyebrow. "His memories record a world called Alysia, and he says that you know the location and course. I need the vectors and flight trajectories that will lead us there. You have that knowledge."

She leaned back away from him. "You're not Joel. You're Lucien. Where's Joel?"

"Don't think of him. He doesn't have the knowledge, but you do. We should strike a bargain, you and I."

"No," she answered, trying not to show her fear. "Never!"

His voice made her shiver.

"Don't say 'no' until you've heard what I offer. I have certain abilities that might interest you." He smirked at her.

"There's nothing I desire that would make me betray my world to the likes of you." She firmed shaky words as she struggled for calm.

"Ah, you use the word 'desire.' Such a wonderful word. Strange you should mention it. It's a strong human emotion. You humans expend a lot of energy on that emotion. I have only one passion: hate, and that fills me entire. I know who Joel desires, but I wonder what or who you desire?"

The direction of this conversation frightened her. Despite the terrifying powers of the creature before her, she would rather a physical confrontation with him rather than this attempt at mind games, but there was Joel who would suffer if things got physical—so she played along for now.

She glared at the being. "There's nothing I desire that you can offer me."

Joel's mouth pursed. He leaned forward, a grin on his face. "Maybe, maybe not. Not fortune, I suspect. Nor fame. You're not the type." He pointed a finger at her. "Health? I think not." He shook his head and dropped his hand. "You have health." He cocked his head. "Honor? I have beguiled some for honor, and you could be such a one, but I think not. You have forged a shield of honor through tears of loss, whether you realize it or not. Love? Ah, now there's an idea. Maybe pure love. No human can resist the lure of pure love."

"You cannot tempt me with love," she retorted.

"Is that so? What about your most courageous captain? Or the other? The helm?" He stopped to consider. "Joel seems to think that you care for them. But desire and love are different emotions. You care for them, but they are already yours. There's nothing I can tempt you with there that you do not cup in the palm of your hands already.

The creature, Joel, shook his head with a serious expression, and then a small smirk emerged across his lips and a light flared in the depth of his eyes. "However, there *is* one whom you have lost and think never to see again. He's beyond your reach, but you desire him every moment you take breath. Such a deep wellspring of emotion for one that considers herself past any feelings."

"There's no one like that."

"Ah, but what about someone named Yo Chi? Joel thinks the pain of losing him is like a sharp knife that has cut out your heart."

Yo Chi!

A look of triumph swam across Joel's strange features. Joel, but not Joel.

She caught her breath. His words conjured up the image of her dear dead brother. She often thought of him and still missed him. She recalled his easy manner and the feeling of safety he had given her whenever he was around. Her big brother had always protected and cared for her, letting her lean on him when all seemed too much to bear. Angry tears filled her eyes as she remembered his brutal death.

All her life others had made decisions for her life, while she carried the responsibility. She had been told who to marry, and then, her betrothed had tried to kill her. She had been told not speak, and when she finally had, her voice brought death. She had been told to hold onto the alien device, and it had been wrenched from her grasp.

Now, she stared consummate evil and vile temptation in the face, and she was alone. Yo Chi was not here to help her when she needed him the most.

Yo Chi. My brother.

Loneliness threatened to engulf her, but then she saw his image in her mind's eye. She saw his familiar dark bulk. She saw his engaging smile, bane to all women of the Ching T'Karre. She felt his presence, and she knew that he still loved her and would be proud of all she had accomplished. She wanted to always feel that he would be proud of what she did, no matter what the temptation, even if that temptation was him. She had kept to her true self in all that she had done and honored the ways. She had disciplined herself each moment to resist temptation, at painful cost.

The creature shook her arm to get her attention. He smiled radiantly at her and said, "We can make a deal. I have the power to bring back your brother from his death. I can give you this greatest desire: to bring back his pure love, his strength, but first, I need the coordinates that give the location of the world you call Alysia. That's the price. Take me to navigation and show me. No one will ever know. They'll only see Joel, and it will be him they accuse. He will pay the price, and you'll have your brother alive."

Solanje closed her eyes and thought.

Ah, to have him back! To feel his love and support once again.

The temptation was strong, but all her life she had disciplined herself to resist temptation and fulfill her duty. Isn't that what Braden had seen and chastised her for? Shift in and shift out, she had resisted the siren call of the crystals, her love for Bashar, her desire for Braden, the lure of the alien probe, and now …

She laughed and watched surprise flash across the stranger's face. She thought, *Who did this creature think she was that he offered so confidently the unthinkable?*

"No!" Solanje felt her mind go cold. Grief wrenched her. She had been taught to be true to the code, to bear the difficult, and meet the obligation. No crystal, no chemicals, no cyberaids, and no deals had softened her life. She stood as she was and dealt with life bare-handed. She had disciplined herself all her life, every moment of it, against temptation in all its forms.

Out of everyone on this godforsaken ship, this piece of evil has picked the wrong person to try to tempt. The absolutely wrong person!

She bent her head forward and felt a strand of hair brush her cheek as if acknowledging her status as a Royal of the Ching T'Karre. She must banish this creature from Joel's mind, but there was only one way she knew how. She screamed; a scream so strong that it shattered all thought.

The creature rose in agony. Joel's eyes went wide. Solanje felt the pain of the entity's rough grasp as Joel's body yanked her toward the door, heading toward Navcom. Blood dripped down her arm where his nails scratched her.

"We're done with talking," he said harshly. He stumbled and grabbed at a panel as she screamed at him again. He clapped shaking hands to his head.

A commotion sounded in the corridor, and Liana's pale face appeared with Braden not far behind her. All they saw was Joel pulling at her, but he stopped abruptly when they approached.

"Help us," Solanje shouted.

Suddenly Elsinore stood at the entrance.

Solanje saw Joel's eyes fill with terror when he saw her, and he released his grip. Then he screamed and clutched his head. He twisted around furiously and slapped at her, missing her, and flailed at empty air. Then, his eyes rolled up into his head as he slumped to the floor. They watched with astonishment as temptation fled the ship, empty-handed.

*

"Solanje, it's okay now." Braden took her hand to lead her out. Vacant eyes stared at him.

He brushed her hair back and picked her up as she collapsed limply into his arms. He nodded to Liana and Elsinore to gather Joel who lay groaning on the deck.

Elsinore and Liana each took a side and lifted him up.

"Able-bodied male needed on deck three ASAP," Braden announced urgently into his comm.

Voices could be heard as feet pounded down the corridor.

"Braden, I did it," she whispered.

"You certainly did," he murmured. 'Don't talk. Let us take care of you."

Dyra volunteered to stay while Crystal checked out Joel and Solanje.

Once Braden was satisfied that there was nothing more he could do, he took Elsinore back to the bridge, so that she could pinpoint what solar system *the Fallen* would be coming from.

"Thank you for sending him away." He gazed sideways at Elsinore.

"Solanje had already broken his control," she answered smoothly. "I just hurried him along. She's proven that humans have gotten strong enough to defeat *the Fallen* if they need to."

"I wish I had your confidence," he gritted out.

Glaze joined them at Navcom. They were standing by the navigational computer while Elsinore showed them *The Fallen's* star system and how to navigate through the gate when Crystal entered.

"What's that?" Crystal asked sharply.

By the tone of her voice, Braden could tell she was upset.

"What's what?" He looked around.

"Is that *a crystal*?" She pointed to something just past the computer monitor and ten notches from his elbow.

He looked down. An oblong shaped rock with crystal facets sat pushed back in a corner near the navigational computer. It had been glowing but winked out when he looked at it.

"It's probably some old stone Adam must have left behind," he answered unsteadily.

"No, that's part of a Master Crystal," answered Elsinore. "And it shouldn't be in Navcom. They're capable of downloading computer information."

"Braden, that *rock* was wedged dangerously close to our navigational computer that has all the data concerning the ship and the star maps. I thought I saw a glow coming from it." Crystal reached for it.

Braden eased it out and handed it to Crystal. "Okay, get it out of here."

Crystal frowned as she flipped the rock over. There were flat facets and rough indentations on it, but it didn't squeak or blink or purr. It lay lifeless in her hand.

She looked intently at Braden. "Odd that it appeared here while we were engaged elsewhere. If I didn't think I was losing my mind, I would say that Lucien was the distraction and here is the real danger."

"Crystals never harmed humans when bonded on Alysia, that I know of," commented Braden.

"No, just started a horrid war," snapped Crystal.

"Get it out," he agreed.

Immediately Crystal picked it up and left, eyeing it as if would sprout horns and fly away. "Where does Adam keep his hammer?" she murmured.

Suddenly, she yelped and dropped the crystal. "It burned my hand!" She looked around for something to hit it with. Braden reached under his console and handed her a blaster. "Use the handle," he urged.

She smashed the rock. It flashed and shot out sparks. She hit it again and again until it finally cracked and lay still.

*

"Look, Bashar," Adam said. "Here's the technology for the alien's jump drive. You got it figured, yet?" Adam and Bashar were working in an alien ship's systems bay.

"Not at all. But if this baby here can jump the ship a vast distance in a nanosecond, like the Enjelise implied it can, I really want to try it out." Bashar eagerly prodded at the assortment of clustered energy nanotubes and jump drive activators.

"You're insane, you know?"

"Glaze did say it's going to be risky, but Elsinore claims these ships are heavily shielded for high radiation particle blasts, neutrino interference, and multi-sized space debris. They're tough little ships, and I want to drive one." Bashar lovingly patted the installation.

"But you do understand the physics of dark matter?" Adam leaned against the console of one of the newly refurbished ships, waving a partial resonator around. "Joel says that our existing weapons may not work against *the Fallen*. He said that he noticed laser-based weaponry, but he didn't mention that he saw anything like our Synthetic Aperture Dark Matter Ejector!" Adam brandished the device at Bashar.

Bashar laughed. "We called her SAMiE and I'm well aware of her capabilities." He grinned. "Studied it at the Academy. Your name was mentioned." He nodded his head in agreement, and clapped Adam on his shoulder. "A nice piece of research."

Adam tapped the device he was holding. "You bet. I studied dark matter and dark energy theory. My family is also descended from the people of the Deep Forest. In the Craft Hall there, many of my relatives studied sound frequencies, so they could explore new forms of music. My cousin Inge taught me about shaping vibrations through her resonating bowls and a lot about what specialized frequency resonating can do."

"Your project generated a lot of interest." Bashar stroked the console that was going to house the weapon.

Adam continued. "When experimenting with alternate weapons at Sunpointe, I noticed that various points of resonation used in critical ways can be very destructive. In the old histories, a single note started a frequency resonation that initiated an avalanche that smothered and destroyed a horde of invading Islianders. Grandmother used to read me the story of the battle at Crest Ridge. That made me think. If dark matter could be harnessed and directed to certain frequencies, it might provide endless power, both constructive and destructive."

Bashar rubbed his hands together. "Your ideas worked and now we have a really awesome space weapon that I plan to try out."

"It's very powerful, accurate, and fires with incredible speed at multiple targets in vacuum almost instantaneously." Adam gestured with his index finger as if firing a laser. "She's a beaut."

"Joel's dream saw crystal beings on each ship, linking them. By duplicating a few more of your SAMiEs, and retrofitting them onto the Enjelise's ships, we might be able to shatter the crystal being's hyperspace mind link. If we could break that link, it would disorganize their communications."

"All right let me look at the ejector part," said Adam. He took it and examined it in his large hands. "I think I can do it."

"By the way, how's Tessa?" Bashar casually inquired.

Adam shrugged. "Last I heard, she talked the Enjelise into letting the animals off our ship so they could breed better. That planet is unbelievably fertile. Also, there's a large garden that she's cultivating there. The soil is rich, and she can grow food faster and healthier, so she has taken both embryos and seeds down there. She has tested extensively for adverse elements and has found that food grown on the planet has more nutrients than ship cultivated food. She has found native vegetables and herbs that she plans to can and dry for space travel."

"There's a rumor that the Enjelise are disappearing," Adam mused.

"We barely saw them in the first place." Bashar snorted.

"Something's going on. Dyra and Liana are trying to find out what."

"Here, we can retrofit your SAMiE into the facing section of the ship and mount it there. I think you're on the right track using a Dark Matter Ejector. Normal sound waves won't travel through vacuum to penetrate solid matter, but dark matter does. I'll bet that they don't have anything like this. See if you can construct three more, and I'll fit them into the other ships as well. This is a good idea, Adam," encouraged Bashar.

Chapter 28

"You really want me to do this?" Adam's deep voice rang around the room.

"Adam, it's for the survival of the species," said a patient Braden.

"I had thought I'd be in the fight. I come from a long line of mercenaries and soldiers. We're battle veterans."

Braden regarded Adam. "You can win a fight without firing a weapon, you know. This is really important."

Bashar tipped back his head and raised his hands. "You want all of humankind to be destroyed, wiped out? A distant memory if we lose?"

"Well, no. But that's not going to happen."

"There's the possibility these Fallen could defeat us and attack Alysia," argued Braden.

"A possibility, but highly unlikely."

"They're pretty vicious from all Joel says," added Icabar.

"If there's even the possibility, we have to take measures, then you're the man," Braden argued. He clapped Adam on the shoulder. "I need a male volunteer. Tessa suggested you, and since ..."

"You're the most logical choice," chimed in Bashar, nodding. "Besides, Tessa has things already started down there."

Liana smirked at him. "In more ways than you can imagine."

"I agree," added Glaze. "It's our plan B just in case things don't go the way we hope. You would be a last desperate chance for humanity's survival."

"Desperate is the right word." Adam surveyed the group. "What about Icabar or Joel?"

"Joel has to handle *the Fallen,* and well, Icabar as a father and helpmate doesn't really resonate."

Bashar added his agreement to the others. "Robert and I can handle the ship's power systems, now that you've got all the SAMiEs installed."

"The planet is beautiful, and I have nothing tying me to Alysia, but I still feel like I'm deserting everyone here."

"This is far from running away. Surviving there will be hard work. You're not getting off easily, believe me," answered Braden.

"You'll have to deal with Tessa and her cabbage sprouts," piped up Icabar. "She's talking about spinach too."

Liana interrupted any further green vegetable discussions. "She's already had a start on the task. She's been down there planting and cultivating. She loves it there, and it will be best for your child and your children to come."

"Child? Children!" Adam started backing away.

"She's pregnant, Adam," revealed Liana.

"Pregnant! Frag! I thought you women couldn't get pregnant. Didn't they do something to prevent that from happening?" Stunned, Adam could only gape at her.

"We thought so, but somehow she got pregnant." Liana shrugged.

"Are you sure it's mine?" Doubt edged Adam's voice as he stared disbelievingly at everyone.

"It is," smiled Crystal. "I ran some tests. It's yours. You got anyone else who might qualify?"

Adam glanced at Braden who shook his head in denial and warded away Adam's accusatory glare. "Never mind the details, Crystal," he responded irritably. "I suppose you're right." Adam looked away. "Those fragging sugar berries. Made a man, well, eager."

Everyone studied Adam's face. They had all agreed on the idea earlier and hoped Adam would volunteer. Just in case the battle went awry, just in case their world was destroyed and mankind exterminated for all time. Adam and Tessa would be their contingency plan for the human race, just in case they failed to stop the attackers.

Just in case.

Adam's job would be to populate Haven and spread the species after the Enjelise abandoned their world. He had proven that he had the ability. Both had proven fertile. Something in, or on, Haven had made them fertile. Or just the lack of shipboard birth control medication might have done it.

Braden and the rest had to protect Haven by diverting the attackers away from the planet or destroying them completely. A lot was at risk. *The Fallen* might return to claim the planet if they defeated the humans. Then Adam and Tessa would be in danger but might still survive with some remaining Enjelise's help.

Adam sighed. "All right. Both Liana and Tessa suggested the idea to me. I just didn't want you to think that I was a coward. I can't say that it isn't the most wonderful place of all the worlds I've seen so far; it is. I can't say that I don't love Tessa or wouldn't be proud to be her husband; I would. But you guys need us. You're going to be out your best cook and gardener, not to mention the great job I do in the energy matrix and keeping the ship functioning."

"Dispersion is extinction insurance," explained Braden.

"Yeah, I see your point. Well, I'm willing if everyone approves." Adam gazed around at all of them.

Braden clapped his hands happily. "We were hoping you'd say that. Everyone has agreed to the idea. We all thank you."

"You'll marry us, won't you Braden? She'll want to be married. You know how women are."

"Just say 'I do', and you'll be good to go," said Braden laughing.

"No, she'll want a formal, legal ceremony." Adam looked stubborn. "We'll want to start out proper."

Braden put an arm on his shoulder. "I'll be glad to read the formal words myself. As captain of the ship, I have the authority. The girls have some goodies already prepared and ready for a celebration. Glaze will take you down as soon as you're ready," added Braden.

"That soon? You haven't given me nearly enough time to get packed."

Liana put her hand on his shoulder and looked him in the eye. "You want this, Adam. You'll be good there with Tessa as a botanist, and you the geologist and resident handy man. You can fix those ships, too," she added. "It's a fresh new world with a fresh new start for both of you."

Adam jerked back. "I won't miss the mind reading one bit," he retorted. "And the manipulation. I see what you've done to Robert."

Silence as deep as space descended on the group for a shocked moment. Then Joel stepped forward. "It shouldn't take long to get packed," he urged, giving him a pat. "Look, I see this turning out good for you and all of Haven. There's a bright future down there with a planet that needs taking care of properly."

"Yeah, and I won't miss all the future predictions and dreams you scare us with either, Joel. I like my future in my hands."

Joel shrugged. "Now, it will be .all up to you."

Adam's eyes widened. He stepped back a bit and breathed heavily.

So, Adam packed everything he could think of that he might need. The beautiful wood sculpture of a soaring bird, given to him by his maternal grandmother rested alongside one of Inge's resonating bowls. They loaded the shuttle with all his possessions. The others followed in a second shuttle.

Braden pulled Adam aside. "I'll leave one of the Enjelise shuttles with you. Another convoy of mother ships with fighters is still orbiting Haven and sometime, you may be able to reactivate them and return to Alysia ... or explore other worlds. If we're successful in our mission, maybe I'll return and see how things are going. So, do well." He smiled.

Glaze and Crystal piloted everyone down to the planet. The women arrived dressed in their best clothes. Dyra even found Tessa a real dress, and not just regulation ship attire, for her to wear. Solanje combed out Tessa's hair and wove an intricate Ching T'Karre hairdo for her. Crystal gathered a handful of bright flowers for her to carry while Adam came up with a heirloom ring. Bashar stood as the best man and Braden read the vows and pronounced them man and wife. Adam leaned in to tentatively give her a kiss when she grabbed him and laid one on his lips so hard that could be heard back on the ship. Everyone laughed and raised a tube of Tessa's finest.

Food and more drinks came out of the shuttles and the party began. At one point, Icabar tried to sing, but loud shouting and protests soon dissuaded him from that notion. Unfortunately, time was short and there was still a lot to do. Braden congratulated the lucky couple, and suggested everyone retire to the ship, but the newlyweds. Then, Robert and Joel ferried the still celebrating and inebriated crew back to the ship.

Adam and Tessa were left to enjoy their honeymoon where after a long lovemaking session, Tessa asked Adam how big of a family did he want. He asked how big did she want?

Her answer left him choking.

Chapter 29

Joel leaned against the starlit window. "I don't even have to dream now," he muttered. "Reality and dreams blur together and there's no division between them." He looked out into the blackness as suddenly alien ships appeared in the view plate. They were strange vicious looking ships. Then they winked out, apparitions of his hallucinations.

"Oh Joel." Dyra moved up against him and laid her head on his shoulder.

"I'm so tired."

"Lay down and get some rest. Let the others plan. There's nothing more that you can do. All you see in your dreams is space and ships around you. Can Crystal give you an injection, or medicine that will help?"

"No, drugs only intensify the hallucinations and make me vulnerable. Just let me lay my head on your lap." He felt her hand softly stroke his hair. Soon, she was tugging off his top and easing him out of clothes, knowing that they would be left alone for a while by others too busy to bother them. She offered the best distraction she knew. She comforted him with a warm touch of her love. Her soft lips kissed his. He forgot about Lucien and rose in building desire and entered her soft embrace.

Later, he drifted off to a sleep that contained visions of stars exploding and ships colliding. He dreamed of a blackness of space sprawled out in front of him. *Where were they?* He groped and reached toward a burst of light. Then, he felt himself being drawn into a whirlpool. His head hurt and his stomach heaved. Behind him swarmed a horde of ships and together, they were all sucked down like strange food into the gorge of a ravenous beast.

At the center, he saw a lone ship tossed about. His headset crackled. Braden was yelling at him. Braden was trying to say something, to save him, but all around played chaos and confusion. He moved through the air like a swimmer in thick syrup. He moved slower and slower until he could barely move at all.

"Glaze," he mumbled. He had to tell Glaze something important. But Glaze wasn't listening. Glaze was somewhere else, and he was supposed to be with him.

Then, horrified he watched as a brilliant explosion blinded him. He screamed.

He fell off a soft lap. He pulled blankets around him and huddled in terror. Dyra commed Icabar.

"All right tell me about this new dream," demanded Icabar wearily.

"Oh Icky," Joel mumbled. "The Creator help us all."

*

Braden called all, but Liana and Joel, into what he was now calling his "war room." He sat at his desk with a monitor at his side turned out for them to see. Gazing at them, he stood until they quieted. He began, "The

Enjelise have provided four ships that they call Fugare class warships. You observed them as outriders to the mother ships. They're compact, well armed, and contain what I understand is a jump drive." He tapped the screen that now showed the ships' configuration.

Bashar leaned forward. "Should be interesting."

Braden shot him a look.

Bashar nodded and sat back, quieted.

"They field a high yield Synthetic Aperture Dark Matter Ejector that Adam and Bashar have retrofitted into each bow that, for obvious reasons, we have dubbed "SAMiE." He pointed at the forward bow.

Braden displayed the ships' inner layout on the screen. "Because she spits out dark matter, SAMiE can penetrate most solid objects and our objective is to disrupt the Linking Crystals that *the Fallen* are carrying inside their ships.

"Each Fugare Warship has a standard reflective screen and a ship encompassing magnetic field that forms a protective barrier against radiation, neutrino bursts, laser or projectile bombardment, not to mention any casual space debris that might cross our path." His pointer swirled around the image.

"Other stuff too," added Solanje.

Braden nodded.

"What about going through the gate?" asked Adam.

"Elsinore's specialist said that the ships are clad in numonium with extra plating at the front, which along with the magnetic field, should provide more than adequate forward protection going through the gate."

Crystal motioned to get his attention and gestured at her head. Braden noticed, and added, "Ah yes, and Liana will create a mind link with each captain as we transverse the gate, as our normal mode of comm link has been known to fail in there."

Crystal scanned the group. "Standard comms fuzz out in that monster. Alien comms may be okay, but we want to be prepared."

All heads nodded and quiet filled the room. Bashar ran a hand through his hair. Icabar rubbed a forehead nervously, most likely remembering his previous experience. Robert twitched and shifted positions. Several worried glances passed back and forth. Bashar heaved a deep breath.

"Hopefully, their Ion Cannons, if we get them working, will target any following hostiles," added Robert.

"Whoa! I thought they said they were averse to violence," Dyra remarked, sitting up suddenly.

Braden grimaced. "They consider these ships relics from their past that they claim they haven't piloted in ages. These ships are complicated, folks, but the Enjelise have offered to donate several shifts of time where they will show us as much detail as they can on how they work and add in a few practice runs for good measure."

"Why can't they ..." murmured Icabar.

Braden faced him and answered, "They claim violence is against their current belief. They won't fight. They were adamant on that point."

"But they'll let us," grumbled Bashar.

Braden ignored the comment and continued. "If we're going to have a chance, then I want to split us up two to a ship.

"Just two!" Bashar blurted out.

"Captain!" Icabar's eyes went wide. "Who's driving?"

"Well, you are Icky. Also, Robert, Glaze, me, and Bashar. At least for now unless some of the gals out fly you in training." He eyed Solanje and Crystal, who responded with wicked glints in their eyes and wide smiles.

Those named looked nervously at each other. A few faces paled, while Bashar rubbed his hands together. "Opportunity of a lifetime folks," he commented with enthusiasm.

"A very short lifetime," muttered Icabar.

Braden clicked off the monitor. "I'll hand out the final ship assignments after you train. These ships are considered "old tech" by the Enjelise. We found only a few who could remember how they worked, but in the proper hands, they could still be highly effective."

He straightened up and regarded his remaining crew. "All right. That's all for now. Disperse and suit up. I'll come with your ship assignments. As soon as you're on board your assigned ship, an Enjelise will join you and take it from there."

Soon five ships shot out of orbit, dodging and narrowly missing scraping savagely into each other. Loud swearing filled the comm links, but all managed to avoid crashing into each other and returned to the main ship without any severe damage, except for frayed nerves.

*

"Fission bombs! You want to create a super fission bomb? Do you realize what something like that can do?" yelled Braden, shaking his head.

He and Bashar were in the propulsion and power module with Robert, trying to assess what weapons they might use if *the Fallen* attacked and how they could deploy them.

"Yes, they're extremely dangerous," answered Bashar. "And very destructive, but we'll be careful."

"Careful!" Braden rubbed his arm and stared at Bashar. "At the Academy, they're called planet destroyers."

"Do you know how to make something like that?" Robert frowned at Bashar and Braden.

"I do and so does Braden," answered Bashar. "Look I got a doctorate degree in Chemistry. Part of that was due to my work on grand scale atomic theory. We already use nuclear power on this ship. No one has complained about living on board a ship containing a mini nuclear reactor. I know I can reconfigure it. There's plutonium and uranium on Haven. It contains all the materials I need. We can use the nuclear component from the alternate power system and assemble a powerful weapon that might save Alysia."

"Fission bombs are against the code," stuttered Robert. "The government would ...

"The Union is light annuals away," retorted Bashar with wave of his hand. "It's our lives that are on the line right now, and our world, if we don't stop any attackers."

"Bashar, we can't set off a fission bomb," said Robert emphatically. "It's too dangerous."

Braden's eyes widened, and he gave Bashar a puzzled look. "Usually, you're on board when it comes to blowing stuff up," Braden commented.

"Violence is wrong," stuttered Robert and grimaced. He put a hand to his head as if it hurt.

More looks we're exchanged.

"If we want to stop those ships from destroying us, we're going to need something powerful," argued Bashar.

Just then, Glaze came through the doorway and hooted, "Bashar and his explosives. Fire of the Sunglast. Of course, he would suggest a big bomb."

"So says the Ice of Islia," laughed Bashar. "A lethal combination, wouldn't you say?"

"Fire and Ice! The way the world ends, or so I've heard some say."

Glaze laughed. "Let's hope not."

"You approve his crazy idea?" asked Braden.

"Braden," Glaze faced his captain. "Lucien probably has fission bombs and plans to use them. Joel reported that possibility already. If it gives us a chance, an opportunity to survive this, then I vote yes, as long as we don't use them anywhere near Alysia or Haven."

"What if he's using Joel to tempt us to use it in hopes we blow ourselves up," argued Braden.

"No matter how hard you try to prevent it, someone is bound to light the fuse." Bashar shrugged. "It might make the difference."

"I'm reluctant, but it wouldn't hurt to have it in our arsenal. Just be careful. Make sure it's disarmed," warned Braden.

"It's the devil's weapon," quavered Robert.

"We agree there," said Bashar. "So, let's use it on some devils."

*

The other crew were hard at work with preparation and training while Joel stood, staring out the viewport into the dark void. He felt Dyra come and stand by him in the observatory.

As he gazed out into the black universe, images appeared and faded. He could feel *the Fallen's* ships around him and Dyra, a wraith next to him. Images overlapped each other and dissolved. His perception became disoriented. He looked out a window through Lucien's eyes and saw Haven growing larger in the viewplate. The stars stretched and twisted in his vision as he returned to his own ship and felt Dyra grasp his hand tightly, returning him to her.

*

Five ships were all Braden and his crew could operate and that took slim safety margins to extreme limits. Liana was a good pilot and was comfortable in the alien ship, but they needed her free from helm responsibility to concentrate on holding the mind link together while they traveled through the gate. Braden assigned her to Icabar who might need help and felt a bit shaky with the piloting task. Braden certainly didn't want Joel piloting anything. Joel's job was to track *the Fallen* through his link with Lucien. So, Braden commissioned Joel with Glaze who was one of the best pilots next to Bashar, and of course, him. Robert had requested to be at the formation's tail with the heavier artillery.

Braden shook his head. "Suddenly, he's eager to blast them out of existence. He and Liana had a talk he says. That woman scares me."

"We have our old Robert back!" Bashar exclaimed excitedly.

"Be careful what you ask for," warned Braden. "But, yeah, he's pretty eager now to blow things up."

Bashar grinned. "Liana must have taken him off his meds."

Braden rubbed his neck. "I hope that's all it is."

Bashar put a hand on his shoulder. "You're worrying too much over him. He's going to be fine." Bashar tapped his monitor and changed the subject to fighting tactics.

*

Joel ached at being separated from Dyra. He had protested her transfer to Robert's ship, but neither he nor she were competent enough to navigate the gate at helm position, and so they had to be split up.

Watching out the viewport, Joel realized they were leaving orbit when he saw a shift in star patterns and felt the onboard gravity change. His dreams now were mostly of ships pulsing through a dark void, hurtling toward a familiar, growing, star system. He was so sleep deprived that he would dream even when wide-awake, not knowing whether he was awake, or just dreaming that he was awake.

Finally, five human-piloted ships left orbit. Listlessly, Joel glanced at a monitor, gazing at the swirl of distant galaxies and the pinpoints of light that indicated billions of stars, thousands of light annuals away. Sharpening his attention, he noticed a dense cluster of moving objects in the distance. He was used to them by now, appearing and disappearing as hallucinations. But then, he heard a gasp from Glaze who sat next to him at helm. Joel leaned toward him. "What? What's the matter?" He blinked at Glaze's excited expression.

"Ships!" Glaze croaked. "Those moving objects are ships coming in." Glaze pointed at the viewscreen and then looked down.

Joel swung toward him, gripping the console with white knuckles. "You see them? You really see them, too?"

"Yep, my instruments just confirmed those are real ships." Glaze gave him a meaningful stare.

"Glaze, I no longer know what's real or not anymore," Joel said wearily.

"They're real; they're here, Joel. Grab a seat. Buckle in. Battle stations. They're coming."

*

RED ALERT! RED ALERT! Everyone to battle stations. Prepare for tactical maneuvers. This is not a drill. Repeat, this is not a drill. The ship's intercom blared a warning throughout the ship.

"Enemy craft approaching," Braden snapped out over ship wide comm. "Report in when ready."

"Ships on scan," informed Bashar. "Ready two."

"Ship three?"

"Right behind you," answered Glaze. "Three ready."

"Icabar?"

"Fragging power setting is giving me static," complained Icabar in a panicky voice.

"Flip the power relays now!" ordered Bashar.

A pause.

"Four ready." Icabar's voice warbled.

"Ship five, Robert?"

"Five ready. On your signal, Captain. Lead us out."

"Commence Alpha Delta 3 defensive maneuver. Make sure the holographics are online," commanded Braden. "On my command, engage now!" barked Braden. "Light 'em up."

Five ships screamed out toward the incoming swarm in a Delta formation. Braden and Crystal commanded the lead ship. Bashar piloted the second ship with Solanje as his copilot. On the port side of the formation, sat Glaze and Joel, while Icabar and Liana settled in the center. Robert and Dyra hung back at rear position on the starboard side. Five ships were all they were able to man. The high intensity training was barely adequate, and this was their first actual battle in strange alien ships. More than one person prayed.

Braden had gotten the Enjelise to work up a series of holograms that would make it appear as if a fleet of ships clustered around them. Other defensive measures were the ability to cloak nearby asteroids out where the alien ships would be entering. They also deployed proximity antimatter mines that read energy and heat patterns of the enemy ships, moved next to them, and detonated.

The fleet would maneuver at high impulse speed in and out of the holographic images, trying to evade direct enemy fire and detection, while attacking the enemy's central formation. Large asteroids blundered throughout the field carrying deadly packages of explosives often tumbling treacherously close by their own ships.

Braden barked out, "They're coming in on vector 03674. Hold formation. Hold fire unless they fire first."

The Fallen's ships flew in, each synchronized to the other, thanks to the Linked Crystal's communication. They were sharp angled, v-shaped, and looked like predatory birds or insects swarming for a kill. Each moved in perfect rhythm to the others. Flames gouted out of their bows and projectile bullets spouted from the front edge of their forward wings.

*

On the bridge of the alien ship, Braden studied the boards and unfamiliar equipment. He was concentrating on the navigation display, trying to compute the alien's counter move when he heard a gasp from Crystal, who sat next to him, staring out the view plate.

But she was staring in the wrong direction. She was looking back toward Haven.

"Captain!"

"What?" He tore away from the lines of complicated data flashing across the monitor. "Busy here." He scowled at his boards. He tapped a switch and tossed a sideways puzzled squint at her.

"It's disappearing."

"What? What's disappearing? Aren't the holograms working?" he asked distracted.

"Haven. It's disappearing. It's getting fainter and fainter. What's happening?" she asked, her voice shaking.

He peered over at the rearview monitor, as the planet winked out of sight. He found himself staring at empty space where a whole planet had just been.

"Frag! They did it! They really did it! Elsinore wasn't sure. She made those Enjelise sound so defenseless, yet it seems they can move planets around like toys," he choked out. He blinked and shook his head. He ran a hand through his hair. "Frag!"

"What's going to happen to Adam and Tessa?" She put her hand to the rear-view monitor and gazed over at him in concern.

He leaned forward and touched her shoulder to reassure her. "Elsinore said they would be fine. She said not to worry over God's chosen creations."

"And we take her word for it?"

He nodded. "I would, given her lifelong concern for humans. Do you comprehend the magnitude of energy it takes to move a whole planet? Yet they run from *the Fallen* like scared children. Terrifies me. She said they didn't want the contamination of negative vibrations from *the Fallen* spreading to the remaining Enjelise. Something about disrupting their spiritual progress."

"Negative vibrations!"

Braden nodded and rolled his eyes. He toggled a switch and leaned into his comm. "Check your rear viewport captains," he advised.

"Captain! What happened to Haven?" shouted an agitated Bashar.

A flurry of exclamations and comments jammed the link.

"They warned me they were going to try it, and they succeeded," Braden explained. "It appears Haven has been moved to a safe place."

"Holy Lady!"

"Yes, most likely," answered Braden wryly. "We're on our own now. Pay attention. Move into our Pi Theta formation. They're coming in," he commanded. "Haven's gone, but we have a more immediate problem. The count's thirty. Confirm the count."

"Thirty confirmed," responded Bashar.

"Thirty," answered Glaze.

"Three-o." Braden recognized Icabar's voice.

"Thirty on mark," Robert confirmed.

"Mark now. Head out and report to me at meet point."

Five ships swooped out and spread apart in a line.

"At meet point," responded Bashar.

"At meet point." Glaze's voice came on.

"That's the number four vector spread, isn't it?" queried Icabar shakily.

"Liana, help him!"

"On it, Captain."

"In place," answered Robert.

"Affirmative Pi Theta, Captain," sounded Icabar's voice. This time he sounded a little more confident.

"Stage One. Full power. Go, go, go." Braden took up the lead as the five ships scattered into a planned dance.

They angled in, slipping between Holos with the agility and quickness that was the strength of the Fugare class warships. They began firing at the incoming aliens, using the asteroids as cover.

Missiles streaked through inky space to bounce off enemy shield in pyrotechnic splendor. Streaks of light flared and angled off the jagged wing-shaped enemy ships.

"Blast! I'm having a hard time getting through their shields and their hulls are made of some composite material and not metal. Most projectile missiles are just scratching their hulls," swore Bashar.

A volley of projectiles followed his words doing minimal damage to *the Fallen* as the shield deflected any serious damage.

"Switch weaponry over to lasers and ion cannons to see if we can burn holes through their defense screens," commanded Braden.

"Switching over to lasers and ion cannons," acknowledged four separate voices.

"Watch out, Bashar. You've got two on your tail."

Two hungry enemy ships converged on Bashar.

Heavy breathing and grunting sounded in the comm as Bashar pulled up heavily and peeled left, barely missing an asteroid. As he tore past, the asteroid exploded behind him, taking out the two enemy ships that were pursuing him

"Frag, that was close!" Bashar panted.

"Heads up, Icabar. Enemy coming in on your left."

"Got one." Dyra's voice sounded exultant. Their screens lit up, as a ball of light burst in the dark void at the far left of the fight.

"Nice shot, Dyra."

"Frag, missed one," Robert's voice cursed.

Braden wheezed as he came around and pulled heavy Gees. "Easy, Robert. Take sure aim."

"Arrgh, too close," Glaze muttered. "At least you distracted them, Robert."

"Lasers are working," commed Robert excitedly. "The cannons are slowing them up too, but the high energy lasers are melting their screens."

Five ships dodged and darted at the incoming enemy as their defense screen blazed in a multi-colored, incandescent spectacle, but they held.

"How many, Crystal?" asked Braden, turning to his co-pilot.

"Twenty-five, and the count's coming down," she answered, looking over at him. "A debris field is building up. Sound alert."

"Some are passing by the Holos," Icabar pointed out, coming through comm.

Two enemy ships on Braden's heads up display ripped right through three Holos as Icabar spoke.

Glaze came on. "Joel says Lucien has gotten a read on the hologram trick and has ordered his captains to ignore them. He thinks the crystals can detect the difference in mass of the Holos and are tagging them for Lucien's pilots."

"That was quick," Icabar grumbled.

Braden came back on. "Okay, then. Time for Stage Two: Crystal Destruction. Arm SAMiE Pick your targets. On three ... one, two, three. Fire at will!"

Braden aimed SAMiE at the ship that Joel had suggested contained Lucien and tapped the igniter. The focused dark matter beams swept out and bore into the alien ships. Each fired on as many enemy ships as they could, in order to disrupt or shatter any crystals on board. They watched as the controlled formation of the incoming enemy ships started to founder.

The beams began shattering the linking crystals in the ships. Now, the enemy would no longer be instantaneously connected by the crystals, but would have to rely on a slower, standard form of communication.

"The net just activated," Crystal remarked.

"Stage Three," Braden advised on comm.

A glowing field sprung up around where the planet had been and washed out toward the advancing aliens, passing through Braden's team.

"That net will slow them down enough to give us a head start for the gate," Braden barked. "All ships turn to heading 653.34. Go for the gate. It's go for the gate. Your coordinates should be preset."

The back end of the enemy fleet began to crash into the abruptly slowing front formation, impacted by the net. In front of Braden, space erupted into a magnificent display of high ion bursts and proton flashes. Braden felt a surge of elation as he saw some alien ships lose power and ram into each other while other ships went inert and became dangerous speeding space flotsam.

"SAMiE is doing the job!" Joel reported. "They're splitting and destroying the crystal communicators. Lucien is furious. He cut all communication to me."

"Fraggin' awesome!" announced Icabar.

"Some are running into their own ships," Joel added.

The enemy formation broke up. Then, they began to regroup. They were down to a rough count of twenty.

"Stage Four, the gate," ordered Braden and swept his ship to the gate's coordinates. "Everyone activate coordinates and commence next stage. Gamma A formation."

They turned while some of the incoming crafts still fired relentlessly and wildly at the holographic ships that now surrounded them.

"How does this fragging thing turn again?" shouted Icabar frantically.

"Monitor three on the right console shows your output from your tactical navigation computer, your course, and a place for course corrections." answered Bashar. "Controls are at the right. Push the green gate preset button."

"Thanks," answered two voices at once.

*

All managed to get turned around as Braden led them toward the gate, putting space between them and the incoming ships. But it didn't last long.

Ahead the mouth of the gate yawned open before them and the whirling outer rim came into view. Polarity reversed. Red numbers began to spew across the monitors indicating the gate's transit codes.

"Speed increasing," informed Glaze over comm as they approached the edge of the gate's vortex.

"Crystal, check our speed," ordered Braden. Pressure changes and heavy gravity soon pressed down viciously on Braden and Crystal.

"Velocity increasing," announced Crystal in a strained voice.

"Strap tight," commanded Braden. "Liana, mind-link us. I'll be entering the Event Horizon at 0:100.

Everyone check your time for :0500 following intervals." Braden looked behind him to see the enemy ships ignoring the Holos, regrouping, and surging after them. Realizing that the Enjelise world, their original target, had vanished, Braden saw Lucien angrily pursuing the fleeing Enjelise ships, most likely thinking they were escaping Enjelise.

Confirm the link, ordered Braden.

In the link, Bashar answered.

In the link, Glaze confirmed.

In the link, Icabar responded.

In the link, Robert added.

Gate ahead, announced Bashar.

"Gate ahead," breathed Crystal next to Braden. She tossed him a brief glance and a nod, then shivered.

"Are they following?" he murmured.

They're following us, reported Robert.

They must think we're the Enjelise, retorted Icabar.

These are their ships, confirmed Braden mentally.

Here they come, answered Liana, firming up the mind-link. Braden felt her presence and the presence of the others penetrate his consciousness and take hold. He grabbed them and strung them out in his conscious mind like wash on a clothesline.

"Keep comm contact as long as we can," ordered Braden. "I'll use the mind-link to time ahead the coordinates to each helm."

The Stargate loomed ahead. Around its edge swirled space debris. Clutter from fine dust to bits of broken up asteroids and pieces of shattered ships made the entrance extremely dangerous. Inside the eye, the endless center lurked, twisting and swirling with violent flashes of light and energy, and finally past that, deep space and the other side of the universe awaited.

Braden read the coordinates off the monitor and tapped the numbers into his board.

"Speed accelerating. We're in. Hold on!" He plunged his ship into the circling maelstrom. Speed picked up, and tossed the ship roughly around, but the alien ship had been built to survive the gate and held solid.

I'm in. Follow in sequence.

Braden saw Crystal blur, separate and snap back. The walls around him buckled as space/time distorted his reality.

"Han n n nnggg ooonnn..."

He tried to say something to Crystal, but the words stretched and contorted and became indistinguishable.

It was the Alysian ship with Bashar and Solanje onboard that they had to worry about most. It had not been made to survive the gate. Braden and Crystal led. Bashar and Solanje came behind them as Glaze and Joel followed. After them came Icabar and Liana. Robert brought up the rear as if he had the devils of hell on his tail, and in fact, he did.

The way appeared ahead, twisting, and turning, zigzagging back and forth, but now, Braden understood the path. Red reverse coordinates flashed across the monitor and his mind expanded, tapped into his Tellurian Time Talent and jumped ahead in time, to capture the coordinates and feed them back to the others at a dizzying rate.

Coordinates 435-6785-9835. He threw out declension, ascension, and drift vectors that flashed from a future monitor only he could see.

Speed increased, approaching light speed. Reality began to stretch like pulled taffy and warped backwards and sideways as the tremendous velocity twisted with time itself. The letters blurred in front of him until he almost couldn't see them. His head ached under the strain of the tearing energies and trying to maintain concentration in the link.

But the link held. Crystal's fingers followed Braden's instructions precisely and accurately, dancing wildly over the console, as she monitored the ships and he managed helm. While time and space gyrated around them, all ten minds meshed as one.

The Fallen weren't doing as well once they got sucked into the gate. As Braden had hoped, they were unused to the high speed, the violent shifts and sharp vector changes along with strange glyphs dancing across their monitors. The long narrow vortex strung them out like beads whirling on a twisting string. Their ships, while powerful, were not as agile and the sharp angles and wing like structure was more unstable in the violent turbulence. Several crashed against the sides of the vortex and ricocheted into fellow ships, creating havoc and deadly explosions within the gate for any following ships. Some ships seemed to lack the crystal's link and were probably relying on the primitive standard transmissions that became garbled as time and space stretched and contracted around them.

Braden's strategy was paying off.

Distantly sensing the explosions behind him, Braden could not afford to lose focus for a nanosecond. He prayed his ships were surviving the violent energies.

Speed increased.

More explosions, behind him, but the path leveled out ... then plunged.

Had the gate gotten longer? Was this the right path? Did the vortex have just one path, or did it branch out and lead into other universes, too? Wayward thoughts skittered in and out of Braden's mind.

He refocused. With flickering flashes of light and the red glow of burning ships surrounding him, suddenly Braden saw a hazy pale blue emerge ahead, then it gathered intensity becoming a black canvass with a sprinkling of stars, as he popped out the other side. Swirling energies hit the ship, skewing it sideways. Braden wrestled for control of the helm and his seat. Time rolled back and forth, stabbing at his mind. He felt distortion and disorientation roil his thoughts. He wanted to throw up, but he had no time for it. He coughed instead and blinked back watering eyes. He braced himself on the console, peering into the other side of the universe.

Robert, report. His urgent thought raced to his last ship. "Robert," his comm crackled, sputtered. He pushed full power, trying to clear the gate and the ships that would soon spurt out after him.

"Robert's in trouble." Crystal voiced concern. *He's been hit badly.*

Bashar out.

Coming on close, Glaze reported.

Almost out, Icabar's thoughts teetered on the edge of panic.

Robert! Braden called.

In gate. Came back the strangled thought. *We're hit! Ship's breaking up. Getting too hard to control. Dyra's going to launch the anti matter missiles.*

Not within the gate! shouted Icabar. *You'll destroy the gate!*

Exactly. No gate. Alysia will be safer.

Dyra! Joel sent a mental scream. *No! No!*

The ship's breaking up! Dyra's thoughts came back frantically. *We have no chance. This is the best action.*

No! Violent protest shook Joel's thoughts.

Robert's thoughts calmed with resolute purpose. *Tell me when Glaze is clear, and we'll light the candle. We'll take all those around us with us. Won't die in vain. I'll make a difference at last.* Robert's thoughts shut off abruptly.

Everyone keep moving, Liana's mental shout interrupted abruptly. *Don't slow down and stay alert. They're still on our tail, and what's left is coming out fast!*

I'm clear, but ...

Glaze's ship shot out and then Icabar's. All but Robert's spewed out of the gate, coughed up like pieces of bad meat.

Get away from the gate. Immediate explosion. Full speed away! Go! Go! Go! Braden sent out the warning.

Crystal's voice cut into Braden's yelling. "Braden, debris field ahead," she warned as she glanced at the outside monitor.

"Frag!" *Debris field ahead. Alert! Alert!* Braden gave a mental shout to all.

He found a small open area, pushed through, and zigzagged past boulders and floating asteroids that loomed in his path and thankfully slid by. Sparks struck off the magnetic field and the defensive screens as bits of space matter bounced against it and crashed into each other.

Looking out the back viewport, Braden saw a tremendous explosion rock the gate. Shock waves roiled the ships at the gate's edge and tossed them roughly about. It looked like a huge worm throwing up.

A series of explosions incinerated those near the jump point. Others that had made it out far enough from the gate, slued and bucked out of control, damaging the integrity of their ships. A bright light flashed and then suddenly the gate shimmered and coughed. All matter around the outside edge reversed course drawn in as the gate imploded, wiping out everything around its mouth and then sucking everything back in with a vast inhalation. An empty blackness and scattered debris took up the place where the gate had been.

An energy wave rolled out toward Braden, buffeting everything before it like a violent tsunami. The huge wave flowed toward them, lifted them up and tossed them forward out over the debris-filled sea into clear space.

Braden clung to his harness for dear life.

Oh frag!

The lights flickered and Braden felt as if he were moving in slow motion, yet the speed on his console indicated that they were pushing light speed. The viewport looked out into a distorted tunnel of stars. The headsets no longer functioned. Sound waves blurred and became indistinguishable, but the mind link held. Braden applied back thrusters. Ship speed decreased. The viewport cleared and smoothed out as the velocity came down.

Looking at his back monitor, he saw two remaining Fugare ships and one Alysian ship clear the debris field and splay out behind him. Time to regroup, take count, and assess losses. Red lights flickered and then settled to yellow. Braden tapped the reverse thrusters again and brought the speed down further.

Headcount, he sent out.

Bashar and Solanje here.

Icabar and Liana here.

Glaze and Joel here.

Robert and Dyra?

Silence as deep as space.

You will be missed, rang Braden's thoughts.

Amen responded eight others as one.

Joel?

Here Captain. A dazed mind struggled to answer.

Damage?

Joel's a bit shaky.

We're severely damaged.

That you Solanje?

Yes, Unfortunately.

Icabar?

I'm losing oxygen. Sealing affected areas now.

At least ten enemy ships are still functional and appear to be following us, Glaze announced.

Frag! That means we aren't done, folks. Head for the next objective. Glaze, give us the coordinates, commanded Braden.

Affirmative. Setting now and sending through comm. We need quick repairs. The enemy is still on our tails, and this next stunt could severely stress our ships.

The Enjelise assured me that they could take it, commented Bashar.

We'll find out soon enough, Braden rsponded.

How much time? Icabar's thoughts felt worried.

Twenty-four duros more at this speed until we approach the decision point. Glaze's thoughts broadcasted to all.

Not enough time! Icabar protested.

Make the time count. Glaze fired back.

Copy that Glaze, thought Braden. *Commence rapid repairs, everyone.*

Chapter 30

It seemed far less than four shifts before Braden felt the first stirrings that they were approaching something unusual. Behind them, ten enemy ships had regrouped and still doggedly followed.

Three of his ships set the autopilot and alternated catching up on sleep and completing repairs. For Bashar and Solanje on board the Alysian ship, however, they got little sleep. Repairs were vital and having only two on board meant no one could be spared for long.

Braden expanded his consciousness. He reached out with his mind and saw the stretching and bending of time and space around the invisible gravity well that lay ahead, lurking like some rabid beast awaiting an unsuspecting prey. Unless one was looking for certain anomalies and energies, the spinning mass was almost invisible. The ships plunged ahead and started picking up speed, drawn in by the dying star's gravitational spin.

Thousands of kilospans away, the gravitational force was already pulling masses of material toward it. The small, nearly invisible, star spun silently ahead while Braden's ships followed him like innocent ducks. On their tail came Lucien's ships, either unaware of what lay ahead, or too intent on destruction to notice.

Behind him, lights flickered as Braden sensed Lucien's attempt to fire on them, but the intense speed made it difficult for an accurate laser or projectile hit. *The Fallen's* heat-based weapons couldn't get close enough to target lock their lasers. Lucien couldn't use mind control unless he linked to Joel—and that was a two-edged sword at best. Besides, Braden figured that Lucien didn't have the extra attention to spare nor want to become vulnerable again. He couldn't use the ship's communications system left to him because they were now traveling faster than the signal was able to follow. Braden grinned despite the serious situation he was still in.

The ships' speed increased and then suddenly there it was—looming ahead of them. Braden's subliminal senses picked up the whirling anomaly that crouched not far away. Glaze pointed it out and Icabar confirmed its existence. A gravity well forming around a newly dying star, warping time and space, spun in dark space like a deadly wheel. That was why Braden had sensed it. He alone could feel the distortion of time at its center. Around its outer edge spun altered time and within its maw swam debris from near space—the garbage of destruction that, in time, would make new planets and worlds. It sucked anything nearby into what appeared to be nothingness.

Braden headed his ship to a precise distance just outside the rim where the energies swirled. If his calculations were correct, he wouldn't be so close as to be sucked in, but close enough to bait the trap. His ship slowed. Comm crackled back on and stuttered. He saw the enemy ships positioned behind Glaze, concentrating on him, oblivious to the peril before them. They had been so intent on pursuit, and then, recovery from the gate, that the enemy appeared to have failed to notice the gathering strangeness that now rippled through space in front of them.

Icabar, sixty intervals and copy me. Bashar sixty intervals after Icabar. Glaze, at your discretion ... just take them in and get out safe. Braden shot out instructions.

I don't know if I can hold them off. They're starting to gain on me. Glaze's thoughts felt contained but intense. *Soon I'll be in target range.*

This must be done precisely. Braden sent, *Set your turning point carefully!*

On it, Captain.

"One, two three on the mark. Mark! Turning now at 873-1064-356, came Braden's shout, both mentally and audibly over comm.

He piloted directly toward the whirling mass and then with exact timing, rotated ninety degrees, skipping along the outer edge of the vortex, using it like a slingshot to throw the ship out and away, driving it to greater speeds by the immense energy, swirling along the outer edge of the whirling mass. His ship felt as if it slammed up against something incredibly powerful energy that flung him away like a discarded toy.

He and Crystal sank deep into the protective webbing that held them. Their bodies groaning from the stress of the tremendous acceleration forward. Lights flickered again; boards flared yellow, and then some red. He felt the skin of his face press and distort against his facial bones. His teeth hurt and he couldn't close his gaping mouth. He found he couldn't move his arm and hoped the shield held, the seals stayed tight, and nothing drifted in the ship's path.

After the initial violent thrust forward, the ship began to lose forward momentum. He felt drag from the star clutching at him, as its gravity began to pull the ship, causing slower and slower forward progress. His ship soon strained against the pulling forces. He lifted a now unstuck arm and pushed the propulsion system into full forward power. They hung suspended in space, even while his engines approached maximum thrust. The monster behind them sucked at his ship, stalling it, calling it back.

No, came the unbidden thought. *Where had he gone wrong?*

"No!" He heard Crystal shout as she watched the monitors. She pounded the board with curled fists.

"Turn sooner, Bashar! Now!" he yelled through comm. "Time it sooner!"

Captain! Braden! Icabar sounded frantic.

Turn Icabar, now! He threw out the command. *Turn before 873-1964-300. Get away!* He had corrected a fraction too late and was in serious trouble.

His ship began to drift backward, toward the swirling mass as two charging ships catapulted past him. He engaged his engines to full power, up past the red line. He couldn't afford to hesitate now. He could feel the power system screaming and straining against the forces that grabbed at his ship. Forward power would soon be down to a dribble.

Braden! Glaze touched his mind in alarm. The remaining ships were focused on Glaze, but suddenly realizing their peril, they frantically tried to alter their course and escape the sprung trap.

Braden saw the following ships caught against the swirling abyss, trapped by its gravity.

I'll take them in, Glaze's mental voice said calmly.

Braden saw Glaze go past the turning point. Bashar looked to be out and free, while Icabar shakily followed on his tail afraid to lose sight. Coming last, Glaze had deliberately waited too long to correct so as to draw in as many enemy ships as he could toward the trap.

Closer and closer, the whirling mass grew larger and nearer, as it tugged on Braden's ship. His engines were no match for the sucking energies of the dying star. He saw Glaze's ship hit the edge of the intense swirl and wobble. The enemy ships began to swerve wildly away, but most got caught in the trap.

Glaze! Teleport! Teleport! Teleport to Icabar! screamed Braden, as helplessly he watched his own ship slide closer and closer to the whirling mass and certain death.

*

Aboard Glaze's ship, Joel stared at the whirling dervish of his dreams as it sucked them toward its heart. His head felt ready to explode by all the shouting of the others that became an indistinguishable din within his mind. Around him, reality moved lazily, as if he were underwater.

Glaze floated indolently over toward him.

Joel, buckle in for hard launch. He yanked down on Joel's harness and moved to the helm in a stop motion action, jerkily punching in a series of coordinates on the autopilot's control board.

"Glazzzzzzz. Whaaaaaatttttt?" The sound of his voice drawled out until it made no audible sense.

What are you doing? Joel asked struggling to think.

But Glaze ignored him.

He watched Glaze move away from the board. The closer the ship slid toward the edge of the event horizon, the slower everything seemed to move. An eternity passed as he watched Glaze float toward the shuttle bay. The ship's autopilot executed a labored 90-degree turn, angling away from the drawing energies and positioning the ship nose outward.

Joel remembered then that Bashar had stowed the fission bomb aboard their shuttle. As disjointed time swirled around him, Joel saw the small shuttlecraft release out of the ship and knew that Glaze rode in it toward the visible edge of the vortex like a beetle skating on top of a whirlpool. With little or no power in its engines, the shuttle would be unable to escape the heavy pull of gravity.

"Teleport Glaze!" croaked Joel to an empty bridge. His ship ignited into full throttle, and he was pushed down deep into his webbing. His face felt like a monster's hands smashed it hard against the bones of his face. His chest crushed inwards, stopping all breath. His words were inaudible. *Teleport before it's too late*, his mind screamed, as he watched the shuttle become a swirling dot amid the violent energies. *Oh God, teleport now, Glaze,* sobbed Joel. But Glaze was somewhere else.

Joel could feel his ship's engines straining to full power, trying to burst free of the dying star's hold, but they had gone too far in.

*

In front of him, Glaze stared at the control board and mentally shut out the wild buffeting energies that tore at the small craft. The noise reminded him of the wind howling outside the ice cave so long ago. He scanned the shuttle and saw the package. Moving was impossibly hard. Thinking was slow and fuzzy. He had to concentrate. He had to concentrate, or all would be lost.

"Do not be afraid," she said.

He gyrated around and saw Angelique in dazzling glory before him. The shock of her being there defied rational thought. Stupidly, he gaped at her. Her voice came through the wild tearing energies, as if she were whispering in his ear.

"The ultimate control over the physical is to claim your own time of death," she murmured softly.

He stared as his mind locked in astonishment, and then, he caught a breath. "Death would not be so hard if we could be together," he murmured as he reached out to her. He heard Braden screaming dimly within his mind. Liana's voice was also in there, somewhere. Joel echoed their words, but he only listened to the Enjelise's soft whispering in his ear.

"Death is only a new reality," she sighed. "God gave humans the capacity to choose. Only you can decide your destiny. You make your own fate. It's time to choose, Glaze." She smiled radiantly at him. "And you have always made interesting choices. That's what I love most about you."

Glaze smiled back. In front of him was the console holding the gift that Bashar had created. *The world-shattering fission bomb*. He needed to draw in Lucien's ships a little more,

And then light the fuse.

Joel could never have done it. He would have refused the evil of atomics, but Glaze didn't have that compunction. He would do whatever was needed. He had been trained to acknowledge the necessity of the extreme choice. A few more heartbeats to wait as the enemy ships slid past the event horizon, and into the gulping abyss, and then....

A few less for Braden to fight off, a few less for Alysia to defend against. His world was too vulnerable to what was out here. And, Braden and Joel had to break free ... had to break free. Must. There was only one way that could happen. I must dare it. After all, they are my family in the final analysis. The crew...frag... The entire human race is my family to protect.

Funny, how past hurts evaporated with that revelation. It cleansed his mind of useless concerns. Time floated in a place like this. It expanded, contracted, and then ceased to exist.

His small ship buffeted violently in the dim twilight, as he tried to keep it intact just a little bit longer. He was a small mote on a roiling stormy sea: infinitesimal in size, but potent with power. His hand groped toward the button, slammed down on it, and then he closed his eyes. He teleported and exploded outwards for the last time in an incredible blaze of light and matter. He would try to teleport at this last, but it wouldn't really matter in the end if he did. As the light blossomed and then expanded outward, he felt himself begin to break up into a million dazzling particles, and he saw her smiling face among them.

And reached out to her.

Chapter 31

The shock wave roiling ahead of the atomic explosion hit Braden's ship with a hard smack. His ship had been drifting backward, drawn in by the whirling energies of the dwarf star. Soon the beast would once again have them within its grasp, but the tremendous explosion, and the shock wave that sped out ahead of it, were enough to knock his ship out of the vortex's grip, much like a bear would swat a bee. The power of the wave threw the ship savagely forward and shook it clear of the vortex's deadly hold.

Both Crystal and Braden sank deep into the chairs' protective webbing, feeling heavy Gs pressing down on their fragile bodies. Their breath stopped and the temperature around them climbed. The enormous acceleration burned the front of the ship, tearing and fragmenting the shield as the ship hurtled forward.

Loosed from the dying star's grip, Braden's ship spat free. Behind him, the fission bomb erupted into a multitude of explosions that started a nuclear chain reaction. He hadn't realized that Glaze had positioned the shuttle between Joel's ship and the dying star's throat. Stunned and dizzy, Braden saw Joel's ship on the crest of an energy wave, like a surfer riding an enormous tsunami,

Joel's ship hurtled outward from the explosion toward them.

"Our Holy Lady, what's happening?" Crystal gasped, blinking at the monitors.

"Bashar's dreaded fission bomb," responded Braden in a drawling stretched tone. "Glaze set it off." He could barely work his mouth to form the words.

He wanted to stare after the phenomenon taking place behind him, but his attention became distracted by the critical condition of his ship. His fuzzy brain recorded red lights flashing everywhere, and the emergency signal blaring a shrill warning of imminent hull breach. The hull's integrity was in jeopardy. Shuttle bay blatted out damage. And they needed to jump out now if they wanted to survive. He had to clear his mind and attend to his ship immediately, or they would be lost here in a dark void, drifting in space forever. Not a death he preferred.

He ordered Crystal to run a systems check while he adjusted and realigned the helm. He brought back power capabilities and sealed off any severely damaged areas. They weren't safe yet. They had a long way to go and much to repair, but they were free and on a countdown to the spatial jump. He ran his eyes over the jump instructions, swearing as he read. Gradually red flashing lights went yellow. A few became green or blue. He heard Crystal breathe out a heavy sigh of relief.

The impact of the first explosion soon passed and dissipated like a wave expending its energy upon the water's shore. It lunged on ahead, seeking other objects to perturb ... planets, asteroids, moons. A second wave hit the ship, and then another, but these were less violent, and he and Crystal were braced for them. The vortex shook them with swirling violence, but they held intact. Still, each wave sent them further outward and away from the exploding nightmare behind them. Staring back at the swirling mass, the chain of nuclear reactions began to ignite the dying star. Braden saw another light blossom, and quickly get snuffed out, and then another spark lit. They looked like small winking fireflies within a brightening, expanding mass. Debris collided and sent out flares of desperation as the forces swallowed back their explosions and vomited up new ones. The chain reactions soon transformed the dark well into a bright ball of unimaginable energy. The rebirth of a dying star.

My God, what's happening? Liana asked.

Liana?

We're out, Captain. But what happened?

Not sure, answered Braden. *But get away as far and as fast as possible. Glaze has started a chain reaction and reawakened a dying star. The thing's growing. Get clear. Activate your spatial jump to the Alpha A preset coordinates now!*

"Did he teleport in time? Where could he teleport to? Oh Glaze, have you saved yourself?" murmured Crystal. Her fingers tapped out coordinates as tears splashed on the console.

He waited too long. Liana's numb thoughts wavered through their minds. *He waited too long and then deliberately set off the atomics.*

On purpose? asked Braden.

To save us. Yes. To save us all, answered Liana. *I don't feel him anymore. Braden, he's gone. He's gone.*

Grief washed over them.

Two of *the Fallen's* ships had also won free, but they were tearing away from the exploding mass as fast as they could, no longer thinking about attacking, rather more about surviving.

"Comm's back online," reported Crystal. She thumped the console and a crackling sound filled the bridge.

"Bashar, report in," ordered Braden.

A static burst and then Bashar came online. "We're clear and activating Alpha A jump procedure," answered Bashar.

Good to have you with us, sent Braden.

We're not in good shape. He heard Solanje's thoughts wavering.

Solanje! He took a relieved breath and began firing out orders. "All ships engage jump drive using prearranged Alpha A coordinates as soon as capable." Braden crossed his fingers and activated the spatial jump that flung the Fugare ship across a vast distance of space to win clear of the blooming nova. Looking at his rear monitor, Braden saw a single ship soaring straight toward them, spat out by the awakening star and Glaze's preset autopilot instructions. *Joel.* Joel's ship had broken free and jumped behind them.

Joel. Joel! Are you alive? Crystal screamed the thought. *I feel his life force flickering. He's alive. Joel's alive, but he's in serious trouble.*

Braden's thoughts came in hard. *We're clear of the star for the moment, but it's still expanding. We need to move fast. I'll see if we can catch his ship, hook up, and get you on board. If he's still alive, he'll need immediate medical attention.*

Behind them, Joel's ship grew larger and larger in the viewport as Braden engaged back thrusters to brake his ship. Behind that, a star's feeble glimmers were getting brighter and brighter.

"Suit up for an extravehicular," he ordered Crystal.

Her face paled and her eyes grew wide. "What?"

"Crystal, you can do this," he urged. "It's Joel's only chance. Take the medical pack and hook it onto your suit. There's a lead line with a magnetic disc on the end coiled near the bay door. When I get close enough, open the bay door and attach one end securely, very securely, to the edge there. Take the magnetic end and jet toward Joel's ship. You can open the door from the outside using 1,3,5,7,11 as the code."

"Seriously?"

"Prime numbers are easy to remember."

"Not that part. The jetting over part."

"He needs immediate medical help. You're the only one who has the healing Talent. My slapping on a bandage won't do it. Then, we need to bring him here. You can do this. You must."

"I'll die out there." She glared at him. "You're sending me to my death."

"No, you won't. You're made of tough stuff. The suit's good and will protect you ... just don't go on holiday. Work fast. You can do this and save a life. Joel's life."

He steeled himself.

Was he made of the right stuff? Could he get her to do this? She might be right, and he didn't want to lose her, but he felt in his gut that this was the right thing to do ... that she could do it. Was he sending her to her death? Could he command her to take such a risk? Would trying to save one, kill two?

He cared for her and didn't want her to die, but Joel was crew. His emotions twisted in agony, but he gave her only a blank face to look at and blocked thoughts.

She stared back at him for a moment as if he had lost his mind and then her shoulders firmed. "You're right." She closed her eyes, pinched her nose, and took a deep breath. "I'll get suited up."

He could only nod mutely, afraid to speak, afraid to think.

She soon returned with a medical kit clipped to the outside of her suit and a determined attitude on her face.

Braden started the delicate process of matching his speed to the runaway ship's speed.

"I'm going to go open the bay door now," she said jamming on her helmet.

He waved a hand and nodded, his attention solely on his board and the dance of the two ships. She left. He stopped for a moment to stare after her and shivered.

Be careful with the line. Keep it straight. At these speeds, any small tug could cut you in two if you get tangled in it. He threw the thought at her.

"So nice to know," she muttered into the suit's comm.

*

She passed through their ship's inner decompression and sterilization chamber out to the exit bay and zero gravity. She floated over to the outside bay door, found the line, secured it tightly to the hatch, and muscled the outer door open. Brilliant stars against deep dark space greeted her sight. One kept getting brighter and brighter with every heartbeat.

You can do it. Liana's calming support flooded her thoughts.

Out of the corner of her eye, she saw the hull of Joel's ship ease into view. Black char covered it. Its shields were down and dead. Space debris pitted the outside surface. It swam to her like a wounded leviathan out of the Deep.

She plunged toward it.

*

Braden checked his velocity and then darted a glance at the large monitor. Crystal floated out between the racing ships, flailing a trailing line in her hand. His other eye he kept on his board as he made minute adjustments to his speed and position while the two ships crept closer and closer together. On the monitor, he saw her line snake out and snap onto the exit bay's door.

"These gloves make me clumsy," she complained through the comm. "I can't punch the numbers." She fumbled with the code, and finally, yanked on the burnt and scored door.

"It won't open."

"Pull harder," he answered.

"I am, I am."

He could hear her heavy breathing and then an exclamation as the door cracked open.

She was in.

"Get control of the ship," he ordered.

"I'm at the boards now and releasing the autopilot," she answered irritably.

"Ease off the speed," he instructed.

"Doing it now."

He matched velocities with gentle braking as both ships bled off speed. He hadn't realized that he had been holding his breath until black spots began dancing in front of his eyes and he felt light-headed. He took a deep breath and shook his head. The world went into a blurred double vision. Another breath and it cleared.

"I got the speed down to 20,000, so I'm locking the panel to autopilot and going to check Joel," she announced.

"Copy that. Proceed."

He set his speed to match and wiped sweat from his forehead. "How is he?" Concern coated his words.

Working here, was her tart response.

He left her alone and directed his thoughts to the remaining ships. Two had jumped clear. He gave his position and ordered a rendezvous. Each responded that they were on their way.

He's going to live, but he'll need time to recuperate, she finally answered. She sounded exhausted. "I'll need help getting him onboard."

He sent out the good news.

Cheers were heard all around.

Now to get back home, thought Braden wearily. The two other surviving ships drew near and fell into formation on either side of his ship.

Eventually they got Joel stabilized, on board, and the three ships set course for Alysia.

Chapter 32

"The Beta Centrex Galaxy is ahead. Home is that-a-ways." Braden smiled at Crystal. They were on the bridge of the last alien ship. The other two had begun to break up and staying on board was dangerous. Because of the damaged condition of the other ships, Braden had consolidated them all into one. Once alien, given numbers and letters, were now becoming familiar. Alien technology assumed understandable functions. Well-known colored lights winked from boards and wall panels: red, blue, green, purple, and white. Mostly green and white now. The once blaring intercom stood silent.

"The Enjelise put the gate near Alysia to have a shortcut back home. They probably have gates near all of their seeded worlds," suggested Braden.

"How many do you think there are?" asked Icabar.

"Elsinore never said," he answered.

"What will Alysia be like when we get back?" asked Crystal.

Braden shrugged. "I honestly don't know. Tessa confirmed that space/time runs slower than Alysia's time. My brother appeared older. Who knows what technology they have now, or who rules the government, or what kind of government even exists? It's probably changed, though."

"Politics ... bet on it." Icabar looked up from the alien communication board that he had been trying to fix. "In addition, we have changed."

Crystal nodded. "After so long in space, lighter gravity has influenced us. Alysia's heavier gravity will be hard on our bodies. Our bones have gotten brittle despite the calcium pills and exercise wheel."

"I've certainly gotten used to the lighter gravity of space," drawled Icabar as he got up and drifted over toward Braden and Crystal.

More than your bodies have changed. Liana glided onto the bridge, as if on cue. *We're not the same as when we left. I wonder if we're even human anymore.*

"If Lucien and his people are called '*The Fallen*', then I think we should be called 'The Risen'," drawled Joel as he entered behind her. "We're a new evolved species of human."

"You've certainly risen," commented Braden as he waved at Joel, "from the nearly dead."

"Thank Crystal and her Talent, or I would be dead."

"And Glaze," added Crystal.

Joel regarded the panel in front of him and rubbed it with his hand. "Yes, and Glaze," he murmured and then blinked. "Too many lost."

Liana gave him a hug.

They all knew he thought of Dyra.

"And how will our fellow humans handle our new abilities?" asked Crystal, changing the subject in order to give Joel a chance to regain his composure.

"Our powers would terrify those we left behind, but as you say, maybe they have changed too," answered Liana switching to vocals.

"I'm not sure that I want to have billions of minds invade my thoughts constantly. I might not stay sane," answered Crystal. "And we should practice using vocals more."

"Thinking what you want to say is easier," protested Icabar.

"It's laziness," retorted Crystal tartly.

Joel cleared his throat. "I have become used to the comfort of close quarters and the ship enclosing me like my mother's arms. The thought of all that open sky terrifies me. Out here the void is vacuum, and deadly. That's our learned instinct now." He joined the group staring out the ship's view plate. He touched it.

Solanje came and joined them, drawn in by their thoughts and broadcasted emotions. She added, "The unpredictability of weather and all the outside forces where you no longer have control over your environment is going to feel strange. And then the people who want to control you ..." Her voice trailed off.

Icabar turned to them. "Remember that Elsinore told you that we were capable of evolving even more. She said not to judge the Enjelise too harshly because we may be in their position in the future. We may be called upon to parent our own world now, or those leftover ships may find a habitable planet and we may have to shepherd them along better evolutionary lines than where *the Fallen* led them. Or, we may find some other species as we expand outwards that hasn't evolved as far as we have that need our help. For humanity will continue to expand out into space, you know. It's part of our nature. We have just opened the door a crack." Icabar eased over next to Liana.

Liana peered out into starry space with them. "I wasn't sure I would ever see home again. I'm as frightened now of returning, as I was of leaving."

Liana closed off her thoughts to the others as she thought to herself, *What am I going to tell Kat? Mother Kat has sacrificed her whole life preparing for Elsinore's return and now the Enjelise aren't coming. There will be no Second Coming. No Judgment for Alysia.* She was surprised at the relief she felt.

"Has a meeting been called?" asked Bashar as he came into the bridge, stretching and yawning. "I don't know if I can give up navigating among the stars now that I have had a taste of it. Can you Captain?"

"There're others out there. We know that for certain. Maybe human colonies like ours. Just what they've become we have yet to discover. There's so much more to do. I don't know, Bashar," he answered. "I expect I'll return to space again some time, but now I just want to go home."

"Do we have to go back?" murmured Crystal. Braden caught a wisp of a sigh and worry over her father. He patted her arm to comfort her.

Crystal paused and looked at him. *I'm much stronger now, aren't I? I've walked in space and saved a life.* She heaved a big sigh and smiled at him. She flung an arm around his shoulder and leaned her head against his, shocking him. He didn't move. He didn't even flinch.

Stronger, but also more compassionate, he thought to her, throwing in strong proud feelings for her.

Oblivious to their mental conversation, Icabar blurted out, "The media will have us for lunch." His thoughts idled on the commotion their arrival would create.

Not to mention what the Tang will say. They all felt Solanje's sudden concern.

Do you even care? intruded Bashar.

After a soul-searching pause, she responded, "No, not anymore."

Bashar nodded and pulled her tight to him. Grins lit up the room.

Then, Braden's face got his stern captain's look. "We were sent to find those who belonged to the alien device." His voice projected firm conviction as he looked around. He cleared his throat. "It's our duty to let them know what we found, so we must return."

"Duty, oh great!" mumbled Icabar.

Braden admonished them, "Remember that we went through a timegate that might have changed time even more. I have no idea what era now exists on Alysia. Time was pulled and twisted and altered when we went through that gate. Alysia may be many annuals in the future and may have evolved even more than we have, or we may come back to a deep past where only wild animal roam our world, and we have to start all over again like Tessa and Adam. I couldn't begin to wonder what awaits us."

Shocked, Crystal spoke for them, "We can contact them when we get closer and find out, can't we?"

"This is an alien ship. How will they know it's us?" Solanje asked the burning question.

Icabar looked over at Braden. "You did tell Richard to prepare to defend against an alien invasion and now here we come. What's to stop them from thinking we're some aliens come to attack Alysia?"

"We tell them it's us." Braden appeared as if it would be no problem.

Solanje responded exasperated. "But we lost the halo when we transferred ships."

"The device was lost, maybe for a reason. I don't think The Creator, or the Enjelise God, wants us to play too much with something that powerful," answered Braden firmly.

"Or use it as a template to make more," added Bashar.

Icabar looked up and made a face at them. "I have yet to master this communication board. It's in an alien code using alien technology and damaged from the vortex." He slapped a hand on it in frustration.

"You'll fix it," soothed Crystal.

"That reminds me. What of the Crystal beings?" asked Icabar. "Do we tell our world about them?"

Braden looked over at Liana. She nodded. "Of course, we do. The Crystals have access to our navigational and systems information which means they may eventually pay us a visit. First, however, they'll have to find a species willing to transport them. They'll come for the silicon, if for nothing else, but that may be a long time away, or maybe never."

Braden said, "I want to set up a program whose purpose is to locate and evaluate other alien species. Besides, I like being captain of a starship. There are worlds out there to discover yet."

"I imagine we have created a whole new universe ourselves," added Icabar.

"What do you mean?" asked Crystal.

"All that nuclear material sucked into a dying dwarf star that was dense and heavy. You saw the explosions. What if those explosions ripped a hole right into a new universe? Or created one? Glaze set off a chain reaction that looked like it was re-igniting a dying star," said Icabar. "Didn't you notice what was happening?"

Bashar rolled his eyes. "I was too busy scrambling to get away from it."

"You mean Glaze might have given birth to a whole new universe? Sort of like taking the big bang into another dimension?" asked Solanje.

"Why not?" Eagerly, Icabar thought about it.

An explosion that would spew out tons and tons of material into a pristine new universe, creating whole new worlds. Wow!

"Creation all over again!" exclaimed Liana.

"Do you think The Creator planned it that way all along?" mused Braden.

"Ours is not to wonder why, ours is just to do or die," pontificated Icabar with a grin.

"Oh, I think we were made to wonder and be amazed," countered Liana.

"Enough philosophy. Right now, I propose we set course for home. We might find an adventure there worth having," concluded Braden.

Yet, they all paused a moment to think of Dyra, Robert, Tessa, and Adam ... all no longer with them.

And finally, Glaze with his last act of love.

*

As they thought of Glaze, and as they moved farther and farther away from him at unimaginable speeds among the stuff of stars; Glaze hurtled past the event horizon into a whole new dimension of space. He fragmented into an infinite number of vibrating particles, all crashing into each other, growing and expanding outward, as he pulled along the reigniting star in his wake. A thermonuclear chain reaction from Bashar's fission bomb was re-igniting the once dying star, and eventually, in the fullness of time, would create whirling planets, soaring asteroids, and burning stars to fill a waiting void. Through an altered reality, Glaze's consciousness looked out onto the birthing universe and saw that it was good. Because of him, new worlds were in the making.

He felt akin to God

Thank you for reading the fourth book in the Alysian Universe series.

If you want to find out about the development of Alysia's space program and how *The Seeker's* crew got selected, read *Cosmic Entanglement: book 3*

Space Song book 5 continues the adventure and is the story of Richard Steele preparing Alysia for an alien invasion. Once again, politics, murder attempts, romance and mystery try to stop Richard from building a space station and a fleet of spaceships. What happens when Braden heads home in the alien ship and can't communicate with Alysia?

How will Richard know not to shoot down and kill his own brother and human crew as Braden returns home?

OTHER STUFF

For more details, character descriptions, vocabulary, and a map of Alysia go to:
http://www.AlysianUniverse.com

For ideas on other science fiction books ideas and the process of writing, for science fiction and fantasy, check out my blog at http://www.scifibookreview.com

Or tweet me at http://Twitter.com/Sheronwriting

Science fiction has been a passion of mine for many years thanks to my father's love of the genre.

After I graduated from the University of Florida with a Master's in Education, I taught creative writing and literature at Bradford High School. I married and held day jobs as high school teacher, banker, stockbroker, art gallery manager and artist.

One night during a long boring ride home from a vacation weekend, I began to construct a story based on a passing name off a billboard. That quick glance, while traveling at sixty miles an hour, turned into years of stories and characters. No wonder I write about time and its effect.

Over the next few years, I attended workshops and continued to write. One story led to another as I fell in love with the Alysian Universe and the wonderful characters that inhabit their universe.

Jump in and experience their adventures.